Only Shorter

Ross Feld

North Point Press
San Francisco
1982

Copyright © 1982 by Ross Feld
Printed in the United States of America
Library of Congress Catalogue Number: 81-83971
ISBN: 0-86547-061-8

March 18. I was wise, if you like, because I was
prepared for death at any moment, but not because
I had taken care of everything that was given me
to do, rather because I had done none of it and could
not even hope ever to do any of it.
　　　　　　Franz Kafka, *The Diaries 1910–1913*

. . . to recognize the good in the bad, the bad in
the worst, and so grow gently old all down the un-
changing days and die one day like any other day,
only shorter.
　　　　　　Samuel Beckett, *Malone Dies*

Prologue

He hates that she came along. It's even in the way he's grabbing at, angrily yanking, the stickshift. They fly down the slanted streets of the student section; and once, when he makes an unnecessarily sharp turn, she wonders if he doesn't mean to see whether she can be flung off, like a fat pulled drop of something.

They leave the town limits. She enjoys this road, the same one that the bus took her in and will take her out on. A few ranch-style homes tail off into a small field of corn, which in turn is suddenly jammed up against a wide garage for school buses: bang bang bang, rich warm yellows. A little further on: a *yurt*, where a crew of local hippies lives in all but the worst winter months. And next—already—the cable TV station, where the taping is to take place. Jack is turning in.

The building, low and cinder-blocked, is the color of mayonnaise. Four cars—one of them a long, dark blue Mercedes—are already parked around back, and Jack seems to be putting the truck as far from the imperial car as possible. After shutting the engine he stays for a minute staring, foggily, in the direction of her knees.

Waiting, she supposes, for something like an apology.

But look now, after all, what is it she's done that's so terrible? She's relapsed, true, is being given drugs again, has slipped a notch unforeseeably—but if there's anyone who ought to know that a notch can be regained, it's him, no? Besides, he was the one who originally wanted her along for this, who thought it might be amusing—but then again he never had much talent for complication.

So she waits him out until, finally, he opens his door and sullenly leaves the truck.

Inside, the small reception area sports aging posters, scotch-taped to the panelling, for local rock concerts; on an end table sits a glass jar containing a single pair of wrapped sourballs, the cellophane clouded with old sugar. While Jack knocks at the access door, calling hello, she sits at the edge of a hard vinyl chair, proud of his bravery and suddenly forgiving him everything. She's pleased to find she's not even all that tired. She pats to check her kerchief. (She'd seen some blue pressed high and back in the sky earlier in the morning, but it had given way to grey overcast—so perhaps it would rain, and then no one would think the kerchief strange at all.) A buzzer frees the door; she rises as fast as she can to follow Jack in, down a short hallway to the control room.

Introductions. With two fingers at the base of her spine, Jack is pushing her forward slightly, as if she's on casters, toward the director, a sweatered boy wearing a headset:

"This is my friend from New York, Judith Kornbluh."

"Hi, Judy—Mark. And that's"—the director pointed through the plate glass at another headsetted boy, this one bent behind a camera— "that's Lex. Why don't we go out and everyone can meet everyone and we can get a key and a base-scoop set on Jack."

It reminds her of a beach, the actual studio space. First dark, the floor littered, then a gleaming strip of scrubbed, mineral light. When she passes by the cameraman, her hello draws no response. The air has a sweetish electrical aroma. Three people seated in canvas director chairs right under the worst of the glare, they rise.

The program's host, a narrow young man with an expensive haircut and a buttoned-up jacket, introduces himself and the others: the woman who wrote the book ("a professional victim": Jack's assessment when he first called weeks ago to tell her about being invited on), and a tall, square-built, blue-suited man: Dr. Something-or-other.

Jack never mentioned any doctor—had he known? She can't see Jack's face to find out, however, because the cameraman was already busy before him, clipping a tie-tack microphone to his jacket lapel.

The Victim was meanwhile making conversation, asking Judith if she's from the area.

"Jack is. I'm from the city." A new light goes on directly overhead, one so immediately hot and harsh that it's making her skin feel superfluous. She can hardly open her eyes in it.

"Oh, me too. We should have lunch! Where abouts?"

Before Judith can answer, the director, open armed, is herding the panelists back to their chairs on the set. And saying to her: "You'll sit with me in the control room."

In the control room the boy quickly rolls a swivel chair her way. She sits, then is waved closer to the console and the window. Their chairs, hers and the director's, are arm to arm as he points around the small room.

"The VTR: we use one-inch tape, just like the real guys. This is the switcher, from one camera to the other. These, obviously, the monitors. What else exotic? Not too much. This thing, this is called a tel-e-phone."

She smiles.

Mark bends toward an intercom box. "I'm getting a slick off the doctor's glasses on one, Lexie, you too? Better. Good. Two is good. Let's give it a try. We're about ready, everyone. Take Lex's downbeat, Tom, and we'll roll. Stand By With Sound."

The room is momentarily quiet, except for the hum of the equipment. Then Mark says, "Hit The Sound"—a direction, it turns out, to himself: he presses a button on the console just as one of the monitors is showing a card that reads: *Community Report*. The room expands with a disinterested sort of string music; Judith sees the cameraman pivot; then another card appears on the monitor: *With Tom Nestora*.

"Fade Out Sound." The cameraman is pointing his finger at the host, Tom, whose voice then proceeds to drive away the strings. Mark now sits back, suggesting she watch the monitors. His hand, though, stays on the switcher console.

One monitor frames an unvarying portrait of the four of them up there, head-on, like Leonardo's *Supper*. The other tiny TV set is completely the host in close-up. Judith alternates: watching through the window, looking at the monitors, then through the window again.

"—are getting it, it's true, but more and more of them also are surviving longer, even to the point of living out normal lives. Our guests today all have experience with the facts of this most frightening of all diseases. I think they'll be able to tell you and me what it's like to know you have cancer, to have it treated, and then to go on living your life afterwards. To my right is Leatrice Cahn, and the book she's written is called *Letter to My Daughter: A Woman's Days with Cancer*, and this is it right here—"

The book jacket eats up an entire monitor. On the other is the woman's face, a tight shot, looking polished and prepared above a wine cowlneck sweater. Judith again starts to watch through the glass, now just in time to see Jack, who's been sitting stiffest of them all up there, to see him turn around . . . looking for her? Yes! She waves back at him with two excited fingers, like a little idiot. He turns again to the others.

"—Roswell Park Memorial Cancer Institute in Buffalo, and Dr. Spering has this week been appearing with Miss Cahn throughout the state—on Friday night here in our own Masonic Hall—to answer questions and provide the medical viewpoint on this very important subject. Thank you for coming on 'Community Report,' Dr. Spering."

The doctor nods. Judith's palm itches faintly: doctors who won't smile.

"And to the right of Miss Cahn is someone who may be familiar to some of you, one of our local businessmen and realtors—"

Judith feels that now she had better look solely at the monitor. If not, if she doesn't get some quick distance, her heart is going to commence to drum, Mark will hear the thumps.

"—Jack Richmond, a young man who's been through his own battle with cancer, getting treatment down in New York City, and who we're glad to see back home and healthy."

For some reason, the camera is not trained close on Jack, as it had been on the others when they were introduced. Instead, it's staying on Tom the host.

Mark mutters, "Ah, shit," and says quickly into the mouthpiece of his headset: "Please, Lexie, no games."

"—lcome, Jack."

(But only a moment of Jack—then the monitor is right back on the host. Had Jack been nodding? His chin, she thought, was up awfully high, as if to dodge a blow. Judith resolves from here on to watch only the group-shot monitor. What does "games" mean?)

"—falls apart on you, of course," the Victim was saying, "and suddenly you're thinking about something you've never seriously thought about before: that soon you might not be around anymore. Can I tell you something that's a little embarrassing? During the first days in the hospital, after the breast had been removed and I lay there realizing that this malignancy had actually been inside of me, and perhaps still was, capable of killing me—I kept on having the most trivial kinds of thoughts. Because of this cancer, I would think to myself, I'll be missing so many wonderful concerts and recitals and operas at Lincoln Center. It'll be just my luck for a great Broadway play to open exactly the day *after* I die."

The doctor sails in at this, as if cued, smiling for the first time, with indulgence. "Patients, Tom, often report feelings of guilt over what they regard as the trivial nature of their initial reactions."

"It's like," the Victim is quick to take over, "looking at the sun. You only can for a split second at a time. It's always been curious to me, you know, that while people are so very anxious lately to learn how to live—another method, another philosophy being marketed every day, it seems—that there is at the same time this paralyzing fear of learning how to die. Everyone dies, after all; and if we gave just a little more thought as to how to best go about it . . ."

Oh my, Judith thinks, dismayed: it's all just talk. For all she's saying, the woman still doesn't truly believe it's ever going to happen to *her*. At least not without some say in the matter, a chance to steer or at least bargain. We're sisters in delusion.

"—we'd live better, fuller lives. I honestly feel this. I live my life more completely today than I ever have. I live it minute to minute, hour by hour, day by day. I savor it, the way someone taking small sips of a very fine wine savors the . . ."

Judith watches the monitor intently. Beneath that excellent make-up, and despite the fashionably perky cap of short, streaked hair *(Am I just jealous?)*, that's mostly a tired woman. And it *is* tiring: minute by minute, hour by hour, day by day . . . like the games solitary drivers play. At the next billboard, a cigarette. Four more gas stations and I'll eat the banana.

"I think it's important not to forget that, thanks to advances in treatment, what we're here to talk about today is *living* with cancer. Leatrice had the good fortune and, might I add, the good sense to seek out and receive the kind of prompt, quality care that has most probably saved her life. And in Mr. Richmond's case, with a malignancy such as Hodgkin's—"

Out of the speakers set into the control room ceiling, and overriding the doctor's words, comes a dripping of loud, unaccountable sounds:

Tup-Tup-Tup-Tup-Tup-Tup-Tup-Tup . . .

"I don't believe this," Mark the director moans; his chair, pushed away with the backs of his knees, rolls skitteringly away as he jumps to his feet. "Stop the sonofabitch, Lex. Signal him to cut it out!"

Through the plate glass Judith can dimly make out the cameraman angrily pointing to his own chest, then making slashing *stop-it* motions at Jack. She consults the group-shot monitor. Sitting tightly in his chair, Jack has his fisted right hand resting against his throat, his thumb sealing his lips—while his pinky is unconsciously tapping the microphone pellet jawed to his lapel.

"—living five, ten years. And with cancer we call ten years—we do this totally statistically, since there's no sure thing—but we at least call it a cure."

The *tupping* has stopped. Mark, recovering his chair, makes his apologies to her: "'Sonofabitch' was only excitement. Sorry."

Tom the host was turning to Jack. "You went through some fairly rigorous treatment for your Hodgkin's disease, Jack . . ."

Pinched and averted, that of a man having trouble with a jar lid, Jack's face finally is filling the close-up monitor.

More of a nudge from Tom: "Didn't you?"

Jack's weight is pitched so far over to one side of his rickety chair it's making her nervous. Eyes fixed off on some edgy nowhere, he at long ·last speaks, a mumble:

"The standard, I think."

Everyone's waiting for more. There isn't any.

"Hodgkin's, Tom," the doctor takes over smartly, "is a sort of feather in the cap of oncologists. It is a neoplasm that only ten years ago was pretty much uniformly fatal sooner or later. Advances, though, in radiation therapy and the putting together of a number of very potent drugs . . ."

The close-up meanwhile has remained on Jack—a leaning Jack, a get-me-out-of-here Jack. She wonders if the cameraman bears him some grudge, a disgruntled tenant maybe. First "Please, Lexie, no games"; now this overattention. Whatever the reason, Judith really can't take seeing any more of Jack pinned like this, and she closes her eyes.

When they open again, Jack's face is thankfully gone. A scratching sound, though, comes through the speakers overhead—he is playing with his mike once more. Mark the director swivels to his left and hits a button on one of the machines.

Leatrice Cahn is saying an additional word about the gift of life. Dr. Spering brings up the need for emotional support all around, patient *and* family, and Miss Cahn is agreeing: counseling is so very important. The ranks of the cured are being swelled every week. The doctor personally prefers the word "recovered." (Mark the director is saying into his headset, "Lex . . .") The Victim understands, of course, but still believes that it is important for people to get used to the fact that there are real cures available today.

Jack appears to have moved forward in his chair, poised to stand. When Tom the host notices, he takes it to mean that Jack anxiously wants in on the discussion. "Jack?"

But Jack stays as he is: no response. Resourcefully, Tom turns to the doctor. "What about job discrimination? Are employers getting the message of what you've been saying here today?"

Mark repeats another time: "Lex . . ."

"I wish I could tell you they have, but unfortunately the situation is regressive. In strict actuarial terms . . ."

Mark the director turns to Judith and, for some reason or other, gives her a goofy look of helplessness.

"But the statistics show," Leatrice leaps in, "that cancer patients who do come back on the job are just as productive, if not more so, as other workers."

The doctor, halely nodding, agrees. "What we have to deal with, as all of us here well know, is the word itself. Cancer. To most people, that's another way of saying death sentence, catastrophe—"

With a laugh—a small feverish whinny, startling—the Victim cuts in:

"Do we look—Jack and I, for instance—do *we* look like catastrophes? We're back at work, things are good again, we—"

"The man was in the middle of his sentence. Let him finish and don't interrupt."

Jack has said that, it takes Judith half a second fully to realize. Mark the director is now slumped back in his chair, grinning and muttering, "This is wild."

And Jack isn't finished yet, either:

"The man knows what he's talking about. You ought to just listen," he scolds the authoress.

Nonplussed, the doctor starts up again falteringly. "We have . . . It's a double-edged sword, er, we deal with in cancer. People—still, sad to say, the majority—die of it—"

"And many, many live, too," insists the Victim.

"But most of them *die*," Jack intones severely, bringing the word down upon the woman's head like the back of a spoon.

Judith isn't sure she can handle all of her sudden shame. Closing her eyes won't help anymore. This is her fault entirely. What she's put him through by insisting on coming here with him—too, too perverse: she being a bad bet he now feels frantically obligated to cover at any odds.

The cameraman has maliciously awarded the close-up to the authoress now—and the woman appears stunned to the point of hurt. She's pressing on—"True, it seems the unhappy situation is that most companies still aren't hiring remitted patients, or rehiring the ones who . . ."—but clearly her heart has gone out of it, it sounds like a soggy chip of the speech she's probably been delivering all week.

"We've got only a few minutes left," Tom the host was saying, "and I'm interested in finding out from the doctor what exactly are the advances now being made in treatment."

As the doctor obligingly begins with this, Jack suddenly rises to his feet. The cord leading from his microphone has accidentally looped, however, around an arm of his director chair—and this is stopping him. On the group-shot monitor it looks like a taut guywire that is keeping him from floating up into the air.

"—leukemia—again with potent drugs in combination—and Burkitt's lymphoma, which is quite rare here but in Africa—" As the doctor distractedly catalogues his good news, he glances up now and then; only Tom the host seems professionally obligated to make believe Jack still is seated.

He looks, Judith thinks, like a dancing bear in the circus. Towering over the others, caught by the wire, but not yet making any desperate move to disentangle himself . . . as though he wanted to hear the doctor out first. His arms hang straight down, like a sleepwalker's—which is also the expression on his face. Momentarily out of his head like this, he's both spectacular and queerly invisible.

"Miss Cahn?"

"Well, these obviously are very heartening facts. I hope I didn't give the impression"—her eyes rise to Jack—"that cancer is anything to take lightly. I'm the last one to be a Pollyanna. There's an element of luck in survival—"

Trying to bribe Jack into looking at her, giving in point by ghoulish point?

"—plus the caliber of medical care used in treatment. But far and away the greatest danger is fear. If people don't go promptly to seek help when they suspect something is wrong, they're negating"—her voice turns more brisk, she's convincing herself all over again and to hell with Jack—"the wonderful advances science has made on their behalfs. So I *am* willing to sound like an evangelist—after all, simply the fact that I'm sitting here today should say *some*thing; and that Mr. Richmond can be here, a younger person who only ten years ago would have been given up as . . ."

Jack, pricked out of his trance by his name, has finally managed to unclip the microphone from his lapel. Then he walks off, out of camera range.

Hoping that the exhausted look on her face will serve as apology enough, Judith turns to the director. But Mark is smiling to himself. "Watch the shitstorm now, telling Tom. But that's my problem."

"Tell him what? What do you have to tell him?"

"When your friend began to hit his mike a second time, I stopped the tape. Had to." Jack has arrived outside the window of the control room. Mark gets up to open the door, letting Jack in and himself ducking out. Judith is dazed. Jack's hand when she takes it is freezing cold.

Tom the host enters the control room a minute later, saying to her, "I don't imagine Jack would want to rest twenty minutes and then give it another go, would he? I realize it's a strain. But the others are amenable. Jack?"

Jack shakes his head no, flicking away the question, asking her instead, "Are you ready?"

Judith can't find where she put down her bag. She panics. Where is her bag? She can't find her bag! She finds it, and hurriedly slips her sweater through the strap. She's all set.

"No," Jack says firmly, "put it on"—taking the sweater and arranging it around her shoulders. On his face is a savage look of relief: *it's over.* She's seen him leave the clinic exactly this way, brutishly happy to be set free.

She only wishes that that bastard Mark would come back in, so she could say something to him—but Jack is already leaving the control room and she has to follow: down the corridor, through the reception area, out into the parking lot under blue—surprise—skies. Energy is sizzling in his strides. She tries to keep up.

PART ONE

Looking at the Sun

1

One fall night, when he was still new to Delphi, as he was driving up his street after work, Jack raised his eyes . . . and there—finally, in the flesh—was his neighbor, the Pakistani: sitting on a bridge chair set up, of all places, just outside his window on the overhang that roofed the porch below. A section of the same porch roofing lay outside Jack's kitchen window as well, but the idea of sitting out on it had never occurred to him. How sturdy could it, tar papered and unlevel, be? There the Pakistani was, though—reading a book, taking the air out on his private, makeshift balcony.

Inside the house, mail in one hand, keys in the other, Jack hesitated at his own apartment door—then turned and walked across the hall.

"Just one minute, please!" Obviously the Pakistani was still outside on the ledge: the voice came fluffed with outdoor air. Shortly after, the door opened. "Hello?"

"I saw you from downstairs. My name's Richmond. Right here in 2B."

"Ah, we meet!" Thin, small, very smooth-cheeked, the Pakistani was wearing aviator frames and a terrible paisley shirt. "I am Tariq."

Jack met the offered hand. "I was intrigued by your terrace."

"Oh—no—yes?" The Pakistani, taking this as terrifically funny, let out with a spangled run of giggles. "Oh, oh: my terrace!"

"Your porch, whatever."

The Pakistani subsided. "It is simply that the person who had lived here previously"—he was off at an amazing clip, whiffed Vs for Ws, a chewiness to the accent that made it sound as if he were saying the word *sandwich* over and over—"had done this conversion of sorts. He originally was the one who showed me how to use it in the pleasant weather as a veranda of a small kind. I would be pleased to show it to you . . ."

The apartment was a mirror of Jack's, with even less inside it. A blue sleeping bag lay unrolled in one corner of the carpeted living room. A card table, covered with notebooks and loose papers, adjoined a window. Books, stacked bellywise, were here and there, and a pile of neatly pressed, discount store clothing mounded up on the seat of a chair. A traveller's iron rested upon a small metal safety base at one end of a towel-draped trunk laid flat on its side. The bedroom door was shut, so Jack couldn't see in there.

"You were at the University for the summer session. I would see your car on the campus," Tariq said.

"Someone else's, not mine. I'm a management analyst at the Scofield plant out on Fifty-one."

"Better! Good! Originally I am an agronomist, but I came eagerly to study here. It is a superior department, this is probably well known to you."

They were passing now through the kitchen—which was bare of anything but the basic appliances and shelves. Taped to the refrigerator door was a color photo portrait of a smiling, swarthy general, his shoulders dripping in gold braid. On a narrow open shelf above the sink stood a lineup of brightly colored, brick-like tins of spice.

"It is a common experience that when we return home—this is very-very common—we find that we have learned met-uds and modalities far too sophisticated for the actual situations we must face. Professor McKay, you know of course, has written fine papers on this dilemma. Technocrats like ourselves, he is stressing, we go into 'overdrive,' we 'spin our wheels.' Please now"—Tariq had one leg through the open window, then the other—"be quite careful, taking it easy."

Jack followed him out. At first the surface declined sharply, and you went down best if you held on to the window frame and skidded slowly against the side of one shoe. Then it ran horizontal for about three feet—and here Tariq had put down four short pine planks. The bridge chair took up almost all of this platform. Technocrats. But Jack, glancing up, felt refreshed by the closer sky. Glancing down: the street looked immense yet innocuous, like a stage backdrop.

"Adjustments in time, though, will be naturally made, I am sure. The met-uds and modalities proper to the situation will develop. Yet now and then I am sometimes questioning if this is the work I still wish to undertake in my country. So *much* to do."

"Can I?" Jack lifted two textbooks and a clipboard off the seat of the bridge chair. The chair rocked as he sat, the boards beneath it warped. He stood up, replacing the books.

"Not very often do I get the opportunity to come out on my little veranda," Tariq confided, as they made their way back through the window into the kitchen and through the apartment to the front door. "I am usually in the library. I hope I am not disturbing you excessively when I return at night."

"I hear your car come in. It's no real disturbance. You're as good as a clock."

"Like Kant for the people of Königsberg, similarly!"

Jack extended a hand. "I appreciate your showing it to me. Good luck on your work."

Giggles again. "When it is the fifteenth of the month and I must pay Mr. Pellegrino his two hundred and fifteen dollars, I so very much wish I would be able to *sleep* in the library as well. But . . . !" Tariq gave a guileless, amicable shrug.

Which, when Jack thought about it again, back in his own place, was interesting. The Pakistani was being asked to pay twenty dollars more in rent than he was for the identical apartment.

It was not the kind of house he had at first imagined himself living in—but what in Delphi had yet met his expectations? When, in New York, after the transfer, an envelope from Personnel came to him containing a fact sheet and brochures on living arrangements in the northern town, Jack had gone along with the suggestion they featured: newly built garden apartment complexes. (Though a good word was put in for mobile homes, too: "For those who like to wake up surrounded by a little country.") The fruity ink smell of the brochures, the precision of their folds: he picked out a pamphlet for one apartment complex, no better or worse looking than the others, and sent off a note on Scofield stationary reserving a one-bedroom apartment and enclosing a deposit check for one hundred dollars, applicable towards. Like his decision to accept the transfer in the first place, simply the swift making up of his mind about this, he sensed, would be salutary and hygienic. A sharp slash.

The drive upstate, on his first day of relocation leave, had been promising. Even though the sun was out strongly, the day was shot through with a whickering coolness. Whoever had planned large stretches of the wide main roads seemed never to have known what nervousness meant: wherever the highway cut, it cut, slicing into a loaf of hill or switching back twenty times across a glassy, stone-floored river that cleaved to the right, then the left, then the right again for miles. The road went on looping or ramming ahead at will, and whether you were off it or on it was strictly your problem. Invigorated, Jack stopped only once in the six hours, for coffee that he didn't really need. He entered Delphi by three in the afternoon.

The garden apartments stood a little back from a booming six-lane expressway, the same one that, a few miles north, would deposit him at the gates to the plant. No complaint, then, about convenience. The complex had looked about as he expected it would. The unit buildings were low and buffy. There were widely spaced evergreen bushes instead of trees. A couple of children rode the swings in the play area but otherwise no one else was in sight. Following the arrows to the rental office, Jack's heels came up slow off the black asphalt walks, their crusts already gone in the sun of only May. A gentle greasy wind that seemed local to the walks and small lawns between buildings whipped no higher than knee-level.

The manager, late-twentyish, with a swatch of vascular blush on each cheek, had kept Jack a long time appreciating the kitchen, the copper-toned stove and refrigerator. "And your outlets: on *both* sides of the sink. Put your toaster in this one, say, and your blender over here. You eliminate that whole jumble of cords." In the living room he spoke at one moment standing; at the next, he was suddenly, passionately, on his knees: "Feel this pile. Brand new. Come on, feel it. You could sleep on this—forget a mattress—couldn't you? And it's in the bedroom as well. Brand new. I love it. I wish I had it in my apartment."

Four of the windows, Jack had noticed—two in the bedroom and the two in the living room—looked toward a solid brick wall thirty yards away. "That's what?"

"Brand new! The Ramada Inn. So you've got complete privacy, no nosy neighbors looking in at you. And if you're worried about noise, please don't be. Anyone in this unit will tell you that the motel is totally soundproofed: you don't hear a peep. We had our own engineers check that out, it was a condition of their zoning permit."

From the kitchen, Jack peered outside. Spluttering between the close-by corners of two neighboring units, a snip of highway was visible. When the window was opened, in blew a distant but constant airy whisk: cars. Jack shut the window.

"Any questions you have, I'll be happy."

The rooms were good sized. It would be convenient. "No, not especially."

The manager straightened up off the refrigerator. "Great, then. I already have your deposit, so all we have to do is get the rental agreement filled out and we're set. We can do that back at the office."

Yet Jack, all of a sudden and to his core, had known that he would never be able to live in this place. He stood staring at the shiny chrome sink, mentally trying to countermaneuver—*Hardly ever be here, so what does it matter?*—but not succeeding. "I tell you. I've got a few appointments up at work this afternoon that I'm already running late for. Let me call you later."

Sensing something, the manager said, "It'll take us no more than a minute—it's on the way to where you parked your car."

"I really have got to run."

The challenge had seemed to rouge the young man's cheeks a shade brighter. "Give me your number and I'll call you."

"Better I call. I'll be running around a lot."

The manager raised his hands, smiling, acknowledging defeat.

Five minutes later, Jack was sitting on the sun-hot seat of his parked Valiant. All along his mind had been made up to take whatever was shown him, no ifs or buts—yet in a minute he'd be pulling out of the parking lot with everything still up in the air. Exactly the kind of person he had never wanted to be: the I-like-it, I-don't-like-it type, one of a vast fraternity of whimsicals thrashing around in a world they saw as one boundless maze of equal choices. Jack usually followed what he thought of as a better policy: you accepted any errors you made, knowing that, inevitably, somewhere down the line, they'd naturally be undone and put right. There was little to lose in living slightly ahead of yourself.

Usually he felt that. What had happened?

He went driving aimlessly around the town, his not-quite-yet new home, not exactly sure now what to do with his double-crossed time. Near the University he entered a neighborhood of leafy, vaulted streets and Tudor-style houses: faculty homes, he guessed. Sunlight was chunked like gelatin by nets of overhead leaves, and the green and secure placidness calmed Jack some. Still further east the houses were older, large and wooden; then the streets took a dip downward until, stopped at one corner, Jack had found his car poised to descend an astonishing hill.

Slowly driving down, riding the brake, he looked around him. All the houses were set in to compensate for the substantial grade. Alongside of each, where side yards would have gone, were small blacktopped parking areas: the houses were multiple dwellings.

Jack turned corners to double back on certain of the streets again. The grades were so striking to him, some of them easily fifteen percent. To trudge up or lean against these streets by foot; to steer a car down them in winter—what would it be like to live somewhere that insisted upon itself so unmistakably, at every moment? A tautness, a resistance. When he spotted a realtor's sign nailed up to a peeling porch post, Jack brought the Valiant to a curb and jotted down the number.

By six that evening he'd been taken to see three different apartments in the hilly section. All of them were equally suitable, but Jack had asked to see the second one again—in what the rental agent/handyman, an elderly Scandinavian named Karlyn who dressed in soothing janitorial greys, called a "sixplex," three apartments to each floor of a chesty two-story house painted outside in a double shade of green. Standing in the empty flat (which was larger than he truly needed), Jack had begun to feel restored, feel that pickiness was finally being defeated. The place was a dump compared to the spruce garden apartment out by the highway—but it was dumpy as the sum of small and individual faults. Someone had apparently once stored a motorcycle in the entrance hall downstairs, and the carpet runner there was blotched with motor oil. The wooden stairs were splintered in places and the plumbing yelped with age. There was a detectable angle to the kitchen floor; the drafts of winter were sure to snake in around some of the rickety window frames. But it was an honorable house: a chipped-off oval of molding next to the bedroom door revealed a layer painted pink, then blue over it, and pink again, and ultimately the present paint, beige. Would it be so bad to help use this place up?

At the end of June, with little enough furniture and effects so that he was able to do it all by himself with a rented U-Haul trailer, Jack moved in. Later, looking back on it, he would think of it as his last honestly satisfying day.

He had always understood that the Scofield plant in Delphi was in a bad way. News of it, in cold figures, used to come across his desk regularly in New York, where his job had been to recommend that hard lines be taken, radical surgeries considered. The Delphi segment—packaging—had been the company's weakest for two years running now. A Swiss firm had shown some interest a year earlier in acquiring the polypropylene-film operation, but it then had backed off. Disappointed, headquarters apparently was going to give the Delphi plant a last shot, not with films but with what it had always been geared for best, containers and extruded packagings. Jack's assumption all along was that he'd been sent up to be the bastard with the whip.

But he'd never expected to find what he did. The underutilization was horrendous. Whole lines were out. Inventory piled up on pallets, and just sat there—as the lines still in operation overproduced today, underproduced tomorrow. Along with Jack on his first walk through the plant tagged the plant manager, Bonsell, and his assistant, Nesby. Stepping down off the stairs of one of the catwalks, Bonsell turned to Jack and in all earnestness said: "We've got a cozy operation here."

Jack thought, Not even meanness is going to help. He took notes and notes on nothing; he ran through a few efficiency studies, the disheartening results of which he could have foreseen at the start; he even searched the faces of secretaries for a single lidded eye, a shrug or a sneer, any sign of realism, of owning up to the operation's miserableness—but he saw only the blandest vegetable self-satisfactions.

So, in the middle of August, lying on his Hollywood sofa after supper, he had begun his first report back to New York. "Mismanagement," "untenable," "illusion"—he'd glance up from the pad and be happy to see some of his things still in boxes, not unpacked. "A no-win situation, as it stands at the present moment . . ." After about an hour of this, he broke off and went down for some air. The light above the steep streets was thin, filtered, the color of white grapes. By the time he returned, the room needed lamplight. He went back to it: "Change of command, *at least,* although probably not even this will fully stem . . ."

Expecting no real response until after Labor Day and the end of everyone's vacations, Jack had gone to the plant each day in an almost dreamy state of curiosity, like a scientist checking his petri dishes for new and disgusting molds that might have grown up overnight. It was a queer, sludgy few weeks, as though he'd fired a gun that had no recoiling kick.

September trailed away, still without an official response to—or even semi-official acknowledgment of—Jack's report; on the phone to New York, the best he'd been able to squeeze out were various "We're picking it over"s and "It's in the hopper"s—after which the conversation on their end would duck down witless alleys, into jokes and bullshitting. It made Jack nervous, but he continued to wait; he had no choice. Nor did he much care for the return migration of the students: they made the small town seem crowded, hectic, artificial; and Jack tried keeping to the perimeters as best he could. Someone at the plant could provide him with cigarettes by the carton, pirated and untaxed; and when Jack wanted a drink, he drove to The Ranchhouse, a bar near the plant that on weekends featured live Country and Western music. Here too, though, more and more students were beginning to appear, sharing the bar and tables with the Scofielders. As for food, Jack used the supermarkets less frequently, taking most of his meals at a Burger King on the Delphi Road. This was where he was returning from, in fact, the night he first caught sight of the Pakistani up on the porch roof.

During the week, he had taken the measurements, then went early on Saturday morning to shop for what he needed at the lumber yard. Instead of loose planks, he had in mind two wide sheets of medium-grade plywood—which he'd joist below with two-by-fours and then hinge together so that the whole deck could easily fold up and be brought back through the window each time. At the lumber yard, on a whim, he also purchased a four-foot section of calf-high picket fencing, as well as a few shims to nail it to. Slip the shims flat under the plywood: he'd have himself a little balustrade in the bargain. Real money was spent, while he was at it, on a good set of screwdrivers, a six-foot folding rule, a hand drill, a smoothing plane, a twelve-point crosscut saw, a nail set, a good hammer—all of which made Jack feel good to have, here in a place where his constructive purpose was otherwise so vague. Besides, nothing that he'd bought was so bulky that it couldn't go back with him—as doubles—when he was soon returned to New York.

Boards and nails and tools were spread out on the living room floor; but even after five minutes of preliminary furniture moving, the space still seemed too cramped to work well in. So Jack fed the materials and tools and lastly himself through the kitchen window and out onto the porch roof.

He maybe could have used one extra pair of two-by-fours, to better even out the balance, but it wasn't crucial. The hinges sank in with satisfying ease, after which Jack stood up, folded the deck, reversed it, and laid it back down. At some point, depending on how ambitious he was, he might yet paint it—green? white?—but for the moment it would be left raw. The afternoon was low, cool, pearly, but every now and again the sun would slit sharply through, concentrated heat furring up beneath Jack's shirt. He took it off. He next set to nailing the pickets of the balustrade to the shims.

Nice.

Now the shims had to go under. Jack worked on his knees, heels to his ass, his back to the edge of the roof. He shoved—

—And right away could sense an excess, a tipping imbalance, that he'd pushed at it too hard. He scrambled to adjust his body weight—luckily there was time, plenty of time . . .

Except that he was wrong, there wasn't: his right foot was already showing its sole to the sky, then the left one—and Jack was sliding: on his belly, backwards, his knees asking desperately for a cradle in the rain gutter at roof's edge, but the trough there promptly cracking off under his weight. Like spaghetti slipping over a pot rim, he was irrevocably dropping down to the ground at an angle very close to the house. He'd held onto the fencing half a second too long—so it too was coming down with him. To shield his head and face from the falling pickets, Jack brought an arm up before hitting the ground.

All told, this was what mainly cost him. The fencing landed nowhere near, but the ground—the broad, calm, even earth—sharpened itself into a needle that went lancing into his bent arm, sending a boiling squirt of pain to scald each bone connected inside there.

Everything after that was shamefully quiet. Up on the porch roof, a corner of the deck jutted out as though it had leaned over to watch Jack clatter down. A pair of pants came up from behind, asking him if he was all right. *(Oh, fuck off.)* "Fine, Fine," mumbled Jack, and finally the pants moved on. Thankfully, none of the three students who had collectively moved into the apartment below Jack's the week before were coming to their windows. *(The self-absorbed shitheads.)* Jack stood up. At first his arm was painless, a hunk of strange weight was all; but then, poking at it, he nearly launched his scalp. He hobbled like a scared old man into the house and up the stairs.

A knock at Tariq's door brought, as expected, nothing. Jack then managed to get his own door open (his keys had stayed inside his pocket as he fell) and, once inside, he stood for a moment, suspended, staring at the plywood splinters left on the living room carpet, at the kitchen window's derisive maw. After telephoning for a taxi and torturing himself into a shirt, he went out the door without bothering to lock it behind him. The stairs he took quite slowly.

The picket fencing lay outside on the tanning lawn, smugly intact. A red taxi soon pulled up, the driver leaning across the seat to yell out the passenger-side window: "The hospital you?" Seeing the pursy way Jack was coming down the walk, the driver, who wore his greying hair in a Marine-type brushcut, got out and opened the back door. "Arm?"

"I fell off the roof." Jack's original plan was to plate this with an italicizing chuckle, but it didn't come off; the driver's mouth winged out in a sincere grimace. Under way, he turned his profile to Jack: "How you doing?"

The entire arm felt numb yet illuminated. A little self-pity? Why not? "It's fucking unbelievable."

"Just hold on," said the driver as Jack gazed out the window; ingenious shortcuts were being taken, most of them illegal. "And if you can stand a story—talk about holding on . . ."

Before cabbing became the way he made his living, he had driven the town buses, was one of the original drivers. He'd been doing the Mac-Millan Park route one morning when he felt a pain: "ass-puckering, excuse the French, straight down my arm. And a real queasy stomach." He'd had the presence of mind to order everyone off the bus, slam shut the doors, lean on the horn straight through downtown, swing up the lake like they were doing now, and head like a bull for the hospital. A week in the cardiac care unit plus two more in a semiprivate room gave him plenty of time to think of what might have been if he hadn't been driving. At home, an ambulance would have been called, he would have had to just lie there. But in the bus, at the wheel, scared as he was . . . well, that was his point: *at the wheel.* "First I had to get there, you know? Then I could die." If need be, he probably could have driven straight on through to Syracuse.

Jack was moved—though anything at that moment might have moved him: a horn hitting flat, the first russet leaf on a tree. Already they were at the hospital, with its spectacular view high above the lake. The cab, with drama, stopped short; Jack, in back, sloshed forward like a water balloon. "Here," he said, handing up his wallet. "Take out what I owe you, plus whatever for yourself." Stiffly he began removing himself from the car.

The wallet was returned to him through the window: "Get soldered back up there, will you? And stay off those roofs. Have our number for the ride back?" After the taxi drove off Jack checked the wallet by holding it open against his belly: the driver had picked out twenty dollars. Disgusted, mostly with his own soupy disappointment, Jack slammed through the doors of the Emergency bay.

X-rays were taken and then the fractured wrist was set with no great finesse by a grumpy, older doctor wearing a tie peppered with horse-heads, who wrapped only enough plaster-impregnated bandage around Jack's hand and forearm to establish a general shape. After that he left the room, and the rest of the job of wrapping fell to the nurse to complete.

"A born charmer," Jack noted aloud to the girl.

"They're that way sometimes on Saturday afternoons: not liking it a bit. He's a good guy, though, really he is." Each time she swaddled another bandage length around him, the breast badged with D. Mehring, R.N. pressed warmly against Jack's shoulder. She was short and very slightly plump, a coat of surprisingly dark hair slicking her forearms. Jack's first impression had been that she was being professional, which translated into half-there—but the more he studied her the more he sensed that it was instead that natural and constant calmness of face to which a pair of open, unjudging eyes and a relaxed mouthline can sometimes sum up. Her brown hair was flipped up in back, held in place by an oval tortoiseshell barrette; and around a tiny nose, over briskly rising cheekbones, and under the big eyes were freckles, small and distinct and tan: on an animal they would be underside markings, too delicate for first rude sight.

When she was done, after she had peeled off the rubber gloves, she left the room for a minute, returning with a clipboard. "While you dry, I might as well get this filled out. Any chance you have your student I.D. with you?"

Wearily, Jack said, "I'm not with the University. I work for Scofield."

"Good. Then I don't need this"—she unclipped the form from the board—"and it's less work. If you have your insurance number with you, I can take that up to the desk; that'll be fastest. Have it? Wait, let me help you." The second time today that someone, a complete stranger, was handling his wallet. "This compartment here? Okay, found it; I'll take this up front and then be right back. Ruin my masterpiece there and I'll break the other arm—so don't move a lot. Be right back."

Eyes glued to the swivel seat of a stainless steel stool, Jack could almost feel—as though it were a physical process—his loneliness increasing, a pasty glutting of his attention. Soon she was back.

"All set. Aren't you happy you didn't wear a tee shirt today? How do men stand having their buttons on this way? Don't they know they're backwards? The buttons, not the men. Maybe the men too. There. Doctor left a prescription for pain for you." She slipped the paper along with his insurance card into the shirt's breast pocket.

Jack was standing in the main lobby ten minutes later, about to move dazedly from the phone book to the phone booth to again call for a cab, when he felt his shoulder being tapped.

"Is someone picking you up?" D. Mehring had on a thin blue cardigan over her uniform and in one hand she was holding a soft, top-bunched leather bag: she was going off shift.

Inside the cramp of her green Volkswagen, she said to him: "I'm Donna. I already *know* you." The small amount of spin she put on the word, making it sound like a crime—Jack liked that. They were driving down from the western heights above the lake. "Here I'd always thought," she said, "that most Scofield people lived in the Hampdell Village apartments." She herself preferred to live out where she did, in Priory, in the country, mostly for the sake of her animals; she'd tried the Slope once but had felt hemmed in. She needed as much space as she could get.

Jack asked her what she raised—giraffes? He'd already looked at her hand on the steering wheel: no rings.

"How'd you guess?"

Downtown, on Main Street, she pulled the car over and parked, shutting the motor. She addressed his puzzlement:

"Brenner's, right? Your Percodan? In fact, let me." Reaching over, she drew the prescription out of his shirt pocket.

In the silence and abrupt abandonment, Jack began to be aware of his wrist—a cored-out heat that pulsed when he paid enough attention. But he didn't pay much. Instead he was thinking that any girl or woman he had ever liked, he liked simply because she had been kind to him, kindness being a sort of availability. He never dared to like anyone who he wasn't sure beforehand would like him back at least doubly: the too thin or too tall or too lonely—and then the race to see whose choicelessness and vulnerability disgusted whom fastest, a race that he always saw to it he won by good margins.

Donna returned, holding a slick white paper bag, a cylindrical bulge at the bottom of it. "You owe me eight seventy-five."

Kind. Not sappy, though—the difference. Awkwardly, after pulling his wallet out yet one more time today, Jack raised his plaster-shelled arm; touching the windshield with his fingertips, he pointed to the marquee of the movie theatre up the street: "Have you seen that one yet? Would you like to, right now?" Then he felt absolutely exhausted from the effort, tremblingly almost.

". . . Eighty-five, ninety-five, and a nickel makes nine. And one dollar is ten." She snapped her change purse closed. "My dogs have to be fed. Besides, you're supposed to take one of these pretty soon, and you'll be so zonked you'd never keep your eyes open. Look here, I'm putting

this"—his wallet, the coins already dropped into the bill compartment—"on the dashboard for now. Remember to take it."

She drove him directly home without asking the address, evidently
remembering it from the insurance form. As she handed him his wallet, which Jack had fully intended to forget to take, he asked if he could
call her.

"Since I'm working swing, my hours vary." She unclipped a pen from
her uniform's diagonal hip pocket and wrote "Donna M." and a number
on the prescription bag, the shiny paper requiring a few write-overs.
(Jack was sorry he hadn't been quick enough to suggest his cast.) "But
try," she said, "and keep that dry."

"I'll be calling you," Jack pledged. "Definitely," he added.

"Enjoy your goofballs."

Jack watched her car chug up the angled street.

At the Twelve-Thirty Club there were the expected jokes. Galore. "I
can see you miss the big-city excitement quite a lot, Richmond, to get
plastered like that." These upstate businessmen loved to deadpan, and
the cast was a golden opportunity. Bonsell and Nesby meanwhile kept
flicking in and out of Jack's side vision, circulating energetically and
getting into as many photos as they could.

Headquarters in New York finally had answered his report (if you
could call it an answer; to Jack, it was like he and New York were oppo-
sitely charged magnets pressing against, slipping to different sides of,
an invisible barrier). Over the phone (not on paper, so no copies to Bonsell and Nesby), Jack was told that his analysis of the Delphi plant was
"especially acute." Haxlin, in charge of the divisions, then suggested
that he, Jack, "knock together a pick-me-up, something short and neat
P.R.-wise" in the meantime, while everything was still being chewed
over in New York. "Can you do that for me, Jack-o?"

Jack-o did it for him, with boredom and loathing, proposing a time-
sharing plan involving use of Scofield's in-house computer by the larger
local firms, such as the lamp factory and the dairy co-op. It brought on,
of course, an avalanche of brownie points, like this luncheon; forelock
tugging on a grand scale. "Barrett's out of town," one after another of
the Twelve-Thirty-ans stopped Jack to say, "but he thinks it's a great
idea and he wanted me to let you know"—Barrett Krem being a former
mayor and still the owner of three-quarters of the town.

Over chicken croquettes, mashed potatoes, and peas, the conversation at the table where Jack had been put revolved mostly around an adult bookstore that had opened on the easternmost, fraying end of Main Street. One man, slight and straw colored, was especially agitated: a young dentist (as Jack later learned from Nesby) with offices in the Savings Bank Building, a church deacon to boot. "Those lawyers in New York City who handle Ted Boole's estate, they don't know what's going on in town and they don't care—they just want to see rental income. But they've got a surprise coming to them, believe me. If Paula Locksley gives up her beauty parlor next door, what sort of tenant—and at what kind of rent—do you suppose they'll be able to lure in there, with that place right next door?"

"He get anything new in lately, Tim?"

Dr. Tim Sleighlin said, "Sure, Ham, you can joke about it—it's not your property. But three down the street are; and this filth, what do you think it makes them worth?" Jack had been inside the bookstore once—mild stuff compared to city standards—but he kept out of the discussion now, didn't say anything. Sleighlin started to get big nods as he ran down the new district attorney, a putterer the University crowd had put into office to make moaning sounds about industrial pollution of the lake; *he* was never going to do anything about this bookstore matter. "It's a shame," someone said in the pneumatic style of a last word—but Sleighlin was quick to correct. "It's a *problem*. Problems find solutions."

There he was—when he returned home that night—smiling up at himself from page three of the afternoon newspaper: a rank of suits, Jack's own in the middle, and the end of his bulbous cast sticking whitely out from one sleeve like a boxer's taped hand.

He went in search of scissors. Four times previously his name had been mentioned in the *Chronicle* in connection with Scofield—this being the second time there was a photo—and each time Jack had sent the clipping back to his father in Bethpage. He found the scissors on top of the refrigerator, next to the vial of Percodans. More fearing pain than experiencing it, he had swallowed a single pill that first night after the fall (something sharp-pointed was needed to pry open the vial's cap) and in the safety of his bed the drug had sent him skimming over dopey, unpleasant clouds; in the morning, the backs of his eyes felt weighted down. Why right then he hadn't dumped all the rest of the pills down the toilet he couldn't say—but he took a moment now to do exactly that, flush down the bowl the goodies the doctor likely had thought he was giving to a student in compensation for a boo-boo. But Jack was no student and he hated drugs: the winks, the music, the stupid bliss, the undermining, the surrender. The nine yellow tablets went swirling.

A knock came at the door while he was busy cutting out the newspaper photo. Though right-handed, Jack had been having trouble with sympathetic coordination ever since the cast, and his fingers weren't escaping the scissor holes that readily now. Another knock—and this time a call along with it: "Landlord!"

The man Jack finally got the door open for was neat and chunky—in a gold golf sweater and light blue slacks. Dark straight hair was combed wet into a just-so sweep and there was a hint of cowlick in back, like Fred Flintstone's. Under his arm he carried a brown expanding file.

"Mr. Richmond, I'm Pellegrino. A friend of mine was passing by last Saturday and saw you fall."

Jack interrupted, invited the man inside.

"You told him you were all right. He had a feeling, though, that you were only estimating." When Jack conceded a smile, the man promptly relaxed into one of his own. "I was a little worried. Was it a very bad break?"

Jack motioned for him to sit. "Not too. At least I can drive. A hairline fracture of the wrist."

The landlord plucked at his pant creases and lowered himself to the Hollywood sofa. "Hairline's good, I gather—or at least better." Then, to Jack's discomfort, he pointed to the half-clipped newspaper photo on the coffee table, the scissors alongside it like an instrument of shouting vanity. "I missed the meeting down at the Grill, but it's good to see someone being alert around here. You've probably seen this for yourself already, but good ideas don't exactly come hot and heavy to some of our locals. We got the buses going downtown in 1955, and I swear there were people thinking, Well, wouldn't want to strain ourselves having another sensible business idea—good night! They're still snoring away. Do you do the actual programming too?"

Jack didn't catch on.

"The computers."

"No, that's a whole other thing. I'm not involved."

"Because now you'd have trouble punching the keys. Lefty or righty?"

Jack lifted his good right arm.

"Still, it's a nuisance, right?" Since entering, Pellegrino had been surveying the apartment bit by bit, discreetly, a landlord's little trick. "I see you have the cable," he said, raising his chin toward the black cord running from the rear of the television and into a small hole in the baseboard. "What I thought, maybe, was that you'd been putting up an antenna. Which, if you were, would have been a waste of time and money and your wrist there, since it wouldn't pull without the cable—and if you've got the cable, there's no call for an antenna anyway. But I see you have it."

A pause. "You understand, I just wanted to come by and discuss the fact"—here he opened the expanding file and began removing papers— "that, according, to the lease signed by you, no improvements are permitted without permission—"

"I don't intend to sue," Jack stated steadily. He tacked a touch of insulted pride to it, for good measure. "My fall—my fault."

A boy's shapely smile came to Pellegrino's whole face—pleasure— and the papers were instantly repocketed in the file. "I've had some who would jump to it, let me tell you."

Jack said, "I shouldn't have been out there in the first place. But one question: where do you buy your leaders and gutters, the ice factory?"

Pellegrino straightened a crease. "I know the Indian sits outside— that's not news to me. The kid who had the apartment before him began this business. All this"—he gestured toward the kitchen, where the evidence of the debacle, the hinged platform and piece of picket fence and the tools, were sitting in full lighted view—"was for that, wasn't it? Sure."

Not wanting to screw Tariq, Jack answered loosely, a wiggle of the fingers, not yes not no.

"It'll be eight years this December that I have these properties and I don't think that there have been two consecutive seasons that some ambitious kid doesn't knock down a wall or try to put an extra one up. They do nice jobs, even. But it's still bad policy, because let the kid get beaned by some lathing and his parents' lawyer is writing to me the next week about negligence. No one needs that." He snapped the elastic band around the file once for emphasis.

"Usually, though, I've got to say, there isn't a problem. These kids sleep in the apartments, study in them, smoke their pot, blast their stereos—there isn't much time for interior decorating. Basically they're good kids."

"But in a fog," said Jack, reminded of what Tariq across the hall had said he was paying in rent.

"Some. But there are always some, am I right? Colleagues of mine in the Realtors Association make a hobby out of moaning about the Slope. Not me. Right now I have commercial sites vacant—*those* are worrying—but the Slope should never be too much trouble. If you screen for decent tenants and keep the properties serviceable, you do all right. It's only too bad that when something needs doing it takes so long to be done. I'm in over my butt with the new Mall out on Ten, so I have to rely on Karlyn to see to everything. But you know how it is: he's an old man, been wanting to retire for years, certain things he just lets slide . . . Well." Pellegrino wrinkled his nose, slapped his thighs, and stood. "That's my problem, not yours." He pointed again toward the kitchen. "You handy?"

Jack said, "Not at the moment."

Grinning, Pellegrino cocked a finger: "Got yourself a point there."

Jack left the Valiant in the hospital parking lot and walked across the spacious, mowed, rear lawn. He stopped for a moment at some benches, placed where they were certainly with the view in mind. From inside the building, a few floors up, it had to be even more breathtaking: the straight continuous rip of the narrow lake, like a blue-green seam that had pulled open on the valley floor. And the angled afternoon sunrays leaning against the surrounding green hills. Even at night, Jack had noticed, when it was a lustrous, plasticky black, the lake seemed naturally to adjust everything near it down a full turn with its long calm.

He was already halfway back to his car when he saw Donna emerging from a side door of the hospital. She had changed out of uniform, a civilian as he'd never seen her before; she was wearing charcoal pants and a blue cowlneck sweater.

Right off, with his best studied nonchalance, too nervous for the preliminaries, Jack said: "I want your honest opinion. Do you think a view like this is absolutely appropriate? Don't they lie up there, looking out the window and cursing their rotten lucks not to be outside?"

"You mean the patients?"

"It would salt *my* wound."

"I don't know that I've ever thought about it," she said.

"Think about it now."

"Well . . . I don't know." She took a bit of lower lip between two teeth. "The ones who even notice—I would say they probably like it. But most of them are too busy being sick. It could be wallpaper for all they know. The others, though—sure, I guess it's calming and nice for them. How's your arm?"

Last night, when he phoned her, Donna's voice had carried across the connection so much intimate, casual caring that for a moment Jack imagined pressing the receiver to the carpet and then picking it up to discover a circle of warm moisture left on the pile. "Super-Arm! Can drive and everything."

They went, in his car, to The Ranchhouse, where they drank vodka tonics and ate chopped steaks.

She had been born and raised on a dairy farm west of Syracuse. She went to nursing school in Buffalo and had lived in Delphi for the last three and a half years. She was the youngest of four children, and now was twenty-five. "That's old, you know, for around here. There are some places downtown, and everywhere on the Slope, where they call me 'Ma'am.'" She shared a trailer out in Priory with two friends. All this information was offered to Jack in a tone of *Well, let's see,* like someone reading an outline aloud, clearing the decks to get down to the important stuff: him.

"How did you come to work for Scofield?" The restaurant, comparatively empty until then, was filling; a group of students had entered, frat brothers, and they were beginning to make noise around the bar and the pinball machines. "There are more popular companies around here, I guess you already know," Donna went on when Jack, distracted, didn't answer immediately. "A lot of people are just waiting for them to foul the lake, but I guess it hasn't happened yet. Maybe it won't ever." She touched his hand. "Am I putting you on the defensive? I don't mean to be."

The students' presence bothered Jack. He took a sip of his drink, and inside the glass his nose chilled quickly and he felt inexplicably and unpleasantly *young.* What, it suddenly dawned on him, could he say about Scofield? That he was a sheep in wolf's clothing? He didn't want to appear a bumbler in the service of other bumblers.

Before he gave it much thought, then, it was out of him: "Theirs is better than the reputation of the company I worked for before."

"Which was that?"

Jack looked at the students by the bar and drank again from his glass, all at once thirsty. "You see, nurse, it's like this—don't shoot me. Dow."

"Dow Chemical?"

He put his glass down to bend raised hands into a bogeyman's threatening claws.

"Oh, boo," she said. "Truly?"

Jack relaxed. Profoundly. Gristle popped at the back of his neck and his shoulders slipped their knots. A shocked stony silence from her after he said it would have dropped him. As it was, his teeth were feeling hollow with post-leap stupidity.

"For how long?"

"Right out of college. Then for almost four years."

"You're an engineer?" When Jack shook his head, she said, "No, I didn't think so." She had stopped eating. She was looking directly at him with those very open but placidly selective eyes. (Jack, who had never been able to postpone his plate, was intimidated by food ignorers.) "Then why Dow?"

Other times, with other people (with fools, and when he was acting fool and faint too), Jack liked to tell the story under a nervous, jokey heading: How I Became a Fascist—but now he left it off. He had been a history major, he told her. A generally bored one—this was at NYU—but in his senior year there had been one seminar he enjoyed and tried never to miss, "The Rise and Fall of Ideology." He'd written a long paper for it, on Machiavelli and early Fichte.

Donna shook her head—didn't know one or the other or both—but with a brief and telegraphing quickness: he should continue.

Usually, he said, he was a day or two early with his papers (an indication of his boredom) but, because of family problems at home, this one he came right down to the wire with, finishing it early in the morning and a few hours later taking it with him on the six-fifty out of Hicksville so that he could reach school by the nine o'clock class.

When he got to Washington Square and the building where the class met, he found the halls clogged with campus security guards, hastily done signs in Magic Marker taped up everywhere, and all the classroom doors locked. Blared cries through a bullhorn outside kept settling over everything like a cooling wax. Dow Chemical, it seemed, had come on campus to recruit, but since Jack didn't live on campus he hadn't paid much attention beforehand, if he'd known about it at all. Taped to the door of the classroom where his seminar met was a note about the cancellation.

So: standing in the corridor, this jerk with a paper he'd stayed up all night to finish—and that he liked, besides. While some barbarous garbage got raved through a bullhorn eight floors below: "Dow, Dow / How many babies burned anyhow?"

He went outside to stand in the park and watch. It was still the winter, but one of those freak mild days that had people shouldering their coats like resentful ten-year-olds forced to look after Baby. Students were chanting, holding aloft large blown-up photo posters of burned Oriental children, and baiting the cops with curses. In between chants, they sipped take-out coffee from the Chock Full O'Nuts across the street, they munched apples. Someone must have then thrown something at a cop, maybe a core, because a small phalanx of police charged one group of kids, some of whom went down. This substantially upped the excitement level. Jack had been to enough baseball games to recognize when thrill was in the air: a hole bored into a mood and waiting for a filling; and when he overheard two girls talking, one telling the other in an isn't-it-just-fabulous voice that "Someone from Mobilization is going to douse him . . . and PL will come up with the match"—then Jack had the feeling they were more than only kidding, and he made his way over to a sergeant and told him what he'd heard.

The policeman smiled. He said no one was dousing anybody, because the Dow guy was inside the building a half hour already and going about his business. "Your big mistake was coming this way. You should have gone down Broadway and in that back entrance. Don't let these little fuckers bother you."

Seeing Jack's suit and tie, the cop simply had assumed.

Jack told Donna that what happened next seemed all very automatic but oddly inevitable: making his way over to Broadway, going in the back entrance of the Chem building, being asked to surrender his I.D., and then going right up. Only three other students were in the waiting room, all filling out the questionnaire; and Jack had reached Question 23—"Describe briefly your career objectives"—before giving any conscious thought to how strange and unprovided-for it was that here he sat, a clipboard on his lap in a room stuffy with steam-heat which no one that day wanted.

The recruiter, a curly-haired man who had kept his jacket on and given an Armenian name, liked it that Jack was a history major, having himself been poli-sci as an undergrad before going on into industrial personnel. He thumbed toward the shadeless windows facing west overlooking the park. Jack, he said, could probably put all this into good perspective, history mostly being a matter of recurring cycles, right? The sun in the room was fierce, assaulting; the man pinched the bridge of his nose, pressed his index fingers heavily against his eyelids once.

Jack told the recruiter that he hoped full combat pay came along with his assignment.

"Do you think I was drafted into this?" asked the recruiter.

"Probably not," said Jack. And he had to disagree, by the way. History seemed more like a pattern of human character variations than a cycle of events.

The recruiter smiled. What were Jack's grades? Would he be able to relocate after graduation? Did Jack know that Dow had a full tuition-rebate program and that it in fact preferred its management trainees go on and receive higher degrees? In Jack's case, that would probably mean an M.B.A. Industry didn't snare too many liberal arts grads lately; the ones it did, it liked to make sure to brand early.

"There's room, in other words," said Jack, "inside the jaws of Mammon." The recruiter stood up and took off his jacket. Jack opened his own collar and loosened his tie. The recruiter asked him how come NYU had never heard of blinds.

A month later, in the mail, came a grade-request consent form. Then, three weeks after that, there was a letter offering a position which would be held open for him starting in August of that year.

When he was done, Donna said nothing. For a hulking, enormous moment she drew lines down through the condensation on her glass.

"You wore a suit and tie to college every day?"

At first Jack felt slapped with ridicule: her taking the mingiest, least germane part of his story and hitting it back at him. But then he realized how close her attention had been. "Everyone on the Long Island Rail Road wears a suit. You wouldn't know this, but the line's logo—they're actually proud of this—is Dan, The Dashing and Harried Commuter. So that was me too: Dan, The Dashing and Harried Commuter." He hoped she was going to smile.

Instead she had begun to play with the hair beside her ear. "I used to work in Pediatrics," she said, with a soberness that was almost downy.

"I know, the napalm."

Her fingers left her hair and came to her lips—as if even the word spoken aloud was devastating.

Jack exhaled. "When you drive somewhere, you try to be aware of alternate routes, right? If there's a jam-up, you go around it, you don't hit the gas and try to break it free.

"Okay. Alternate routes. I had two of them—two, as my neighbor would say, methods and modalities. One was the cop-out method and modality, but still legitimate. I worked in industrial sealants, about as foreign to napalm as the medical research division was—and they, by the way, were at that same time developing an artifical skin for use in grafting. Villainy isn't usually that schizo.

"Anyway, true as that is, it's still the cop-out. There's also this, which people like to hear less. When there's a war on, industries produce war materiel. It's the nature of the beast. Clubs. Gunpowder. Mustard gas. Atom bombs. The nicest companies too, not just rapacious meanies. The country that's at war comes down with a fever—and history likes to see a sweat worked up. Then it breaks, cools down, and everyone starts asking: What happened?

"If you were alive during that time of war, no matter what you did was probably more wronging than wronged. I don't buy this complicity stuff. *Everybody* complies. All I can tell you is that if I had ever once personally witnessed someone pouring napalm on a child or on anyone, I'd bash that person's brains out."

Donna allowed herself a wide and wandering breath. "It sounds like it all might have been simpler if you had lived on campus."

She meant nothing mocking by it, just a friendly diagnosis—but Jack, too hiked up by the risk he'd taken, too much at the far ends of his nerves, was still in high gear. "I've never been too big on simple. It doesn't do much for me. If someone called *you* simple, would you like it?" Then he only prayed it had come out sounding half amiable.

Donna pushed her fork all the way onto the leaf of garnish lettuce on her plate. "If you're done . . ."

"Ready when you are." He'd blown it. Fool.

"Those two over at the bar," she leaned to whisper, "do you see them?" Jack looked. A pair of country types, one bearded, both in John Deere caps, was sending up taunts to the bar's TV screen, where stick-thin young Mexicans were hurling themselves off sheer rock faces into Acapulco waters hundreds of feet below. "They're terrible—and I mean really. I was in the E.R. one night and they came in: they'd shot each other in the hand, some game they were playing."

Jack made a face of fright. "Then let's by all means."

On the way back to the hospital Jack asked if she'd mind his stopping at the 7-11 for cigarettes. She came into the store with him, but everything he offered—popcorn? pretzels? Slim Jims?—she declined with a smile. Jack paid for his cigarettes. Why had he ever told her?

In the parking lot of the hospital Donna got out of Jack's car and into her own. In his rearview mirror he watched her follow him out of the lot. On the road down into town: still following. And then, into the Slope, she was still there.

Tariq's Volkswagen hawked, then ceased, below the window at twelve midnight. It woke Donna from a brief but deep sleep. "Hhh?"

"It's nothing," Jack whispered.

She sat up. "Am I blocking his space? I'll go down and move."

"It's all right. Go back to sleep."

"No, I'm up."

Then, shortly after, and with a logy kindness, she began to suck on him. He'd never wanted much of this, but it was nice. Her breasts were large for so small a girl. Before, when his fingers had been inside her, she was languid and unfocused; when he got on top of her, though, both knees had whanged back quickly, like a released trap. It happened that way again now, a second time.

The things you could forget: rhythm, speed, the sheer attention that was required. The new continuous hardness of himself was notable also.

And she was *different.* In all his years at Dow and at Scofield in New York, the girls he'd known were from inside the company. Cousins, of a sort. They shared gossip with him, and personalities, and salaries—it made them seem somehow tamed. But now, naked and slippery, he was with someone totally other, someone who was calm, generous, unfazed; the initiator, the relaxed expert . . . someone truly *strange.* He didn't know what to think.

Jack spurted, half-died. After dropping off to the side of her, he touched one of Donna's amazing barbarian-girl nipples—like someone who stops to read the menu posted outside *after* eating in the restaurant. She smiled.

2

After what had happened at the TV studio, Judith swore to herself that from then on she was going to be mortified and pliant. Invisible. As much out of Jack's way as possible.

But he didn't make this easy. All the rest of the day, and through the night, he was a hoverer. Once, she awoke to find his fever-searching lips against her forehead. "What are you doing?" "Just kissing you." "No, you're not." "I was." "Leave me alone!" Acting stymied and insulted (but actually victorious), he lay there quietly for a while, then got up from the bed. She heard him turn on one of the gas burners in the kitchen. Then she smelled the marijuana she'd brought up from the city for him.

On arrival, right off the bus—this was her big blunder—she should have come directly out with it: I'm through with Anthony, I'm all yours for the having. While she was still rested from the ride, energetic, prior to his first good long look at the kerchief and the thinness and the steroid moon of her face. Seconds count—and she had waited too long, letting him figure out the lousier part of her news instead. Coming along with him to the TV studio was merely the final nail in the . . .

He wasn't coming back to bed. Judith moved her feet over, getting comfortable. She closed her eyes again. She was not the most subtle of engineers, that was all. Last week's maneuver, it hadn't been so very graceful either.

Chuckie Gold had called the loft around seven on a Sunday night: Felice Dacey was at The Nest for one night only, did they want to go. Without consulting Judith, Anthony had declined. She raised a squawk ("Oh, that's right, I forgot: our vigil.")—and he went to call Chuckie back.

Felice Dacey, who turned out to be a touch wattley under the chin, wore a black dress with long sleeves, sipped between songs at a drink that had five chunks of lime in it, and smiled only at the bass player (which Judith had found a mite snobbish). Anthony, though, enjoyed himself. He and Chuckie pulled contentedly at their beer bottles through "There's a Small Hotel" and "Round Midnight" and "How High the Moon" and "Yesterday" and "The Shadow of Your Smile" and "All the Things You Are," each of the melodies ingeniously bent according to the famous Felice Dacey style. It had been kind and smart of Chuckie to think of it. A Sunday night's properly minuscule crowd, all *cognoscenti,* like a service in a private chapel: right up Anthony's alley—and good for him, especially now. His hurt had been awful for her to see. He was so nakedly sorry that he'd ever believed in her remission; and now he didn't know which was the more indefensible: to have bought the illusion or the illusion itself. The going out and the music had cooled him a little—but, then, much too soon, Felice Dacey was saying "All right, one last song."

Things began to go downhill only after they had left The Nest for a nightcap at Lynton's. The lights in the bar were brighter than the club's, and in place of music was raucous, gaudy bar talk from Judith's least favorite brand of drunk, the Sunday night one. Anthony, too, seemed to worsen in the change of atmospheres, turning sentimental over his brandy, making some swoony remark about how "incredibly goddamn beautiful" Felice's face was; which Judith—so ungoddamn beautiful and guaranteed to become even less so in the near future—thought crude of him, and so she'd said something back about how thankful Max Factor must be, Felice having kept them in business all these years.

Chuckie had tried to mediate, admitting that yes, Felice did use a lot of makeup, but it was to hide the facial scars: Felice had been beaten in the Forties, he explained, down South. By cops. While Chuckie labored to explain the circumstances ("Jacksonville, I think. Which was the wrong place—to say the least—at the wrong time, you know?"), Anthony had sat back, holding his snifter, wearing one of his cool and jazzbo looks; and only when Judith asked enough of what he clearly thought were dumb questions did he, the foreman, finally step in, taking it away from Chuckie:

"They stopped her in a car. That right there—the sight of a white woman driving the South in a car that expensive, while a nigger sax player was sacked out in back—did not endear her to the constabulary. I believe she was also wearing a mink-collared coat."

Endear. Constabulary. Nigger. All meant to rile Judith.

Chuckie added, "And of course she was carrying, too."

Heroin, Chuckie meant—and that had brought the talk immediately down to ever pickier levels: Judith saying that she had, in that case, less sympathy for Felice; Chuckie, looking pained, protesting that it still hadn't been right to hit her around the face with a club; Judith, wondering if that's what really had happened, drug addicts being well-known liars—and, even if it had, it wasn't exactly the Sacco and Vanzetti affair, was it? heroin being illegal and harmful and an evil thing; Chuckie countering Evil? That was a sort of hard thing to define . . .

"We're finished here," Anthony meanwhile had informed the waitress, getting to his feet and pressing a twenty atop her order pad before she had a chance to total up the bill. Without waiting for his change, he started down the bar for the door.

Chuckie stood also—but Judith had remained seated, watching Anthony go out the front door. He'd do it, too—leave her here, make her walk home alone. Poor Chuckie by then didn't know what to do—and for his sake alone Judith rose.

Mr. Lucky had been waiting at the corner, reading a bill pasted to the fire-alarm box there. Not a word from him as they came aside. Since Chuckie lived on the way, there were three of them for half the walk east. But no one spoke. At Chuckie's door, Judith lunged for him, taking him aback as she kissed him affectionately.

As she was stepping down off the curb at Fourth Avenue, Anthony finally took her arm—which she shook off vigorously, leading him to say, "Had yourself one grand time of it tonight, didn't you?"

"The holiest connoisseur himself deigns to speak! And the smuggest!" Judith had slowed down so that he would gain a few steps on her, allowing her the target of his back. "I *did* have a good time—to answer a supercilious question."

Surprised at the new distance that had sprung up between them, Anthony turned his head—but didn't slow up. "Name two songs she sang."

"Who taught you to be so good at missing the point? I just like being with *you*. I don't much care where." She hadn't planned to say this but it slid out, a loose silky lining to her anger.

"Foolish attitude," he said.

He'd brought her back to the desired state of huff. "If it is, it's one you certainly depend on enough."

"—and foolish conversation."

"Admit it for once: you take me for granted. Even now. If I'm well, I'm supposed to be well—no deviations. If I'm sick: be sick, woman. Men think that way—that you have to be one thing at a time."

Anthony had stopped before a doorway (dark and grundgy looking;

she wished he hadn't): "It's tiresome. This whole lib thing: tiresome. You're beyond it; it's a waste for someone like you. Maybe not for your friend Somogyi—she has need for bullshit, it's what she thrives on—but for you it's perverse. Yet you don't see that. A terrible shame."

She had neglected to halt in the meantime, so had passed him—and now *her* back became the target. It had been better the other way. "You want us to take whatever comes along submissively, and then you criticize us for being will-less. The old story: the woman comes too close, the man tells her to be more selfish. No wonder you wanted to go tonight—she's your ideal. A woman heroin addict."

"Who was the one who wanted to go?" But he was getting bored with it. She could tell by his voice.

"I'm extremely sorry that I'm not a junkie—and that, compared to yours, my self-involvement is very undeveloped." Why doesn't he speed up and pass her already? She stopped dead—and he passed, muttering *"meshuga"* as he did.

"With his little Yiddish words, folks, that everyone gets a big kick out of." She raised her voice. "Phony like the rest of him." They were entering his block now; the whores clustering at one of the far corners looked, in the dark and fog, like short sticks of condensation.

"Quiet," Anthony ordered.

"Neat little loft, neat little enthusiasms."

"Calm down, Ophelia."

"Neat little *failure!*" The sheer reckless unfairness of what she was saying allowed Judith the best breaths she'd drawn in weeks. Rip apart his retreat! "How did I ever get stuck with such an old fart?"

Anthony had reached the entrance to his building and was getting the steel front door open. He grabbed for her arm. "Come inside now."

She had twisted away. "A fart!" At this, the *Whoo-weeeee!*'s from the whores on the corner flew back down the street like long pennants. Anthony again tried to nab her, but she stepped away. "Or maybe a fruit—someone who likes everything to be just so. A picky old fruity fart." She turned on her heel and headed back in the direction they'd come.

"Where are you going? What are you doing?" Anthony had caught up with her.

"Going home to *my* house. Right now I'm waiting for a cab."

Shaking his head, Anthony had stepped into the middle of the traffickless avenue, looking north and south—while Judith waited by the curb, shivering with excitement. He finally saw and stopped a taxi (not a Checker, not now)—*and then was helping her into it!* Never once looking at her while he did so. If he'd looked, the ass, he would have been apologized to, by face or word. But he had never looked.

In the morning Jack was up and dressed before she was. A day at home, just the two of them—he with his fear and his grass, she with her infinite capacity for mistake—would have been unbearable; so, over breakfast, she cajoled him into taking her to an apple cidery she'd read about in the local paper. He made excuses—the weather; it was far—but in the end he took her. (He had a pipeful before leaving the house.)

"What did that sign back there say? I missed it."

"'Chicken Dinner. Sunday Night, 7 PM. First Hanaford Congregational Church.'"

Jack nodded tightly. Not the type to admit to being lost, he was the type to make them both miserable if that in fact were the case. But finally: "Lettors Falls Apple Products. One Mile Right."

Three wooden buildings of differing heights but painted the same color—red, naturally. Outside the lowest, longest shed was a weighing scale and a conveyor belt (REMOVE LEAVES AND TWIGS. DO NOT OVERLOAD), which sluggishly moved the apples through a cutout in the wall of the middle of the shack. The apples got a forceless, hot-water shower there and continued on the belt into the last and tallest building, where they were tumbled into large rectangular frames. Two workers were dropping heavy cheesecloth over each filled frame, then stacking and pushing them five at a time under a hydraulic press. The cider that came out dripped down into a copper catch-trough, and lastly into a big tank. Visitors could follow the whole process from behind a railing.

The smell in the pressing shack! Whenever people would open the door to enter or leave, the fresh air they let in was dull and bleachy by comparison. Who would want to exit? Jack was touching the back of her neck tenderly. Was he going to kiss her, here amidst this hurricane of fragrance? She nearly yipped with pleasure as she turned to him.

"I'll be outside," he said.

After they had the two empty plastic jugs Jack had bought filled with cider from a nozzle, they returned to Jack's truck. The rain that had made most of the morning metallic, like a spoon left too long in a soup pot, had cleared, and better weather was bringing more people out. One of the cidery hands was playing traffic cop, but not very logically: he was holding back the people who were leaving in favor of the newly arrived. Jack was inching the truck in queue when he was suddenly cut off by a van driven by a bearded father, two small boys his passengers.

"Look at the sticker," Jack said. "'I Brake For Animals.' Being one myself."

Judith was opening one of the jugs and tasting. "This is so delicious. Mmm." (Although in no more than a second it repeated on her.)

Jack had his head stuck out the window. "That's a hopeless kid, the one waving everyone in. No one's paying any attention to him—and if they can . . ." Bringing his head back in, he cut the wheel sharply and zoomed around the van in front, jouncing over mud furrows and out onto the road.

"Try some of this."

"When we stop." Jack rose off the seat to see something better in the rearview mirror. "He's got one in front too—this ape's a regular saint. Cuts me off, almost causes an accident, could have injured his own kids—but don't you forget that he loves the furry creatures."

Judith capped the jug and looked back. The van was following close behind on the narrow road. Another sticker—I PAUSE FOR PAWS—was pasted over the trademark circle on the front grille.

"So." She turned around ahead. "He's showing off his better and his worse traits, that's all. Be happy there's a range."

"I'm not happy." The truck slowed a bit as Jack let up on the gas.

Craning around again, Judith strained to catch a glimpse of the children through the windshield of the van. She could only make out the beard.

"And where to do you suppose the mother is?" Jack said. "Probably home nursing her own crash injuries. Or filing for divorce."

A horn blat from the van—and Jack promptly slowed down more. Flatly, as they started to take a curve—quietly—he said: "So pass, jerk."

On the very next straightaway, still too narrow for one to yet get ahead of another, the van rushed up almost within bumping distance of the truck's taillights.

Judith looked around. The beard's mouth within all that hair was pulled closed like a string bag's. "If there's a fight," she warned Jack, "I'm running."

"Brake for *me*, asshole!" Jack hooted. He began to tap at the brake pedal.

"Jack!" Now she was scared.

"I want to see him pass me."

"Jack, children are in there."

"Takes two to tango. You see how much *he* cares." The truck nonetheless edged a little to the right, toward the shoulder. Judith looked back: the imbecile beard was maneuvering likewise, not letting go in the least.

"Besides," she shouted desperately at Jack, "you're making *me* very nauseous."

In two seconds they were off the road completely, pulling to an urgent stop on the berm. The van flashed by, braying, the beard heaping on insult with a finger raised above the roof.

But Jack was concentrating on her. "Are you all right?"

"Fine."

Very seriously: "I'm sorry."

"I'm *fine!*"

At the house again, she asked if she could lie down a while—"With you." When she started to undress, Jack's face closed into that vacant piety men frequently think is appropriate; and she had to get up—"Oh, no"—and gruntingly remove his clothes as well—"you wouldn't want to make this easy, perish the thought."

He suffered it, floppy and uninflated. She even bent to him. "Stop," he ordered. "But I get pleashure"—slurping a rope of drool. "I said stop." He drew her down flat to the bed again, hugging her more in constraint than out of any passion.

But a hug's a hug, and a solid thigh wins out over principle any day: "Oh. Oh. Yes, oh—keep your leg like that—don't move it, yes. Ohhhh."

Then he was back into his underpants in a flash, warning, "You'll be cold like that." Her slipping under the covers as she was, still nude, wasn't what he'd had in mind of course—and it was then that he'd brought up the matter of the bus schedule.

More passengers were coming down the dim and narrow raised aisle, but so far no one had to sit next to anyone else—which is how Judith hoped it would stay. From the high smoked windows of the Scenicruiser, she had Jack dumpily foreshortened, his hands in his pockets, his breath visible in the autumn air. The front door was closing, the pinch of the airbrakes released, the transmission convulsing and settling:

they began to roll slowly backwards. He looks like a twerp, she instructed herself to think. A twerp with twerpy reasons ("I don't want you unloaded into an all-out psycho party down at the Port Authority terminal. Any later bus back, and that's what you're going to find."). She wasn't going to look at him down there anymore.

She looked. Jack was waving and blowing a kiss. Judith put her lips to the window, excitedly sending back two to his one.

She could now have a good trip back. Very small towns bunched up near the interstate; and the bus was having to crawl through the center of one of them, two policemen keeping traffic moving past some sort of ceremony on the town green: flags, children, amplified music, citizens in checked woolen overshirts making neighborly conversation while standing on a floor of mustard-colored leaves. Someone on the bus took out an Instamatic for a picture. The bus, though, was now past the delay; it reared back once before regaining speed, an effect Judith felt profoundly at the bottom of her stomach.

A dramamine now? She hated to. These two-week intervals between treatments were supposedly her state of grace. Drug-free—but never exactly: the dramamine had to be as close at hand as the nausea was, even-steven. But she was going to hold off a while now, she decided, and see how it goes: it'll be her time-killer: her crossword puzzle, her granny square, her novel.

Anything at all can become a hobby. At one of the group-therapy sessions for Hodgkin's patients, the Puerto Rican furniture salesman, Eddie, had strained to describe his fantasy: the ultimate puke. "Enough—and real hard—so that you could, you know, be like inside out." Herzberg the psychiatrist went Eddie one better, imagining it as grabbing a corner of a pillow you wanted to fling—only to have the pillow fly but the case remain in your hand. Further analogies tried to beat out that one, everyone clamoring to add a piece, like to the zillion-part Jackson Pollock jigsaw puzzle in the solarium.

That particular session was the one and the only Jack had attended. He hadn't said a word, though, the entire time, slithering away from every invitation. Herzberg—tall and paunchy, big dog-eyes, the group his baby thanks to a government grant—plucked tirelessly at everyone's cork—"How you feel, when you feel, what you feel, undergoing this experience"—and the only ones who didn't oblige him and talk up that night were Jack and herself. As the only inpatient at the

sessions, the sole one in robe and slippers, she was frankly pulling rank.
(Too shy anyway.) And Jack—Jack clammed up because, as she'd later
realize, he was Jack.

They were also the only two who left immediately afterwards; the
others milled around Herzberg as if marks would presently be distributed. Through the clinic's waiting room and out into the corridor, Jack
had kept a constant three or four steps behind her. Semi-introduced
situations like this one always made her nervous: being aware of one
another but not sufficiently to produce conversation. His face—which
was uncannily like young Picasso's: fleshy features, green and intelli-
gent eyes, brutally sharp brows, sandy straight hair—wasn't unknown
to her, she'd noticed him before on clinic days. He would come to the
clinic wearing a suit and tie, which was either stupid or spunky of him
since all his clothes would soon have to come off anyway. New patients, of course, were often that way: starting strong. Put back together after the shock of diagnosis by the word *curable,* they were humble,
happy, vulgar rays of light.

Judith had made it to the lobby elevator banks, with him at her heels,
when all of a sudden she heard him saying something to her back:

"You're upstairs?"

She turned. Dry-tongued as an unpopular schoolgirl rarely spoken to
at recess, her eyes losing focus for a second, she smashed a high-strung
question right back at him:

"What did you think of that in there?"

He scowled tightly, the look he'd worn occasionally during the session. "I thought it was—"

"Interesting?"

"No. That's not what I was going to say. I was going to say that it
wasn't in good taste. It was heavily weighted, in fact, I was going to say,
toward bullshit."

She pressed the button for the elevator. Too astringent for her: good-
bye.

"Now I know what it means when they say someone is 'dumb-
struck.' The way he kept on calling it 'an experience.' And 'Does that
scare you?' What's he expect—that it doesn't scare us? It's like a parent
coming into a dark room, yelling out *Boo!* and then turning on the light
to show the kid it isn't a monster after all but only Daddy. Either way
the kid has pissed his bed."

She found his vehemence, as if they weren't in a hospital lobby but coming out onto a nighttime street after seeing a controversial movie that he'd hated, entertaining. The elevator doors—*bing*—had slipped open.

"You can have coffee, can't you?" he was asking.

She had let go for a moment of the rubber gasket of the elevator door, which closed, and watched him point across the lobby in the direction of the coffee shop. Pushing a fist inside a pocket, producing a bulge of display, she said, "But I'm in this."

"Why, do they discriminate against robes?"

In the coffee shop he told her that were he ever to go back to one of those (which he'd never) he would stand up and say, Oh I love having this disease, love talking about it, losing hair on account of it, love every wonderful minute of the experience, the adventure. "And do you think that quack would even blink?"

He was a frivolous person. Judith was sorry she hadn't guessed as much right away and gone directly upstairs as planned. They were seated at the elbow of the only counter still serving, and he had ordered two coffees, forcing her to say no to the waitress and change that to one coffee and one strawberry malted (think weight gain). She had already looked around, not entirely comfortable trespassing here, in a zone of the well; and she was wondering too at what point she'd have to say something to him about not having any money on her, which he surely hadn't thought about.

"All we are to him are data."

You could tell somehow that his hair was usually kept shorter, that it had been recently let go. It made him seem even more aggressive. "Are you always so committed to your first impressions?"

"So are you, Judith. So is everybody."

"But I'm willing to go back for a second impression. That's the difference." How did he know her name? She didn't know his. "And is it possible that Dr. Herzberg was as nervous as the rest of us?"

"I wasn't nervous—and you're just being fair."

"*Just?*" Strictly to amuse herself, she unscrolled a theatrical, grand dame's laugh. "Then it must come easier to you than it does to me." She remembered now. Everyone had had to introduce himself at the start of the session. People who remembered strangers' names, though, were pushy.

He was rubbing those razor brows of his, calmly. "Things can seem more interesting and more acceptable than they are. You're in bed all day, reading, watching television, not much to do . . ."

What a detestable person! "Tell me about you. Like your name and how you're staged. I'm Four-B."

He smiled. "It's the draft board all over again. Jack Richmond. They tell me—and who knows if it's true or not—that I'm Three-A."

He wasn't, then, all that less sick than she was—only newer to it, untrusting, and this was what she'd taken for cockiness: the anger. She herself had it too. Back then. But it wore off. (How could it have? It did somehow. *Why me?* turning into *Why* not *me?*)

"You had a spleen operation, right?" he was asking. "The reason I know is because I was in the next cubicle while Dr. Wellitz was explaining it to you; I heard him say 'Judith.' How was the splenectomy? Very tough?"

"If you can, order the lambchops instead." But all Jack did was nod, the way that people without senses of humor do, waiting for you to get past the foolishness, so she relented. "It hurt more afterwards than I was expecting, but it was also less of a big deal. It's a fairly routine procedure here. They know what they're doing, and you knowing that they know helps. That's not the universal case, of course." She heard herself: the grizzled veteran.

"You've been in other hospitals for this?"

"One other."

"And they didn't help you?" The tip of his tongue appeared between his lips; he seemed shocked.

"Not out of any meanness. Either they didn't know about the newest methods or they didn't use them very well."

"Well, which?" He looked at his fingers. "So then they must have made it worse. Jesus!"

She was beginning to like him a little, for his kid-like innocence or his empathy and probably for both. It hadn't been lost on her either that, as they talked, he had very deftly palmed the check, which had been set down closer to her than to him.

"Where exactly upstairs are you?" he asked her.

"Oncology."

"I know that—I mean what room." A pen was pulled from his jacket and held poised over a napkin.

"Two-twenty-four-B."

He wrote it down—no name, just the number. Clicked-up, the pen was put away. "Since when?"

"It'll be three weeks. But I think next week I'll check out." The making it sound like it was her decision—was this his influence already?

"So you'll go home—" Jack said. "Where's that, and what do you do?"

Anthony would absolutely hate him. Anthony, who was generally accurate to no particular purpose about people, would say that Jack had "the soul of a salesman." "I'm an associate curator at a museum." She waited for *Which museum?* and the inevitable being-impressed; even in robe and slippers she was still what she was.

Instead he asked, "How long have you been sick?"

She pushed away her half-emptied glass. "I ought to go back up. Thanks for the malted, Jack . . . It's Jack, right? I do vaguely remember seeing you before. In the clinic."

"You have," he said, rising gallantly with her, "but don't remind us."

The next afternoon, to her total surprise, he appeared at the door to her room.

It forced her to pull herself from a deep slouch in the bed and quickly try to become presentable, all the while making elementary introductions: her parents were there at the time.

Did he know Judy from the museum? Daddy asked him. Co-workers? Without hesitation, naturally as can be, Jack said, "No, from right here. We're shipmates on the same boat"—and with a forefinger and thumb, he encircled his neck at the latitude of the lymph nodes. (For a moment it had looked to Judith like he was going to make a throat-slashing gesture.) Horrified, her father's tumbling expression was netted at the last second by a flabby, polite smile.

Bernice, ever the tougher cookie of the two, had been eyeing Jack carefully; but she too was quickly brought to heel: "You look fine, though. Everything's working out for you?"

The smile Jack turned on her was sky-bright. "Everything's great. I'm getting treatment, your daughter's going home soon—it's all on track."

Daddy got up, relinquishing his chair. Jack, as she hoped he would, accepted it, pulling it closer to the side of the bed. Anthony's small teak-and-fruitwood chess set was on the bedstand, and Judith asked Jack if he played.

"Not offense *and* defense I don't."

"Oh, I know, I know," chuckled Bernice. "I'm not good at games, either." (Judith thought: Is that so?)

Finally her parents were making to go. Jack got up from the chair also, pulling a railroad schedule from his pocket. "If you need a lift . . ." Daddy offered, but Jack said no, he was all set. Out in the corridors the nurses were beginning to come around for afternoon temperatures—and Judith couldn't wait for all of them, Jack included, to be gone.

The next day, though, around noon and before visiting hours, he was at the door again. The violation! No doors to knock on, not a phone call first—he's just suddenly there. She could have wept.

The morning's blood count had come up short, a transfusion was ordered and begun, and all morning she'd been feeling like bread dough punched down after a rise. And now him. She watched his eyes registering the I.V. stand, the bag, the black line of tubing, the wristboard. He walked directly to the chair he'd sat in the day before and pulled it close. (No! The blood—literally—smelled like shit, and she'd been having trouble standing it herself.)

But once he began talking, Jack never at all mentioned her transfusion. His concern, briefly and exclusively, was with himself. Downstairs, in half an hour, they were going to start *the big push*—radiating his abdomen. They'd told him to expect a certain amount of nausea. What was "a certain amount," he wanted to know. If it meant only feeling fragile for a few hours, he figured he could handle it. "Am I being a big baby?" He got up and paced. Did she have today's newspaper around? Judith motioned with her one free hand to the chair near the metal clothes closet. "I might as well see how I did. I may not remember later." He explained that, to pass the train ride home, he doped out the racing charts, making paper bets out of a pool of a hundred imaginary dollars.

"I would have expected the stock market instead," she said bitchily.

"Can I use this pen?"

She wished he'd go. She didn't like him, he wasn't paying any attention to her. "Do you come out ahead?"

"You tell me. Here." He folded the paper to half its width. "This is who I think I like best today. Ducky Joy, in the fifth." He studied the paper another minute and put it and the pen down. "I'm nervous, can't sit. I better go." He touched her hand and left—left just like that.

By suppertime the needle was out of her arm. She was bruised, but at least the gloomiest band of her mood was loosened. While she ate her meal, Anthony sat watching the TV news and massaging her ankles.

"What's this?" The newspaper had caught his eye. "Picking ponies? Since when?" He gave the page a fluid scan. "Poor choices"—a foxy smile.

"It isn't my paper."

Anthony squinted at the page. "Your pen's ink."

"It isn't," she insisted—"and shhh, I want to hear this." The weatherman had come on.

"*Why?*" Anthony sat molding the newspaper over his kneecap, looking at it but not looking at it, insensible to the tasteless thing either he'd just said or she'd just heard. The racing page seemed to have put him in one of his antsy periods—his heels were clicking on the underrung of the straight chair he was in—and these were often volatile. Who knows, maybe he was fantasizing: If she ever got out of here . . . Belmont . . . Saratoga in August together . . . A pure, sweet, inane hospital-room reverie.

At home, surrounded by certain empty walls of the loft, Anthony could never have afforded to entertain such thoughts. In order to cover debts run up by just such "ponies," he had been forced to sell off two large, valuable, almost mystically precious-to-him paintings painted and given to him by his master and idol and as-good-as-father, Walter Dornish. This occurred a few years before Judith had met him. The sale of the Dornishes had been effected with great discretion and greater pain; for a long time Judith knew about it only from what she could piece together from odd, cryptic remarks. A two-day-old baby would be found, for instance, in a Gristede's bag in Central Park, and Anthony would turn away from the TV, muttering, "Ought to be shot, not forgivable." Then: ". . . Look who's talking." One night, with a lot of wine in him, after a radio broadcast of *Turandot,* his favorite opera, he finally dribbled out most of the story to her—what he loved most bartered to clean up after what he could help least—but not the whole thing: "There's more, there's more, but it's too shmucky to tell."

Judith was able to piece out the rest by herself. Only a matter of months after selling the Dornishes, Anthony had put down his own brushes and opened a frame shop. His friends, some gone on to the fame and riches he was renouncing, kept him liberally in work, often stipulating that Terrezza be the one to do the major framing when they had a show at a gallery or museum. The night Judith first met him, at her museum, it was an opening of a friend's show that he had framed. People were surrounding Anthony all night; someone who didn't know would have thought he was the artist. He was small—Judith didn't think she'd ever seen such an impossibly elegant man. Greying hair, cut short, none of the long sideburn and flowing locks with-it style that was then popular. Thin. Dark skin—darkest around the eyes, which paled when he smiled. A pullover and loden slacks where most everyone else was in a suit or even formal wear.

The way he smoked a cigarette. The buttery leather of his shoes, step-ins. Challenged to it, as a social game, he was providing a rundown of the titles of every movie Ida Lupino, his star of choice, had ever made. The list was delivered with a shy, hip confidence that moved a few listeners to applause when he was done. By the time Judith was formally introduced to him, later that evening, she already felt powdery with infatuation.

What she didn't know until later, of course, was that the main element of this perfect balance, its crosspiece, was guilt—unremovable, too. He still gambled; now and then she found OTB slips stuck into books as markers. But she would have been surprised *not* to find them: the special mark of all his friends, it seemed, was their faith, especially in what bashed them around. Compared to Anthony, Judith herself felt like a snowflake, transitory. Selling the Dornishes was his atrocity, but she pictured it as a crime of love and of the past, as romantic. Maybe she was a terrible person, but other people's shame she often thought of as their best quality.

She finished the fruit cup, pushed away the swing-out table, and drew her feet back up and onto the bed and under the sheet. The arm into which the blood had gone was sore.

Anthony was giving the newspaper another appraisal. "You're right. The way the letters next to the races are written, even the circling—it's not your handwriting."

"So kind of you to believe me."

He rubbed her shin from above the sheet. "A long rough day for you." He kneaded. "Tomorrow's going to be better. How was the chicken?"

Jack Richmond didn't reappear the next day, although until four-thirty, when she knew the machines down in Radiotherapy stopped for the day, she vaguely expected him. Just as well: she needed a visitorless day. She changed nightgowns and balanced her checkbook. She called a few people at the museum at an hour when she knew they'd be lolling about in their offices, not working. She put on some blusher and sat awhile in the solarium, among hot limp ribbons of western light. Supper—fish Italiano—wasn't inedible, and on the portable TV which Mrs. Petrile's son had brought in on the sly rather than pay the hospital's costly rental she then watched junk long into night.

She had to grab, panicky, for her hairbrush when, at ten-thirty the next morning, Jack again showed his face.

He thoughtfully said a few words to Mrs. Petrile until he heard the click of the hairbrush against the formica-topped bedstand; then he turned and dragged a chair over to Judith's bed. She'd been planning to jump out of it, but wasn't quick enough.

"No more blood—good, congratulations." Jack settled his elbows on the slatty armrests. "You have to congratulate me, too. I'm now a full-fledged member of the club: *The Sickies*." He smiled. "The minute that machine shut off yesterday, I had the feeling—and whoever saw me in Penn Station afterwards will be telling their grandchildren about it one day. World-class upchucking. So today I'm not taking any chances. I'm here *before* treatment. I wanted to ask you something. How did you—"

"Everyone reacts differently."

Like a little brother, he nodded docilely. "A while ago they gave me pills," he said, "for the nausea. Not too effective."

She softened. "Pester them, then—until they give you something that does work. If it'll hold you until you get home, it works."

"They mentioned suppositories once, Compazine suppositories—although I'm not eager . . ."

Judith's prissiness surged again: suppositories. She wanted more of his abrasive, spit-in-the-eye charm, not talk of suppositories. But before she could say anything more, he was standing. "Well . . . into the fray. If I'm early, you don't think they'd take pity and ray-gun me with less, do you?"

"Ducky Joy came in second," she said quickly.

It stopped him. "You checked? That's right, he placed."

"Would you have won anything?"

"Zip." His eyes crinkled sweetly. "But only fools are cautious with imaginary money, or someone else's."

"Which is why, I suppose, the expression *a poor second*."

"You suppose that, do you?"

She was sorry when he left. Flirting: how much fun. Even with someone scared half to death.

Except on weekends, he came every morning after that. She had to admit that it secretly made her proud: able to lure him back daily. Her discharge was postponed a week, but since it coincided with the worst of Jack's cobalt (they were treating his midabdomen) she didn't mind too terribly. Although there were mornings when his hands trembled as he turned to the racing page, laying it out on the bed for them both to study; mornings when, instead of coming upstairs to see her, he could have spent an extra half-hour at home resting—Judith was never able to work up enough unselfishness to tell him not to come to her. After Mrs. Petrile was discharged, her bed was taken over by a Queens schoolteacher with a sarcoma that smelled evilly; curlicues of demoralizing odor ruffled the room always. Jack took one whiff, the first day, and immediately ran down Ritter, the chief resident on the unit; Judith was moved to another room that afternoon.

She floated in the luxury of the security. Nothing had to be explained to him.

After she left the hospital they saw each other only on clinic days. Most of the contact was by phone. Usually she did the calling—but, one time, he did: nervous-voiced, quavery (afraid that Anthony might have answered, jealous?). He'd had his first chemotherapy injections and had vomited for sixteen, seventeen, maybe eighteen hours after. (Judith's lips numbed to hear it, as if they'd touched a cold pane of glass. Her own drug treatments had been a little less bad but not much; with Jack now, she felt like she was watching from a high window a blind man step off a curb into traffic.) One of the doctors had recommended marijuana to him as a tool against the nausea.

"Which is just dandy," Jack said disgustedly to her. "A great, great idea." (This was a first: a frazzled Jack.) "Where am I supposed to find that in my father's house on Long Island?"

"From friends?" she asked.

"Not here. Not there, either—I don't *have* those kinds of friends."

"Then forget it, don't take it, you'll manage." She was almost positive he'd never smoked before; it would go with the rest of his generally reactionary attitudes.

"But what if it really works? If it works, I want it."

"Let me see what I can do."

"No, I don't want you to be involved."

Tom, one of the art handlers at the museum, came through without any problem, even offering to make a gift of it, which Judith refused. When she called Jack back he sounded—against the imminent fact—twice as jumpy. Everything was a huge problem. How would he get it from her, feeling as weak as he did? And when? Where should he "take" it? How much?

She offered a proposal. The night before he was going to get his next injections, he would come to her house and smoke. He could stay over, and then go directly to the hospital in the morning from there.

"How would your friend feel about that?"

"No, not here," Judith said. "My own apartment. I don't stay there very often—though lately more." This all swam up, cohering, as she said it. She would tell Anthony she needed a night alone.

Jack, bleak, sorry for himself, said, "All this *shit.*"

It was raining again. Not so hard that it was giving the bus driver any trouble; just steadily, juicily, enough to sound like a celestially amplified noisy eater. On the seat next to her the plastic jug of cider *chunk-chunked* every time the bus took a curve; she placed it down between her feet, where it cooled her ankles. Hundreds of new cars were sitting like colored buttons on the wet lots outside an assembly plant in Mahwah, and mile upon mile of shopping centers and roadside businesses were set to begin.

Judith pulled out her compact, touched herself up in the soggy half-light: looking a lot less than great in the small round mirror—but who was going to care anyway?

(No no, none of that now: small sips of a fine wine—she had to remember. Small sips.)

Nestled between a Dunkin' Donuts and a carpet outlet was a piney semicircle of cute gingerbread cabins: the Swiss Lodge Motel, its chained plaques—Vacancy, Day Rates—swinging in the shower. It was easily the oldest looking place along the road. Wouldn't it be fun to call up an image of her own mother and father fancifully checking in to this same Swiss Lodge Motel nine months before the famous date?

She tried. But it wouldn't come—no image, no small sip. Rubbing like a mad person against Jack's martyred thigh: *that's* what came to mind instead, without any coaxing, bounding right up like a happy dumb hound.

Is she depressed? She wondered. She's dealing with elemental rules here, after all, and who is she to alter them? Everyone hates the sick. *We* even hate the sick. So Jack hates me. Exiles get touchy among themselves like anyone else. In Jack's shoes . . .

But, ah, isn't that the very problem. She *is* in his shoes, he's in hers— if you looked beneath her bed you wouldn't find, even there, in the dust, shoes that are so badly confused.

3

Staticky snow was drifting on the diagonal, like the real thing, across Donna's small-screened TV. Since her trailer sat in the deepest part of a dell—and since out back behind it, beyond a steely, now-frozen stream, was a scrubby, medium-sized hill—that she got any picture at all was a marvel.

Outside the closed door to Donna's room, Rafe and Doughnut were crooning softly over doggy banishment. On TV, beneath the interference's white tweed, Joel McCrae said, *Maybe so, but if I'm expecting that man to*—when the phone rang in the trailer, drowning him out.

After a single ring, silence. Then Tina's voice, cottony lumps, carried from the other end of the trailer: "Bigup, Donna! For you!" Tina, like Donna, was a nurse, in the intensive care unit of Delphi Community. When she was home, between shifts, she scuffed about—big-boned, blonde, not neat—in puffball slippers and a quilted robe hairy with threads. A safety pin kept one of the temple-pieces of her eyeglasses united with the rest of the frame. Slightly allergic to Donna's long-haired dogs, she sniffled constantly but had apparently never stirred her mind around the idea of moving out. As Vic Pellegrino's new part-time handyman/agent (old man Karlyn had retired down to his eldest daughter's in North Carolina), Jack was becoming familiar with the Slope tenants' laid-back lifestyles—but someone quite as gone-to-lunch as Tina was still new to him: casualness oversprouting to the point where it matted down and snuffed out sense completely.

For a time Tina had been involved with Bert, the other trailermate, who taught third grade at Delphi's only experimental public school; but Bert had then dropped her and married someone else. It seemed to make no difference at all in life at the trailer. Donna and Tina and Bert were old friends from back in high school days; that loyalty prevailed. And Bert himself set a kind of tone: he was a truly genial person, something that you guessed from looking at him. His beard—red, in a no-mustache, sea captain's style—was the perfect emblem for him: lively and fuzzy, with parts kept open. A look into his tiny bedroom in the trailer gave the same impression. Counterculture posters and volley-balls, piles of completed workbooks and dozens of water-colored weather charts done by his students: Bert didn't discard gifts, someone else's proud achievement—and the temperament operated both large and small in his life, no difference. On weekends he shared his closet-sized room with Sue, his wife, who during the rest of the week lived in town with a studio-arts professor at the University. Donna had explained to Jack that she too used to go out with this sculptor, Larry Vashagian, which was how he and Sue eventually got together.

Donna was clambering over Jack to get to the phone. Breasts to breasts, her coined tips cool and weighty on his skin for a moment, Jack was restirred; his hand moved toward the smooth and desirable back of one her thighs, but she was already on the other side of him, grabbing for the extension. Jack turned away, onto his belly. He sunk his cheek heavily in the pillow and from under a torpid lid eyed a few of Doughnut's red hairs on the slip; he blew them away.

Jack had had an unusual day, queer but satisfying. Leaving the plant at midafternoon, he'd gone down to Main Street; and with a group of Twelve-Thirty-ans—Pellegrino, a printer, an insurance man, and Sleighlin, the dentist—had gently harrassed the owner of the adult bookstore: they stood conspicuously together just inside the store, a deterrent to browsers, while Sleighlin agitatedly dueled with the store manager ("If you knew how closely you're being watched, you'd never scratch your behind." "I'll scratch all I want. This is a legal business." "Was. *Was* a legal business!" "Well"—the manager grinning, leaning over the counter to tap at the poster affixed there—"As the sign says: *Keep on truckin'.*"). Jack had wandered around the store again. In front were trestle tables piled with comic books, posters, used records. The porn in the dim back area consisted mostly of paperback novels with steamy covers. A table held a set of plastic drink tumblers: add liquid, and the clothed body of the girl on the glass turned nude. There was a display of novelty buttons and a rack of magazines, each magazine wrapped painstakingly in Saran-Wrap, then sealed with cellophane tape.

But Jack had been discovering that in a small town nothing ever was really too small. It cost him nothing, besides, to be active in these civic charades. What did it matter where he sat: in his office at the plant, stringing together necklaces of paperclips; or at some committee meeting with a bunch of storekeepers?

Also he felt obligated to—and liked being with—Vic Pellegrino. Jack felt that Pellegrino, by offering him Karlyn's job, had saved his sanity. He had inherited the old man's fine assortment of plumbing and electrical tools, as well as the Toyota pickup truck Pellegrino leased long-term; and the job so far had proven quite do-able part-time and on weekends, blessedly separate from Scofield. Vic was friendly, too; he'd taken Jack to his mother's Italian restaurant near the north campus (a bachelor, Vic lived with the old lady in a large house out in Canora); he wasn't pious about his fellow Delphians ("The University looks at a guy like Sleighlin, making the kind of ruckus he's making—they put him down for a nut. Maybe he is a nut. But while the nut gets what he wants, other people also do a little maneuvering into better positions behind him. That's what this bookstore stuff is all about, you know. I don't know specifics, but I don't have to."); he seemed to respect Jack, and had stopped accepting any more rent payments from him. After the bookstore delegation had dispersed, he had driven Jack out into the newly snowed-on country to show him some commercial properties he might keep in mind: a ramshackle garage, a Quonset-hut bowling alley, and back in the Slope a row of four empty stores. "Accept them for what they are and are going to be: dead. You won't be luring any-thing into them that'll involve even a medium-sized investment. All I would like is to keep them warm for at least one more school year. By then the Mall will be open and I'll be in a position to unload; but until then, see what comes your way. Don't be choosy: sell hard and fast and don't let them realize what they've done. I don't have the heart to ask for the three-year lease I should, so offer a single. People tend to figure, What's one year; they take a shot."

Jack left the pillow to turn around, curious after hearing Donna say into the phone: "Did you ask him to use his hand? And?"

Donna continued: "That's not true. If you won't tell him, he can't be blamed for not knowing. All right, go. . . . Sue," she explained to Jack's inquiring face. "She's upset. There was a small fiasco with Larry. He's lying there asleep next to her, so she had to whisper. But now she went to change phones.

"I'm still here. Fine—but slowly, please, and one thing at a time, okay?" Donna had lifted herself upright against the headboard, hugging her naked knees. Jack covered her lap with the blanket, to a smile. "Could it be that the unreasonable one is *you*. No, I haven't—I'm just asking; once you tell me the sides, then I'll take one. Well, so what? All the time. Uh-huh. But you know that's vanity: he isn't seventeen and he never will be again. Well—that's another story. I didn't know you demanded formal compliments after every meal you make. I under-stand.

"Have you seen it? Well, you're going to have to—that's how creative people are. I think you also a tiny bit resent it. No. Watching television. A movie. So-so, at least what we can see of it. Old. Who's the guy?"

Silence—and then Jack realized the question was being addressed to him. He sat up. "Joel McCrae."

"Joel McCrae. Put it on. Channel Eight, I'm pretty sure—Jack is nodding. Yes, right here. Yes. *Yes.* To everyone. That's right."

Jack's breathing slowed: they were talking about *him* now.

"It isn't soap, Suze—uniform each and every time. You aren't dealing with machines, remember."

Jack got quietly, quickly, out of bed, putting on his pants and shirt, hoping all the while that Donna wouldn't say another word until he was well out of the room. She was looking at him, her fingers across the receiver; Jack whispered to her, "Those crackers," and put out a parched tongue. Donna jabbed a finger toward her breastbone twice: water for me, too.

Rafe and Doughnut churned deliriously at Jack's feet as he closed Donna's bedroom door behind him. "No food, no food, nothing for you guys"—but they continued undaunted to slobber and leap. The frays of the rope rug biting at his bare soles, Jack had gotten halfway across the long narrow living room when the trailer's front door opened—a rushing block of frigid night air—and in came Bert.

"Hey, Jack, good to see you again!" Raising one mittened hand like a Roman, then the other, which held a brown lump in a clear plastic bag, Bert said, "I've brought us back some *fine* bread." He leaned in the direction of Donna's closed door and warned loudly, "Anyone wanting some of this better get a move on."

While Bert shucked parka and sweaters, Jack took pains to be greatly interested. "What kind is it?"

"Whole wheat-raisin. Boss stuff. Everyone!" he called.

"Tina may be asleep. Donna I know is," Jack lied, picking up the bag of bread, warm and soft. "Where did you get it?"

"You know down on South Ferrier, the drive-in dry cleaners there? Right behind it, that tin-roofed building? Folks are using it now as the distribution center for a second food co-op in town. I was down there tonight helping them out with their books. One of the women—Lois—just baked these and brought them over: our pay. Let me get us a knife."

Jack followed Bert into the galley-like kitchen. "Any butter in here? There's not much point to fresh-baked bread if there's no butter." Jack's voice, as he bent to the half-sized refrigerator, was pal-like, bouncy, utterly false.

"I doubt it," answered Bert. "The girls are real down on animal fats. There should be margarine, though. And if you see the jar of apple butter, grab that too. Wow! To cut this! Did you get that blast of aroma? Where are those girls? It's too early to sleep. Not when you have something hot and fresh like this in the house."

"They both said they'd had long days."

"I'll just yell softly."

"This is what again? whole wheat and raisin—?"

"Tina! Fresh-baked bread—before Jack and I glom it all up! Donna!"

"Does she bake any other kind?" Jack asked forlornly, stalling for time for Donna to get off the phone.

"I know she does a pumpernickel—I've had that. And a wheatberry-rye combination that I haven't had but that everyone says is extremely fine. This girl can bake."

"Any interest by her, you think, in baking commercially?"

"She's got three small kids, but I could ask."

"Find out. The Slope really needs a bakery of its own—"

Tina had emerged from her room and was staring with slow, moist interest at all the activity in the kitchen: Bert sawing away at the round loaf, Jack covering slices with different spreads. After a sniffle she said to Bert, "Suzie's on the phone."

Bert put down the knife. "Suzie? I was going to call her tonight, since I was in her neighborhood, but I didn't get the chance."

Jack's look, homicidal, bounced off Tina totally. He turned last-ditch efforts on Bert: "Because if she can get some capitalization, I happen to know of a perfect property—"

But Bert was already out of the kitchen, reaching the phone on the floor by the living room couch in three long, excited paces. Tina padded sleepily into the kitchen and took his place, to pick at a bread crust. It was all Jack could do not to smack away her fingering hand.

Bert, after having listened silently awhile, was saying into the phone, "I wish you'd come with me to yoga. You're under a lot of stress. Thursday nights. Then at least let me teach you what I've learned so far. We'll do the positions together and I guarantee that you'll feel better. You know that tension I always got in my shoulders at school? I don't have it anymore."

Donna was now out of her bedroom, wearing a nightgown and knee-socks, Rafe and Doughnut calming instantly at her silent command. She walked right by Bert and into the kitchen, joining Jack and Tina in the jammed tiny area. Jack looked feverishly at her, wanting to lock understandings, but her face was free of dismay; she picked up Jack's slice of bread, which he could not eat, and began nibbling at it; she ran herself a glass of water. Standing, eating and drinking, listening and looking hypnotized as they all were by Bert:

"You *are*. No, no, you *are*. But it takes time, owl. A lot of different things have been coming at you very fast. You *are*. Do you know what that implies? You're saying that I don't have good taste."

Jack had to look away. To the loaf of bread. Why am I here? he asked himself. Who are these people?

"Would you like me to drive over there now?—because I can. Fine, tomorrow—but it'll have to be late: I'm taking my kids to the ag labs in the morning, then out to the winery. Figure on ten or ten-thirty. Is that too late? Of course I do, what kind of question is that? Because you're my owl. Aren't you my owl?"

Tina suddenly shouldered past Jack and Donna, on-course for the couch. She sat down next to Bert, taking his hand in both of hers as he went on speaking into the phone:

"Too bad you aren't here now. You'd get a slice of fine whole wheat-raisin bread someone from the co-op baked. We're all chomping away. I'll save you some. Now go to sleep. You will. Yes, you will—I guarantee it. No more tears."

Tina rested the side of her face against Bert's hunched back.

Bert said after hanging up, addressing no one in particular, more the air: "I'm not really too concerned. I don't think he would deliberately set out to hurt her. She's not the kind of person you could *want* to hurt. But she surely is blue."

So simple—so amazingly, dancingly easy!

He had been down the street, having coffee and a cruller among the late-breakfasting weekend crowd at the Hearth, and when he returned, as he was walking in the door, Tracy said to him, "These gentlemen are here to see you, Jack." And to them: "Didn't I tell you he gulps?"

Two young men were seated in the heavy wooden chairs up front, both bathed in the jaundice produced by the sheet of antiglare plastic drawn down over the window. Jack asked them back to the desk he used on Saturdays at the realty office.

The taller and darker of the two wore broad, solid black eyeglass frames and looked to be in his early thirties. The other one was fairer and younger. Jack read the business card the one in the beetling glasses had handed him.

NEW MORNING PRESS
OFFSET MIMEO PASTE-UP DESIGN
29 LYLE STREET CORNLEY, NEW YORK
RICHARD SALCO, PROP.

They wanted a look at one of the empty stores on Woods Street that were advertised in the paper. Jack had them trundling up the Slope in his car in no time.

The store they had in mind was the middle one, once a jeans shop. Jack played his red-tipped flashlight around the space for them, but there was light enough through the window at that hour to see with just fine. Both young men paced out the length and breadth of the space independently, the Salco person having a peculiar walk: part of it a glide, left foot pulling and riding ever so slightly, but toe-ahead, so that it seemed he was about to bend his knee like a tango dancer coming onto the floor mid-tune. He wore a narrow maroon tie over a wrinkled chambray shirt, no jacket, black chinos.

Jack was busily hyping—"With the student walk-by, your Xerox machine will draw and draw . . ."—when Lex Parmenteer, the associate, interrupted: Who were the neighbors left and right? Yet even while Jack hemmed about this, trying to sweeten it with talk of a short lease, Salco was already pulling out a checkbook, beginning to write. They had in mind, he said, something longer, like three years or two at the least. Was that possible?

Possible? After Jack had deposited the two with Tracy down at the office, to have the rental agreement drawn up (he had to go on to the lumber yard and pick up a load of copper flashing), he whooped aloud to himself in the truck. Less as in *You poor suckers*; more as in *Thank God, thank God, it may actually—I can't believe it—be starting to turn for me here.*

The morning, which began as pale ash, had been darkening by the hour. Around lunchtime the tiny points of cold in the air suddenly went flat; and, any hour now, what they'd been predicting seemed about to be: a major snow on its way.

When Jack made it to the downtown Greyhound terminal shortly after four, the ticket agent's portable radio was turned up high; the half-dozen students waiting for the New York City-bound bus were being warned of what they might be in for. Jack planted himself down at the end of an empty bench. Soon the city-bound bus pulled in, on time, from further upstate; the students boarded; Jack was left alone with the ticket agent, who now went around turning off certain low-watt bulbs at one side of the drafty brick building, turning on others nearer to Jack. The in coming bus, he said, might be either a little late or a lot.

Jack wasn't worried. Even if she were stopped by five-foot drifts, his sister would be able to manage. Since age twelve, Sandy had owned the knack of inflating a full adult within her at a moment's notice. Where was the sense in being a motherless child in the first place if you couldn't militantly cope?

When their mother was sickest—breasts, bones, even at the end her brain surrendering to the fester—Sandy, without announcement, took to going to the local Young Israel every weekday afternoon, directly from junior high and usually walking the distance, a good two miles. The volleyball team she played pivot for that first year went all the way to the Long Island community center finals. She swam breaststroke and anchored relay for the swimming team as well, and in school joined the girls' basketball squad. In her freshman year of high school, she cap-tained both the JV volleyball and swimming teams. From the bleachers above the turquoise pool, the whooping echoes blowing like gas, Jack and Irwin one night watched her win first place in freestyle in the downstate eliminations for the All-State championships, the two of them sapped and glassy with the helpless pride that inmates on the in-side must feel when they see a fellow prisoner slipping past the gates and guards.

Rising from the bench to stretch his legs, Jack saw by the wall clock that Sandy's bus was already ten minutes overdue. He walked across the floor, stopping at a wooden wall rack: local giveaway newspapers, Jehovah's Witness tracts, ads for student tours to Europe, single mim-eographed sheets of pale brown paper ("THEY'VE GOT YOU WHERE THEY WANT YOU—ALONE AND ISOLATED!!!")—one of which Jack took back to the bench with him.

> After we punch out, we think our time is our own. With fellow Workers, we relax over a few beers before going home. Depending on the season, we hunt or bowl or play in the summer leagues in MacMillan Park. We enjoy our families, take outings & trips. We've worked hard all week & want to enjoy our leisure. We've earned it.
>
> Lately, in the Courier, we've been reading how the Bosses spend *their* leisure time. They get together after work too, but their all-year-round league is for the purpose of consolidating & boosting already criminally

high Profits. Their trophies are considerably more valuable than ours
are: they share their technical knowledge & facilities—while we as
sume that our interests as Workers are being watched over by reformist
labor union elements who in reality merely serve as lieutenants of the
oppressive Bosses.

THIS IS EXACTLY HOW THEY WANT IT TO BE.

All five of the major industrial operations in Delphi are physically cut
off from one another. Workers in the different means of production therefore rarely recognize common interests. This alienation, the Bosses realize very well, is to their advantage. They however regularly meet, keeping in cross-industrial touch, SO AS TO PERFECT OUR EXPLOITATION.

With the wide spectrum of Delphi workers—industrial, agricultural,
academic, clerical, retail—we have the perfect opportunity to develop
not one but MANY strong & independent Workers Councils that will
serve to keep our interests viable and will not be sabotaged by reformist
elements bought off by pitifully small infusions of ruling-class Super-
Profits to function as A LABOR ARISTOCRACY. Workers Councils, in co-
operation with vanguard elements of the Student Movement, will have a
growing & eventually predominant say in how this area develops, as
well as

The station agent was turning back on the lights he'd shut before:
"Twenty-one minutes late. Could have been worse." Jack got up to re-
place the leaflet. The glass front doors of the terminal were being filled:
huge tire, metal sidetrim.

The restaurant Jack had chosen was a windowless converted railroad
car fitted out with gaslamps, barrel chairs, and a salad bar. "All your
clippings," Sandy reported, "are stuck into the frame of the mirror on
his dresser."

"That's nice"—yet Jack's heart had, in a second, begun to hit and
miss.

"Although I don't think he exactly knows what to make of the real-
estate advertisement. I think he wonders why you're working another
job in addition to the one you already have."

Jack sighed tiredly. "I wish he'd spared you the trip and just sent his
questions up in a pouch. I would have written back my replies and you
could have done without six long hours on a bus. It would never of
course occur to him that I might *like* real estate."

"No one's attacking you," Sandy said, unruffled. "I'm certainly not."
After she'd picked at the chickpeas and greens on her salad plate and

before the entree arrived, she—the athlete—did something Jack had never seen her do before: take out a cigarette, begin to smoke it. "Your other job, Scofield—they don't mind?"

His sister looked inexplicably different to Jack. It had even taken him some time to locate the birthmark on her jaw, that nebula of birdshot which barred her from being truly attractive. Also, her hair was longer than usual, freer; she didn't look as normally dark, wound up, alert. Jack shook his head. "It's useless . . . Tell him for me that the world doesn't watch any one person that closely, despite what he thinks. To walk around like he does on eggshells all the time, sure that the Powers That Be are on the downswing of sledgehammering you—"

"Okay, but we've changed the subject. We're not talking about him."

"Yes we are. We always are."

It had taken Jack a few years of working in offices himself to see that it wasn't only Irwin—there was a whole classifiable subbreed of these "gentle souls," "lovely men" who were awash in absolute, constant terror. Against the darker, more purposeful background of business they showed right up, yet they managed to remain and persevere, being carried on payrolls—as Irwin was carried for twenty years—and earning token keeps while providing services more tangential yet original than a few puny sales.

In Irwin's case, it had been his reputation for being the fastest birthday card in midtown Manhattan. Wives, children, even the bookkeepers of customers—no one was ever forgotten; birthdays, holidays, anniversaries, children's weddings, condolences. Toward the end of each October he'd get busy with a first draft of the firm's master Christmas gift list, a job no one else would dare tradition to usurp. He also was usually the firm's representative at funerals, frequently off to Brooklyn and the modern parlors on Coney Island Avenue, stopping off sometimes at home after a burial at one of the Long Island cemeteries for a quick grilled cheese sandwich before returning to the office for the afternoon.

He was born, in other words, to be a widower: it was his pinnacle, his triumph.

Yet at first Jack (in what he still thought of as his last true act of innocence) believed Irwin when he said he was all right, when he insisted Jack still go, that he had Sandra at home, that things in life settle, they go on. Bespelled by this twinkly dust of reasonableness thrown in his eyes, Jack went ahead and occupied the room in the freshman dorm at

NYU. One morning in November a secretary fetched him out of a sociology class, urging into his hand a slip of paper with a phone number on it. He was supposed to ask for a Sergeant Bosco.

Sergeant Bosco, at Penn Station, gave the details over the phone. Irwin had come off the Hicksville train with the rest of the crowd, but had only made it a dozen steps before he sat down on the station floor, weeping and unable to move. They had him in the first-aid station now, where he was resting. The nurse doubted it was physical. Oh, and if possible, Jack would want to bring down a change of clothing: he'd had a little accident, too.

Working from books and totally on his own, Jack built a separate downstairs bathroom for Jean, the Rumanian housekeeper whom the family agency had sent to live with them. Though always the handyman of the house (Irwin did nothing manual and was always proud of the inability), Jack had never attempted a job so ambitious. As he worked at connecting copper pipes, as he dripped sweat onto the resinous tiles lifted out of boxes with Italian words stencilled on the sides, he felt himself getting older with a distinct acceleration: each pipe fitted, each tile laid, slipped some sort of lift under his life, jacking him up to a new and tenuous height.

The disparity in their attitudes—Irwin at his lowest, Jack shakily up there—perhaps accounted for the hellish arguing between father and son. Sandy knew to stay away, at one team practice or another, well beyond the seven o'clock TV news each night. It never took more than a single minute of film—jungles, helicopters, senators, protesters—for Jack and his father to be off and at it: Jack pro, Irwin anti. Each image of a kid going boneless in a policeman's arms aimed Jack's thoughts right back to Sergeant Bosco and Penn Station. And for all he knew, Irwin was reminded of the same thing, his sympathies naturally flying to the supported, not the supporters. Daily—on weekends it could be three or four times a day—the arguing flared, untamped, hurtfulness snapping through the house like an air-dried sheet. Irwin's trump—*If you like the war so much, how come you don't drop your student deferment and join up and go?*—was played only in segments, never wholly—for how could he suggest another possible loss for himself? It was a genuine game, then, with handicaps and everything. In private, in public, it didn't matter; Irwin's younger sister Rae and her husband could be visiting and yet the rancor would still beat above their heads like released canaries. Nazi. Simp. Terrible words. All out. Sam and Rae watched in fear as Irwin's face would boil, the veins tom-tom in his neck—would he have another breakdown right here and now?

No, he wouldn't. Both Irwin and Jack knew that. The more his father apologized for the world, and the more Jack despised it, the greater and surer the perch each had upon its tricky motion.

"So do they or don't they mind?" One of Sandy's eyelids was clamped down against the smoke.

Jack took and lit one of her cigarettes for himself. "They sent me to Siberia up here, Sand. To an exile—and I'm not being dramatic." To finally say it out loud to someone was a small, real satisfaction. "The operation is a disaster. I know it; they know it; everyone knows it. If they closed down overnight, it would come as no big shock. But they want to make it seem like they're serious for a while longer. I futz around, I'm visible—those clippings. It's meaningless."

"How's your wrist been? That was a pretty funny-looking picture: you with your cast."

"So the real estate is the only thing I do that I actually enjoy. I do fix-ups and collections and some renting. It's real, the work. Since when do you smoke?"

"You couldn't ask for a transfer back to New York? Scofield must know how you feel; I can't see you keeping it a secret."

"I wrote a report. Silence. Or as good as."

"What are you going to do?"

"I've been putting off thinking about it. Eventually I'll have to. I might be content managing real estate full-time."

"In a college town?"

"Don't people in college towns need places to live? In the order of things, a place to live must be almost as important . . . let's see . . . as a three-piece herringbone Harris tweed suit." Since recovering from his breakdown, Irwin sold men's suits at a department store in Huntington. But Sandy said nothing; she smoked and picked at her food; she looked indistinct, clouded. Jack asked how her shrimps were.

"You probably don't remember 'tents,' do you?" Stubbing out her cigarette, lighting another, Sandy brushed the hair back off her forehead. "Mommy let us use that light green blanket, the oversized one. Once we made a two-roomer: you managed to get the dining room table open, and we pulled the middle of the blanket down through the gap. That was my all-time favorite game. You got tired of it—I realize you were older and all—but I have this very vivid memory.

"You either had a cold or the grippe or something—you'd been home from school for a whole week. You set up the tent. We started playing, then you said you had to go out and hunt and I should stay and watch the fire.

"You went out to hunt and I watched the fire. You were out a long time. I continued to watch the fire and cut up clay into small pieces for our food. Finally I went out to see. Do you know where you were? You were in your room, reading. You didn't see or hear me come to the door, or you weren't letting on that you knew I was there. I went back to the tent and got under again and made believe that you had gone out hunting but that cowboys had found you and shot you and you were dead. Now I'd have to be all by myself and do my own hunting. Eventually, when you were finished with or tired of your book you came back; but I already had pulled the blanket down off the table and stopped playing. Do you remember any of this?"

"A little" Jack said, voice thick and quiet.

"No you don't—but that's all right."

When they left the restaurant Sandy cried, "Oh, look! And only since we were in there!" The cars in the parking lot supported white loaves. The street lamps made temporary thumbprints in the steady windless fall—snuffing out, on, out. Already there'd been one plowing of the streets, and the silence all about was tube-like, walled and curved. Jack blackened his brown gloves in clearing the windshield.

The Valiant could only crawl along the streets, headlights all but worthless. Passing Woods Street, Jack rolled his window down to point outside. "Those, for instance, are all my properties. I just rented that middle store."

"With the coffee-colored paper taped inside the window?"

"They're setting up. A print shop."

The answering service had only one call to relay when Jack got home: 26 North Adams, apartment 4; they'd called three times, a broken radiator which the tenant was afraid was going to explode. Jack told Sandy he was sorry. "Can't I go with you?" she asked. They took the truck. "I never rode in one of these little jobs before. Cute."

Because Jack had only lately started to collect rents in person, names and faces of individual tenants were not securely matched yet in his mind. But when she opened the door after his knock, he recognized the girl and the apartment immediately.

"Oh, thank *God!* It was driving us *crazy!*" There was a steady soprano song of steam in the room: the radiator's pressure cap had been jarred loose. It was nothing to drag him out in a storm for. When Jack went down on his knees with his tools and a replacement cap, a must of cat dander, baked by the radiator's heat, billowed up in eye-tearing clouds from behind the fixture.

"I'm Maura," the pudgy girl was telling Sandy. "Would you like some tea?"

Sandy politely declined; Jack thought, Good. From close to the floor, he was getting oppressive eyefuls of the girl's bare feet, white with bumpers of thick horny callus at the sides, almost black at the soles, the nail of one big toe greenish and ribbed like stone. Cats, at least four of them, had begun to re-enter the room, investigating the strangers. After the new cap was on, when Jack went to wash, he found under-wear—stained bikini panties and diaphanous brassieres—in incredibly large piles on the tiled floor of the bathroom. The barest dingy ghost of a soap bar lay in the dish, and the single towel had a nap as stiff as burrs.

Sandy was playing with two of the cats when he returned to the living room. "Your lease says no pets," Jack declared to the girl.

Instead of at him, she looked at Sandy and smiled. "These aren't. I'm theirs. They own me more than I own them."

"Well, then," he said, "you work it out between you. You or they have to be out by the fifteenth, when I come for the rent next."

Sandy grinned, but the cat-girl's mouth had dropped. "I've always had Gina and Schmaltz. Mr. Karlyn never bothered me."

"En-oh pee-eee-tee-ess."

"No one's complained before," the girl whined. "And what about Lem, Donnie's dog downstairs?"

"Concern yourself with what you have to do. I'll worry about the others." Jack checked a final time to see that the radiator cap was on firmly.

The girl was pointing a finger at him when he turned back. "You can't harass me. I'll go to Community Aid."

"Bring along your lease." Jack returned his tools to the box, closing and clasping it. "And no cheating now—escort them back here for a tour. And a sniff."

She picked up one of the cats, pressing it to her large front, saying hoarsely, "This isn't fair."

Jack lifted the heavy tool box. "Do you rent or do you own? Is this or isn't this someone else's property?" Sandy, hovering at the door, looked eager to flee.

In the truck she said to Jack: "Tell me you hated that. She's a poor lonely thing."

"Can I tell you something about that poor lonely thing? Can I? She makes candles. The first time I was over there—she needed a new faucet—there were hundreds of empty frozen-juice containers on a table in the kitchen and she obviously wasn't exactly obsessed with washing them out fully. The entire building, on her account, was crawling. Every apartment. I had to get an exterminator in there, for a nice piece of change."

"Not your money," Sandy rebutted.

Jack negotiated the slippery streets very slowly. "That's the final criterion—whose money? The point is she's a slob." Making a left at the next corner the truck skidded a little and kissed a parked car. In the tufted vault of the ongoing storm, it seemed much less than a big deal, and Jack steered out and away without even an exclamation.

As they were pulling into the driveway, Sandy said, "That girl: it happens to people you know. To women." Jack had stopped the windshield wipers; the glass crusted over in no time and created a milky fastness within the cab. "I could be like that too."

"I highly doubt that. You just want to think you could." He opened his door to get out. But Sandy stayed where she was.

"Have you even asked me why, on a Thursday in the middle of January, I'm not in Boston but here?" Her eyes were filling. Jack shut his door.

There had been a boy. She'd met him at a party in Cambridge. He was an M.I.T. graduate but worked only part-time in various labs so that he could support himself but also have time enough for his main activity, which was blueboxing. In case Jack didn't know: small radio transmitters that sent out tones through a telephone receiver and fooled the automatic switching system into putting the calls through without charge. Mark's whole group, all M.I.T. geniuses, had the best boxes. A big evening for them, with her along, would be to drive along until they found a booth they liked, dial a toll-free number, and then use the box. California was always the first call, used to "tune up" by.

She was flattered, in case Jack was wondering what fun it was for her, that people as brilliant (although childish) as they were would like having her around.

"That's stu—" Jack started to say, but she stopped him: "Don't." Mark, her boyfriend, always carried a map and time-chart around with him. During the day he would have already picked out some numbers from the International Industrial Register: in Singapore, say, or Hong Kong, or the Philippines—places where English was spoken. Then he would pretend to be a buyer for an American firm—and the amount of follow-up material he'd get was unbelievable. Gifts too: fabrics or teas or little figurines, all of which he'd give to her.

Sandy lit a cigarette, fogging the cab further. A few muffled cries travelled up from an adjacent street, late-night gambollers in the fresh and still-dropping snow. "Something you said in the restaurant: about the world not focusing only on you, on any one person—I agree with that. Maybe it's just a big myth, disaster. People adjust to anything. Although being pregnant seemed unadjustable-to." She wasn't, by the way. But she did, one afternoon a week ago, have a sanity attack and make arrangements with the dean's office for a leave. "And here I be."

Jack later turned uncomfortably on the Hollywood sofa all night, snowlight keeping the living room undark. Sandy's story was like a jumbo ball to him: he could belly-up onto it, but then couldn't move it off its mark. Comparing herself to the cat-girl—he couldn't rid it from his mind. Sandy, whom he'd counted on to avoid a messy life, a poor lonely thing? Each time he thought of it, it crowded him farther and farther back from sleep; at five in the morning he was still holding his small transistor radio to his ear, listening to the AM station. School and business closings were announced, Scofield's among them. There was fourteen inches of snow on the ground already. Jack closed his eyes.

"Hooray. I was afraid you were going to miss it completely. Great, isn't it?" The room now was light. Rolling on his side, Jack looked at his watch on the floor: ten-thirty. Sandy was wearing a robe. She had pulled one of the Danish chairs over to a front window; a spine-furrowed paperback book lay over one of the arms. "You didn't even hear the phone the two times, lazy. From your job—don't come in, they're closed—and from a female. When I asked who it was, she was interested in the same thing: 'who's *this?*' Oo-la-la, Jackie. She's going to come by here later this morning, this Donna."

Jack stretched while Sandy continued to tease: "Vehhhry in-ter-esting."

During breakfast, Tim Sleighlin phoned, so upset he sounded nearly giddy. He wanted sympathy. "I had a patient—I *had* to come in, an emergency. But where does *he* come off opening up on a day like today? His sidewalk is clear, he's shovelling." Clear sidewalks reminded Jack of his job for the day: the snowblower sitting in the back shed. "Can't he bear to be closed a day? That filth has to be available all the time?"

Donna was at the door a little before noon. She and Sandy were introduced. Would they like to come out for a ride? One of the nurses owned a four-wheel jeep and Bert had volunteered to shuttle people around all day. Sandy rushed to dress in the bedroom while Jack explained that he had to clear sidewalks. Donna touched his face. Sandy, all set, returned.

Jack watched them leave the house together from the window. Cross-country skis were lashed to the top of the brown jeep, which looked crowded inside with at least three other people. Bert's red beard flashed in the air, a crackle, as he stepped out from behind the wheel to be formally introduced to Sandy. Jack moved away from the window before any of them might think to look up at him and wave.

He dressed in an additional pair of socks, long underwear, his heaviest corduroy pants, a wool shirt, sweater, watch cap, two pairs of gloves. In the backyard, heading for the shed, he raised his knees like a circus horse, making wells in the drifts. The metal housing of the snowblower chilled his hands through the gloves as he filled the tank with gas. A shovel was needed to start a first swathe in the snow, after which Jack pulled the cord on the machine.

His impression was that the snowblower's roar was *scaring* grey out of the sky: while Jack worked the air gradually gave up its hoariness, until finally, just after one o'clock, the sun came belting out and wild glares began to rule. All green-painted things—garages and cars and signs—looked especially brilliant against the snow; icicles hung from porches giantly pure. An unexpected brush of wind threw back powder in his face, matting it. Jack put on his sunglasses.

He took his time, was in no rush. The din and rhythm of the spiral path-making covered over Jack's thoughts until he no longer had any. Lack of sleep made him feel puttyish and quirky; he could have driven the augers of the blower into the very concrete of the sidewalks and thrown that up as a talc too—who cared? Next door to one of his buildings, on East Temple, was a student ecology commune. At two in the afternoon their walks were not only unshovelled but seemed barely trod on. Jack angled some spray in their direction.

His last stop was Woods Street, the row of stores there. By now the light was emptying out of the day, the wind had dropped, and the streets were turning dull and leaden. Jack approached Woods via Temple and started up the blower around the corner. The only established store, the

laundromat on the corner, was closed, but the new printing shop had
its lights on and its portion of sidewalk already cleaned. While Jack
pushed the machine over the street, no one from there even stuck out a
head to see who and what was making all the noise. Jack decided to
knock—to let them know that, with a snowfall this large, they didn't
have to do their own shovelling.

The light brown paper taped to the inside of the front window was
not, he discovered, blank after all; it was printed on, and the typeface
was familiar:

> growing & eventually predominant say in how this area develops, as
> well as

Jack killed the motor of the blower. No one still had come out of the
store.

> Let's not bowl ourselves out of jobs. While the Bosses plan, we can't sit
> back & think that economic and social improvement of Workers' lives will
> come about magically through polite agreement & the Bosses' "good
> will." In search of always greater Super-Profits, they are much more
> likely to push us out of our jobs completely. OUR LEISURE TIME &
> THEIRS—NOT THE SAME.
>   THIS IS HOW THEY WANT IT TO BE—BUT WITH STRONG WORKERS
> COUNCILS IT CAN & WILL CHANGE!!!
>   Workers Committee for Economic Coalition

The other sheets in the window also had writing on them, but Jack's
eyes could only swipe at phrases, too electrified to read the whole
thing. "CAPITULATIONIST EISEN FACTION REVEALS ITSELF AS
ANTI-REVOLUTIONARY." "Vicious methodological dualism and
subjective idealism . . ." "class-against-capital—*not*, as the renegade
Eisen revisionist rump faction would have it, class-for-itself . . ."
"trans-historical fetishism . . ." "We intend to address this split at
the forthcoming plenary session of the CUWF-S at its new Delphi,
N.Y., headquarters in the near future . . ." In a corner of the window
were five magazine-sized portraits: four beards and a woman. The
predictable two Germans, the two goateed Russians, and the woman,
whom Jack the history major recognized as Rosa Luxemburg.

First he knocked at the door, then tried the knob. He *shook* the knob.
Shaking and shaking, worrying, jangling it—shake the whole goddamn

place down! Through a crack between two printed sheets on the inside of the window Jack saw a little of the inside: a section of a poster: the ubiquitous burned Vietnamese child . . .

He gave up. They weren't going to open. *He told me to rent fast and not be picky.* Excuses. As Jack walked away, pushing the snowblower down the cleared middle of the street, past snowy houses turning fuzzy in the twilight, the air smelled more and more of smoke. Trotskyites. It made him want to hide.

A car, tire chains clanking, nearly nudged Jack from behind before he could move over into a drift and let it pass. He was inclined to strike out, slam a fist against the moving back fender.

Listen, Vic, I seem to have made a mistake . . .

Trotskyites! Not even a disgrace you could shut yourself up and get cozy with, like Scofield. Jack pounded down the streets behind the snow-removal machine, the lumpish clop of a fuck-up.

Sandy wasn't back yet when he got to the apartment. No beer, no whiskey in the house—he'd even have settled for those bad Percodans. Jack's fingers rattled in the holes as he dialed the answering service, but Sandy's was the only message: she'd be back late-ish. The streets outside the windows of the living room were abysmally silent and tucked-up. Later, at ten, the phone rang: not Sandy—worse: Pellegrino. Jack's tongue grew immediately huge. Vic was inviting him out ice fishing on the lake Saturday. Clippedly Jack said he couldn't. "You all right?" wondered Vic. "Fine," said Jack. "Just tired from snow clearing."

Sandy returned after midnight. Jack had fallen asleep where he was, in a chair. While he came dejectedly awake, his sister was taking off her hat and coat and gloves; she was humming and her eyes were bright. "You sleep a lot, know that? Something new. Is it the late nights, Donna wearing you out? I'm going to put up some tea."

Pinned to the back of one of her gloves, which lay on the coffee table, was a day-glo button: SNOW BUNNY. Under the lettering a cartoon rabbit, floppy eared and pink pawed, wearing a parka—but it had the body of a woman, swelled out at hips and bust, nipped at the waist. Only a couple of stores in town dealt in these lewd-cute novelties—and because he'd passed by there this afternoon, Jack knew that one, The Student Depot on East Temple, was closed because of the snow.

"We went absolutely everywhere." Sandy stood at the doorway of the kitchen, combing her hair and waiting for the kettle to boil. "Bert had skis, but also snowshoes—and after we dropped everyone else off we hiked around. It was so beautiful. Were you ever up on snowshoes? First I was terrified: you think you're going to sink down immediately into the snow. But you don't. I thought it was fabulous."

Jack stared at and through the button, thinking, *Trotskyites!* "Donna, by the way," he said, "just so it's understood, is a whore." The cat-girl. Bert. This button. New Morning Press.

Sandy came into the room: head on an angle, sardonic pull of mouth. "You wouldn't want to overreact, would you now?"

"Were you out to the trailer, too? If not, you're still in for a treat."

Sandy sat down on the Hollywood sofa. "I'm only smiling because I'm not used to this—you opening up."

"I'm not opening up. Getting back to the trailer. There's Bert, there's Donna, and there's Tina. There used to be Sue, who is Bert's—pardon the expression—wife, you should know. But Sue has been living with a sculptor who teaches at the University (and also used to shag Donna). Although Sue does show her face every once in a while. Don't worry, though: she isn't really missed by Bert. Because you know what I think? I think that they're all *very* good friends out there. Just for your information."

"Big brother to little sister: watch out! watch out!" Nevertheless, Sandy's eyes were setting more seriously—into her shunted, her independent look.

"*Very* close," Jack repeated poisonously. He picked up the glove with the button on it and played with the limp fingers.

Sandy stood and left for the kitchen silently. She was back a minute later.

"Keep in mind that I'm not one of your tenants, okay? I'm not that pathetic girl with the cats you can bully." She swooped down, whisking the glove out of his hand and stamping off into the kitchen with it. Jack could hear the tearing sounds of her tea being sipped (none for him) and placed them by the kitchen window. She returned to him five minutes after. "Your targets are so weird. They always have been. Donna is a *good* person." Something had peaked in her—maybe the consciousness of being a visitor and a guest—and she was calmer now. "One day maybe I'll understand you."

The Scofield plant opened on Saturday, to make up for the lost time, and Jack was at his desk. Already, earlier that morning, he'd been up to Woods Street—where he found that, yes, the stores all shared a common basement but that they also shared a common boiler: to cut off Salco's heat would cripple the laundromat at the same time. It had been his only idea for a remedy so far.

Sandy called shortly after one. The buses to New York were again running, and Bert—she paused for effect—was picking her up in ten minutes to take her down to the terminal.

Guilty and relieved, Jack said, "That's ridiculous!" Sandy went on: "I'm leaving the key inside your mailbox. You people are more warm-blooded than I am—too cold here. Thanks for everything."

"Sure," Jack said. "For everything."

4

Today?

Today. One more. Up. Feet off the bed, onto the floor—a hippo at this compared to Anthony, but who wouldn't be? Before moving out on him she used to like to lie there in the morning and just watch. Off with the covers and onto the floor in one fluid motion, he'd be moving through the loft, passing alongside Beauty (his 1937 floor model Stromberg Carlson, big as an office safe in its honey oak chassis) to slip into "the can." Out never more than five minutes later—for a shot of tomato juice—and then back in, to shave. Out again (and this for Judith had always been *the* part) to dress. The perfectly folded clothes perfectly unfolded. *Draped* on. A noiseless slap to his pant creases. A goose with his thumbs to his collar (he rarely wore a tie, but when he did, it knotted with lubricated ease)—and on to the last item, like a monarch settling his crown: the shoes. Soundlessly soft Italian gondolas: a wipe, a spit, a buff, another wipe and buff. A tiptoe out the door. The end. Bravo. She really did use to love it.

The insides of Jack's shoes, she had noticed while upstate yesterday, were fitted with charcoal cushions. And it was true: sometimes his socks did smell vinegary. Still the sight of the Odor-Eaters was disheartening. That he should have to worry about such things. And on her account. A fierce thing, male vanity, though—she knew, having lived with a grand master, a Michelangelo, an Escoffier of it. Anthony's reliance on dry cleaners, on only Checker cabs, Picayunes by the carton, phoning for the weather when he needed only to turn on Beauty for it: fussings and crotchets all of them, but kept so well polished that they all passed for strengths, for character. People admired him even for remaining on that hopeless ugly block, where not an artist lived any more, where there was only the heavy past in addition to the lumber yard, the welfare center, the corner whores (the Sisters Scuzzo: Anthony's name for them, saying they reminded him of Rome. People ate that up too. Dapper and secure enough, it seemed, you got away with anything).

In the shower Judith kept her head carefully away from the spray. Fixing dry hair was bad enough, having to dart at it timidly with the comb like someone icing a cake—but, wet, whole hanks were liable to tug out. She pulled the accordion-arm mirror that Anthony once installed on the wall above the tub (Why? He never stayed here even once) and wiped away the steam. This was the face that Jack had beheld all weekend. The cortisone-chubby cheeks (what she'd hated, too, the last time they gave her chemo) and the eyes like ash pits, the beginnings of a cold sore ruining her only good feature, her mouth. Was it any surprise, then, that he was limp? For all practical purposes, Jack—she kept on forgetting this—was well again. And healthy people make certain demands. She should have worn the wig. From now on she would, everywhere and all the time. She'd wear it today.

Towelled dry, robed, she went back into the room and put on underwear. A first shiver of weakness was apparent while she was on her back, struggling into panty hose; then, after spotting a bad run on the right stocking near the calf and sitting up before going to get the bottle of nail polish remover, she really felt it: tremors in her legs. *Good morning, hon, here we are.*

She had to lie back down a second. Why fool herself? She had one day left before the next round of injections, and she hadn't gone in to work the whole two previous weeks. Officially she was on sick leave, unsalaried so that she could collect disability benefits, but her office was still available to her. To do what in, though?

No, she would go in. Finding the nail polish remover, dabbing it on, stemming the run; while she waited for it to dry she regarded the wig on its stand across the room, all of a piece and shining like brassy metal in the sun—and it weakened her resolve. But no, she had decided: going in. She wouldn't fall prey to the Anthony Terrezza philosophy of steering into skids, she rejected that, it was why she had left him in the first place.

Terrific sun out, and the wind when she got to the bus stop was deceptive: sudden scrolls of it went straight for the face, right after which there'd be nothing. Judith would normally have waited in the doorway of the jewelry store, but that spot was occupied now: a pair of lovers, Puerto Rican teenagers, the girl dressed in layers of dark, soft clothing (Danskin top, sweater, elastic tights under a skirt, black cloth Chinese slipper-shoes), the boy in jitterbug-wide pants and a leather coat of red and green patches. Both held chewed-up spiral notebooks and were peering in fixedly at the rings and the bracelets and the Omegas. The girl was positioned behind the boy, against his back, her chin weightily resting on the perch of his shoulder. Even when pivoting to check for the bus, her chin stayed right there—in a socket that didn't move, that she could depend on.

Judith could not remember the last time she had put her own weight down like that—in heaviness and total trust. With Anthony? With Jack? Maybe at first, but then they both turned into wobblers.

She must have been staring, and the teenaged girl, full of herself, had noticed. "What's *your* problem?" As Judith quickly turned away, the boy whispered to his Juliet, "Cool it," but smiled with pleasure all the same.

Fair question, though: What *was* her problem? All Judith wanted was a socket too. Love's small click—and you're fastened in, can swivel around at will.

She had been—the getting up and going in today had been worth it for this revelation alone—she'd been too timid. She'd just have to find someone who wouldn't have her only as a special case—and when she did she would be demanding and bright and usual. Right now—the hell with waiting any more—she was going to take a cab uptown.

On Mondays, since the museum was closed that day to the public, the staff took its time drifting in. Judith was alone in the elevator going up to the fourth floor and alone in the corridors. Her office door was locked, but someone had recently been in: a pile of mail sat on her desk; mostly staff memos but also a mailing envelope that probably contained the slides of an artist who wanted a viewing, someone who out of ignorance thought Judith still wielded some authority.

She threw away a memo on cafeteria hours, one on I.D. cards. Stragglers were starting to come down the hall, past her open door. "Judy! You look great!"

"As it's only fair I should"—she put down the mail. "Being merely the latest in an entire line of great-looking Kornbluhs."

Missy Hoadsworth, taking off a glove, stuck the bare hand past the door and into Judith's office. Frowned. "Every Monday lately he's been doing this to us—freezing us in order to save money. Maybe we *should* be unionized."

Judith realized that all her outer clothes were still on; she got off as much as she could while sitting, but had to rise in order to remove the cape—and when she did, her legs buzzed. "How goes it with the dashing prince?"

Missy slumped against the jamb. "You don't want to know. It's old news, besides."

"Tell me anyway. Aging imparts a flavor. Like fine wine."

A hand still on the doorframe, Missy committed herself to a single step further into Judith's cubicle.

"It isn't really fair, is it, Judes? They all seem to have this inborn antenna that only picks up what they think are threats. We go to an absolutely wonderful party . . . God, was it a week ago already? It'll be a week tomorrow, yes. He's involved, you know, with the planning board of the Zoo, and it was their dinner dance at the Pierre. We had a ball. And you know how I am when I drink champagne. In the cab—terrible sin of sins—I tell him that I need him and I love him and that I always want to be with him—"

Judith hummed the "Dragnet" theme. Missy's eyes goggled attractively: "Don't I know it. And I'm still paying for it. Crumb by crumb, he's been getting friendlier each time I see him since, but whenever I kiss him I know he's sort of wincing."

"Crumb by crumb is nicely put," Judith said, W. C. Fields-like. In this lover's complaint business it was better to not cast too serious a die: the game could change in ten minutes' time, with the arrival of flowers or a makeup phone call.

"Like *Uh-oh, here it comes again.*"

"I then have a suggestion."

Missy took one more brave step inside. "Do you really?"

Unfortunately, a sweltering wave of interior heat rose up just at that moment through Judith's thighs, a parallel curtain dropping south from her shoulders. It was followed by a glacial shiver, focused in her stomach muscles. She had meant to be cute—say something about sprays of Mace that fit in pearled clutches—but had to settle for a plain "Kick him."

Missy smiled tepidly. "Bachelors. I mean, how do *you* manage? With Tony. He's never been married, has he?"

This was really sweet of Missy—to consider her, Judith, as still on the active roster. It supported her conclusions of the morning: that people will generally think what you want them to. Oh, Missy (if I had only had my Wheaties this morning I would say), don't fret it excessively, this free-lance Manhattan love stuff: it will all be fine. You're a clean-limbed WASP girl, you'll marry and have children and wear man-tailored shirts. "Shin-busters, Hoadsie, and more shin-busters, it's the only way."

Missy was retreating, out into the corridor again, sighing. "It just seems needlessly complicated, that's all." She gave Judith a lengthy, stupefied stare. (The wig on straight?) "God, Jude, you look so great," she said mournfully. "So great. I've got to run now and call my super and just pray I catch him in. I wanted him to accept a package for me, but smart me forgot to leave him a note. I love your hair that style."

The very second Missy was gone, Judith tore off her sweater. She was on fire. The heat was making a long continuous S, like the element in an electric broiler, especially in her thighs, which felt rucked under the skin like a bunched slip.

Think of other things. She opened the mailing envelope, taking hold of the tag near the pointing finger and ripping downward, kapok flakes jumping free onto her lap. Besides a box of Ektachrome slides, there was a sealed envelope inside. Usually, in her experience, these envelopes contained a resumé and a handwritten plea for attention by the artist. She put the envelope aside—saving it for a later time when someone else's desperation would make her feel better.

Unlocking the bottom drawer of her desk, Judith took out her hand viewer. The first slide in the box was identified in pen on the cardboard frame as *"At the Counter, 119" x 74", mixed media and acrylic."* Judith dropped it in the viewer.

Painting, collage, sculpture—a little of each. It was a thread and notions counter in a five-and-ten-cent store, slanting and gridded with greenish panes of glass to make compartments filled with buttons and zippers and fasteners and thread—all of which looked to be real and pasted on, as were packages of Rit dye.

Instead of watching so much TV, Judith thought, reminded—I ought to sew more.

The slide slipped from her fingers; she re-pressed and the bulb went back on. Behind and before the counter were two figures, women, middle-aged: the one behind the counter only a torso in a blue print dress; the one in front, the customer, wearing yellow dotted swiss. The faces were made of flat wood, painted. The expressions were remarkable . . .

"*Ju*dee, *Ju*dee, *Ju*dee."

She looked up. Henry Jacoby was pulling the cubicle's extra chair to the other side of her desk. Judith pushed the slides aside. "Someone," she said to Henry, "thought to come in and deliver my mail—which was very kind of someone. Was that nice someone you?"

Henry put two long thin fingers against his cheek. "Oh my. Well, yes, I'll take credit for it—despite the fact that I didn't do it. But it's a di-

lemma of breeding, no? Which is worse: to turn down a perfectly serviceable compliment or to be ungraciously scrupulous. What have you
there?"—Henry reached forward for the viewer.

"Personal." She put the viewer and slides into a drawer.

Henry settled relaxedly back. "You being here today—that means
they're done with you for a while? the white witch doctors? Ever see
that one? Rita Hayworth, and don't. The time you can waste on efflu-
via. You say to yourself, Just one more—to keep the willies away. So
you watch 'Young Mr. Lincoln' which isn't half-bad. But then you go
on, stay up, watch more, some rock of craperoo with Ward Bond."

"I didn't realize you and Ward were such night owls."

"With luck," Henry went on, "it should be enough to get you to Sun-
rise Semester. And *that* means"—collapsing his shoulders, miming
relief—"you've made it through another one."

Super-awake on prednisone, steroidly flying, Judith also had these
endless nights lately, the television a clock made out of gargoyles.

Encouraged by her recognizing smile, Henry pressed ahead. "Someone was also telling me the other day that the stuff they're giving to
you acts like Antabuse—a touch of the sauce and you pay unforget-
tably. That I hadn't known."

Henry—fervid, curious, a sufferer himself—had been one of the few
here at the museum who seemed unafraid of Judith since the relapse,
who didn't treat her as her own not-as-good (and temporary) replacement. It was clear that he thought of himself as a parallel soul. His
spells at the Connecticut drying-out farm—Judith's hospitalizations.
His hand tremors—her throwing up. Both their pallors. Their leaves of
absences: Henry would get gibbering at an opening, make a gross pass
at one of the student bartenders, and then not be seen for months; his
aunt on the board of directors rescued his job again and again.

But Judith had no patience for him now. A player-with-things, his
hands were all over her desk, shaking her marmalade jar filled with
pencils, sifting her dish of paper clips. "Living on Thirty-first still? My
offer holds, you know. I have the room, you could move right in with
me. That bitch nearly eviscerated the place when he left—so there is, to
put it mildly, space enough. Wouldn't it be marvelous? I wouldn't be
able to get away with a thing with you there."

"Flattering, Henry, flattering—what am I, a Doberman pinscher? I
have to take a pill," she fibbed, standing.

"Should I bring you some water?"

"That's all right."

"You take it dry? Of course not. I'll walk you to the water cooler."

"Not necessary."

"I'm going in that direction anyhow."

Missy was right—the building *was* cold, especially the corridors. Judith didn't quite know how she was going to do this: take a pill she did not have. Her legs had at least stopped shaking. Henry was letting fly with puffs of gossip as they walked; she'd never be able to stop him. *The ladies' room.* A few steps before the water cooler, Judith waved goodbye to Henry, interrupting one of his revelations, and ducked inside.

In the small antechamber, between the inner and outer doors, she pulled up short, mentally estimating the time it would take for Henry to turn the corner in the corridor and be gone.

Then—*watch out!*—her nose was nearly mashed by someone pushing in the outer door: "Oh, shit—sorry—someone is going to get killed one of these . . . Look who's here! *I* didn't know you'd be coming in. Fantastic! Don't leave. In. Go." Judith let herself be herded through the inner door, into the yellow-tiled room, by her boss, Alexandra Somogyi.

"I called you Friday night." Alex had gone directly into a stall, leaving Judith alone by the sinks, her back to the mirrors. "But your pal said you weren't there."

"Don't call me there anymore."

"Finito? Totally? What are you doing when you get your treatments? Who helps you? *Shut up, Alex, not your business.*"

"Don't shut up; my parents; and otherwise, like a big girl, I stay by myself. What did you want on Friday?"

"That dancer I know, Julio Stein? His company was putting on a thing out on Long Island and he sent me two tickets. I rented a car."

"Any good?" When Judith closed her eyes for an instant, she could feel her jaw shimmering back into place after each time she spoke. The morning so far—and Henry Jacoby especially—had been more of an exertion than she had expected; she was wet under the arms and worried about her turtleneck.

"Wonderful. Degenerate. Where is Merrick? Four people in the company, Julio included, share a house there: the flamingest freaks—on this very old, staid, suburban block. You had to see it. And this, this was wonderful: instead of a ping-pong table and a washing machine in the basement, they have the floor down there covered with red dirt—it's where they practice some certain exercises. Pink fluorescent lights overhead."

Judith yanked two paper towels from the dispenser, folding one into a rectangle and wetting it, leaving the other dry. She took both towels into a stall two over from Alex's. "The dance performance was in the basement?" She pulled off her turtleneck, washed, dabbed her armpits dry. From her bag she removed her pocket spray of Norell: a double spritz under each arm.

"No, that was at some college, but the party afterwards was back at this house of theirs in Merrick. They had these thin plastic smocks in case anyone wanted to roll around in the dirt. A very primal crowd, though—the hell with smocks, people just took off their clothes."

"You?"

"*My* thighs? But Paul did—I went with Paul Bose, you know him, don't you? Stan had a Knights of Pythias installation, and it was hardly his type of thing anyway."

Alex's current (but not exclusive) beau was Stan LeVeen, a bathrobe manufacturer in his late fifties, married, with grown children, sporter of gold neck jewelry, owner-of-record of a pair of trotters. His showroom (Judith once had been there) was filled with works by artists Alex championed: a fifty-foot coiled length of hawser, two red-painted walnuts on a pedestal, a painting of a submarine beached up onto Canal Street. ("My girl out front has to bite her fingers at the people's expressions when they come in and see, especially the out-of-town buyers. They plotz.")

Alex's art-world friends were turned off by Stan ("Is this a nut? I love her!"), but his gaucherie was doubtlessly part of his attractiveness for Alex, who liked to keep a roguish step ahead. At a women's-group meeting in SoHo once, when, midway, the hostess brought out coffee and English biscuits and a glass dish of multicolored sugar she'd prepared—crystals of green, red, orange, blue—a gleam had entered Alex's eye. Suddenly she began to make a big, appreciative deal over the sugar—and soon enough everyone was up and clucking, asking for the recipe, a gaggle of bohemian Betty Crockers. At the next week's meeting, Alex moved that the group disband: the sugar incident, she said matter-of-factly, proved that the group's function was met or else its energy was spent. She herself promptly took up scuba diving instead—and a few months later she was putting on a small exhibition in the museum's basement gallery of work by a woman in her scuba class who painted directly on the plastic shields of the facemasks. Receiving the announcement in the mail—"Twenty Facemasks: Investigatory Paintings by Dottie Kerns"—Anthony had cried: "Mama!"

But Alex could and did get away with it because she was the star—no one at the museum was better known. Her gypsy looks—deep-set eyes, a beaky nose, black hair cut into severe bangs that fell across her forehead like a café curtain—made her recognizable. And the art she went to bat for was so previously thought-out and self-effacing that you saw straight through it directly to Alex. Her first major exhibition at the museum had even made Reuters, the artist having been a young Californian who out of plastic formed what looked almost exactly like human bones—which he strewed sparely over one whole floor of the museum, mainly in corners. A film crew and reporter from the ten o'clock news were dispatched pronto; and even Anthony, who considered Alex "a culture killer, an assassin," had to admit that she had handled herself with skill. "Be honest with me," asked the TV reporter— "You really consider this *art*?" "I consider it a wrench. It turns your eyes and your mind to a new position." "But you don't actually expect people to care about stuff like this, do you?" "They care. They care very much. They look very carefully. If only so that they don't step on anything. No one likes to crunch a tibia." "All right, level with me now: this is a put-on, isn't it?" "I'm sure you sincerely hope so." In the four years she'd been curator of contemporary collections, Alex had repeatedly proposed a show called "Questionable Art"—lousy art being art too, she said—but she could never get it past Lee Morrowing, the director. A foe of the spiritual and the priestly artist (everything Anthony most revered), she believed most of all in adventure. She treated Judith's illness as one.

"So where were you Friday?"

Judith, tucking her shirt into place, left the stall. "I went upstate."

"And?"

"And not too much. I don't think I'll be going back anymore. The light, I'm afraid, has been seen. Are you ever coming out of there?" Alex could sit on the seat for an hour, content over her cooling broth. "I can't talk about this to a door."

"A minute."

"I'm not what he needs now." Her legs were starting to tingle once more; she leaned back against a sink. "Backing him into corners he's familiar with enough, all by himself, without my help. I'm not surprised that he doesn't respond."

"Still soft city? Maybe he's gay."

"He isn't."

"Should he be?"

"You stay and be flip—I'm leaving." But she made no move to push herself off the sink.

A hollowed roar from inside the stall, an opened door: "I know what you're saying." Alex came to the sink to wash her hands. "Though maybe you're being a titch oversubtle."

"I've considered that. This morning, in fact."

"He's had the same medicines you're taking. That has to be a factor right there, doesn't it? All those heavy chemicals? They've got to act somehow on a man's, as they say, physical capabilities. You yourself told me that you once didn't have a period for months."

And still don't have them—a castrata. Why do you think I'm so frenzied and rash? "It isn't that. It's that no one makes love to his own nightmare."

"*Anthony* loves you. Hard as it is for me to recommend him." Alex was slicking her brows with water. "Stay two weeks with him, two weeks by yourself—an arrangement. It'd be so European."

"No, that's over. I made a big to-do. The only thing back there now would be honesty: twenty-four hours a day, continual. I'll pass."

Alex weighed her own sharp features in the mirror. "Then the answer is obvious—you need a new man." She put her hands to her hair, giving it a quick, tempestuous mix.

Looking on enviously, Judith spared Alex and didn't demand a list of candidates. "Possibly." She turned fully to face the sinks, ran cold water, and plunged her hands in. Her nails grew icy. She was revived.

"Consider it settled, then," said Alex. "Have I seen you since I got that invitation to that studio down on Twentieth Street? I don't think so. Wait till I bring this to Lee. A c.v. came along with the letter: the guy had a brochure made up about himself, a picture of himself on the cover: leather, early forties I'd say; you know the type: handsome but in that perfect gay way, a belch would ruin everything? In the c.v. it said he used to teach in Oregon and had spent a year in Japan, where he got the chance to see a private collection of ivory phallus stiffeners. So guess what he does now."

(Of everything, Judith might miss this most: bad taste. No one except for Alex dared it around her anymore.)

"He makes them out of plastic, then paints right on them. Nothing overtly pornographic. Sweet, in fact: people, imaginary animals. I wish

someone would snap a Polaroid of Lee's face when I get around to proposing the show to him—I'd send it to you."

But Judith had drifted off. If the problem with Jack was only physiol-
ogy, that wouldn't be so bad. Patience would lead to better, not worse.
But it wasn't that, no. "He's well, Al. Or weller."

"Lee? The cock-ring guy? Oh—*him.*"

"He's putting his life back together. He was wearing Odor-Eaters in
his shoes."

"Painted Odor-Eaters—who could I suggest that to? Look, we decided already—on to greener pastures." Alex stepped back from the
sink. "Look at this belly. My health spa at lunchtime—want to?"

"I know that you're right—someone who . . . Anyway. No, I'll be
going home in a little while."

Back in her office, the door closed, Judith took out the box of slides
again. It was good once more to be sitting. *"Uncle Lou's Lunch,* 110" x
68", mixed media and acrylic." She dropped it into the viewer. Hunkered down in the depths of a green woods was a single figure, a man
wearing hunter's camouflage. A shotgun was resting on the ground by
his side and he was rearranging a sandwich that lay unwrapped upon
the flat of one thigh. The top slice of bread was removed, set over to
balance near the knee—and the man's fingers, raw pine dowels, were
pushing at wooden pucks of liverwurst to make for a better distribution
on top of the bottom slice of bread. Like the Woolworth ladies, his face
was painted on a flat wooden board slightly wider than a paddle. The
eyes were aimed slightly to the left and up, the lips were drawn so
that it looked like he was blowing maddened air over his top lip. *(She
never makes it right, always bulging. I can't eat it that way and she
knows it.)* The trees and bushes around him seemed to have been cut
out of cloth, dense green spoons of it.

The next slide in the box was of another scene: two little girls riding
in the back seat of an old car, wearing the same dress, the same black
polished Mary Janes. Next slide: an old man sitting shoeless, in white
cotton socks, inside a shoe-repair stall. Same combination of materials: wood, painted canvas, sewn cloth.

Where was that Woolworth one again? The faces of those women!
The saleslady was wearing a look of vicious forebearance, the customer
lady one of absolute concentration: being pains to one another, and
both of them loving it.

This is a portrait of two ladies, Judith thought. Not girls and not women but *ladies*, as in "You want cherries, lady, I do the picking for you," or "A group of us, just a few ladies, once a month we go on an outing together, it gives our spirits a lift." Out of the sexual crossfire, slightly despised, allowed to crank about moderately. Who—Judith fumbled open the envelope containing the c.v.—who did these? who knows all this? who longs for ladyhood like I do (one minute the Horny Harridan, the next wanting out altogether)? who understands how pleasant it would be only to be tawdry and culminated and uncalled upon?

William Huft. Born: Virginia. Age: 35. She was flabbergasted that it should be a man. An address downtown, below Canal Street. According to the c.v., one previous gallery show, the date coincident with when she had her spleen out, which is why the name was unfamiliar. His attached note was surprisingly decorous and ungrovelling: *Dear Ms. Kornbluh, Would like to know what you think of these. Best wishes, Bill Huft."*

What I think is that I think they're wonderful. She lifted the viewer again. No outer world for these ladies, at least not until they're done with the transaction involving the spool of No. 3 green thread. They've got time by its neck; the world will have to wait until this particular sale is completed. A better lesson than small sips.

As she dialed, Judith kept the viewer pressed on in the other hand, for encouragement. She had no firm idea of what to say to William Huft. *(They're beautiful, but since I'm the lamest duck you'll ever find . . . ?)* The phone was picked up at the other end before one full ring.

"Hello?" The voice was Southern, light vanilla. When she said who she was, he cried "Oh, *yes!*" And if she proceeded to disappoint him from there on, he never showed it in his voice. She was simply calling to say that she'd received his slides, looked at them, loved them. The pause that followed she hoped would convey that that was it, there was and would be nothing more. He waited a second, then said, "They're all down here, if you want to see them in 'real-life,' you might say. I'm at your disposal."

"That isn't possible, I'm afraid. Perhaps in a few weeks, but—"

"Two weeks—say the eighteenth? That's two weeks and two days."

After hanging up, Judith was chilled and put on her sweater. What she'd do, the day before, was call him and cancel. But keep the slides. She looked up. Alex had opened the door without knocking. She was wearing one of her purple smocks, a dozen of which she owned and wore around the office, making her look like a kindergarten teacher. "Leaving?"

Judith pulled her briefcase close with a foot—"Few minutes"—dropping in the box of slides, the c.v., the viewer.

"What we were talking about before, about you calling it quits upstate?" Alex closed the door, stepped in, and lowered her voice. "Even if you don't change your mind, you might want to consider one final act of mercy."

"Everyone waffles. Even you." Judith stood to put on her scarf. "How disillusioning."

"Did you notice that Tom's grass wasn't so great this time? Did your friend comment? It was very harsh but also weak, I thought. I ran into Tom just before, down in Storage; he said it was lousy too, he agreed—he had bought last month from a new source, and never again. He feels very guilty about selling it to you, under the circumstances. He may be up later, in fact, to apologize."

"I won't be here." Her cape went on. "Is what he sold me harmful or is it just bad?"

"An inferior grade. I said you might be gone, so he told me what he would have told you. He has someone upstate for your friend." Alex took out a slip of paper from one of the smock's large pockets. "This will save you the job of being a courier each time, too."

Judith looked at the paper on her desk. "There's no name on it."

"He says just to call the number and have Jack say he's a friend of Tom's. He insists this person is very honest, gives good weight and high quality, and won't burn him."

Judith stashed the paper into the briefcase—then took it out, not liking that it shared space with the slides. She put it into the pocket of her cape.

"They shoot you up again tomorrow? What time?"

"Seven-thirty A.M., as usual. Thank Tom."

"Are you taxiing downtown? Because I'll ride with you as far as the spa."

"I'm sorry I'm pooping out about that."

"Like you don't get enough exercise as is, right?"

5

Mrs. Krem, petite and blonde and grandmotherly pretty, wearing a string of seed pearls as though she were the one who was visiting, answered the chimes. After taking his coat, she led him down a long strip of translucent rose-colored carpet protector, past a large, antique-filled living room, and toward the very back of the house. "Any trouble finding us?"

Jack said no, he'd just followed the directions.

"Don't think that stops some people—they get lost anyway."

The Krem house, built at lakeside, probably was more easily approached by boat than car: the road had been a narrow, switchy one. But being an ex-mayor and the town's grey eminence brought with it advantages. Nearly every foot of road, Jack found, had been plowed as clean as Main Street.

The hallway ended at a closed, polished walnut door; Mrs. Krem knocked, opened it a few inches, stuck her head in, and said like a secretary: "Mr. Richmond's come." Then she flattened against the door to let Jack pass.

He was entering a den, a room identifiable only by the lowest lamplight. A large picture window gave out onto the lawn, where spotlights enamelled the snow pinkly and then abruptly went no further, a dropping off into invisibility with the margin of the lake. A fire was going in a grate. Framed bird pictures hung on the walls. In a corner of the room sat a grand mahogany desk, a large switcher-console telephone atop it looking like its control panel.

"Jackson." Krem came sucking out of a deep leather armchair. Also in the room, just dimly to be seen, was Tim Sleighlin, as well as a middle-aged woman Jack did not know; she was wearing a green turban on her head.

No Vic yet.

"Let's have orders here," Krem was saying. "Bourbon your poison?"

"No, nothing for me," said Jack. His elbow was being taken by Tim Sleighlin, who'd risen to lead Jack toward the turbaned woman. "You two know each other, don't you? Paula Locksley, Jack Richmond."

Keeping her seat, the woman offered a bony hand and cleared her throat, a high-pitched sluice that never quite went on to spill a word. Sleighlin said, "Paula's is the hair salon on East Main."

"Sure," Jack nodded, smiling. "Of course." Turning, he scouted for a place to sit and chose one end of the leather chesterfield sofa, which held him low to the ground and pitched back steeply. Chin-level to him, on an end table, was a color photograph in a silver frame of a boy and a girl—Krem's grandchildren, most likely—being hugged by Dumbo at Disneyworld.

"We were just throwing the ball around," said Krem, back in his cave-like chair after refreshing his drink, "whether or not Timmy should open a second office out in our friend Victor's new Delphi Mall."

Jack interrupted. "Is Vic expected tonight?"

"He called me late in the afternoon," Sleighlin said. "Tied up."

Krem said, "That's one busy son-of-a-bee lately."

True—and the suspense was starting to kill Jack. He'd gone so far as to buy himself a bottle of Jim Beam a few nights ago, something to iron down the turmoil, only to find that the very first sip brought with it such a spell of intense stomach knifings—they lasted almost twenty minutes—that it had to mean the whole misadventure had left him with the start of an ulcer.

His mind lately changed by the hour. Vic knew about New Morning but didn't particularly care. He knew about it and did care but wasn't saying anything, waiting to see how Jack (whose miserable fault it all was: *No application? No checking with a bank? Anyone can print up business cards, open a checking account*) would extricate himself. Or he didn't know at all: that was always still possible. Trouble with contractors out at the Mall had been keeping Vic away from the latest flurry of meetings Sleighlin had set up between the business task force and city officials. (Jack and some insurance man had been sent earlier in the week to the Glenn Road firehouse for a tour in the company of the chief; but Jack had been as good as not there.)

Whatever the reasons now were, though, Vic wouldn't be staying out of it forever. Time was wasting, the margin shrinking—and the simple fact remained that Jack did not know what to *do*. In some of the books on real estate management he took out of the library, the advice was to offer to buy Salco the Trotskyite out: a few hundred dollars out of Jack's own pocket as the first month's rent on another store, one not owned by Pellegrino. But that seemed too clumsy. Other ploys mentioned in the books didn't exactly apply: Salco paid his rent on time, fit badly into the "nuisance" category, and had, besides, the vaguest, stretchiest of leases.

"My opinion," Krem was saying, screwing up a you-old-coot eye at Sleighlin, "is he'll never do it. This man is frightened to death of his bracket rising any higher. Another office, and the government'll have to make up a whole new set of IRS provisions just for him."

Paula Locksley, her legs crossed tightly at the ankles, said with reserve, "I'd be one of his patients out there, I know that."

"Victor could rent him a little booth right in the middle of the parking lot, like a Fotomat. 'Drive-in Drilling.'"

Looking as foreign to Krem's banter as Jack felt, Sleighlin leaned forward in his chair. "Vic's got Paula ninety-eight percent sold on leasing space out at the new Mall."

Jack offered the woman his congratulations.

"Thank you," she said. "It is exciting—even though I'm too old for it. Big changes are for mommas, not grandmommas."

"Baloney," countered Krem. "I've heard about the tee shot this gal whacks."

Sleighlin went on explaining to Jack: "But this is all tentative."

Krem scratched one foot with the other. "Paula's been where she is now a long time."

"You get used to a place," the woman agreed. "When I think of moving . . . "

Krem leaned across the arm of his chair to touch her hand. "Don't I know, my darling, don't I know. Guess how long I've been in this house."

Krem was one of those people who really wanted you to guess. Paula said twenty years. Krem pointed a finger at Jack, who ventured thirty.

"Thirty-seven. Thirty-seven long years. Of *course* it's hard to think about pulling up and going somewhere else. But Jack is going to tell you in a minute why you're smart to do what you're doing. He's been doing a great job with the downtown businessmen's Main Street group—and he just finished a service-delivery study: police, sanitation—"

"Fire, too, I think," Sleighlin added. "Right?"

Not too securely locked into the drift, Jack nodded anyway. "The chief, Gowall, seems very competent."

Paula Locksley turned to Sleighlin. "Does he know John McGee?"

"Who does—Jack or Walt?" Krem asked. "Jack was with John down at the meeting with Walt Gowall. And John and Walt are old hunting buddies for it's got to be going on something like twenty years now."

Just at that moment, something must have bitten Jack—right above the collarbone. A hardy winter mosquito? A flea from the couch? He rubbed at the itch through his shirt.

Paula Locksley's calves uncrossed for the first time that night. She took a sip of her highball and watched as Tim Sleighlin rose and began stiffly to track back and forth across the royal blue Antron. "Your class of customer will improve," he stressed in his deaconish way. "All the studies of shopping malls—"

"Studies, hell, Timmy," Krem broke in. "She doesn't need to hear about studies—she knows that already, don't you, dear? You've seen ladies go to the supermarket. While they're there, they browse in the adjoining stores. A beauty parlor, though—that's positively bringing the mountain to Mohammed. Surefire. I see your volume doubling within six months."

Jack's bite had begun to itch savagely now. He slipped two fingers down his collar, encountering a swelling distinct as an egg, and raked it good and hard with his nails.

"My niece Ginny's girl, Marlene, graduates Delphi High this spring. The child's turned out to be a good colorist—this isn't only a proud great aunt speaking—and I'd know that this way I could take her on. It's been one consideration."

Krem told Jack: "That whole family's seen rough times. Bill Herkett, wonderful guy, worked for Scofield, in fact. He woke up one morning, feeling poorly . . . Six months later . . ."

The woman was looking at Jack—staring at him, in fact.

"So you *are* saying that John McGee and the fire chief *do* understand one another," she questioned concentratingly.

Because it seemed to be what he was here for, Jack nodded; he felt the bump on his neck pull as he lowered his chin.

Paula Locksley said seriously, "A big undertaking."

Sleighlin assured her that God watches over. "And so do I," Krem added with an impious grin. The Locksley lady stared at her hands, then slowly got up. "I was telling Ginny before I came tonight: If I can't get good advice and guidance from these people, I wouldn't know where else a person *could* get it."

Everyone was starting to rise now.

Was that going to be it? Jack felt heavy-handed, as though he'd overly waited out something; as though whatever was going on had gone on while he was enduring a buzzing spell of itch. While to keep himself from wildly scratching he'd gazed slackly at Krem's blond granddaughter sheltered by one of Dumbo's giant ears—somewhere along there he must have missed the very purpose. Sleighlin was picking up his briefcase: the meeting, everything indicated, wasn't going to continue after the beauty parlor owner left.

And so Jack, feeling badly lapsed, stood up too.

Four, five, six times during the night his fingers went to it, checking. The itch was mostly gone but not the swelling. That, if anything had increased, become defined and hard. Before dawn he went into the bathroom, turned on the light over the sink, and looked at it in the mirror. Only when he pressed at it did it redden, buzz against the air faintly; he painted the entire area generously with calamine lotion. Hours later, when he drove to work, it was tieless.

Just by turning his head he'd feel it immediately—and by eleven o'clock it had made him already tired: in and out of the men's room to look at it in the mirror, in and out. A little before lunchtime, exhausted, all his attention covered by a thickening membrane of worry, Jack made his decision.

He had to knock repeatedly at the trailer door. Barks—one tentative, then two sure, then a whole tripped clatter of them—were the only response he got at first. But a curtain at one of the front windows moved.

They both had the dogs to gratefully contend with. Doughnut and Rafe were in raptures over seeing and smelling Jack again after all this time. Donna, her face slightly puffy with the broad stains of a recent nap, cautioned the animals weakly; while Jack discreetly tried to keep the leaping and slobbering going: it got him inside the trailer while postponing first words. Finally, with wagging tails and happy looks back, the dogs returned to Donna's bedroom, to the secure and sunbaked bed Jack seemed to have roused both mistress and animals from.

"They're surprised to see you," Donna said. "Also."

"I called you at the hospital. They said you were here. You have a cold," Jack told her.

Turning away from him, she walked to Bert's rocking chair and sat down. But not well into it: tipped forward, the chair's back was a formidable image of impatience.

Jack hadn't allowed for any kind of preface, knowing none would ever be right. Instead, he began to unbutton his shirt, saying, "There's something I want you to do for me." Eyes stretched by disbelief, Donna brought her legs up and hugged them, retreating into the well of the rocker, not even wanting to share a floor with him.

Jack left the remaining buttons alone, to pull back the right wing of his collar. "Some stupid thing bit me last night and raised a hard bump. See it? Over here?"

She didn't leave the chair. "Scofield has a nurse."

Tiny shingles of dried Calamine were coming off, sprinkling down his shirt as he fingered the swelling. "It itched last night, but that stopped. Now it's just very hard—two or three small marbles. What could have bitten me at this time of year?"

Donna slowly left the chair. As she walked to him, Jack was struck by how short she was; in the month since he'd broken off contact, could she have slipped so free of his memory? She only came to a little above his chin. But right before him now, starting gently to probe the bite with her fingertips, she seemed taller. Jack lifted his chin to allow her a clear field.

"Is there a doctor in town you see?" she asked.

"Just the emergency room that one time. You know that." Her dry distance, in the beginning understandable, was now annoying to him. Her hands had gone down. "What was it you think got me?"

"I'm no doctor." She was still looking at it.

"Yes, I know that. But something bit me and I thought you might have an idea about what to do. Christ!"

Her eyes moved slowly away from his neck; she gazed out the glary window. She was the one with the advantage, and she was using it. It was starting to make him fairly nervous. "So dramatic," he said.

Donna looked at him again. "I can't tell you what it is because I don't know. If it bothers you, why not see a doctor? Dr. LeMoyne, in the Savings Bank Building, is who I go to. I'll call him for you."

"Wait—I don't see why I need a doctor to tell what this is. It's a bite, plain and simple."

"In that case, you probably wasted a trip out here, too. Since you're already so sure, there was no reason to come."

"I came to see you."

Bad of him.

Donna didn't twitch. "I'm going to call Dr. LeMoyne." She headed for her bedroom.

Jack, not wanting to hear the call, went into the kitchenette and ran the water tap. Rafe and Doughnut ambled out to join him, and he rubbed their bellies: "How've you guys been, huh? huh? huh? Huh? Good dogs?"

"He can see you at three o'clock," Donna told him when she came out of the bedroom. "Please turn off the water."

"What day?"

"Which day do you think—today. And he was able to fit me in, too, right after you. I must need vitamins or something: I haven't been right for a little while."

Touché—and Jack thought, *I should be saying something, making amends, to her now.* "Did he mention what he thought it might be?"

"I only spoke to the secretary. I'm going to change clothes now. I'll be a few minutes."

LeMoyne, long limbed, white haired, easily into the start of his seventies, looked like the type who'd be excessively folksy: his office chairs, his desk, the fountain pen in his coat pocket were all old-fashioned. Yet his examination turned out to be as efficient and well designed as the new stainless steel table and equipment taking up three-quarters of the long sunny room. His fingers had gone immediately to Jack's bite as if quickly covering a boiling pot. He got the swelling to move, to roll back and forth. He pressed firmly into the other side of Jack's neck, under his arms, into his belly, groin, at his ankles. "Another?" Jack asked as LeMoyne fitted yet a third, empty vial to the needle stuck in one of Jack's veins ("Well, I know I don't *look* like a vampire, but . . ."). And while Jack dressed, LeMoyne came back for one last feel of the bite. He shrugged and walked back to his desk, holding the tubes of blood.

Jack sat in one of the high-backed chairs across the desk while LeMoyne scanned the large index card on which he'd jotted down Jack's history. "You're twenty-seven. Yesss. And you've been well in general. The only thing new, then, would be that you've got yourself a nice fat lymphadenopathy there."

"Which is what?" Jack had known all along it was no bite. That LeMoyne knew it too was cheering: two negatives equalling a positive.

"A swollen node."

Jack's muscles fitted tongue-in-groove into the back of his chair: the relief! Only swollen glands.

"Considering your age, I think it just might be good to have someone

pop out one of those bubs for you and have a look at it under some mag-
nification."

"A biopsy?" A voice from behind Jack.

"I think it would be a good idea."

Jack wrenched himself around in his chair. Donna, having entered
the room silently, was standing back by the examining table and smiling at him bravely. One look at that smile and dread inundated Jack.

"Is my opinion worth anything here?" he asked her. His voice was
shelved high up . . . and why was he asking *her*? Her appearance and the
word "biopsy" had him suddenly rocking at angles like the drug-
company toy on LeMoyne's desk, a semi-abstract figure balanced on a
pointy pedestal by way of a lead ball at the end of each arm. "It's just an
insect bite."

"It isn't an insect bite, that I can tell you," said LeMoyne. "It also
feels a mite hard for mono. It could be a strangulated node, but that's
weak." He had begun to doodle on one edge of Jack's history card with
his venerable pen; Jack felt like reaching over and grabbing his wrist.
"It's hard to exactly know, simply to look at it. But I have a wonderful man up in Syracuse, a head and neck surgeon, who'll be able to get
some out of there so that we *will* definitely know. And that'll be that,
end of mystery."

Jack turned and looked to Donna, catching her nodding to LeMoyne.
Once again she aimed a kamikaze smile at Jack, and again it made him
boneless.

He faced the doctor. "*Assuming* I'd have this biopsy"—the word was
a monstrous sausage he fed to the air—"which frankly I'm leaning to
not having . . . Why Syracuse? Couldn't it be done here?"

"They've got pathologists up there who are crack."

"You're telling me that if you yourself looked at a slide under a mi-
croscope, you wouldn't know whether it was mono or a strangled node?
I just love that about this place. Everyone thinks, going in, that they're
just poor yokels in need of outside expertise."

LeMoyne set down his pen softly and advanced himself further into
the well of his desk, his long frame crouched like a downhill skier's.
"You're a twenty-seven-year-old man, Jack. You've got a history in your
family. You've experienced recent pain upon ingestion of alcohol—"

"That was nerves. A situation had been bothering me, a business
situation."

"What I'm saying to you is that it's possible—though without examination of tissue it can't be determined for sure—that it could be Hodgkin's disease."

From behind, Donna's hand came down onto Jack's shoulder. His initial impulse was to shake it off violently—how could she have let him humiliate himself with talk of insect bites when, at a glance, she'd known better?—but nothing in him proved dry and flinty enough for a response. He felt spongy, pooched out with sacs of emptiness.

LeMoyne said, "I'll set it all up for you, and Laurel will call you with the details." Pushing himself away from the desk, he stood and came around near Jack; when he leaned against a corner of the desk his elbow almost toppled the balancing-man toy. "Remember, it can as easily be nothing at all. But don't wait on this, please. It isn't something a person diagnoses himself. The way to put your mind at rest is simply to get it all over and done with."

Jack opened his jacket for his checkbook—"How much do I owe you?"—but LeMoyne bent to pull the jacket closed. "Laurel bills monthly. You both scoot now and let me call Matt Weisening in Syracuse. Chances are anyway that I'll have to leave a message—being the best means also being the busiest."

Donna thanked him. Jack was silent: thanks for what? Waiting together for the small elevator in the hallway of the building, Jack turned to her. "*Your* appointment? The one you made for yourself, for vitamins—what ever happened to that?"

She looked unwaveringly back through his steam. "Another time."

In his bed that night, sometimes holding him and sometimes not, Donna snuffled and snored, tied in congestion. Jack slept little; when he did he was fired straight into lousy dreams. Salco the Troskyite barging in while Jack was with LeMoyne, staggered by pains from a false pregnancy. *Want to help me get him on the table? Thataway. We see more of this than you'd think.* Salco then being excised of something greeny-white, like cooked cabbage.

Jack would awaken and not sleep again right away. When he was lying down, the lump seemed to tantalizingly diminish but never completely go. As arranged for, the alarm went off before daybreak and Donna left to drive back to Priory and pick up her uniform. Jack rose with her, disgusted with the horizontal.

After three insupportable hours at the plant, he was the first one at LeMoyne's office. Even the nurse hadn't arrived yet.

"I knew this was going to happen!" he shrilly squawked, while Le-

Moyne calmly slipped into his white coat. "When a production is made out of nothing, it's the same thing as asking for it. And so now it's spread—now it's in my throat also! Right here"—Jack held his windpipe at a spot above the Adam's apple. "I can't swallow! It's an egg."

LeMoyne nodded, said, "I know," but made no move toward Jack to examine it.

"Shouldn't you really have told me? I have the right to know how fast it's going to spread." Maybe best, Jack realized, to die right now, here in LeMoyne's office, rather than go through this cavalcade of horrors, one after the other, a domino-fall. "This is part of the same tumor, isn't it? *Shit.*"

LeMoyne sat behind his desk. "First: even if it's Hodgkin's, it's not strictly speaking one 'tumor.' Secondly: that thing in your throat now is what's called a *bolus.*"

"I can't swallow around it."

"I know you can't. But it'll pass. A bolus acts that way. Your throat's very dry?"

"Sandpaper."

"Classic fear bolus. It's going to disappear. I know it's tough, Jack, the waiting and wondering."

"This throat thing, you're saying, is fear? You know that for a fact?"

LeMoyne assured him.

"Well, then, okay. That I guess I can handle. That's nothing. Not anything physical. You're sure? Okay. Fine. Good. Okay."

The night before they were to leave for Syracuse, Jack lay listening to the radio through the earphone all night, waiting—once he'd heard the midnight news—for each subsequent report. Donna, her cold gone, slept quietly. Toward morning, the fire marshal's preliminary report was read over the air on WDEL. According to Chief Walter Gowall, old wiring in one of the stationary hairdryers had shorted out, melting the plastic shell of the bonnet and in turn setting the wallpaper afire. The large amounts of hairspray and other combustibles appeared to have fed the blaze, which then spread quickly. Both the hairdressing establishment, owned by Mrs. Paula Locksley of Cornley, and the adjacent store, A and B Books, were totally destroyed by the fire despite the best efforts of Delphi fire fighters to contain it.

In the morning, on their way out of town in the direction of the interstate, Jack had Donna drive by there. Beams and supports were gnawed by char into fingers of black cookie. The roofs of both stores were down. Though a Delphi cop was posted by a barricade, no curious were present to keep at bay.

Jack couldn't tear his eyes away until Donna had left it far behind and Main Street slipped from sight completely.

PART TWO

The Course

6

So piteously early. Anthony's heart feels for them, actually. Whose desire did they possibly count on at six-thirty on a Saturday morning? The salmon-colored streets were deserted: few ride-bys, no other walkers except himself. Michelle and Daranna, like coffee-shop waitresses after the lunch-hour rush, were leaning against a parked car, looking slumped and workable as clay. Sunny, opposite, stood slightly more erect in the doorway to the lumber yard office. Tired bodies had a charm. Walter used to claim that only a model sick to death of posing was a model indeed, one worth drawing. The three of them wore the standard short jackets of fake fur, the over-the-knee boots. Cheap gold- and silver-plated chains, hip-slung, winked under the faded street lighting. His eye, a nonconsumer's, was touched.

Still, he kept himself strictly to the middle of the sidewalk, not overly close to the buildings or the blind spots between cars. You never could tell—a string of bad nights, lousy johns, the distemper of some drug or other . . . Normally he avoided this corner altogether, but Saturdays he liked to have his first cup of coffee take-out, from the Greek's: an old habit. And the Greek's was east.

"Mist. A."

Anthony, approaching, didn't slacken. He wasn't, he decided, even going to smile.

"Mist. A.!—you believe this? He deaf? Got to raise my voice? Mist. A., need your 'vice about a matter."

A few steps past them, and only then did he turn, slowly backpedalling.

"See, what it is. My sister, her oldest child—that's oldest of six, mind you, and she talk about *me* . . . The child's name Turlene, and she say she out*grew* school. Ten years old. My sister she get a letter—if Turlene don't report to school, the mother have to go to Brooklyn or else they be calling up your caseworker. All she need, they go and cut off her check. But she can't go to no Brooklyn with three little ones for no whole day." When Anthony had finally come to a whole stop, Sunny left her doorway, taking a few steps closer. "So Aunt Sunny be the one as usual to take care of business."

"That Sunny," Daranna called out from behind mockingly. "She a holy poor thing."

"Bet your nigger ass," Sunny shot back. "Girl over there don't understand, but that's all right—lot of people don't understand about childrens, about having to be watching how they do. Most people it don't matter shit, just so they makes their money meanwhile. That's the way most people sees it. Like my main man, Franklin."

"Oh, Sunny," Anthony groaned involuntarily. "Still Franklin? You could be *his* momma, you could be taking *him* down to the Board of Ed." Nothing that that kid equipped himself with, not the purple velour fedora and not the glass-heeled platform shoes and not the gold-knobbed walking stick and not the red plaid cutaway coat that came down past his knees—nothing visibly upped his age past that of high school. Yet Sunny was slavish, handing over to him the scant takes from her tricks. This far downtown—and low on the ladder—pimps were a pretension and there hardly were any. But with Sunny it was, of course, that Franklin *was* such a baby, a *pisher:* the urge to parent leaks out where it will. The falling in love with need. Distance in years between them like a third life, room in back where there was less and less in front.

He ought to know.

"Franklin he only care that Sunny might be off the street a whole day. So I got to make it up somehow, otherwise it come right out of poor Sunny's hide. What a good dude like you got to do for *me*, then—"

"Shit, Sunny, here I stop to listen . . ." Anthony turned his back on them and continued to the corner. He felt, surprisingly, even a little insulted.

"You got to come across and give your friend Sunny a little bit of your time right *now!"*

"At six-thirty in the morning," he called back. "Believe it."

"She treat you nice." If he turned around now, he'd find a wicked smile. He could *hear* it.

"*Vaya con Dios*, ladies."

"Doncha like a good time? Oooo-*wheeeee!"* Michelle and Daranna joined in, and together the trio did a job on the street's tender silence.

In addition to his coffee, Anthony bought a *Times* and a *News* from Nestor, but then wouldn't stay to chat: the day was rising much faster than he'd counted on, the streets were already close to fully light. Walter had once declared Anthony the earliest riser downtown, but the truth was that he sometimes never used to go to bed at all, postponing it in favor of getting hold of the streets at this hour, when they were like a newspaper other hands hadn't yet been on. (In order that J. not muss his precious paper, Anthony often bought two copies. The gratuitous distances he'd jammed between them in the past—unbearable to consider.) Tucking the *Times* and *News* under his arm, Anthony pried away the container top as he walked and dropped it into the next trash can. Never Styrofoam for Nestor: strictly the cardboard classic. Twenty years ago, when Anthony was only one of many abroad at this hour, when there were knots of people evicted from the bars after closing time but not yet talked out, heading for home—back then they sipped coffee from containers just like these. He persisted in thinking back on this as a nearly golden memory of virtue. The night would drain, the day fill—we ambled, we acted like guests and optimists on these least chic, most warehousey of city streets.

(J., released after one of her hospitalizations—he forgot which—had sniffed the morning and judged, "It's very out out.")

Sipping, he was getting closer to his block. He supposed he'd have to open up now. The idea less than thrilled him; over the years robbery had thickened as a fear. Now and then he'd find his gates pulled at, and taking into account the sort of trash that came floating out of the old Albert hotel nowadays, you didn't care to be the only open store on the block at any time.

But there was no real alternative. Staying in the loft was out, totally. In the week since she'd left him, Anthony was satisfied to make it to four A.M., at about which time a tickle summoned. (The early rising prodding the tickle? or the other way around?) In any case, awake he'd remain. In the loft, on his back, most prone to the whammies.

Yesterday, for example, it had been to wonder: If I had hit her . . . ? Enough to sting, a small slap, no more than that, a device to recall attention, as the Zens do. Delivered when she had come back that next day after the stupidity about Felice Dacey and when she was packing her suitcases, her skin soap, her Fuzzy Footies—a stinger, very brief, as though to say, *Basta* with this shit, you're staying here. You aren't leaving. She would have relented, that he knew. It was written into her nerve circuitry already: accept each new shock.

She would have relented—and Anthony most likely would have immediately wept, aghast for having impinged. He couldn't stand anymore to see her go (*Who will ever love me again?* was the secret selfish key), but what right did he have to step in? Her life now was running pell-mell. When she gave him the occasional horns with the sick kid, those single nights when off she went to her apartment—that was velocity, nothing else. He had always recognized that, had never complained. To get in her way seemed a crime.

So she runs me over. Me, me, me. The Wop weeps. The selfishness!

There was life—Anthony was surprised to see it as he turned onto the block—inside Lynton's. He crossed over. Sharing the small table at the front window, for light to read the Form by, were Gold and Pigna. Anthony knocked. Pigna, still the most agile of them, sprang up to work the door lock.

Anthony blinked at the gloom as he entered. "A bit early, no?"

"Saturday," Terry advised from behind the bar. Last night's receipts were spread out under an oval of beige light thrown by the piano lamp over the cash register, the only bulb turned on in the place so far.

"But seven o'clock?" Anthony removed his raincoat, threw it on a chair.

Chuckie pointed without looking up from the Form to the wall clock above the ancient poster for Aleurtha Horton's Dance Experiment, September 16, 1958. "Eight."

"No, that's wrong."

"The one who's wrong, *stroonz*, is a you." Terry gathered up the receipts. Claiming to have once written book for one of the Brooklyn Families, there were certain southern accents he thought himself marvelous at.

Anthony went closer to the bar and checked his watch: seven-oh-four. Pigna, once again up to open the knocked-at door, came back in with Howard Rosenman—and now the regular morning conclave was complete. Anthony asked Howard for the time. "Seven something, right?"

"Good morning," Rosenman bowed at all. "Wonderful to see such bright, happy, eager faces. Eight-oh-five. I'm serving today, I gather, by default?"

An entire hour lost. Anthony couldn't afford this kind of reduction. His talent for adjusting the heretofore was becoming *too* skilled.

Howard returned from the kitchen in the rear with a tray: the pot of coffee Terry had started when he opened, as well as mugs. Chuckie stood. "I just figured out what happened to you," he told Anthony as he walked behind the bar to coat the bottoms of his and Rosenman's mugs with Remy-Martin. "You turned your clocks back *last* night instead of tonight."

He had. It was true. Worse still. To be a sacrificer of whole days, that much the anticipator. Who am I, the superfluous man, to even make a bid for her?

"Am I right?"

Pigna folded the Form away and bounced his chair around to face the others. "Tony, you'll get a kick out of this. Know who came in here last night? Perkle. Remember Perkle?"

"What's a Perkle?" Chuckie asked.

"Tell him."

"You know him, Chuckie, but you haven't heard the name in a while, that's all," said Anthony, charitable now about memory stumbles. (He glanced up at the wall clock momentarily. Wasn't it preferable, though, to add hours *on?* He'd have to say, personally, for himself, yes.) "Guy, very loathsome, who owned a small record company."

"Only went out with shade girls," added Howard.

"But saved the screwing for the musicians." Terry entered the conversation in his usual manner, as though he could hardly bear to, stepping disinclined into a mess of incompleteness. "Sammy Otis would come in here cursing the shit out of that guy. There'd be tears in his eyes."

Chuckie's memory was jogged, he cried: "Of course!" Then, embarrassed, he couldn't be stopped:

"Perkle, Explorer Records—and Sammy Otis, Explorer Four-Eighteen, the cheapest looking jacket, but a good date, a very nice 'Do Nothing Till You Hear From Me'—Sammy, and Ten Herbert on piano, Calvin Winston, drums, and Bob—? Sure, Bobby Zaks, bass."

"Four-eighteen," sniffed Terry, walking down the duckboards toward Anthony and slipping the *News* out from under his elbow. "If he put out eigh*teen,* that was a lot."

"Was he with a black girl?" Rosenman wanted to know. Crowding fifty, with two college-age daughters by Gail, his ex-wife, Howard continued attending to the corner of the sexual marketplace that Lynton's, at night, remained. His skills as a trader were secure—for older women he had travel stories, his week with the monks at Mount Athos, his Nepalese climbs; for the younger ones there was nostalgia: *Over there, one night, in that booth,* etc.—but he liked to keep up with the competition.

"Not that I saw," said Pigna.

"You know . . ." A long pause from Howard—a new key: thoughtfulness. "We scorn that guy. You, Tony, saying he's loathsome—and he is. Not only that he's an operator; everyone's an operator—and no *speak for yourself,* because you know what I'm saying is true: everyone is in their own way an operator."

We've become this old? Anthony thought. Listen to Howard: the sort of sincere shit-in-your-hat stuff only excusable late at night, yet here it was, seven . . . *eight*-thirty in the morning.

"But this, when all's said and done, is the type of person who survives. He's oblivious. Those are the conquerors. Obnoxious, but they go their merry way, not caring, not caring to care. Like my landlord."

Lester? Lionel? Luther? Something very re-bop and universally assumed to be false—yet Perkle's first name would not land, could not be recalled by Anthony. On a snowy morning toward the end of last winter, a girl had been steered in here (Frank and Terry both denied it was by either of them, but it had to have been), a doctoral candidate, an art historian—and Anthony remembered feeling that what had ensued was false, for the girl and for the rest of them as well: the past was just not that far enough away yet. But no, apparently it was. Perkle's name lost back in the distance. Even single hours now hurdle me.

Gwen, the doctoral girl's name was—*that* I remember. High heels despite the messy streets, a sheath dress *à la* the Fifties, heaving tits. She's ragging us, he sensed, to dress like this—and when Howard, who obligingly made her that night, reported back that she wore bright red underwear, it only confirmed Anthony's premonition of mockery and derisiveness.

But the others fell for her totally. Pigna pointed out for her the exact spot people had been standing in fifteen and twenty years ago, on specific nights. Chuckie had proved funniest of all—talking about cars. How the painters drove, *if* they drove; the houses in Southhampton, the Jaguars given in trade—while so few of these bastards actually knew how to drive. Chuckie, as they all did back then, had regularly played chauffeur.

As for himself, Anthony had started to talk to her about the aesthetic—she whistled inwardly, a kind of wheeze, as she took notes—only to have it occur to him that she'd of course read all the books and articles before coming here; he wasn't telling her anything new. He had reined up short in the middle of a sentence, and from then on said no more—let the others talk.

She was interested, she said, in the fact that they all now ran small businesses on the street: she pressed for histories. Pigna, with seniority on this score (the business was first his father's), pointed out the window to the store on the opposite corner, the beauty parlor out of which a teenaged Ronnie regularly came busting, *sheesh*ing over paternal bullheadedness, and going straight into Lynton's: a haven of tap beer and an entirely different atmosphere.

Chuckie likewise had been a refugee from adolescence. An architecture student at Cooper Union, he'd found a home in the bar. In those days, devoted energies always gained affection. "I knew batting averages back to 1933, I knew jazz. People here did too." To stay close to the bar after dropping out of school, Chuckie learned enough about antiques—first as a hauler, then eventually a buyer—to make old man Glasser a happy retiree by buying him out. A date was made with Gwen for later in the day to show her through the cavernous gallery: the walnut commodes, the coromandel screens, the drum tables, the Sarouks, the Queen Anne highboys, the excruciating Bougereau imitations, the hummocks of excelsior.

As she rightly should have been, the girl was charmed. Their stories—Ron's and Chuckie's—were, Anthony had felt, hearing them again, blameless. His and Howard's not so.

He had winced to hear Howard tell her that the travel agency was "how I make my buck." Couldn't the girl feel—palpably, like a gnarl—the lie in this? Howard was no painter anymore. He'd seen it fully replaced—for which Anthony respected him. Both of them used to travel downtown together, students at the Art Student's League on the G.I. Bill. Inside Lynton's, the hope was, proximity to the big painting guns might at least waft some creative pollen their ways. For Howard it wafted something else as well. Tall, very thin, his hipster mustache a little like William Powell's, he started catching the overflow of women who jammed the bar those long-ago nights wanting to fuck a painter. Soon he was collecting impressive tallies. Then he married Gail—and shouldn't have. A good girl, Gail, very loving to Howard, but she was a better, more successful painter than he was: Howard eventually walked. At the bar, where women painters were tolerated at best, it never was held too much against him; and shortly thereafter he was back in the swim. An English woman named Lena put him into the travel business originally, giving him a part-time job at her agency down the street to support his painting. The painting fell away, the agency grew. Howard later bought her out.

The only one still touching the hems of art was himself, Anthony. Unseemly. *Mala figura.* Whatever evades and yet still torments you deserves—*demands*—an annulling curse. But he couldn't master the insult, he just was unable.

The radio had been switched on by Terry. Anthony, anguished, made a plea for mercy; he stood up and walked around behind the bar.

"I like the songs he plays," Terry defended.

"John for crying out loud Gambling?"

Terry, elbows on the bar and flipping through the newspaper: "Leave it."

"'Peg O' My Heart'—for all you old farts. I'm not leaving it." Locating the small switch on the side by touch alone, Anthony moved it to the FM position, then spun the dial. "Not when I wait all week for this. This particular announcer plays what *he* feels like on Saturday morning: Monteverdi, early Dvorak—those Bagatelles with harmonium—Clementi. Things you don't regularly hear." Anthony returned to his stool but had to be up again a second later. Bathroom.

Returned from the john, he found that Howard had taken up position at the front window—thumbs locked behind his back, looking out—and that the talk, more grumbly, had shifted to the subject of landlords. They'd all four of them had this problem at some point, and there was a legitimate sad frustration to it that took no feigning.

"He lectures me, the prick," Howard was telling them all. *"You can afford it. All that money you've been saving in rent these years—go ahead and treat yourself. You're a businessman: I don't have to explain equity to you. An extra hearse isn't thrown in so that your money can go out with you, you know."*

Anthony's own block least of all—yet—but, in general, the neighborhood had jumped in marketability; and each of them here had lived long and cheaply in what were the biggest, hence best, local apartments and lofts—the story of their charmed-or-not lives was for things to spring up choice around them. Howard's apartment, the spaciousness and the location, had itself been sufficient bait for some of his sexual conquests. Now, though, his landlord wanted it for his son and daughter-in-law; failing that, he was threatening to turn the entire building co-op.

But Anthony had no taste for this turn of the talk. He knew what was going to happen in just a moment, they'd all be sitting like irrigated grounds in the silently shared idea of only having *lasted,* a sogginess there was usually no pulling out from immediately. He personally couldn't afford it. At the first short pause, then, he asked Pigna, "Did you get to actually speak to Perkle? Anything to say for himself?"

"Nothing much. Wait, no, he did, yes—this is beautiful. He said he'd read in *Newsweek* that 'my friend' Torng had had an exhibition somewhere lately. I told him yes, at some little dink joint, nothing big—called The Metropolitan. He made a face like he didn't know and he was impressed. He asked if I knew offhand what small Torngs were bringing lately."

This was a topic of import. Even Terry closed the paper to say, "Making like he owns one."

Chuckie: "Could he possibly?"

"Perkle?" Terry threw in two more black cents: "He shits a brick before breakfast everyday. Did he ever try, though. You remember how he used to be on Eino's back?"

Pigna remembered. "The album cover."

"Every week he had discovered 'the new Bird,'" Chuckie said, smiling at the thought. "The album was guaranteed to sell a ten-thousand-copy minimum and Eino would have his big break, on the jacket, in the meantime. 'None of you people appreciate mass distribution.' Jesus, this is all coming back to me."

"He thought," Terry came in again, "that because Eino came from the other side, what could he know? While Eino could tell a creep faster than anyone in this place, including all of you bozos."

"I wonder," Pigna said, "who he actually does have."

"Definitely a Dornish," Chuckie had no doubts. "You threw Jack Teagarden's name around and Walter would salivate. And Perkle really did *know* Teagarden, and once introduced him to Walter. Walter said so."

Walter said so. But Walter, Anthony knew, had said a lot of things. It had reached the point where a perverse pleasure got taken in keeping speculation alive as to who'd been given what. A crazy time: success had come to some of them so stunningly—a Weimar, unthinkable inflation—and the more each painting and each sketch became worth on the market the more the painters in their discomfort felt that they could only give others just as good away. Walter had only to invite someone at the bar back to the studio for the rumors to fly. There were twenty people in town whose Dornish was perpetually at the framer, never on the walls. But Walter would never have presented a picture to so abject a cluck as Perkle. Lester? Lionel? Something like that.

"There's your solution, shmucko," Terry called to Howard. "You want to keep your place, sell a painting."

Howard looked out the window. He straightened his tie. Then he went to the john. Never a word.

"I insulted him," Terry concluded impenitently.

Howard, like Anthony, had no paintings anymore to sell. "I've 'de-accessioned' the fucking things," he had admitted to Anthony one rainy afternoon years ago. A girl had got him to do it, a Wall Street broker he was shtupping, a Park Avenue type—Howard found them all over, but uptowners were a frequent taste. The travel agency had grown shabby-looking, business starting to be lost; this was at a time when his girls were freshly enrolled in a new and expensive private school. So he sold the Dornish pen-and-ink and the large Torng oil he owned, he renovated, the girls' tuition was paid. Anthony stopped going to Howard's, and vice versa; instead Lynton's became the agreed-upon neutral zone. No one dared to see what was or wasn't on the other's walls. To find out how negligently each had kept the flame.

Pigna stood and was stretching. Chuckie started gathering the mugs. Howard, straight from the john, stopped off next to Anthony—who couldn't help it, who stiffened knowing what was coming.

"How is Judy?"

"Riding it out."

"But they are beginning to see improvement," Howard led.

"She's only had a couple of courses of treatment so far. It takes longer than that to know." There had been, for a second, the impulse to say, *Yes, she's really coming along*—as if, crazily, this might redound to his, Anthony's, own credit.

Howard's pewter sideburns, long as razorshell clams, hiked up as he rubbed his chin and jaw. "Someone I know who only knows her by sight saw her at the museum recently. This person said that, chemotherapy or not, she looked great. I know one thing: she really has got the guts. You think *we*, at that age, could have held up?"

I can't hold up *now*, Howard; I walk around poleaxed; I lose whole hours. And you: your "someone" and your "this person"—you mean a woman, Howard; new cunt; why can't you just say it? And how much more has she told you—has J. told *her*—whoever she is? Something I never liked about you: this reverence you have for inside information. "What was Perkle's first name? I've been trying and trying to think."

"Stanley," Chuckie shouted on his way out the door with Pigna.

Howard wasn't yet ready to relent. "But they are encouraging, aren't they? The voodooists up there at the hospital?"

"Howard, they're just like painters. First they do. Talk comes after they see results." Anthony slipped off the stool and retrieved his London Fog.

Terry turned to the radio. "Now I can shut this dreary piss." Howard had gone one more time to the bathroom, leaving them alone. *(Prostate?)* "You haven't talked to me yet about an animal," Terry said to Anthony. "So talk to me."

"You saw—have I even looked at the sheet?"

"Then, please, Terso, make it your business to. And call me early— like in an hour, tops. Don't hang me up here."

"I'll try." Quickly, before Howard could emerge from the john, Anthony left the bar.

On a Saturday, whether it was cloudy outside or not, Anthony never hesitated to turn on all the lights in the store, front and back. That way, strollers got a good look in at the wall of moldings, the general neat competence of the place. Once he had the radio tuned in, he washed his hands. Checking Howard like that in the bar had elevated his spirits to some degree and today, he decided, he'd get started on the Alice Stemmack job.

He pulled down five of the tubes from the storage shelf and gently eased them empty of their rolled drawings. This largest one, in conté crayon and able to sustain a strong mat, would keep him a whole morning. After blocking out size with pieces of blank paper, he walked with energy to the materials cabinet, the shallow steel drawers on their good bearings rolling out with a smooth eagerness to him.

Anthony scribed the outline of a window. Alice was someone he had always liked. Which museum had she said these were for—Akron? Cleveland? He took up his knife—Gabrieli *canzoni*, recorded in St. Mark's in Venice: listen to the grandeur!—and sharpened the blade on the oil-moistened stone.

He set about cutting the left-hand side's bevel. The fiberboard ripping under the blade had about it an elementally gratifying sound, like falling water. Alice, it was said, reigned now as queen at the Skowhegan summers, a genuinely fine teacher. To the best of his knowledge no one—not even Howard—had ever succeeded in persuading her into his comradely bed. The knife, like a big sweet thumb pressed up into his palm, slashed and separated with ease. Using a razor blade, Anthony loosened the board beneath, which dropped away, leaving only the window.

He poured and prepared his gesso, then gave mat and bevel a coat of it. While it dried he looked at the other untubed drawings, all still lifes. No larger lesson that was out there to be learned had substantially eluded Alice: she knew how to pull space and when to pocket it; her line was trim but a warmth, even in pen, always lurked. And responsibility. No idle strokes. The night that the freight elevator in Will Georgades' building slipped its catch as they were piling in: that instant when the single bulb overhead flickered and momentarily ground out, Alice had been the one closest to the still-open door and could have gone diving out for safety. Others did. But she had instead turned—all of this in half a second, all instinctual—to see if she could help remove Hannah Torng, who was out of the hospital barely a week following a delicate ovarian operation. The car then recaught, didn't plummet; and there were nervous laughers (myself) and there were not (Alice). Even in the blottiest of these flowers, no flightiness.

I assume everyone to be born to a world of pain—then excuse myself from examining the specifics. Alice had lost two children in an air crash, one of those impossible catastrophes that only happens to people you would never know. Roy Stemmack, the kids' father, divorced her a year later, snaffled by bewilderment. Now she was the wife of Seymour Coopersmith, a fine man, a lawyer for a child-welfare agency—who a few years ago had been obliged to give up a length of his colon and now relied instead on a bag. Would Anthony be able to ask J. to change a bagful of yellow-brown water? Alice had done more than just provide forbearance; she'd gone on working, gradually increasing her sales. Now museum shows. One or two grand every few years to Anthony for framing alone. A house in Maine, a beautiful studio on the top floor of their townhouse on Bethune Street.

The only thing missing from her work was had-to-be-ness. One late Fifties night, while a young and defenseless Anthony was in the loft, Walter had jumped up to finish a canvas. Exalted and nauseated from the cheap spic brandy Walter drank, from trying to encompass the hectic mash of Dornish-talk about Palladio, *marmaligga,* the Lovestoneites, Isaac Luria, Delacroix, Kropotkin—Anthony tried to keep his eyes away, not witness the act, but Walter was all fired up, jabbering and goading: "Don't look away, citizen. You still want to think it's a mystery? It isn't. Look how easily art can be fooled! So what does that prove? It proves the fool is you! Art *lets* itself be passed right by, the Shekinah hides itself deliberately in its veils. A little peek is enough. Look here! Look! From just this butterfly shit, see what I've made here? A goddamn anvil!" "Part and Parcel" had been the painting that night; it was reproduced in most good reference books now, on student slides, even on tacky museum shop postcards.

Alice, it had to be said, made no anvils. But why did it have to be said? A *stroonz* is right. Alice will sell this and probably all the others too; and in the Maine summers Seymour will be partially compensated for the plug in his belly: cool days, a sail, the *Times* a day late. When artificial colons are developed at Hopkins or Mayo, Seymour, thanks to these un-anvils, will go there for a consultation.

Anthony sanded the gesso smooth and put down a coat of shellac. Beethoven now: Kakadu Variations. Standing, he went to the cabinet for dry pigments—burnt sienna, perhaps a touch of ultramarine—and to switch on the hot plate to start the glue going. The phone rang.

I am not scared, he said to himself. Seizing up could only bring delay in right thinking and response. No one's helped that way. He grabbed the phone.

But it was only Terry asking: "Well? Today?"

Anthony mixed the colors with the glue size. "Such a rush—it's only ten after eleven."

"And twenty minutes from now I'm full. It's Saturday, I get other people in here on Saturdays, not only old jerkoffs. Saturday's a young crowd for lunch—hungry and thirsty."

"They're so talented." Working meanwhile, Anthony put the color down on the mat and dabbed the wet fiberboard with a rag, raising a modest texture.

"Shit or get off the pot," suggested Terry.

The pigment provided gravity, his own small improvement to Alice's picture. A combed gesso finish to the frame, and she would have a grabber here. "Go serve your margaritas. I'll look and see. Haste is a very bad sign in a man of your age and condition."

"Hilarious." Terry hung up.

With his thin aluminum pizza paddle, Anthony lifted the mat from underneath and brought it to the drying table. Then, clearing the work area, he opened the *News,* strictly to satisfy Terry. It was the rare horse that looked good to him lately; he played mostly out of a sense of obligation to his own instincts for the almost, the not quite. Besides, small tangible losses might forestall more ominous and abstract larger ones.

Paging through from front to back, he was tripped by a headline. ITALIAN CANCER DOC SLAIN IN PARK. A Dr. Paolo Bettici, from Milan, in the city to attend a conference at Mt. Sinai, had been stabbed six times in the heart while returning to the Plaza from dinner. Father of three . . . resistance fighter during the war . . . described by colleagues as "brilliant and innovative" . . . lab in Milan responsible for developing many new promising drug treatments in fight against cancer . . . a special telephone number set up by police . . .

Whetted by this, Anthony next opened the *Times* and swung through the front pages until he found the story on page 18, where there was also a sidebar biography of Bettici. He had been the Director of Clinical Research at the Instituto Nazionale Tumori in Milan—"one of the most productive and adventurous cancer research centers in the world, primarily in the field of drug development." Adriamycin, a Milan-developed compound, had proved greatly successful against a variety of hard and soft tumors. As well as DTIC—"Dimethyl-triazeno-imidazole-carboxamide." Bettici, according to the story, had been nicknamed "The Sorcerer" by his often more cautious American colleagues. "'He completely believed he was on the verge of pulling the right card out of the deck,'" the chairman of research oncology at Columbia-Presbyterian was quoted. "Said another doctor, who asked not to be identified: 'Often there's been a feeling here that the Italians were doing research the way they drive. But there's no ignoring the INT's batting average. And Paolo insisted he sensed the whole nut coming into range.'" Friends in New York speculated as to the circumstances of the crime. "'He'd seen so much agony; he'd lost a certain sense of self. A bunch of kids could have stopped him, demanded his money and his watch—I can imagine him laughing at them.'"

The *cafone!* So close to a cure—and he laughed? The Instituto Nazionale Tumori, in Milano: this was news to Anthony. Labs and labs full of sorcerers, *cafones.* His neck had begun to stiffen; he got up and checked the mat, which was dry; he brought it back with him to the work table. After unwrapping the chunk of carnauba wax, he chipped small corners off it with an X-acto knife into a tin pan on the hot plate. The wax slivers immediately began sliding and giving up their oily shapes along the bottom like his mother's Sicilian remedy for head-colds...

A red cloth. Placed over his head as he sat in a chair, then a soup plate of cold water balanced with a hand atop the cloth. Fervent, whispered prayers from his mother while she made small marks of the cross with her thumb on the sides of the plate. Then, from a small dish of olive oil, her thumb taking up a single drop and letting it fall into the plate of water. A loud plop signified headcold, nothing worse—and she'd continue dropping the oil off her thumb till the plopping ceased. The cold was gone. The water could be changed only once.

. . . And how he'd worn, with the measles, a rope necklace with five knots in it, a red flannel shirt over that. Sorcerers. Removing the pan from the hot plate, Anthony added turps—then a little more, and some varnish for pastiness—and began to polish the mat with a square of chamois. Circles and circles: Aunt Surzetta's circles, when his mother had the *vermi*—stomach pains. But this had been genuinely frightening: he must have been ten, maybe eleven, no more. A darkened room in the middle of the afternoon, Mama on her back, lying on the red rug with the dark blue flowers—the chuting angle of descent that these were coming back at him on! bombs of remembrance!—with a white handkerchief over her dress at the belly as Suzie bent to set an index finger upon Mama's navel and then walked clockwise, clockwise like the whirlorama that came to Worcester each August; praying, screwing the finger in deeper, stopping only to spit out a specific prayer and rub the belly flesh like a spilled mound of beans toward the belly button.

At the time, repugnant. What if he were to bring Joe Hetschek home from school with him someday and again find this going on? So he complained. "Tell me, so smart, what I can do," was his father's reply. "Tell me." His pop: whose magic was so much weaker—hundreds lost on the White Sox that year, dashing all plans for his own store and the end of bondage to the warehouse and that *melanzan* Volpe. Who was dead at forty-nine—while she, she, a little brown walnut, still now sat in Phoenix and watched "As the World Turns," had seen in color men drop onto the surface of the moon. "The moon is my friend. *Respetto*," she told Anthony when he called her the night of the landing. In her village, she said, the women would go up to the highest roof or balcony and scream out the worst curses at the thunderheads, arms rigidly up and making scissoring motions to cut off the head of the storm and either let the men go out in the boats or bring them safely back. *Respetto.* She, to this day, drank a daily infusion of bay leaf and lemon. Dozens,

dozens of remedies: beaten egg white wrapped tight against leakage inside a cloth, which then was applied to a muscle strain. Sugar on a bleeding cut (though this his father forbade: "You get away!"). Raw lemons for diarrhea, garlic for tension. Howard talking about voodooists. "The Sorcerer."

The phone book, the white pages, lay under some papers in a carton, and Anthony dug it out. The woman at the Public Library's phone information service spent ten minutes searching but could find nothing that gave the address of the Instituto Nazionale Tumori in Milan, Italy. Had he tried the Academy of Medicine, uptown? They might have it.

In middial, Anthony stopped.

Not the way.

The address would do little for him. He would write; Milan would answer (assuming they even got the letter—wretched Italian mails) and recommend the excellent clinical centers in the States, where no doubt J. already was receiving the most up-to-date therapy. No, he wouldn't write. When Irmalinde Doennis, the uptown private dealer he did occasional work for, had discovered a lump in her breast one morning (he wished he'd remembered this sooner), she had her phone cut off, mail stopped, and her best clients and sources notified. She packed two suitcases, booked herself on a Lufthansa flight, and was at a clinic in Dusseldorf when it opened at eight the next morning. With knife and cobalt and drugs and Teutonic efficiency, they had cleaned her out, for far less cost than she would have had to pay here; a year later she was again home and in business. That had been ten years ago.

If he and J. were simply to arrive in Milan, present themselves, could they be turned away? It was unlikely. Desperation. Nobility. The incontrovertible. Things Italians knew about.

So much memory, keen and unprepared for—and now this glimmer of a fresh idea: it all sped Anthony's blood. He slipped Alice's drawing under the polished mat, hinging it there with two spits of tape. Against the richness of the mat, the drawing settled down; the gaiety Alice strove for was checked. Under glass, in its frame, it would look even graver and weaker.

Good.

He was in the midst of pulling his gates shut when, from down the street, he heard his name being called. A man and woman were stamping toward him, laughing and calling out to each other as they ran: "Who said we wouldn't catch him?" "But just, just!" And then they were at his side, happily panting. Stewart Morton, a large rectangular package under one arm, clapped his free hand to Anthony's back— "*Come sta,* Antonio?"—while Jane, the wife, shyly kissed his cheek.

"You have a goody," Anthony said when they were all inside the shop. The Mortons were two- or three-times-a-year customers, "young collectors"—she especially avid and jumpy, it seemed, to cover ground in the arts, with the husband's money from an import-export firm being the supercharge.

Placing the package on a table, Stewart began to wrestle it open. "While I'm doing this, Jane, show the new pictures of Dana."

The wife winced. The minute she'd stepped inside her mood had turned vigilant, irritable, scanning: a hyperalert hash of self-consciousness. Anthony had seen her be this way before. "He"—she meant her husband—"doesn't realize how boring they are to other people."

"Well, not to me—so hand them over." Stewart, he saw, was having difficulty with the tape around the package; Anthony lent him a knife. Five or six Kodachromes had appeared in Jane's hand and were being held out apologetically to whomever might want them. Anthony took the photos from her with a show of eagerness.

"She walks around the house"—Stewart was grimacing, his tongue between his teeth while he ripped at tape and corrugated cardboard with Anthony's knife—"saying to anyone she sees, even the furniture: 'Isn't it a nice day?' Janey says she must have swallowed a bumper sticker when we weren't looking."

"She's great," Anthony said. The Kodachromes of the little brown-haired girl were being immediately repossessed out of his fingers by Jane before he could give them a second glance.

"Ta-da!" The package finally undone, Morton was slipping out the contents carefully, his eye happening meanwhile to fall upon the open page of the *Times:* "Great for the tourist industry, that"—a shake of the head. "Anyway—voilà! Another masterpiece added to the Morton Collection of Rowayton, Connecticut. A Marius Hennert. Mr. Rogoff *hid* it for us. The day the show opened, everything was sold right away; but we were in London. Janey, though, had seen this a month earlier—Hennert had just brought it up to the gallery. She tells me he doesn't work this small very often. Rogoff says he could see in her eyes how much she loved it, and so he put it aside for us."

Jane wanted it made clear that she never said she loved it, she didn't *love* it: "I thought it was very appealing. I *liked* it very much."

"Okay, but the day she first saw it she made me leave the office and cab up to the gallery right away so I could see it. And it's all she talks about lately."

"Let's not make it sound like a Giotto or something," Jane said, venom in the humility. Stewart shrugged his shoulders. "Or a Dornish," she added, looking meaningfully to Anthony.

As much as Anthony hated to agree with her about anything, she here was accurate. No Giotto, no Dornish, the Hennert consisted of a rope of cad red medium, thick as though straight from the tube, which took a shimmy or two a third of the way down the canvas and then bellied out into feathery gills of plum stain. When faced with a piece of crap like this, Eino Torng used to sometimes do a little patter— "Paintings on Parade," he called it—making himself sound like a pinch-nosed Movietone News announcer: "Dis fine American line bakes one fine angel cake, plays the accordion, and, folks, will you get a look at the gams on her, the dung!"

"What do you think?" Stewart was asking.

Jane rotated toward her husband quickly: "You shouldn't ask him that!"

Stewart moved with the painting two steps to his right. "I think the light's better over here. How's that?"

Anthony said, "It's handsome. Any preferences as to how you want it framed?" He took the canvas from Stewart's hands. The way Jane was looking at her husband and at her painting—she might have been about to cry.

"We'll just leave that to your expertise."

"There isn't any rush," Jane said.

"That wasn't your attitude to the poor cab driver on the way down here," Stewart kidded his wife.

Jane dismissed this with a shake of her blunt-cut hair. (Pretty, but this kind of unappeasable woman often was.) "This month's issue of *Plastica*, the English magazine," she was saying to Anthony—"have you seen it? There's a big piece on Dornish. You're mentioned."

The flirt. Arrange to have her come back alone for the framed painting. Grabbing her hair, I would shake her up, I would lean her over the cabinets and fuck her (he thought this with shame yet a filling crotch, letting the idea run on riggishly a moment or two longer) . . . turn her around, lift her ankles into the air, and ream her with the leisure of cruelty, ignoring her yips, bitchy cries, I would . . . No, I wouldn't— a dream. With the obstinately unmollified—like Jane, like J.—only kindness worked. Even a simpleton like Stewart knew this. Kindness, with its sloped sides, its gutters, was the ultimate defense, shield.

"Janey took me down, Antonio, to that big retrospective in Washington of your guy Dornish," Stewart began as Anthony was measuring the Hennert.

Jane: "*Dragged*. And Dornish is not 'his guy.'"

"Oh, sure he is," Anthony said over his shoulder mildly. (Leave, he prayed. Now.)

"At first I didn't really get what was going on—so many shapes and blocks superimposed on top of each other—but you see sixty or seventy of them together like that, and, damn, it makes an impression." Stewart took a seat in the chair next to the worktable. "All *his* stuff, I'd guess, was vacuumed up a long time ago."

An immediate click of disdain from Jane. What a drag she was. But to Stewart, Anthony merely shrugged and mumbled, "You never can tell . . ."

"Because if ever one *was* available . . ." And suddenly there was a hand on Anthony's shoulder: not Stewart's hand, a female hand.

"A small one," Stewart qualified.

"We'd pay a price," said Jane, "that's competitive."

Anthony held up the Hennert. "I'm going to put a grey wood around this, if that suits you."

Jane collected herself. The hand came down, she smoothed a brow. Stewart swore complete trust in Anthony's judgment. "Can you come have a drink with us over at Lynton's?" Jane asked.

More of my time? Fastidiousness rose up and threatened to swamp Anthony like a wave. He made apologies—work to do at home—and finally they left. He gazed at the Hennert dung. The money, the thousands it must have cost. And I don't ask them for a deposit. And they don't offer.

At home, he drank some wine. What they'd diagnosed at Lynton's in the morning had proved to be the pathetic case: all his clocks were slow because he'd turned them back a day too soon. Now he went around resetting each an hour ahead, even though they'd all have to be changed back in a few hours anyway. He drank more wine. He turned the chicken breasts; oil spat up at him, burning a dot onto the back of his hand. The din was fierce. He added chopped onion and garlic, and the bits bronzed. Walter's favorite midnight supper: chicken—but I hadn't known, had I? about a low, low flame and about slow cooking; and so the first time I ever tried it alone, my inaugural meal in my first loft on the Bowery, it was a fryer—you fried a fryer, right?—and when the skin crackled and turned golden, it had to be done, of course it had to be. And I sat down and bit into a bird pinker than grapefruit. Proud and sickened. Funny. He lowered the flame and added the wine that was left in his glass and then some more from the bottle, along with the two peeled and diced tomatoes. He covered the pan.

He polished three pairs of shoes—which he wouldn't dare to do if J. were here, not three in a row, that snotty look that would come on her face. He stripped the bed, though this was not necessary, and put on new linens. He lay back, clothed, on the sheets, then got up and remade the bed. He checked the chicken and opened another bottle of wine. She never understood me. He cleared his throat, and when it sounded like the start of a sob, he toyed with it, clearing his throat again. The day had been working up so nicely to a tangle, an orgy of feeling—and then it had to be interrupted by those Morton fools, whom he would never forgive—

Or probably would. Since it didn't matter. Regrets lately came to him promiscuously, most of them hambone. That she understand him: something that had never been of importance when she was still here but since her leaving cankered him ornately. Where he honored order she only clucked critically over ritual. Right now, for instance, if she knew, she'd be making fun of the chicken. Someone who's hungry eats, he doesn't cook. He went again to check on the chicken. Far from ready, and the muttering simmer seemed to be taunting, taking her side.

He walked to the stereo setup and put it on the turntable, he didn't care: *Turandot*. In Milan, on nights when the drug effects won't be too bad, they might be able to get tickets for La Scala. Another glass of wine. Volume up high. He went to make the bed, finding that he'd made it already. *"Non piangere, Liù"*—I'll do all the bawling for both of us. He returned to the round table and his hand went out for the magazine: he would only read the ads in front. He opened then immediately closed it, excited. In Leitner's, the magazine store where he'd gone directly from the shop after closing and after checking the street to see that the Mortons weren't still around, his heart had been a handball, compact and wild. The ego was a crazed thing: three times he'd taken the copy of the magazine to the cash register but twice he'd walked back and returned it to its place. I don't care—but I do. I do.

The wine was starting to make him a little sick. In a while he wouldn't be able to read.

His finger found the exact page. "Heuristic compositions, they play lightly with the notions of rigidity . . . Any full eidetic reconstruction would have to be based . . . mockery at technique itself . . . Terrezza . . ."

He gulped wine, spilling some on his chin.

"The Museum of Modern Art show in 1958 provided a spur and challenge to an entire underculture of young painters—Henry Bowne, Simon Lepf, Anthony Terrezza (the consultant for the Modern's 1970 retrospective)—all of whom showed at the Piké Gallery, a cooperative, and who to a remarkable extent captured in their own works the sides, as it were, of the Dornish style. A style of hegemony such as Dornish's, both by paralleling and reversing . . ."

As it were. Was it sides when, one morning—was it sides when he and Walter had done a picture *together?* Hung over, O.K., but still a seriousness. An "exquisite corpse." "The Surrealists played this game. One stroke you, one stroke me. Gruesome, isn't it? Let's stop." Sides? The fucking very heart! Hiccupping. Anthony's throat was douched with sourness.

This part: so very lovely—*Gli enigmi sono tre, una ela-vita*—a high C!

"The unshakable disguise of color is Dornish's hubris yet also his veil, a curtain his Kabbalistic interests drew over the awareness that his gestures are unapproachable by other painters simply on neurophysiological grounds . . ."

And I have saved it to this day, that "exquisite corpse." Walter had kept it, and two days after he died, I took it out of his loft with the rest of the little mementi: some brushes, a can of turps, paints, small blank canvas boards. "Take what you want," May had told him that morning, meaning, he supposed, finished paintings. "Better you than the jackals." But a young man's heart is offended sorely by a completed, tied-off memory; I took raw materials, as many paint tubes as I could grab through my tears. (Stuff for Walter to use in case he ever came back?)

"Neurophysiological grounds" is it? Where was that "corpse"? I have proof! Oh boy, a tiny wobble there, as he was getting up—but I'm fine . . . walking to the back of the loft, the storage racks, and pulling and pulling until he found it. This! In cardboard originally, then at some point later (when?) he'd wrapped heavy plastic around it, and rope.

Here's "sides" for you! Right here. He was sweating now. He got the thing open, brought it back to the drafting table up front, under some light. I'll show you.

But where was it, the "exquisite corpse"? All that was here were the old blank canvas boards, the paints, the moldering Walter stuff of potential. Anthony finished what was in his glass and then found that that had done it, too, for the bottle. He put it out of sight on the floor.

Pinching off a dry cap, giving a tentative squeeze to a tube—what had happened to the "corpse"?—the old tube farted but did squirt wet: proof that the past—good—wasn't all that far away after all. Other tubes too were workable. With gauze—all very quickly—he rubbed a mix of yellow, white, green as background onto one of the old canvas boards. The horizontals came quickly after that. So much for the style of hegemony.

Vincero! Vin-cer-rrr-o!

The forms began to accumulate; he swiped them away with a butter knife, let them reclump. A stroke shot out the right side. He smudged the brown leftmost form, then nudged in the green rectangle. Break it, break it, now! Show me the veil! By the testicles, Walter, by the stones—streaking the white, keeping the thickness, the melding, the dotting, the gulleys—would you honestly know this wasn't yours? No. It *is* yours. You, who crippled me. And it's also mine. The Sorcerer.

Ah! Solleva quel velo, guarda, guarda, o crudele, quel purissimo sangue che fu sparso per te! Raise that veil and look, look, O cruel one, at that blood so pure which has been shed for thee!

A little less pissant background—more yellow. An umber cord, vertical, all the way over to the left: a life rope. You were not a flippant man—and nor am I. J., when we're in the box at La Scala, will *see* that, even if I choose to polish *ten* pairs of shoes in the hotel room before. Anthony could feel the very pulses within his eyes. This is for you, then—I'm even putting your name on it—W. Dorn in the lower left corner, as you always signed—it's for you, understand? Justice at last, an act of reunion—see, here, I'm starting another one, I'll use up all these five boards if I don't first puke (Oh J.!)—between what you did and I didn't. Shit on "sides."

7

Three names in a vertical row were on the buzzer board: Acquarius Plastic, Inc.; Temma Reid Creations; and W. Huft. Judith rang and waited. (That was wrong, she was fairly sure: *Acquarius. No c.*) She inched in closer to the doorway. Very nasty streets down here, like wind tunnels: strange weathered, narrow, closed in. To find this one her cabbie was forced to nose into half a dozen others first, like a surgical probe: "Noop." "Noop."

No one was buzzing back. So much for adventurousness; finding a taxi now to take her back home was going to be a definite joy and a half. But then, from the other side of the steel-plate door, clusters of quick clomps. Louder. Louder.

"The buzzer—I'm so sorry. I tried calling you; I left messages. It's on the fritz again. You're Ms. Kornbluh? It never stays fixed long. I'm Bill. Very sorry."

"Hello, Bill. Your neighbors run down each time, too?"

"Mostly we throw keys. But not to someone important like yourself." His accent in person was a little drawlier than she remembered from the phone. He was of medium height, very squarely put together. Hair a box of curls. Face slightly red. Glasses (which for some reason never failed to surprise her: eyeglasses on people obviously born south of Philadelphia or west of Chicago), a thin nose. He was no one she'd turn around after in the street, but he was pleasant enough looking. *Clark Kent*—that was the resemblance.

He was shaking his head guiltily. "You biding your time out here in the cold . . ."

"I live . . ." She corrected herself: "I've lived in lofts myself, I know the problems."

"We are doing real poorly at the moment here: only got the heat back on a week ago after two weeks of it off—lived in lofts yourself? Watch yourself now," he warned, going ahead of her into the vestibule, which smelled of something like pumpkin. "You just follow me."

The door to the street had slammed behind them and he was taking Judith by the hand through the fruity darkness. After a few obscure steps, she felt her wrist being tugged upward.

"First step. Find it? Careful."

Stairs. And now she recalled him saying, that time on the phone, something about the fourth floor.

"Why don't you give over your briefcase here to me."

"Yes, why don't I"—she handed it up.

It was going to be impossible of course. Maybe this first flight, since she had been climbing that much lately at her parents' house, but not more. Already, after five or six *steps,* her knees were beginning to feel overbaked and crumby.

"How you doin'?" he called back.

"I'm doing." Like tiny oily blooms, patches of heat were popping out beneath her clothes; she pulled her fingers from his guiding hand in case they started to get wet. Another step and another. The sudden declarative smell of her Norell didn't bode very well, either; on her, a strong burst of scent like this usually meant it was about to disappear totally.

But at the second flight she came into a small inheritance: air alone seemed to be pumping, working the backs of her knees.

The third flight—with the end in sight—she decided to treat like a dream: vivid, but this really wasn't happening. Tremors were vining around her calves. Under the wig, her kerchief was soaked with an arc of perspiration, drying and cooling like a halo. Huft had already reached the top; light from the open door of his loft was falling around him. If he weren't looking, she'd stick a finger under her fake, second head and wipe away some of the drips.

The final step. She reached it—and exactly there was where she deposited herself. Huft tried to comfort—"If you aren't used to it . . ."—but Judith knew that if she said even a single word back now, she'd throw up; she only raised a mute hand of peace and continued to sit.

"Can I get you some refreshment?" Rolling his lips with voluptuous unease, Huft kept glancing back through the open door into the loft. Judith, taking pity, got to her feet.

In the front section of the loft, nearest the door, wallboard had been built three-quarters of the way up to the pressed-tin ceiling, making for a small comb of cubicles. Huft was carefully hanging Judith's coat on a clotheshorse. Somewhere in the loft a television was on to "The Beverly Hillbillies."

Judith followed Huft down the narrow hallway, stopping abruptly when he did—at the door to one of the cubicles. He raised an arm to gather Judith in more closely.

"This is Ms. Kornbluh, Quinny. This is my daughter Quinton."

Lying belly down on a skinny cot was a child of nine or ten, blonde, wearing glasses like her father. A small portable TV, only a foot from her face, sat on a fiberboard chest of drawers. The little girl shifted around on her elbows and seemed to watch the screen all the harder.

With a strange somber pride Huft announced that Quinny had an upset tum.

"Dad*dee!*"

"Why, am I lying? It's not the truth?" Stepping inside the room to sit at the edge of the cot, Huft began to stroke the golden hair—but Quinny, wanting none of it, twisted away.

Huft rose reluctantly from the cot. "Promise you'll call if you need me, Cakes."

In the loft's main work area stood large packing crates, some dismantled, some intact. The walls of the room were piebald and the fluorescent tubes spaced unevenly overhead soaked some of the Huft creations hanging on the walls into shadow.

"This, by the way, is over here"—he was showing Judith the filing cabinet on which he'd rested her briefcase. "Whenever you want it."

If Judith wanted anything, it was the big paint-dirtied Morris chair she'd noticed in the center of the loft. Her breath was about fully returned, her chest feeling less pigeony, her calves calming down—but to sit would have been heaven. Huft, though, was saying: "Start maybe over there and work our way around? I've got a few crated, too, that I can take out and show."

The floor, grey-painted, was gritty with shavings and sawdust. At the loft's far end, the windows looking down upon the street were covered with a purple burlap that blocked out most of the natural light. Used to the comfort and impeccable orderliness of Anthony's loft (where, true, no work was done anymore), Judith was thinking that she'd hate to have to grow up here, as Quinny must. And was the wife at a job, working to support them all?

"This is one I think you said on the phone you liked." Huft stepped back to look at it with her. It was the one of the old man waiting in the box for his shoes to be repaired. In person, however, up close and full-sized, it made Judith uncomfortable. Real white socks, droopy ones, were down around nude, twiggy ankles that had been planed from raw pine. Anthony's ankles were starting to look exactly like that. "Your materials are what?"

"On this: acrylic polymer—"

"I prefer oils, myself," she said, for no reason at all.

Huft nodded seriously, acknowledging the unacknowledgeable. He went on, hesitant: "Poly foam. Cotton duck. Some tin for this area here." In his eyes was: *Those all right with you?*

"Dah-dee-ee!"

Huft turned back apprehensively toward the cubicles. "Pine . . . Do you mind? I'll be just a second. Sorry about this."

"No, of course not." She watched him sprint away, his tie flapping. He wore a tie for her. She's going to stop the snotty playacting, it isn't fair. She's going to confess to him that she's got nothing to do with anything, and humbly leave.

Huft was back in a minute. "Sorry. Let me show you the one you said you *really* liked"—walking her by three or four other pieces on the walls and stopping at the "Two Ladies."

It was as wonderful in real life as it had been on the transparency. "Which one of them is your mother?" Judith suddenly got the inspiration to ask.

"That one"—he pointed to the saleslady behind the counter. When unpinched by politeness, his smile was extremely pleasant.

"I thought so."

"Did you?" When he laughed—a cough of genuine happy surprise—the fluorescent bars overhead jiggled, doubled, in his glasses. "She sold notions for Grant's for fifteen years."

"I knew that also," Judith said fancifully.

"You did?" Another laugh. "I'll be!"

"Dahdeeeee!"—came the summons from the cubicle, this time with a moan: "*Ohhhh.*" Holding his hands high to ask that the conversation hang just as is, Huft once more took off.

It wasn't bad, Judith thought, to be appreciated—even in the form of a ten-year-old's jealous dramatics.

On one wall, covered with a white sheet, was a work-in-progress. Judith lifted a corner of the sheet. On a love seat, sewn and tufted and buttoned like real upholstery, sat the figure of a teenaged boy. Lying on his lap, belly down, was a teenaged girl (wearing actual blue jeans). Her top, made of painted wood, was dressed only in a bra that the boy was hurrying to undo. Huft, additionally, had taken a photo of Bela Lugosi as Dracula, given it pimples and feral young eyes, and had pasted it on the customary breadboard that was the boy's face. The girl's face, on the other hand, had been painted in almost classically—yet with an evil smile of manipulation and foreknowledge to the mouth. The hair was blond: Quinny's.

Judith dropped the sheet at the sound of Huft coming back.

Absently straightening the drape of that same sheet, Huft said quietly, confidingly, with a whole new demeanor: "I wasn't expecting Quinton, you see, and she wasn't expecting me. It put her a little out of phase, it seems like. Her momma's a psychologist down in Richmond; she got suddenly called to come down to Atlanta to testify at a trial; no one was around down there for Quinton to stay with; and so here we are. She hasn't been out of bed since this morning, it's been paining her that much."

I hate people who do this. "What has?"

"But to pee, she hasn't been to the bathroom for four days now. I've been going down and bringing her back bran muffins, making her eat them—they're supposed to help, right?—but she's had more than her fill of them. Balks."

Judith looked to the file cabinet for her briefcase. "This isn't the best time for me to be bothering you, then."

Huft looked up from his shoes. "Bothering me?" He appeared truly scandalized. "You call this a bother?"

"Dahdeee, come in here!"

"Just a moment, Cakes," Huft yelled back. "Daddy's a little busy right now."

"I think I should go," Judith said.

He misunderstood drastically. "Would you? That would be wonderful." He began a short briefing: "I've made her drink water till it's coming out her ears, and last night we went downstairs to get some exercise: move it about a little, you know? That's when we also bought the Ex-Lax." Planted like an oak in front of her, he was making it hard for Judith to get to her briefcase and thus clarify what she meant to do, which was leave.

"Has she taken that before?" Judith asked.

"She knows the commercial. Have I been mismanaging?" When she moved, he moved. Was he intentionally blocking her?

Judith wondered if something else might not be better, like an enema.

Huft stepped over to a table and restlessly began to stir a Maxwell House can filled with brushes. "My daddy used to give me those when I was a boy, and I can't say it made my day," Huft said darkly.

"I'm sure not." Judith moved toward her briefcase unimpeded. "But they make a bottled kind now, already mixed. You use it all up at once, then throw it away. Very gentle. I think it also comes in a children's strength."

Almost whispering, Huft said, "But they probably don't sell it around here . . ."

"I bet they do." She grabbed the briefcase.

He nodded and silently stirred the brushes, nodded and stirred.

"It's very easy," Judith assured him, "and then she'll feel better." A sucker: that's her. "Would you like me to stay while you give it to her?"

Quinny, now sitting upright at the cot's edge, turning channels, didn't raise her eyes to the grownups who were suddenly crowding the doorway of the cubicle. "Cakes, we're in luck. Ms. Kornbluh, you know, is a nurse—and she's going to give you something that'll do the trick in a jiffy. You'll be jumping for joy!"

Judith looked at him—it had been been a long time since anyone had taken advantage of her—but Huft, pulling on a Peruvian sweater-coat he took from the clotheshorse, had no trouble whatsoever in meeting her eyes. "Write down the name for me, so I get exactly the right thing."

Afterwards, success having been achieved but Quinny napping after the ordeal, Huft insisted on toasting Judith for her efforts. The burlap curtains over the front windows had turned wine-black, it had become nighttime, but Judith stayed only because, while Huft drank and talked, she was getting some time in the Morris chair—which she needed.

"It's all this tricky equilibrium, the three of us satisfying each other's expectations. Jane—after a few days with me like these—counts on Quinny coming back and buying her whole line about me: that I'm not a 'realistic person.' That, granted, may be true enough. And I know that Quinton pities me. I accept that. I've accepted worse than a ten-year-old's pity. I'll swallow down about any damn thing as long as it lets me stay right here and do whatever it is I'm doing."

He poured the contents of Judith's refused glass into his own. "But there are things that you can tell children that just aren't right. Yesterday, when Quin was really having bad cramps and I wanted to take her over to Beekman General or to St. Vincent's (which is better, by the way?), she started crying and crying. I figured she was scared—but you know what she told me? She said she wasn't going to go because her momma had once said that one of the reasons she and Quinny moved back home in the first place was because the doctors up here were all niggers. That's my psychologist wife talking, telling that to the child—believe it?"

Judith asked him for the time, and Huft looked at his watch—but then caught on: "You haven't seen the work, though, yet! We've been too busy."

"I'll come back another day."

"But aren't you hungry? I was going down to get this excellent Chinese food, because Quinny's going to be starved. And she'll hate it if you leave before she gets up, you did so much for her and all." An additional nimble thought lit his face. "And someone has to stay here with her while I'm out for the food!"

She had no luck in resisting this man. When he was gone, Judith went again to the work-in-progress, lifting off the entire sheet this time.

It struck her again the way it had the first time: as all wrong. What teenage boy was that monstrous? would deserve a vampire's face? None that Judith had ever known. Down in the finished basement, in fact, it was usually the boy at the disadvantage. Ricky Lebo's fingers she remembered as smelling of potato chips, fumbling pressuredly with the buttons of her blouse; when he finally groped her little titties, fingers under the Maidenform cups, he'd been as graceful as someone filling an order for a dozen ice-cream cones in a hurry. Anything but Dracula. Only Ricky pressing at her, and she trying to get in line with his fingertips . . . until, when he finally got it right, it was time (one Mississippi, two Mississippi, three Mississippi) to yank his hand out and say "No."

All sweet and dreamy and strictly unprofessional—not like this shark and this little whore with a broiling pussy beneath her jeans. Who even *had* a pussy at fourteen? At fourteen she'd had *He's so gorgeous!* and The Five Satins singing "To the Aisle" and giggle fits and chocolate-chip cookies while watching "American Bandstand" and just maybe a vicious miniature skill now and then at manipulating Daddy. She made anonymous phone calls with Lisa to older boys they liked and she suffered an occasional weepy week. But no pussy. This was solely Huft's problem.

Dinner turned out to be lively. Huft covered a long table—a plywood board atop sawhorses—with newspapers and did all the serving himself. The cartons of salty-smelling food were lined up shoulder to shoulder and made the middle of the table look like a white, modernistic city, a Brasilia. Quinny, face washed and hair brushed and in fresh clothes, wore a large lime barrette and a blissfully more comfortable expression. A joke—based on the word *gunk*—developed between the girl and Judith. "Please pass some of that gunk." "This gunk or that gunk?" "That gunk." "Oh, I'm sorry, I thought you meant this gunk." And Huft would every so often jump to his feet—"I'm the server around here!"—and hug Quinny. He would do this, jump up and hug her, five or six times. A hugger.

It was very festive. "Tell the pukey story, Daddy. Of the you know—" Quinny doubling over, pressing at her belly.

"I just told that to you yesterday, Cakes."

"But tell her"—pointing to Judith. "And yesterday I wasn't in the mood."

Huft's mouth was happy yet drooping. (A glass of brandy stayed close at hand even as he ate.) "Good buddies of mine and myself went one summer weekend to Virginia Beach." Quinny, nodding, had stopped eating and was gnawing happily at her fingernails, enraptured. "We had ourselves a good time—all I need say, right? And one place refused to serve us. It was sort of a café, with tables outside with umbrellas over them . . . I wish you could see yourself. You look like a cannibal."

Quinny dropped her hand into her lap.

"What is it anyway that's so delicious? Really. I'd like to know, am truly curious. If fingers are better than these Cantonese clams, tell me and I'll eat mine too."

Quinny squealed joyfully, "Don't do it, Dads! Look at them!"

Huft played along, sheepishly inspecting his color-flecked fingers, holding them aloft like a booby prize he'd won. "Yuccchh!" yelled Quinny, laughter becoming hiccups.

Judith: "So it was a sort of café . . ."

Huft gave his fingers a last regretful inspection and slipped them quickly beneath the table. He summarized: "Yes, well, a café. That refused to serve us. We left. Bought candied fruit, some cottage cheese, ketchup, a hot-water bottle. Made up a mixture, filled the bottle with it, put the bottle down shirt, left stopper off. Went back to the café. Ordered Cokes, manager came out. I made sick faces. Leaned against the side of the table."

Quinny squirmed.

"Everything coming up over my shirt collar, onto the table. Waiter brings towels, but we say no, not necessary. Would appreciate, though, four spoons."

Quinny by this time was conducting the story with her fork as if it were a symphony. "And tell what you did!"

"She knows, Cakes. She figured it out herself."

"They *ate* it!" Strands of Quinny's hair swept through what food remained on her plate.

When the laughter had flattened, and the sauces in the containers began to skin, Quinny was sent off to change into her pj's. Then there were kisses goodnight: "And how about one for the lady?"—Quinny's knees jabbing into Judith's thighs as she clambered up onto her lap like a baby, then off.

Huft, after removing the plates and glasses and utensils, was clearing the table by making a giant ball of the newspaper tablecloth, the food containers, the napkins: he dumped everything into a metal garbage can by the sink. "Don't ever, if you don't already know this, order sea bass," he said dreamily as he worked. "It looks good and all when they bring it out, and it's tasty, I guess—but it's a dirty, dirty fish, a bottom feeder, a mudder. What did you think of my show at Henrack?"

Judith said, "I'm afraid I missed it."

"But you saw the reviews."

The loft had grown warmer—or else she had. Nothing spiking—a low flame. Judith wondered if he owned a car. If he did, she ought to ask him for a ride home before Quinny was asleep.

"They said I was a sentimental asshole." He sipped brandy. "The exact words."

"I think I have to be going now."

"That my nostalgia was cruel and that my visual irony was 'inert and groping.' I have always suspected that Quinny's mom actually wrote that one and got it printed under another name. She'd be one to think a redneck hog like me would not know that inert things don't 'grope.'"

He shook his head, savoring the injury. "She hated every single one of these she got to see. Jane liked me abstract. Abstract didn't get in anybody's way. She only needed to *wonder* what I was up to instead of actually finding out. I want your opinion. The truth, now. Am I just a baby who's picking up his little shitball to inspect it?"

She would have to take a cab.

"Her idea being that grownups don't need to be that specific. She made this argument, mind you, in front of Gloria Henrack—who was just waiting to be convinced, not having sold a single thing of mine. I'll never have another show *there*. What irked Jane from the beginning—what started the whole get-Billy movement, was this one here."

He led Judith over to the assemblage, then pointed at it like an accuser. "*Ride to Grams*. It's Jane and her sister, that's true enough." Two little girls in starched Sunday best sharing the back seat of a Forties sedan: one of the slides he'd sent. "Jane found it embarrassing, me using her past. Not Thelma, though. Thelma thought it was a real rip; she even talked about buying it. You can just picture that, right? This thing on the wall of Thelma's basement in Durham, next to the Little League trophies . . . But why not? Henrack might have kept me on the strength of a single sale. Naturally Thelma had only said it to get under Jane's skin. I like Thelma." Glazed, he was staring at one of the sisters' Mary Janes.

Suddenly extremely unsure on her legs, Judith had to run for the Morris chair. Rows of chill lay blipping right under her heart like a parade band assembling on a side street. Full-out sick now, it was too late for a cab; her only hope was quickly to lie down; off her feet, she could sometimes find one good inch—and into that fold the feeble rest of herself like one of those plastic raincoats. "Is it possible for me to lie down somewhere?"

Huft had watched her break for the chair, but hadn't moved himself from beside *Ride to Grams*, which he still kept half-looking at. "The food get to you? Sure. My room. Right this way."

Quinny's room was dark, the child asleep inside, as they passed it. At the doorway to the adjoining cubicle, Huft said, "In here. Just make yourself comfortable, get refreshed. Then we can look at all the rest of the work and we won't be tired."

His last *we* disturbed her—but happily there was a door, which Judith reached around and put a hand on, serving notice that she meant to shut it—she in and he out. If he took offense, Huft didn't show it; he stood there an extra second—looking more bewildered, in a pleased sort of way, than anything else; a hipless sentimental Rickie Lebo exactly, lost in the vagarious surprise of females; not one Quinny on his hands, but two—then said, "Okay. See you later. Rest well."

A fiberboard chest of drawers identical to the one in Quinny's room. A ten-speed bicycle. A pipe-rack clothes hanger: shirts and a suit in dry cleaner's plastic—

—And a loft bed. With four ladder steps up. *No place to lie down unless you go into the air first.*

Judith tested one rung of the ladder, and the next. She could have cried. She would never make it, didn't have the strength. Eye-level to the mattress, she noted that his sheets, royal blue, were clean and crisp. She rested her head upon them, but when her legs started to buckle she had to come back down.

Why me?

Don't start that again. Judith took off the wig and laid it down atop the chest of drawers. Over it she placed her removed blouse, but when the sheer blouse wasn't opaque enough to hide the wig, she took her skirt off too and covered both wig and blouse with that. She chose one of Huft's clean shirts from the pipe rack; before putting it on, she sprayed herself liberally with the Norell from her purse. Then she climbed the ladder at her own good-bad speed.

Another, wholly separate world up here. A platform Huft had attached to the bed frame was a kind of night table and bed-tray combined. Telephone; gooseneck lamp with a switch next to it that controlled the overhead light as well; a book on Jean Arp; an apple; a black pebble-grained sketchbook; some pencils; in a glass jar, a single yellow carnation: evidence of some forethought?

She didn't care. A hugger, a drinker, a hoper. All that counted was that she was horizontal at last. There was a top sheet in addition to a blanket. After clicking off the lights, she tied her kerchief tight and rested her head down. Trying not to remember that she was seven feet off the ground, she shut her eyes . . . Oh so necessary—and just in time, too, the deeper colors of being sick immediately flooding her, the ones that mass when fever is trembling on the brim . . .

She later awakened—because she was feeling better, but also because there was new noise in the room . . . and a careening bar of light: Huft with a flashlight. She could hear him, under the platform, undressing, sounds of jiggling change. Now climbing the ladder. Too late to leave now; she quickly closed her eyes.

He was getting in next to her. (She had a moment of terror: can the bed hold up under two?) "Judith?"

First names now. And a hand on her shoulder—which she removed by the thumb, pressing it firmly to the mattress and holding it there.

Again: "Judith?"

"I'm sleeping deeply now," she enunciated.

"Okay . . . Good night." His body seemed to adjust for only sleep, his back turning to hers. So she let go of his hand. A miracle.

She was on her stomach when her eyes opened next—on her stomach and pinned down, his flung forearm sleeping heavily across the back of her thighs. A nightsweat had soaked her; worse, her kerchief was around her neck. In the dark, in the air, with this stranger, it was about to make her hysterical. "Bill? Bill, move your arm."

But *Bill* sounded all wrong. She didn't want a Bill. All a Bill will prove is that she'd been clumsy one more time, close but no cigar. "Oh, Huft, move, you're *crushing* me." She bucked her backside.

"Hhuhh?"

"You were crushing me." She rolled free of his lifting arm, faced the wall, and hurriedly redid the kerchief.

"Sorry. Sorry." But he was awake now and starting to be interested in her panty hose and, under them, her cotton panties. (Only the pure of intention would have worn such large plain bloomers, Judith hoped he recognized—and would act accordingly.) A third thumb was already nudging against her waist. And all of a sudden her pantyhose and pants were down, downer, around her ankles.

No, not in the damp of the nightsweat she wouldn't, definitely not. She shifted slightly in his direction, to find a dry spot; but Huft took this as the invitation it perhaps half was, and he was rising up behind her and being very bold with his fingers. Should she scream? It would wake Quinny. Amazingly, Judith seemed to have wetted up—like an actual real female person. And Huft was on his way in.

She had forgotten—Anthony unwilling, Jack unable—she had forgotten how cute and delicious it is for a minute or two, and then how boring. But the boredom also pleasant in its own way—more, for her, the retreats than the thrusts: her power to possibly not let him back in for more. To tease, draw out . . .

But not this time. Huft sagged, and she could feel it hitting her walls like last puffs of air squeezed from a paper bag. His cheek lay against her spine; straightening up, he removed his weight off to the side of her. "Can I do you now?"—a hand at her shoulder, trying to turn her around.

And see or feel her splenectomy scar? Or the kerchief slipping down? "No, that's all right. I want to sleep." Damp sheet or not, Judith rolled back toward the wall.

"The women I've met in the art world, they're nothing at all like you." His words were bitten-off breezes on Judith's neck. "If only for what you did for Quinny . . ." He was quiet awhile.

Asleep? Though she should have been letting him drift off again, then have been climbing over him and down the ladder, stealing away—she asked the wall: "How come you sent me your slides? Why not to Alexandra Somogyi?"

He was not asleep. "Who is that?"

"She's the curator for contemporary art."

"Aren't you that? I thought you were."

"I'm her assistant."

A pause. "See, I didn't know that. Have I offended anyone? I didn't want to do that. I'd seen your name in a catalogue, you understand, and thought that—"

"Shh. Let's sleep now."

"Geez. Well, still, what you did for Quinton was fantastic."

"Shhh. Sleep."

What time could it be? She wished she wore a watch. For years she hadn't, not since the one she got for graduating high school was lifted in an X-ray department locker room. Any she had tried on since had looked either too small or too big, were too silly, too expensive, too cheap, hard to read.

Drooling on the pillow—shape up!

It could be ten o'clock, it could be four. She would wait it out until morning, she decided. Huft's hand came around and was staying on her breast. Like she'd thought: a hugger. What was he going to make of the wig when he saw it in the morning?

Probably nothing. That's why—she convinced herself—she's still here. Her kind of man. (By default?) The kind who, even if he notices, doesn't notice. A hugger. Immune.

8

He eventually learned not to startle when the machine first snapped on: the *craackkk,* followed by a loud and long whoosh—and here came the rays. His chin raised uncomfortably high per instructions, the back of his head sandbagged by a bolster of lead shot so it wouldn't move, Jack looked down his nose and up into the mouth of the monster, a tiny aperture under a grid and cross-hair scope. He never failed to be amazed that there was nothing whatsoever to see. This was the fearsome experience everything had led up to, supposedly the big thing; and what was it? Angel cake.

Already, in the week and a half previous, there had been the nicking open of his feet. (His *feet!* If they'd told him incisions were to be made in his eyeballs he couldn't have been more shocked or instantly drained of hope.) Two syringes, each cradled in a mechanized vise that infinitesimally advanced the plunger, then sent blue dye at a fixed rate through his thready lymph channels while an X-ray machine above pried around, looking for disease. There had been the riding of a stationary bike while wearing a clear plastic mask. He had had to drink a whole small bottle of thick, oily cascara that brutally cleaned him out in preparation for a kind of kidney test.

Last and most awful, a hematologist sunk a bore into the bone above Jack's ass in order to extract a core of marrow—the doctor, a gaunt and elegant-looking man, putting all the grunting muscle into it of someone undoing the frozen lugs of a car wheel. When he was done he showed Jack the prize: an inch-long spongy cylinder, not white as Jack had expected but red. The doctor's hairline was droppletted from the exertion; and the young nurse-assistant, who'd told Jack before it began that the procedure was all new to her too, looked greenish afterwards. Jack still was sore when he sat.

And there were also the dreams at night, to be suffered on his nervous single bed back in his old room in Bethpage. He dreamt he discovered that each lymph node could, with some jiggling, be pried out from inside his body. A first one came slowly out, and Jack inspected it: a red marble. It had a cap, a carapace, that was removable; underneath was a smooth blue surface of interlocking shapes, like American Indian aquamarine jewelry. The seriousness of design seemed to certify the node's deadliness. He would awake in water, limply positive that he would lose and lose until he used up all losing.

Finally, after all the tests were performed and evaluated, there was the consultation with Dr. Wellitz: the getting-the-news. Wellitz had come personally out to the waiting room to usher them into his office: "I've kept you waiting too, too long." But then the phone on his desk buzzed again, and he raised his arms in helpless apology, revealing a striped shirt over a thin chest under an overlarge coat. Ill himself? As a man, the three Richmonds seated in a row on his nubby couch nodded that it was quite all right.

Jack looked at the shelves of books—*Gynecological Oncology, Cancer Research, Leukemias and Lymphomas, Diagnosis and Treatment of Tumors of the Head and Neck*—and the testimonial plaques, all of them somewhere containing The Word. Euphemism had become obsolete. Wellitz, on the phone, was saying, ". . . a discrete shadow. And when I showed it to Sterling, he didn't like the looks of it either . . ." The chair beside the doctor's desk was empty. Jack left his father and sister at the couch and went to fill it. The hot seat. The office was small, the Venetian blinds drawn despite a sunny day outside. Jack stared with wretched unpreparedness at a set of skull X-rays clipped up onto a shadow box.

Wellitz put down the phone. "Again, my apologies."

Jack stalled for time. Pointing to the X-rays: "I'm going to want that one touched up. It's not my good side."

Wellitz pursed his mouth pleasantly but moved in his chair to reach and pull down the negatives. "These aren't you. Number one, this is a woman—"

"Doctor," Irwin broke in.

Jack, twisting around, glared at his father, ambushing what words were left in Irwin's mouth. He steered the doctor back: "They belong to a woman . . ."

"You'd have to trust me, you're better off with your own set." Wellitz took a large envelope off the floor, removed a handful of X-rays, and fitted them against the shadow box. "Because I have the feeling we're going to be very good touch-up artists with yours." He was standing, pointing out with a pencil the "troubled"—as he put it—nodes. He explained where the radiotherapy was to be focused and what was its likely outcome. "Don't look so down in the dumps, Mr. Richmond," he chided a fragile-eyed Irwin. "I'm giving you good news. You're going to have your son a while yet."

Sandy blanketed Irwin's more obvious weep-sniffles with a barrage of practical questions. Diet—should she feed Jack any special foods while he was getting the cobalt? Exercise? Vitamins? Wellitz was patient; they spoke for half an hour all told, by which time the mood in the sunlightless office had turned springy. His hair will perhaps fall out. Fine. He's likely to get very weak. Fine. He may vomit during the time his abdomen will be radiated. O.K.! No problem!—as long as he lives. By then Jack, the guest of honor, had worked up enough courage (bogus, since he felt now pretty sure of what the answer would be) to ask, "So you'd say the prognosis was . . ."

"Very good. We know so much more than we did even five years ago about Hodgkin's. Be glad you got it now."

"I'm tickled pink." Laughter from all around, except for soggy Irwin. *Only very good? Not excellent?*

Outside the hospital, canyon winds swept down from the tall buildings of the Medical Center. Sandy persuaded Irwin and Jack, both of them washed out and insensate, that they were also hungry; she led them to the nearest open restaurant, an expensive-looking Italian place given to banquettes. Though it was totally empty at that hour of the afternoon, the captain was at first reluctant to serve them, then changed his mind.

"Order this veal here, Daddy, with the cheese—you like that. We're celebrating."

Irwin gave a stray sniffle or two even as he ate. "I should get up and phone your aunts. They're waiting to hear."

By the dim red lights of the place, Sandy pored over the fact sheet for radiotherapy patients that Wellitz's nurse gave Jack as they were leaving the office. She studied the appointment card. She took deep breaths of relief. Over dessert, she led the praise for Dr. Wellitz: his manner, his knowledge, even his eyes.

Sitting leadenly against the velour back of the banquette, Jack weighed the most unusual sensation. That something was happening—or still was to come—which, though, felt like it had already long passed, finished and done. As if he were living in a far-focused world where all of a sudden only *intention* counted.

The machine switched off with a vociferous sigh. Jack lay as he was, unnaturally askew, until his technician, a cinnamon-haired European woman named Celeste, entered the room. She pushed away the cream-colored and smooth-sided machine; she removed the lucite tray full of lead blocks that, like a fat jigsaw puzzle, shielded certain inner organs corresponding to the outlines painted violet on Jack's skin. "Okay, darling, you can get dressed. Your appointment card is waiting on the console—don't forget it. You feel all right, darling?"

Jack felt all right. Apart from a cherry burn on his neck and chest—like a first-beach-day reddening, and which he treated with some of Sandy's skin lotion—there was no discomfort. Had anything ever been done to him this ephemerally?

Yet one Saturday morning he awoke unable to swallow. Fear bolus again? Sandy's breakfast oatmeal went down like swords. He wolfed Sucrets all day, but they did nothing, and he ended up calling the hospital. The resident on duty told him to come in the next morning.

What it turned out to be was his first, temporary, very common side effect: the tissues of the throat had swelled from the treatment. Dr. Nemeckova, one of the Czech residents, conducted the examination in the waiting room, looking down Jack's mouth with a penlight, patting Jack's cheek reassuringly with a bluff, steelmiller's hand.

Sitting next to Jack in a chair the whole time was a boy of eleven or twelve, his mother across the room reading *Redbook*. Jack hadn't known anyone came in for treatments on Sundays. Violet lines were painted not on the boy's upper jaw and back of the neck, like Jack's, but over his ears and up his completely hairless skull. The boy sat quietly, holding a paper cup in one hand and turning the pages of a comic book in his lap with the other. Every few seconds, a rivulet of saliva, clear as water, would come over his lips and trickle down into the cup.

"Stay. Tell me what you'd like."

"I would tell you if I knew. That's why I'm going to get up. To see."

"Please stay. I'll look what's there; you tell me what it is you want, I'll bring it."

"You plan on memorizing the entire contents of the refrigerator?"

"You shouldn't be standing in front of there—it's cold."

"I think I once read that somewhere about refrigerators."

"I don't want you chilled."

"And why is that?"

"Play games."

"No, you're right. Totally. I'm a sick person, and from this moment
henceforth, no games. In fact, maybe I should be lying down."

"Some joke."

"—Saving my meager energies."

"The refrigerator is cold. You don't have your full resistance. I was
going to look. That's all. And you know it. Sandy bought very nice-
looking pears. How about one?"

"I don't want anything."

"There's ice cream."

"Nothing."

"Some ice cream? Sure? Very good."

"Deaf as well? I said: *nothing.*"

While eating from a bag of pretzel logs he accidentally also swallowed
the toothbrush packed as a promotion inside the same bag—the bris-
tles tearing down his throat, the plastic handle dissolving in his stomach into carcinogenic commandos.

He snapped awake, perfectly terrified.

Dow. Scofield. Even indirect contact with the chemical fumes, the
plastics . . . Hadn't Krem once mentioned someone who got cancer at
Scofield? After all that inhaled poison, how could Wellitz and the others make believe that he wasn't going to die? They were putting on
fronts, but they really knew better. The pitch-dark room was over-
warm. Jack's wrists were wet.

Boiling in here.

Excessive sweating: heat, juice, salt—would it biochemically stir the
cancer awake? How long could it sleep, fooled? Jack swung out of bed,
put on pants, and went through the sleeping house to the bathroom,
where he lay his wrists over the side of the basin and let cold water play
over them. He'd sleep this way. He took one hand out of the water to
shut the light again, then he sat on the closed lid of the commode. The
water splashed out of the tap until Jack began to shiver. He dried his
hands and arms.

Where now? He didn't want to pace the house like a ghost, but going
outside wouldn't be wise. He went back to bed, into the outlines left by
his own gush of sweat.

"Good. Superb. Everything I could have asked for." Under Wellitz's
hand, the neck lump felt like a stunted pea, nearly all melted down. "So
now what we'll do is move down and do the abdomen and groin. We'll

start that next Wednesday." The doctor moved a step to the side, pulling the examining room curtain tighter. "Between now and then, I'd like you to take care of something. Marian in my office will make the arrangements and give you the address." He explained that all his young male patients were asked to go do this. "Think of it solely as a form of insurance."

Jack had difficulty exactly locating the place. The address Wellitz's secretary had given him was of a midtown office building, but nowhere on the directory board was Cryotechnics, Inc. listed and Jack wasn't desperate enough yet to ask the uniformed starter at the elevator banks for help. He wandered around the lobby another time, went out, came back in; and on one final reconnoiter, he spotted a door bearing a plaque with only the name—no description—in simple metal letters. The door opened directly out to the lobby the way auxiliary entrances to ground-floor stores do; and Jack passed through it, he hoped unobtrusively.

A staircase led downward. The steps and the stairwell walls were carpeted alike, with a thin unbroken tube of green neon running as a decorative accent a few inches below the bannister. The stairs ended at a spacious basement reception area: more of the same carpeting, more neon spaghetti, and dark, dark as a cocktail lounge. Across the entire width of the rear wall, however, was a partition of glass—and, beyond it, everything was white and tiled and sorely bright: desks, lab tables, file cabinets. Way in the back were four gleaming metal cannisters on their sides, resembling and about the size of the speed-record-breaking cars that run the salt flats. These, presumably, were the freezers.

Unless there were people lost in corners of the murk that he wasn't seeing, Jack was alone in the reception area, which was how he would have preferred it. When he introduced himself to the young woman sitting at the window on her side of the glass wall, she nodded knowledgeably at the mention of Wellitz's name and handed Jack a booklet, at the back of which were forms to be filled out, a task he could do at any of the small writing desks she pointed out in the corners of the room. Elaborately coded identification sticks, with five separate sets of specially matching numbers in addition to Jack's own Social Security number, were to go on everything. His name, the booklet stressed in bold type, would never appear anywhere but in the master files.

Jack was just about done with the forms and stickers when someone else came down the stairs. Raising his eyes for only a second—a man in a suit—Jack hunched tentingly down over his booklet and slowly penned over everything he'd written on the forms. He could hear the girl at the window saying to the newcomer, "You'll have to come back later. I'm busy with a client now and don't have the time."

She was standing, the next thing Jack knew, at his side by the writing desk. "Everything filled out?"—cheerily; in her fist was a capped, though empty, glass vial.

Right behind her was the suited man.

"We guarantee a ten and a four o'clock pickup. SMA-Twelves and -Twenties we can have back to you by four on a ten A.M. pickup, by ten the next morning on a four P.M. pickup—and you know that you're not going to find better service than that from any other lab in the city. We're new—why the name may not be familiar—but twenty doctors in the area are already using us and are very satisfied. We'll do BUNs, liver function, sed rate, urea—you name it. And we're equipped to handle not only blood but—"

The girl was giving him her back: "Please not now"—bending low over Jack (who, still seated at the writing desk, was able to see down her blouse to her black bra), checking that all the stickers were correctly done. Peeling one off from the back of the booklet, she stuck it onto the empty vial. "Come with me now."

"Okay, just take our rate card for the moment, then. Study it at your leisure. Then you tell me when's best: ten minutes from now? an hour? this afternoon?—I can be back anytime." The salesman was bringing up the rear of the procession, right behind Jack, who was following the young woman. They all were heading for a handleless black door at the side of the reception room.

"This afternoon," the girl called back tightly. "And now could you please? I have to take care of this client."

"Say around one? Actually, could I just have that rate card I gave you back a second? The serum lipids rate is in error on there, and I should have changed it . . ."

"This afternoon—would you *mind?*"

"It'll take just a second. I don't want to be giving you wrong prices."

"This locks from the inside," the girl was informing Jack in front of the door. She handed him the empty but now personally identified vial. "It's important that you collect the very first ejaculate. So be careful."

"Better idea—I'm giving you here a corrected rate schedule. There. Throw the one I gave you away. Please keep the pen—our number's right on it. Can I give you the gift of one of our pens, too, sir?"

At the other side of the door was only a small square room: Jack had at least expected a corridor of some kind for privacy leading further away from the reception area. Turning the inside lock, he put his ear to the door but heard nothing. Beige carpeted walls, a beanbag chair, a plastic-lined waste can; there was also a parsons table—on it a box of Kleenex, an ashtray, a *Penthouse,* one of the previous day's *New York Times.* The ashtray, the *Penthouse:* both were impulses that he'd left back in Delphi—but after looking over the beanbag chair for sanitariness, he opened his pants and sat down.

The magazine girls in their glossy vitality were uninspiring. There was a black-and-white still from a porno movie that showed a nurse getting it from behind, her white uniform thrown up over her back—and Jack grimly put down the magazine.

The *Times?* He didn't touch it.

Imagine Donna? (The ride to Syracuse; the biopsy; the ride back from Syracuse; her ersatz optimism. He had asked her firmly not to phone him in Bethpage, but he knew that she called Sandy and vice versa.)

The girl at the reception window—who knew what he was doing at this very minute?

Jack reopened the *Penthouse*—the longer he stayed in here the worse it would look, he needed to be determined. One cartoon was very vaguely of assistance, and he labored and labored, feeling as though he was unfairly annoying an earned deadness in him. Finally he got it done, and all into the vial. After wiping himself with a Kleenex—which he dropped into the thankfully empty waste basket—he capped the jar, rearranged his clothes, made triple sure the vial was fitting totally within his sheltering palm and not a bit of it could be seen, and opened the door.

The young woman at the window received it impassively; she shook it up and down a few times, put it on the desk in front of her. She brought out an appointment book to put Jack down for a time the next day to submit his backup sample. Jack was peering around. Unless he was hiding in some recess too dark to see, the salesman appeared to be gone. But in case he wasn't, Jack, when he left, climbed the carpeted stairs two steps at a time.

The knack reawakened, he masturbated every day, once and sometimes twice. For the first time in his life it was giving him something more than a few seconds' sharp thin pleasure: it became his only real exercise, it left him satisfiedly winded afterwards. The rest of the day

he built models from kits. He put together the USS *Wisconsin,* the
Leyte Gulf. With one of Sandy's emery boards he filed the minute parts
free of their excess edges. He affixed the decals. He even did what he
had never bothered to do as a kid: paint on the camouflage.

The two resurrected activities, one excessively furious and the other
so very slow, gave to his day a meaninglessness that seemed just about
right. And most regularly of all, he got on the train every other day and
went to the hospital in Manhattan. It brought back all those years he
commuted to college. Now the trip seemed like a jaundiced commen-
tary on those unhappy and pressured years—and though someone else
might see it in reverse, Jack felt that what was happening to him now
severely punished the past for its unfairness.

Sandy, who worked not far from Irwin and drove home with him at
night, would put supper on the table and, as soon as she could after the
dishes were washed, would go off somewhere in her car. Up late one
night over a model—a troop carrier, the *Leonard Wood*—Jack sat with
her at the kitchen table after she came home, around one-thirty. There
was alcohol on her breath. Yet she wasn't secretive: most nights, usually alone, she said, she went to a bar in Port Jefferson where the jukebox
was stocked with good country-rock, her favorite music. "Just to be
out. And don't think it has anything to do with you—you were thinking that, right? It doesn't. When I took the leave I promised myself I
wouldn't always sit here, I'd go out even when I didn't particularly want
to. It's a kind of discipline, and I need that."

It was a lie, of course. Because she always made a point of being well
out of there before seven P.M. and the television news. Jack and Irwin
had resumed their old battles as though trucked back in time, not missing a beat. "I know you don't like him. But at least admit that what he's
saying here is true. Plain common sense."

"I wouldn't want to horn in on your pleasure. I leave all the admitting
to you."

"He's simply looking—and thinking—ahead."

"Why not? He's got to know when to get his white flag out of the
laundry."

"Anyone who wants to avoid a war is immediately a coward to you?
This man's been in the Senate for eighteen years. In all that time, you're
telling me that he hasn't built up an idea of what's really going on?"

"A spotless record."

"You're too cynical."

"—"

"Worse, you're proud of it. It's not attractive. It isn't mature."

"And you, with the instincts of a butler—that, I assume, is better."

When invited to take part in the opening session of a discussion group made up of clinic patients at the hospital, Jack first declined; then, thinking of Sandy, he changed his mind and decided to go. After getting his cobalt that day late in the afternoon, he ate dinner in the coffee shop in the lobby and from there went at six to the conference room in the clinic. The hospital had begun to feel more and more like home base to him, and—with the lump dissolving—the doctors like business contacts: less self-contained, more easygoing and buddy-up now that the contract between them was mutually agreeable. The hospital, Jack realized, was what Scofield always should have been.

Faces he recognized from the clinic waiting room were seated around the long conference table. The group's organizer, a psychiatrist named Herzberg, started in by flattering them: they'd been chosen for the group because each was an aware and articulate person. (Jack had come to see that certain doctors put great store in this. Finding a patient who knew how to speak, they promptly spilled all sorts of facts and diagnoses and peculiarities, the thrills of pathology the poor patient wanted to know none of.)

Except for himself and a woman wearing a robe, everyone then wanted the floor. Herzberg, after each wave of testimony, looked up to ask: "Did that—or does that—frighten you?" Jack was so instantly turned off that some of his sighs became audible.

"Mr. Richmond? Something to say?"

"Nope."

"Well, please don't feel constrained."

A Puerto Rican guy said he'd been vomiting so much after his chemotherapy that he was afraid he was going to get a throat tumor too from the irritation. Someone else, a woman, complained about the phone calls she was constantly having to make in order to get her disability payments straightened out. Jack, who had no problems (he didn't feel sick; his disability checks came through promptly if unnecessarily, since his living expenses were almost nil living in Bethpage and since Scofield's medical insurance saw to nearly ninety-five percent of the bills; Vic Pellegrino was keeping an eye on the apartment in Delphi until he got back), had nothing much to say even if he'd wanted to.

Why the woman in the robe—who clearly did have problems—was also mute he couldn't say. She certainly looked less than well: a color-swirled kerchief wrapped in a bohemian fashion around her head and low to her brows was the only touch of decoration to a very drawn face. But there was a lenient, soft look in her eyes that suggested she'd been through worse than this meeting; and after Herzberg called a halt to the evening, and the others lingered in the conference room, Jack invited her to have coffee with him in the shop in the lobby.

Her name was Judith, and she had had her spleen cut out, she said. This was the second hospital she had been treated at—the first team of doctors hadn't known what they were doing. Lonely and bored, she volunteered her room number, wanted him to write it down so he wouldn't forget it.

She was smart, a chessplayer—but she seemed to keep the intelligence lockered while in the hospital, where it did her no particular good. Jack liked this: when people had enough respect for their sturdiest qualities to hold them at bay when the situation warranted. He introduced her to the racing charts in the paper, something to keep her a little busier. He didn't mind the visits: as long as she was the inpatient, and not him, they felt like offerings.

The treatments to his abdomen began and, at worst, his belly would get a little hollow-feeling about five hours after. But one afternoon in Penn Station, waiting for his train home, Jack suddenly began to wilt from the inside out. And nothing helped: he nailed his eyes desperately to a sign advertising monthly commutation tickets by mail—"SAVE THE HASSLE!"—but then the station lights overhead started moistly blinking. The first cheesy wave splatted the side of a waste container as people around him quickly moved. The next hit his shoes. A station cop was prodding his shoulder with a nightstick. Gulping for air, Jack cried, "I'm getting radiation treatments for cancer!"—decrepit curse on the cop for the poke. When Jack called home from a phone booth, his own sour smell wreathed him in the close quarters. Sandy had just gotten in and she drove immediately into the city to fetch him.

After that, Irwin arranged with Men's Suits to be able to drive Jack back and forth to the hospital each day. He would wait in the main lobby while Jack ran up after his treatment to stop in briefly with Judith. Who didn't look so bad anymore to Jack, who himself had lost weight and whose legs were growing weaker.

But still she held a valuable lead in terms of authority. Miss a visit, and he was afraid to find her the next time much sicker, that she'd pulled markedly away, a preview maybe of things to come for himself. This way, seeing her daily, he kept close tabs, he got around surprise, he tried to note what to watch out for and, if at all possible, avoid.

He made the USS *Constitution*, his first sailing ship.

They were radiating around his groin now, the inguinal nodes, but it was the last and very least of it. The pea in Jack's neck was gone totally. On Tuesdays—clinic days—he would see Judith; usually she came accompanied by an older man, short and dark and very well dressed, who stood outside the clinic in the tiled corridor and read the *Times* over and over. She looked better and more feminine in the sophisticated skirts, espadrilles, and bright tee shirts she wore now than she had in the heavy robe of her inpatient days. On the day of his last cobalt treatment she thoughtfully phoned to congratulate him: It was *over.*

It was. And that was why Jack had been hoping when the phone rang that it was going to be Vic Pellegrino calling instead. Jack had had pleasant enough chats with Tracy, the secretary at the realty office, but Vic never once acknowledged the messages he left.

Jack did the USS *Forrestal*, a boring boat. Now that he went to the hospital only once a week, for a checkup, he was more aware of time, its formless abundance. At the clinic, they would only take blood and examine him. An occasional X-ray. Sitting on the examining table, hearing Wellitz's voice right outside the cubicle, Jack smiled to himself and had valedictory thoughts. Everyone had been very good to him here; off their cushion of care he now could bounce. If, as he expected, they told him he'd have to check back here only once a month from now on, he could be on his way back to Delphi by the end of the week.

Dr. Wellitz was entering the cubicle. Three other doctors, residents, were with him. He looked at Jack from under his brows and cleared his throat.

"We've got a small hitch. A spot in the mediastinum—that's your midchest—shows up on the X-ray." He was speaking rapidly and pulling at the skin of his neck. "Either it's a node the betatron didn't get, or it's a small relapse. Whichever, it's an annoyance. We really ought to get it out of there."

"Like you cleaned your house and left one room dirty," said Ritter, the chief resident, a hand on Jack's shoulder.

"So we're thinking in terms of a course of chemotherapy for you,"

Wellitz continued, "as the best approach now. You deserve a little vacation, though, first. Three weeks. That'll build your blood counts back up, too. Then we'll start the drugs. They'll wipe up everything spic-and-span, at which point we'll kiss you bon voyage and you go back wherever it is upstate with the cows and the ridiculous weather."

Climbing up the outside of his cheeks, surrounding Jack's head like a heavy lining of felt, came an oily knowledge.

He wasn't going to Delphi. He was going to die instead, and very soon.

"Phone for you," Sandy told him.

"Who?"

"Take it and you'll see."

"I'm not home."

"Jackie."

"Not home. You talk to her. You always do."

"Jack, you have to."

"I don't have to do anything."

When she returned—Jack was motionless in front of "Columbo"—she sat and, after a while, said, "I like it long."

Jack quickly took his fingers away from his hair, where they'd been twirling thoughtlessly in the back overgrowth; he hadn't had a haircut since Delphi.

"But I realize your horror at looking anything like fashionable—so get up. I'm going to cut it for you right now!" Sandy catapulted herself out of the barcalounger and was waving Jack up. "Come wiz me to ze baathroom."

He stayed as he was.

"I'm waiting."

Jack's look was reptilian. "Sit down. It will all fall out soon enough. What—as I'm sure the designer of the Washington Monument also wondered—would be the point." They perfectly suited him now, these crabby, poor jokes: they made everybody else feel speechlessly terrible.

"Not true! What little fell out from the radiotherapy came right back, didn't it? They say that some people don't lose any with the drugs." Then she began to laugh. "What you just said."

"It wasn't funny," Jack said sepulchrally.

Cowed, Sandy stared a minute at Columbo getting out of a car. Then she turned back to him, insisting, "It *was* funny. *You're* funny."

"No, I'm contemptuous and I'm cynical, remember? But of course I understand—that was back then. Now I'm funny."

Sandy perched at the edge of the recliner and wouldn't look at him but only at the TV.

Jack said, "You can leave the room if you want. I won't be insulted."

"I'm watching!"

"I see. I'll be quiet and let you watch."

"Shut—Shhh!" Her head snapped toward him with great force.

"I'll leave you alone with your program." Jack rose from the couch shuffling; the slight lameness that had been a side effect of the radiation—and had passed—was something he had reinstituted in the last week.

Sandy flew up too, and grabbed his wrist. She was trembling. "Put whatever you like on. I thought *you* were watching the dumb thing." She was damming tears. "You better not leave."

Jack strained against her hand, and the tears came. "The bathroom?" he said. "Make sissy? Do I have permission?"

She threw down his wrist, dropped herself to the couch, and hectically regarded a seam of the den wall.

The resident pulled on rubber gloves before preparing the syringes. "I don't want to get this stuff on my hands."

"Good thinking," said Jack.

Bleakly furious: this charade. A rubber band around his forehead at the hairline, a bottle of saline dripping into him—why go through these fancy motions? During his "vacation," he had perfected a style of mourning for himself, and this now was being interrupted. He resented it—all the more so because it was futile.

Within half a second after the plunger started down, the medicine filled Jack's chest with a walloping cold: his stomach gave a high, shocked flutter.

But all right, he told himself, I'm standing it.

The second syringe was introduced. Sour. More sour. Oh my God —he could taste and smell it inside: something green and mucous and sweet, what death must taste like. The saline solution was continuing to drip, supposedly to disperse the drugs, but it did nothing. Oh my God. Fifteen minutes later, when the needle and tubing and rubber band to keep his hair in were removed, Jack sat up unsteadily on the table, everything inside him morbidly ablaze.

Irwin drove as he probably never had before, a speed demon, doing his best as well to avoid potholes and bumps. In the driveway at home, Jack let go of the plastic garbage bag he'd been holding the entire ride: not a drop in it. "We made it. Maybe I'm not going to be sick. Do I smell, though? Is it me? I have this bad smell in my nose."

But the light inside the house was jelly; each new shirt Jack put on was immediately soaked through; a minute after he lay down on the couch in the den a freshet of saliva began to course through his fouled mouth and wouldn't cease. He raced for the bathroom.

Six hours straight at anything eventually provides a few refinements in technique. Resting his chin on the edge of the toilet bowl, Jack found, made it easier on his neck. Putting a folded towel under his knees protected them from the hard tile. He learned not to stop until he was absolutely ready—swallowing the last acrid juice was no treat. Sandy and Irwin took turns standing a guard of mercy right outside the closed door and Jack croaked encouragement out to them, his voice burnt down to the diameter of a pipe cleaner.

Once, thinking it was over, he left the bathroom and went to lie down on his bed. But after a quarter hour of rinsing sleep, he was back sweatily in the bathroom again. Around three in the morning, Sandy got him to agree to a few sips of soup.

"Go to sleep," he rasped. "You've got to be up for work in three hours."

"You know me—a bon vivant." She took away the soup after he had only a few spoons of it.

Ritter, small and thickset, smiled with hedged innocence.

"I'm not joking. For some people it seems to do the trick: a joint or two four or five hours before the drugs are introduced. It appears to still the vomiting center in the brain. Reports have been popping up a lot lately in the literature."

Jack was offended. This wouldn't be prescribed to the old woman—breasts like flippers, her chest all marked up in violet—whom Jack had accidentally seen through the partially open curtain of the opposite cubicle. The button he'd considered wearing in Delphi—*I am not a student, understand?*—would still have had its uses. "How about an alternative. Something legal."

"Legal. There isn't anything, not that you haven't already tried when the cobalt was bothering your belly. Try this. Let me know how it works. And why do I get the feeling that I'm not exactly going to have to twist your arm?"

A novelty, a cute idea, something that would brighten up Ritter's no doubt depressing daily routine—but how was he, Jack, supposed to go about this? He drove home, plagued. Ask Sandy to get him some and then have to suffer her irony? Sit on his single, boy's bed in Bethpage and suck away on a shriveled cigarette, which Irwin would bring to him on a platter along with the nightly dish of ice cream?

He reported back to Judith immediately over the phone, even chancing—not caring—that the boyfriend might answer. She was the one who usually did the calling, but her games were her business; Jack went along with her fey, career girl, artsy, New York side. He wasn't looking for a lover. She was his scout, more valuable.

"Some people have all the luck," were her first words after he'd told her.

"Yes, sure, this is a big joke to everyone—but the one who has to figure a way of getting it in the first place still is me. And then has to find a place to take it."

She called back half an hour later. When Irwin came home from work and while Sandy was out of ear's reach in the shower, Jack told him. "I won't be sleeping home tomorrow night. I'll be staying at a friend's. At the hospital they told me to try marijuana before getting the drugs. They said it would cut down on the throwing up later. So that's what I'll be doing. I wanted you to know."

Irwin regarded him cheerlessly, opening the refrigerator, then shutting it without having taken anything out.

"Well?"

"Don't go crazy, Jack. It's not easy for someone like you to be sick, your type of personality, and I realize one of the pills you take can make you depressed, but just don't go overboard."

"I really need this." Jack grabbed the wall phone. "Come on. Here. Call Dr. Ritter, ask him to repeat what he told me."

His father removed his glasses and kneaded his lids. "In case we have to get hold of you, there'll be a number there, I assume."

"Not *we*. This you have to promise, and I mean it: Sandy's not to know. Tell her I'm staying over at a friend's, but that's all." Jack hung up the phone. "And I don't know the number."

"I'm a big boy. You can give it."

"Honestly, I don't know it. The situation is complicated. I'll try to
call you once I'm there."

Jack sat with legs crossed, pressing still the wormy, beating vein in his
stomach that lately got to banging whenever he was tense. He was surprised—a little alarmed, too—at how much of it she had been able to ob-
tain on such short notice. Half a sandwich bag full.

Judith was filling a small pipe. In the bowl fit a tiny mesh strainer,
and before filling this she worked the loose marijuana with her fingers,
rubbing it finer, separating out seeds: the sort of excessive, stagy me-
ticulousness Jack always inherently knew he would hate about it.

She had cooked curry for dinner. "Not well, but in detail. If you're
allergic to pretension, think of it as chicken stew." Jack helped her
bring things out to the opened gateleg table in the living room and had
noticed inside her refrigerator little more than the fixings for the meal
they were about to eat. Already he'd had a notion—at the sight of the
hardened, crusted soap bar in the bathroom while washing up—that
she was almost never here. It lent a feeling of her having opened a club-
house expressly for their temporary use together.

The apartment, in a newer building on East 30th Street, was basically
two rooms squashed side to side, and a medium-sized bathroom. In the
large kitchen, oddly, was a rolltop desk, next to the refrigerator. On the
kitchen and living room/bedroom walls were large quantities of jarring
and witless modern art prints, all well framed and making the rooms
seem smaller than they actually were. Jack, accustomed to the abun-
dant layouts of apartments on the Slope, felt comfortable here right
away, patronizingly.

All through the meal Jack wanted to ask her about peeing, which he
did a lot of now, since taking the medications. Had she also? But he
waited. He helped clear the plates off when they were done eating. Judith emptied the untouched portions of side condiments directly into
the garbage pail. Jack offered, but she wouldn't let him wash the dishes.
She wore rubber gloves and the scalding water sent up a face-pinking
steam—but to Jack's mind she was a bad dishwasher, using scouring
pads on the ceramic plates, unthinkingly. He had sat meanwhile on a
high wooden stool by the kitchen desk and was surveilling the walls.
He pointed to one glass-framed poster: a sunlit porch; two young girls

sitting at a blue-covered table, shelling peas—but everything painted very flat, like cardboard cutouts. "That's fairly nice."

"Think so?" She barely gave it a glance. Jack saw that she even was doing the pots: another indication that, tomorrow morning, she'd be gone from here as well.

"But you can't go by me, I'm a baboon when it comes to art. I guess I never learned how to look at it."

Judith turned, the waist of her dress stuck to her skin by the damp enamel slowly unsticking. "Why are you being so polite? We've met. I know you think all of this is crud."

He had to smile demurely. "I do."

"Fine." She turned with satisfaction back to the dishes.

"Since it's on your walls, though, there must be something to it that I'm missing."

"Only taste."

"That you have and I don't."

"True, I'm so lucky." She added, "And what if I'm wrong?"

Jack, rocking the stool from side to side, was enjoying this. "You're the professional. You're supposed to know if this is good or not."

She faced him again. "Oh no. Not fair. I get the same opportunity to be wrong and stupid you so generously give everyone else."

She was done now with all the filling and packing and finally was lighting a match. With closed eyes she drew at the silly miniature pipe, letting Jack closely observe the technique.

Draw. Gulp. Hold. Release.

When she handed him the pipe his stomach flipped up briefly. The blackened moss inside the bowl was throbbing red, crackling, as he inhaled; and he hadn't expected the smoke to be so hot. He whipped the pipe back to Judith, but she took it in no great hurry. Back and forth it went until done. Judith stood up. "I get really thirsty."

It was a fraud. There were no effects. When Jack, though, attempted to ask for water also, he found a lead mask clapped over his face from forehead to chin. There seemed to be some sort of cloud, too, newly balanced on his head, a pleasant heavy business to which he discovered he could refer all the rest of him.

After Judith returned with a pitcher of ice water and two glasses, they shared another pipeful. Jack was beginning to understand the sense behind the whole supplementary caboodle—the music, the candles, the

strobe lights in his tenants' apartments: anything at all that helped
keep the droopy banner waving was good. Judith put the radio on, an
opera. Jack hated opera, but this one he loved, great stuff.

Then, with a thump, it got late. She had gone off to the bathroom.
Jack already had removed his shoes, so now all he needed to do was
lie down on the Scandinavian sofa—he saw this as an elegant, tricky
maneuver—and allow the slab of foam to hold him away from the floor
at every inch.

Remarkable inventions, sofas.

Judith came out wearing a short terry robe. The sight of bare knees and
lower thighs surprised him, and he was as embarrassed as if he'd peered
up her nostrils. Flinging cushions away, she pulled the other couch in
the room into a bed. Jack said, "Wait, I'll help," then settled down to a
drawn-out spell of infantile hilarity over not being able to move.

Within moments the lights in the apartment were off totally. Jack
was hearing the crapey sounds of either dressing or undressing. Then
silence. He could feel himself starting to float out a little widely, divorced from his person and bobbing into some sheer, courseless space
that was only going to get more and more hands-off. To anchor himself,
he tried his voice.

"Good night?" (Worked—but eccentrically; he hadn't meant for it to
be a question.)

"I don't know," Judith answered. "Is that where you're camped?
Final decision?" She sounded rusty-throated too.

Jack levered himself up off the foam and onto an elbow. "Do you
think it's better over there? I wasn't knowing"—words pilled in his
mouth—"if I should come over. I could, I guess. But fine's good here
too."

"Weren't you wondering why you hadn't got a blanket?" she said as
Jack got heavily into the bed beside her.

"Yes, right," he agreed. His feet were wheeling around—he'd been
feeling less wayward on the firmer foam—but then it passed and the
darkness breathed for a while. Jack put his hand (all his motions: he
could see them in his mind's eye like the thrown images from an
opaque projector in a darkened classroom) down in search of Judith's—and she instantly turned onto her side and totally bare skin was
fitted against him. But the cloud over his head had started melting
down over his face just about then.

When he came back awake at some later time it was still dark—

raining out now, too. The sounds of the wetness energized him and he sat up to get his clothes off. All the previous facial weight, lead mask and cloud, seemed to have slipped to his middle, making his penis especially feel like a single large udder needing to be milked: a heavy, moody, itchy, dark demander.

Judith was asleep, but under his unsubtle hands this changed. He got on top of her as if hiding them both from scrutiny. He was jammed in tightly (she was ridged and a little dry; thinking he might have mistakenly entered her anus froze, then additionally excited, him) and as he began to inject and leave, inject and leave, he was feeling like someone whose tongue was nailed to his shoe, at once leading and tumbling after himself.

She didn't want to let him go immediately after; her thighs and ankles trapped him. "I can sleep like this, if you can," her breath smelling of dried flowers.

He couldn't. Nor could he fall asleep again, even on his back. The bedside clock read four. The more awake he became, the more he returned to himself, to what he was doing here, to how he was going to be dead soon. At four-thirty he woke Judith not very gently; it was time for more of the medicinal marijuana. She went to take a quick shower and Jack, his depression in full bloom by now, watched the window shade getting faintly lighter. By the time she came back out to prepare the pipe, he'd lost all faith in this, in her, in the sex (an accident and an error). But he smoked anyway.

"Your eyes are terribly red," Irwin informed his son three hours later, in the clinic.

After the drugs were administered and the race back to Bethpage was completed, Jack did throw up again, at length—but a good three hours less, finally, than the last time. And it wasn't quite so violent.

Sold.

Each time now that he saw Ritter, Jack smirked. The resident smirked back. They both rolled their eyes. All the doctors knew. Jack was the mischievous darling of the clinic . . .

—And, at the desk in Judith's kitchen, when, after studiously sprinkling and folding and rolling and wetting and twisting, he would ask, "Are these or aren't these the neatest little bombers you ever saw?"—and she would go limp with laughter . . .

But what did he care if he played the fool? He was in possession of the

first brand-new knowledge he'd had in a long time. And the chemotherapy appeared to be working: the spot in his chest stopped turning
up on the X-rays. The conclusion, then, wasn't difficult to arrive at. The
drugs—perhaps with the marijuana as the final component—would
only be as effective as he chose them to be: metabolized by will.

He never smoked with anyone but Judith, and always at her apartment, arriving there late in the morning on the day before a treatment.
After smoking, if the day were nice, they'd take a walk, both wearing
hats against the sun, both whacked out, strolling at decorous paces past
fruit stores and playgrounds and in the gardens of the United Nations.

Her apartment, though, continued to disturb Jack. It seemed makeshift, a kind of rigid pup tent. Nothing ever needed to be fixed there,
because nothing was ever used long or hard enough to break; when he
discovered the Hot knob in the shower leaking—a shot washer—he
was pleased, and made a special trip in from Bethpage with tools to fix
it. Working nude, he changed washers on both faucets, then ran the
shower on himself. After he dried himself with a bright orange bath
towel, he put all his clothes back on, socks included. Coming out half-
dressed might give Judith the wrong idea.

"You had a call. Your sister."

Judith was sitting on the stool by the kitchen desk, where the phone
was; she held a slip of paper.

"I'm reporting to you exactly what she asked me to. That you missed
supper. That your aunt was there—and you knew she would be. That
she had roasted a turkey. And that you have some mail at home you
probably want to take care of. Something from Scofield . . ." She
paused; she looked sightlessly at the paper; she pushed the address
book on the desk over an inch. Rapidly she said, "Also a bill from the
sperm bank.

"She was upset, Jack—allow for it. If you left now, could you make it
back in time to eat with them? That might salvage something."

"Move"—he wanted the stool.

"Jack."

"Please let me sit there." He dialed, and Irwin answered immediately.

"I got your daughter's message and I'd like to speak to her."

"Jackie—"

"Put Sandy on."

"Fay is here."

"First I want to speak to your daughter."

Sandy dallied getting on the extension. Finally: "Daddy, you hang up."

Not knowing what to do with herself, Judith was on her way to the bathroom. "This isn't private," Jack called to her roughly. "You can listen." Then, into the receiver: "What kind of shit—"

"Daddy, please get off!"

"Fay sends her love, Jack," Irwin said morosely.

"You were saying," said Sandy.

"The sight of you, puffed up and pleased with your bitchy self, must be something to see."

"Oh, that's perfect. I'm the one who thinks she's really something. That's wonderful. I'm the selfish one—me. The one who doesn't give a damn about anyone else in the world."

Jack was calm. "I forgot about dinner. That's true. And after you get off, you'll put Fay on and I'll apologize to her. But that's secondary. The main thing is that I don't need this bitchiness from you now."

"Who cares what you do or don't need? You're always saying that lately. What if we don't need you?"

"Fair enough."

"We're sitting around here like three dolts, this stupid giant turkey . . . !"

"You want to manipulate people? Manipulate ones your own flaky style. There are other things on my mind. I'm not your phone-freak—or Bert."

She hung up on him then—though for appearance's sake, Jack went on talking a few seconds more into the dead phone: "We'll straighten this out later."

Returning to Bethpage the next morning, Jack found no one home; they'd both gone off to work. When the car pulled into the driveway at night, only Irwin stepped out. Sandy, he told Jack, had called him at the store around noon, saying she planned to leave directly after work for Boston, to spend a few days there with friends.

"Yes, that seems to be her time of day to spring news." Jack sat clicking his thumbnails at the kitchen table. Irwin, changed out of his suit into slacks, slippers, and an undershirt, was starting to fix supper, cutting slices from the notorious bird of the day before, cooking a package of frozen broccoli spears. "She went to see that jewel of hers, Peter, didn't she?"

"He isn't so bad." Irwin didn't turn around. "I met him."

What glumly bothered Jack was not Sandy's attempt (successful) to make him feel guilty. Guilt itself surprised him—cancer should have blown that away already, shouldn't it have? "So you know he's a sicko, then. That he places calls overseas for the thrill of not paying for them—about the same thing as pissing in phone booths, only technological. So you already know that. That they're going to lock him up one of these days. And who'll be implicated? Your precious daughter."

Irwin still hadn't turned away from the countertop. "The boy moved to California three months ago. She went up to Boston to get away, for a rest."

"And her job? They allow leaves for R. & R.?"

"If they fire her, that's okay with her—and with me. Her leave from school is over, she's ready to go back. I called the dean a week ago and explained the situation. He was very cooperative; the little I spoke to him, I liked him."

Jack shook his head. "No one would ever believe this. I'm sick. She's deeply depressed. You, God only knows what you are . . ."

Irwin turned; the tomato he'd been about to slice was clutched tightly in his fist, and Jack expected to see it burst. "You cope the way you have to, I'll cope the way *I* have to. And since that's got nothing to do with you, why not shut up." His face had at some point become as orange as the tomato.

"And all the problems will go away." Jack had lost; he knew it even before he looked into his father's fiery and sickened eyes; his own grip had slid, and Irwin had gotten purchase instead. "How nice."

"You blame us. You blame the girl upstate—Sandy told me about her—who only cares for you. You blame everyone for what's happened. But it's all twisted in you now. Your sister and I are doing fine, the best we can, we try. You can't come down here and destroy what we've managed to make over. I won't let you."

"I'll be out of your way—and everyone else's—soon enough."

Leaping from Irwin's mouth came womanly shrieks:

"I said shut up! Not another word! Shut up! Shut up! This is my house and I say be quiet! Shut your damn mouth!"

Jack's skepticism threatened constantly to shake him apart like the shot transmission of an accelerating car—yet every second, then third, then fourth week—when he went to the clinic for checkups, verdicts—he was found clean. Spotless X-rays, perfect bloods. The six months of chemotherapy had left him thin but whole.

He waited, holding his breath for relapse—and when that didn't come, all the interest flew out of his days. The first big waves of oncoming death had crippled his capacity for thinking ahead; now he was stuck in an unbearably baggy present. Sandy had returned to school and Judith to work at the museum, quarter-time. More and more often, their weekly smoke-in was subject to cancellation—always by him, too embarrassed at always failing in the embraces Judith seemed to expect as a part of his visits.

He listened to radio talk shows—dull occupation. A seed catalogue, addressed to Sandy, came in the mail; he studied it. He thought about a garden: vegetables he wouldn't be around to see come up? Or, maybe worse, would. Playing his most satisfying role lately—the ironist—to the hilt, Jack went to the garage, found an old hoe, and took it back to the yard.

He began experimentally to chunk up some earth. He chopped harder, making a mess. Since the end of treatments and the start of his "second life," he had had many manic mornings like this, when he wondered if nervous breakdowns were hereditary.

The phone was ringing inside the house.

Black and tan earth came crumbling off the sides of his fingers as he lifted the kitchen receiver. "Hello?"

"Hello, Nat."

Before Jack could say anything, the woman at the other end must have caught a sense of not-quite-rightness. "Wrong number, I guess."

"Yes," Jack said.

"The house was what I wanted," the woman explained obscurely. "But it looks like I dialed the store instead. I'm not awake this morning, still asleep. Made a mistake."

What house? What store? Jack said, "Yes, a mistake."

"Well, sorry to have disturbed you, Nat," the woman said—and then hung up.

Jack replaced the receiver. He wasn't Nat. He walked back out to the shameful podge of earth he'd made. Grimy clouds were flying. She *thought* he was Nat. As Nat, he'd been short and discourteous to her, offering not a single pleasantry, quick to get off. Thanks to him, the woman would never feel exactly the same about Nat again. And this was all his, Jack's, fault, the non-Nat but as-good-as-Nat.

The accidental violence, cause and effect putting on such a quick but frightful show—with Jack himself as its star—appalled him. He, who according to all recent evidence took up so little and evershrinking room in the world—obviously he took up more than he thought.

He got down on his knees and began to refit the clods. If he didn't watch out he would strangle on his own loose ends. He would have to live more carefully. That meant only one place: Delphi. There, he could choose his spots, press only them; undo the botches and start clean. When the plot of yard looked less ravaged, Jack went into the house and got Tim Sleighlin's office number from Information.

Sleighlin's secretary resisted but finally gave in to Jack's demand, the maybe slightly crazy urgency in his voice. Tim got on, saying he couldn't talk long, he had a patient in the chair, how was Jack feeling? Warmed to be remembered at all, Jack said, Fine, and told the dentist he would be back in town within a week or so. "I'd like you to go check something out for me, though, first, if it isn't too much to ask."

9

"Nice, Fred."

"Yes? Probably," the art dealer said, studying himself in the triple mirror. "But what problems we've had with it, no, Maurice?"

The fitter, on his knees eye-level to a vent flap and himself in a suit fully equal to the one he was working on, the fitter discreetly allowed, "Mr. Mallelieu has altered his waistline." The ramrod posture as he pinned and chalked, and the fleck of a smile in his eyes, added silently: *the pig.*

"It's Eee-taly. I don't even try there—the pastas. Rome I'm pretty good. I eat with friends at their homes. In Bologna, in the restaurants, I am bad. This is a third fitting. Poor Maurice. He wants me to look so good in this."

Anthony, from where he stood a few feet back, squinted at the fabric. "Is it olive or grey? I can't tell."

"For Mr. Mallelieu here, olive is the better choice. In a pin stripe by all means." The fitter pointed his chin in the direction of the open manila folder in which were stapled swatches of earlier Mallelieu suits. "He has a blue or two that he's fond of, but I prefer the olive in a suit like this." Handsomely black-haired, trim and neat, with a touch of Long Island creeping under what was probably the genuinely Continental accent, Maurice was that not completely bad thing: the gentleman greaser. Wife and kids in a split-level and the lawn on Saturday morning, but during the week an arbiter, Pope Urbane. Real condescension, Anthony had thought more than once, was a talent and perhaps even a gift.

Mallelieu was smiling inattentively at his own reflection, a cuticle-free hand coming up to smooth back his longish, limestone hair. As long as Anthony could remember, Mallelieu's coif had never varied: the same ridgy mudguard, not quite professorial, and which swayed from side to side a little when he talked. In a profession of the short and frequently bald, his aristocratic height and mane were standouts. "All this labor to cover up a . . . what is the word? Years ago it was *dirigible*"—he gave it the French glaze.

"Blimp," provided Anthony. Not in a position to take part, Maurice only bit down on his grin, opening a few last basting stitches with a razor blade. He straightened up and stood back—"I think we are done"—then dipped forward one last time to smooth a lie.

"Excellent. I want so much to get out of this," said Mallelieu, retreating to the dressing rooms. Maurice, resting a hand on the bolts of suiting cloth racked horizontally, asked if there was anything he could help Anthony with; told no, he moved off to wait near the narrow walnut door Mallelieu was changing behind.

When he would next be able to buy himself clothes and shoes Anthony couldn't say. The small hole of hope punched into the future by Milan had also suctioned up any real thought of spending the kind of monies required in a place like this. At the bank yesterday he'd asked for change wrappers, a first for him. But besides thrift, his plan to take J. away also seemed to have seeded a moralism. Going to Lynton's in the morning, drugging himself with that old, comfortable company which made the rest of the day seem like a vulgar afterthought—he'd cut that out. He no longer looked at the racing charts. The pale blue hundred-dollar alpaca cardigan that had held him briefly on the way in here, for a closer look and a caress: frippery. The next time he'd buy clothes and shoes it would be with liras.

On the phone Mallelieu said that he'd rather Anthony didn't come up to the gallery; a show was being mounted, too noisy, too busy. Dunhill's, where he was due for a fitting at two, would be better, if that were all right. It was all right—despite the temptations. Anthony couldn't afford for it not to be. To save cab fare he had walked uptown, interested especially in all the cut-rate electronic stores that had opened unknown to him along Broadway below the Empire State Building. A bazaar of plugs and jacks, they were modern cousins of older, forever-on-the-brink rug shops. Hustlers—Howard was right—always survived. Anthony had always known this, though he had never wanted to know, but now he was hungry for the fact in any guise. Mallelieu was notoriously cheap (except on himself, whom he lavished) but every few years he would put up a show of some of what was left by his old-timers. Reframed, these—usually drawings—could add up to a respectable check for Anthony. So to Dunhill's he went, as any good in-a-hurry hustler would.

In shirt-sleeves, tie, trousers, and blue and red suspenders, Mallelieu stepped from the changing room. Maurice had a ready-to-wear sports jacket waiting. "And this, Tony?"

The fitter identified it—"Oatmeal cashmere"—and so that Anthony could feel the goods, Maurice was leading the art dealer over to him by the coat cuff; Mallelieu, comfortable enough with functionaries to obey their temporary wishes, was letting himself be led tractably.

"Ummnh," Anthony was tepid.

"Ah, see, I am always going to have you shop with me. I too had my doubts."

Maurice was expressionless. "It can be held for you still longer, sir. I put it away for you specially since before you took your trip to Europe—I can hold it yet a little longer."

"Everywhere the hard sell," Mallelieu lamented, slipping off the jacket. The fitter blushed. "Hold it no longer. The fabric feels greasy to me, and that would annoy me. Beautiful to look at I grant you it is, and worth the price, but not for my touch. Sell it to Mr. Terrezza here perhaps—he's an art dealer now, he can afford it."

Anthony locked, frozen, then quickly unstuck—he wasn't unprepared for this, of course. Mallelieu had to have eventually found out, even perhaps be miffed, maybe enough to jerk Anthony up here for that one single zinger.

"Would you care to try it on?" Maurice was gamely asking Anthony as Mallelieu gathered up his suit jacket, top coat, and hat.

"I'll pass, thanks."

Mallelieu, now dressed in his outerclothes, hooked an arm through one of Anthony's: "Come." To Maurice he called back, "Ring the gallery when it's ready. Oh, I wanted to remember—I need hose. I'll come in again maybe tomorrow. Good-bye!"

On the street, the dealer stood bestowing benignly patrician smiles upon the passersby, at the traffic of Fifty-seventh Street. Anthony said, "Fred, I've got to get back," but Mallelieu ignored him. "Do you still go to Azgré for your suits?"

"Not for years." The wind was lashing and forced Mallelieu to grab for his head. Anthony mentioned liking his hat, and the dealer removed it and looked at it himself: the felt—rabbit—creamy as cheese, the feather as color-marvelous as a jeweled pin. "In Bolzano, this trip."

He put the hat on again. "I would like a sports jacket, though, really I would. Your man Azgré doesn't cut quite correctly for me, is the problem. On a reed like yourself he is fine. Someone suggested Barney's to me. That would even be on your way, yes? There's a cab. No arguing—we haven't talked business a little yet. Come, I have one!"

"I can't, Fred. I'll have to call you tomorrow. I'm up to my ass with work."

"You can, you can—here, he's stopping, no arguing, I won't buy anything unless you see it first—do me this one favor. Look, he's waiting."

"Wave him on. I see a Checker—that's roomier."

In the taxi, Mallelieu gripped the side strap, a little boy enjoying himself. Then he heaved a sigh. "How is your Judith?"

Anthony, perhaps infected by the dealer's European manner, answered by undoing a fist: slowly, not sanguinely. "But there are other possibilities for treatment." (Bolzano was not all that far from Milan. Ask for tips.)

Mallelieu shook his head. "A nephew of my son-in-law has the same thing. They just . . . found it—the word in English . . ."

"Diagnosed."

"They just diagnosed it. As you say, though, they come up with wonderful cures today. A new one daily. She will be all right, I know it."

Anthony shrugged fatalistically.

"No, she will be. She'll enjoy much more of life. Speaking of enjoyment"—Mallelieu shifted around, not quite face-to-face with Anthony; he seemed to be looking out the window above Anthony's right shoulder—"that young couple, they are ecstatic. Like they won the sweepstakes. And everyone they talk to then calls me. When I got back from Europe my director, Alan, had a boxful of messages."

Anthony said nothing, sat calm. It wasn't pretense. Evasion—making as though there were no feelings to have—had been his usual first response to challenge for so long—not fight and not flight but anesthesia—that it was perfectly natural to him.

"I had them come in this morning, these Mortons, at my request—to show it to me. They were a little uncomfortable, as you would think."

Anthony spurred himself to say at least something. "The impression I get is that's the way they are. All the time."

"But they are sweet kids, aren't they? I became just as excited as they were. I would say that she is the more spirited one, wouldn't you, Tony? She was the one, I could tell, who wanted to know—and yet also not know—if they'd paid a fair price. I didn't see why I should be mysterious—I told them. I said that their arrangement with you was *more* than fair, considering the extreme rarity. *Then* you should have seen them smile! Are we going the right way? To Barney's?" Mallelieu bent to call through the hinged money-exchange tray at the partitioned-off cabbie: "Did I say that before, driver? Barney's is what we want. I don't know the way." He sat back. "I've never been there," he told Anthony. "Watch that he's not cheating us."

Jane Morton, that morning of the sale, nearly was hyperventilating. Stewart made the chitchat. What each of the three of them wanted, of course, was for the check to be written, the painting grabbed, and then the running-like-hell in their respective directions. Still, a certain ceremoniousness had seemed fitting and necessary; the Mortons might otherwise have been suspicious.

"It's a very beautiful one," Mallelieu was musing aloud, "very beautiful. The October of that year was when Walter did also *Claustral.* These must have been just before that. Would you know?"

"Who said anything about there being others?"

"They told me you did."

As Anthony unfortunately had—a slip. Because he was greedy to banish any qualm at all remaining in the Mortons; because he wanted them to go beyond belief in the picture and to actually *grieve* with him over its sacrifice—because of these he'd said a hokey, unnecessary thing while he was wrapping the picture. "I liberate these and they liberate me."

Jane, sharp-eared even when wild happy, had picked it right up. *"These?* There are others?" Stewart broke in: "We'd have to auction Dana off first to buy another"; and Anthony quickly laughed, saying, "How about an even swap"—but the damage had been done.

Mallelieu touched a finger to Anthony's knee, immediately withdrawing it. "You know very well how I feel about this. You know that Walter for me is finished and that I like it that way. Today is today, not twenty years ago—I have artists now, who can know? who maybe are about to be Dornishes as well. What I feel now, with any Dornish . . . How do I put this. It is my *responsibility:* his dealer for so many years, after all.

"I don't mean the estate—May handles it her way and I no longer have anything to say about it. But history is involved, isn't it, Tony? That's the responsibility—to history. Not to money. I have young artists, alive ones, to make money from now. And if I can't, that's my fault—it means I didn't make the good judgments I did with Walter and Eino."

Judgments? Mallelieu, pillowed by the past, was flattering himself. Lucky and tactful he'd been—but never any judge. Walter had sometimes not been a nice man: when the money began to run flush, he every so often would deliberately bring a painting to the gallery that he knew was weak, that barely looked like a Dornish at all. Mallelieu's habit was never to comment on quality to his stars, thinking it might insult them ("I'm not the one to rank genius"—a line used so frequently that it turned into a bar joke); he accepted Walter's wooden nickels with grace—making Walter rush back ten minutes later and feign upset: "It isn't finished! Going down in the elevator I realized it! This may be the beginning of the end, Fred—it's starting to desert me!" Cruel, arrogant comedy.

The cab had stopped. Anthony said, "Here's Barney's, Fred. I'm going to go on home, though."

"We're here? Already? No, you must come in." Mallelieu quickly stuffed bills into the money exchange. "I don't know what's good, what's bad, it's new to me. I won't be long. You must come in with me."

"I've got Judy's supper to fix," Anthony lied (and wobbled tremendously within the falsehood a moment).

"A few minutes, that's all! To help me find my way around. I insist. Then I let you go."

Just inside the store, Mallelieu headed decisively left—then caught himself; he stopped to ask a salesman where better suits were put out, consulting Anthony too: "The Burberry or the Oak Room—which do I want?"

In the elevator, he said, "My son-in-law's birthday comes next week. He's exactly your proportions. What size shirt do you wear?"

"I knew once, Fred, but now I think I don't remember."

In the Oak Room, Mallelieu waved away a salesman who, smiling familiarly, was making straight for them. He drew Anthony over to a dark green love seat in a corner.

"We realize—you and I—that money only can be made from the past for a specific, short time. By me, I mean, of course. But history asks us—those who know—always to keep an eye on the reputation. *We're* the real curators, Tony, I'm one and you're one, not the museum people—history chooses *us*. That's why it's a thrill for me when a Dornish shows up unexpectedly on the market, even when I'm not involved in the sale, like I was for you the first time.

"Isn't it a mystery, how an artist works? He labors alone. One day he can do nothing and the next day he's turning out fifty things: great, not so wonderful, some in-between, and many that he probably forgets about. And some that he prefers to keep for himself, that he has his reasons for not acknowledging."

Mallelieu had begun to speak more softly and slowly. Anthony had to hand it to him: how many paintings had he sold here in the Oak Room? The lines of expensive, muted suits, the carpeting, the mirrors all around—it all provided an atmosphere of deferred interest, like a court that was consciously ignoring talk of state in its midst.

"With an artist's work of a whole career there is so much we don't find out till much later. Such a private world. I give you an example. Do you remember that little girl Walter was so crazy about?"

"Denise?"

"Not his daughter, I don't mean his child. No, a girl he met in Lynton's: Agnes. Do you remember? Such a small face. A few years ago I found in a box a picture someone took of the two of them in Pennsylvania. Walter looks brave. May, he once told me, knew about it and was very upset, threatening to leave him. You don't remember her? I have the photo—I'll send it down to you tomorrow by messenger."

"I can see it some time at the gallery—no need."

"The sweetest, smallest features on that Agnes—like a doll's. *Agnes.* I don't think, do you, they would name a *jeune fille* in America Agnes anymore? She sat for him, you know. Portraits—that's right. But abstract, he said. Imagine. He never said another word about them, never showed them to me; I don't know what happened to them, or how many there ever were. One thing I am sure of is that May doesn't have them—she would have burned them immediately. But he did do them. They were nineteen fifty-fours, like your painting that you sold to the young couple."

The waiting salesman, hanging back, edged closer, and Mallelieu put up a restraining finger. "He never said anything about them to you? I must be, then, the only one he told. What they say about great geniuses—that they never die—that's true; the people around them keep them alive afterward; we *become* them. We perpetuate their wishes, we know their secrets.

"When the young couple were in to see me this morning, I had the sense—very light—that the husband—he's a lawyer, yes?—that he had something he would have wanted to ask if it were not so terrible to. So I looked him right in the eye: I said that if Anthony Terrezza has sold you this, then it is a genuine Dornish. Even if he did it *himself,* it is a real Dornish! They laughed, they understood. Stay right here, let me have a word with this man." Mallelieu went over to the salesman, a low conversation commencing, the dealer making hand motions to the throat.

The two other canvas boards Anthony had done that fevered, abhorrent, triumphant, wine-drunk night were now in jeopardy. Milan was threatened, J.'s only hope was threatened. Mallelieu, faced with a paper loss running into the ungenteel thousands, was playing hardball. While I've been playing, Anthony thought, strictly for the painted grapefruit league.

The dealer returned to the love seat and to a motorless, benumbed Anthony. "You'll frame it up for me, the photo? In the morning I send it down to you. I'm not in any rush, keep it as long as you need. The second you see her face, Agnes', I know you'll remember her. Tiny nose and mouth—the kind of face Walter would love to draw, to paint. Kiss, I assume, also. I don't know, you know, if they ever slept together. I'm prudish; I prefer to think that it was merely an infatuation. For the wife, though, an infatuation is worse, don't you think?—Walter told me that May was furious. Better never to mention any of this to her, of course. Of course, he told me many stories that weren't totally true. A shifty life, you know? That's why we have to take care of it. What's this?"

The salesman was approaching, a bag in hand, which Mallelieu routed to Anthony. "For you. One curator to another."

Anthony looked in. He reclosed the bag and placed it on Mallelieu's lap.

Mallelieu pushed the bag back at him. "Can't I buy you an ascot? Take it home, wear it during dinner—Judith will like it, so dashing. I've seen you wear them before. Now go and start your cooking, and thanks for bringing me here. I'll just look around a little more on my own."

Anthony removed a twenty-dollar bill from his clip, pressing it into the dealer's surprisingly cool hand.

"Why are you insulting me?" Mallelieu said sadly. "Two respectable men, making a scene in the store—how can it look." He opened the bag and put the twenty inside with the scarf.

Anthony stood. The bag crackled: his fingers were cramping. "And Fred—about the other? No also. Don't send me any photograph. Not interested." One last time he thrust the bag at the dealer but Mallelieu had risen to bend out of the way like a bullfighter.

"This nice man"—pointing to the salesman—"has been so patient, I must let him show me some things now. Don't feel you have to stay, Tony. And don't be so proud. Whenever you want to see the photo, I have it for you. That elevator, that one over there, is the one to take to the ground floor."

Out on the street, Anthony lofted the bag into a sidewalk-parked dumpster, only remembering half a block later the twenty-dollar bill that was still inside. But, no, he must discipline himself: hardball from now on. Nevertheless he swayed like a drunk for a moment in indecision, whether to go back and get the twenty or not. He walked on.

10

Answering Judith's knock (the door buzzer had been fixed some time back but still not the elevator—so another breathless entrance by her), Huft said "Hey, great!"—and yet five minutes later, zip, he was gone: out to do his party shopping, be back in an hour, not one questioning word as to why she was here after she originally had said she wouldn't be.

Unforeseen developments just did not deter this one, Judith had come to realize. He couldn't touch her hair while they make love in the always darkened room? *Wow. Interesting.* (Dead asleep with a brandy hangover, he never got to see her rewig that first morning.) The reason she wouldn't drink, and sometimes was pale and weak, was on account of an "irritable colon"? *Got to watch that.* She wouldn't be around for the next two weeks? *Okey-doke, have fun whatever you do.* Himself a collector, the daily enlargement of human prejudices and particularities only fascinated him, wasn't something to be challenged.

"When you go to the delicatessen, don't ever let them start a ham for you. You'll only get the smallest slices, off the tip—and they're not real hams anyway: water's shot into them, then they're molded. That tip is just a bunch of gristle and fat. Everybody knows that."

"Ask any doctor. He'll tell you. Right at either side of your nose, behind, are sinuses. Pick a pimple there, and if it gets infected, those sinuses leading directly to the brain . . . You'd be in some trouble."

"They have a meeting. They sit around a big table and they take out the applications. Maybe they look at a slide or two, but probably not. They read off the names. William Huft. Anybody know this guy? Or know somebody who does know him? No? Back in the pile. Andrea Mantegna. Anyone heard of this guy or know someone who has? No? Back in the pile—no grant."

A question, whenever he had one, would be no less specific. "I've finished *Bib and Tucker.* Does the museum want to buy it? No gallery commission—so that much cheaper." "Temma needs an honest mechanic who's also good. For her jeep: the transmission gave out yesterday. Call people you know who have cars and find out some names." "Tell me what you know about Hoboken. I have a feeling my rent is going to go up." "What should I do? The loft feels kind of . . . flabby, since my girl left." (Not for a second did Judith misunderstand; he meant, of course, Quinny.)

Her replies had to be as directly to the point. No; unless Alex is very wild over it, they weren't acquiring lately. Three Gees Automotive Specialists, 593 West Fifty-first Street. It's in New Jersey—beyond that I can't help you. Why not have a party?

An hour later he was calling her back: "I'm having a party." Like those wire ties that came with plastic bags: a twist—and he held in that position until twisted next.

Alone in it now, the loft did not appear exactly ready for a party to Judith. Not that she expected vacuumed, nuts-in-full-bowls, pillows-plumped perfection (or perhaps she did)—but after sitting in the Morris chair for ten minutes, recuperating from the stairs, she rose and got to it: she pulled the purple burlap curtains back. The grime on the windows, inside and out, was bad; but with a bottle of ammonia that she found, with water and sheets of newspaper, she was able to get off at least a top layer. She scrubbed the grey of the refrigerator enamel considerably lighter. Paint that had dripped on various surfaces she was able to scrape or pry off with a sharp-tipped knife. Wrapping and rubber banding a rag to its end, she ran a long piece of thin doweling around the corners of the ceiling, collapsing dozens of webs.

At the bottom of a green metal storage cabinet she had discovered a new-looking yellow plastic tablecloth that was long enough to cover the board-and-sawhorses dining table. In the same cupboard, ironstone plates—but since Huft had never said how many people were expected, these she left. It was while Judith was snapping out the felt-backed cloth, though, that her strengthless arms gave out, felt as though they were about to leave their sockets. She stopped, sweat beginning to burst from every pore like fire engines on alarm.

In the stall of Huft's steel shower, the spray helped paste her back together again. Blood was bumping and sawing through her like spilled sugar underfoot; when she breathed she could feel air play around her ankles, as though she had gills down there—yet, all in all, she was proud of herself for trying, for doing what she'd done at least, for not having given in. Still fragile from the bad clinic scare of two mornings ago, she figured that any energy, even if the fuel be pure-grade fright, was an achievement.

A new doctor, never seen before, howdydoo. Not unusual: she regularly got the new man rotating in, the visiting fellow like this one (the idea being that maybe *he'd* come up with something). Short, expertly groomed, wearing an English shirt of robin's-egg blue with contrasting white collar under the white coat, salt-and-pepper hair (she's partial to this in young men), tortoiseshell glasses. He gave the duplicate of that morning's blood report from the lab a long, thorough study. He looked up, studying her face in the same way.

Quick smile. "I tell you what I think we might do," said N. Krans, M.D. (His chunky ivory name badge reminded Judith of tiles in her mother's old mah-jongg set.) "Your platelets are kind of low—low enough to want to watch them. I think what we might do is try to get you a bed upstairs. We could give you your next course of chemo there—or not give it, depending. In any case, we could keep an eye on you. That sound acceptable?"

Judith could tell right away that this was not the truth—probably not even close. His look was too unswerving. Anyone with a chart as thick as hers deserved at least the considerations of semiprofessional status, and N. Krans (Neal? Norman?) seemed distinctly uncomfortable dishing out code words to an old vet like herself. The cubicle walls were thin, privacy minimal; and Judith had overheard too many corridor consultations—"infiltrative spread . . ." "bone pain now . . ." "palliation from here on in . . ." "a white count like you wouldn't believe . . ."—and the pap then told to the patient, to be fooled now.

Her legs, unconsciously twitching, had begun to swing back and forth, banging the sides of the examining table, almost kicking Krans, who took a step back. She had always intended to keep a reserve of loyalty to the idea of disaster—just tell me from what direction the tornado will be coming and I'll start revolving now—but where was it? "Upstairs," she echoed weakly. "That means admitted?"

"If a bed's available, why not?" Taking her hand, he fingered one of her rings: "Navajo?" He said, "You know, I like to think of myself as a devil-may-care kind of person, but deep down I must be cautious. Do it for me." He winked. "And we'll get to see more of each other this way."

"You'll have to pick me up, you know, and also take me home."

Krans laughed too robustly. "Deal. Well?"

For a demented moment she had actually thought to tunnel out from under with jokes. "Do I have a choice?"

"Thatta girl."

Rita, the clinic nurse who'd come in while they were talking, leaned over Krans' shoulder for a look at the chart. Then she hurriedly left, scowling. Headed for the staff ladies' room and a good cry, Judith expected—wished.

Certain things were most definitely sad. It was much too beautiful a day out, for one, for this to be happening: skyey and bright when she'd walked from her apartment to the hospital. If only she'd paid more attention. The thin slices of what she'd noticed—dogs being walked and garbage picked up—were melting too quickly. From here on her life would be only rooms—sucked from room to room to room. This morning, her last one outside in the world, had therefore been almost totally wasted.

Krans, consulting the chart once more, moved to the phone on the wall. The number he dialed didn't answer. "I'm going to run up there myself: be faster. Sit tight."

When he was gone, Judith stood up and went to the same phone. Because Krans was new to the case, he wouldn't know her father, who was sitting out in the waiting room; and Daddy wouldn't know him. So she still had a few last minutes alone. She dialed.

He was at the shop, as she'd figured, and his hello sounded busy.

"Hi?" she said smally. She had no knees.

"What's the matter? Where are you?"

Tears filled her throat; it was impossible to answer.

"At the hospital? Today's your day. Is anything wrong?"

How occupied he'd sounded when he first answered. How much readier for the worst he was than she, too. Which sin was the more real: to imagine someone else's death before your own, or vice versa? The tears evaporated, leaving a touchy coating to her voice: "Have any packages come for me?"

"What's going on? Are you at the hospital? I hear sounds. What's the matter?"

"Nothing is. If any packages do come, forward them. Thanks."

"Something's the matter. You're sure you're okay?"

"Yes. I have to go."

And now? Call Jack? Call poor Huft? That song she liked—"Love the one you're with . . ."—as if she'd ever had any choice but. She called neither.

The cubicle curtains parted just as Judith was getting back onto the table. In first walked Rita, disappointingly dry-eyed. In tow behind her were Dr. Wellitz, Dr. Sanders, and, bringing up the rear, young Norman or Neal Krans.

Rita righteously grabbed up the chart, opened it, and after passing it around to the white coats, set to preparing the I.V. pole, the syringe and the vials.

"A small foul-up," Dr. Sanders informed Judith.

"Not so small"—a loud mutter from the unshrinking Rita.

"You've seen the lab forms lots of times, Judy. They're in triplicate, pressure-sensitive like deposit slips in a bank. Today, instead of being printed out as usual, the values came down handwritten. Whoever did the filling in didn't do it too neatly—so, on the copies, what belonged to what box was hard to read."

"Your platelets are within range," said Dr. Wellitz. He looked furious.

She asked, "No hospitalization?" Sanders squeezed her knee—as though she'd said something adorable, about God's birthday or if there was such a thing as a puppy factory. He left along with Wellitz, who patted Rita's shoulder approvingly on the way out.

Immediately Krans bustled. "Show on the road and all that rot!"—a mock-English accent. He was moving around so quickly, jumpily, that he had trouble getting the gloves on: his error was an altar, and he was burning calories on it.

She took the chemo, was driven to Greenburgh by her father (who never knew what he had missed), and was sick that night longer than usual. In a way it had been thrilling—*Here it finally was*—but she shouldn't have made that phone call to Anthony. He had called Greenburgh that night, of course, and Judith had been obliged to get on. Be terse. But he was being pretty strange himself. Asking her if her passport was still valid. She had gotten off quickly. The next day she remembered Huft's party.

She closed the faucets, stepped out, and toweled herself. Her new purchase, the very small portable hair dryer, was in her overnight bag, along with her clothes. Saronged in a towel, she went down the hallway to Huft's room, where she climbed the ladder to the bed, the overnight bag over one shoulder, a fist inside the wig.

She hadn't remembered, though: no place to plug the hairdryer into. The cord to Huft's Tensor lamp, taped to the wall, led to an outlet under the loft bed, near the floor. So she was halfway down the ladder again—when she heard footsteps outside on the stairs, and had barely enough time to jam on the wig (no time for the kerchief first) over her damp head and scramble back up.

"Boy, lay-zee." Huft looked up at her on the bed: half in and half out of her party clothes: blue silk blouse, long brown skirt, textured hose.

"A minute and I'll be right down," she stalled. "Do what you have to meanwhile."

"No minutes given, come down now. I've got spoils—which could spoil."

"One minute." She took her good shoes out of her overnighter, flung them over the side to the floor (causing a shocked Huft to yelp, "Hey! You could break the heels like that!"); then, coming as quickly as she could down the ladder, she rushed past Huft for the bathroom and a mirror in which to see if she was on straight.

"That's better," Huft declared when she left the bathroom. He was referring not to her but to the table: he had stripped off the cloth she'd laid at such cost of energy, and out of one of the shopping bags he'd brought home he had pulled a long piece, maybe four yards worth, of cheap dress fabric: printed roses. This he unfurled over the plywood board; straightening the sides, he commented, "Looks very Puerto Rican, doesn't it? They'll like it."

"Are the people who are coming Puerto Rican? You haven't told me who you've invited." Judith moved to lift the shopping bags onto the table, sensing while in motion the heavy wetness of her hair under the wig's cap. She worried about chill, even mildew.

Huft sent a last admiring gaze at the revolting table covering, then moved fleetly to remove the bags from Judith's possession. "Mitts off these, step back. Something in here for you." He turned away to rummage. "Stepping back like I said? Go on."

"Two questions first. Does it bite and can it explode?"

"Close your eyes."

"I don't do that—not for surprises. Not for anybody. Sorry."

He'd got a hand on what he was looking for in the bag but didn't pull it out; he peered back at her through his bent arm, face upside down. "Waiting."

"Tell me first what it is—then I'll close them," she sang nervously. "I need a medium amount to a lot of warning."

"She's just dithering on," said Huft, shaking his head, now with some tinder to his tone. "Postponing it. *Ruining* it."

Judith wondered if he'd been drinking. "But you have to promise you'll just hold it and not put it in my hand or anything. You're sure it's not alive . . ."

"Tight—and don't open them till I say."

Her heart trilled. Something was coming down *over her head! the tops of her ears!* Though nothing hurt her, she squeaked in pain anyway.

It was a hat—that much she could tell from feel alone: a baseball cap with a stiff bill. Company's coming, so dress Baldy up in a funny hat. If she could be sure the wig wouldn't pop away with it, she'd tear it from her head. (What of the wig? How badly askew was it now?) She had to open her eyes.

Huft now wore a hat also. A baseball cap of green satin. Hers—she pulled it carefully off—was the same color. He was smiling, waiting for comment, but Judith needed to get to a mirror first. The wig, she found, had held, knocked maybe half an inch rightward. She straightened it. Huft—clearly, she decided, a little buzzed already—probably hadn't noticed.

By the time she got back from the bathroom Huft had also donned a buckskin vest, shaggy, with preposterously long fringes. Thankfully there didn't seem to be a mate of it for her to wear. He was beginning to unpack what else was in the bags. Lump after lump emerged—what must have been easily thirty dollars worth of imported cheeses. Even inside the plastic wraps, they stank to the ceiling, most of it being the chalky-rinded, aged, runny sort of cheese that she couldn't eat because it reacted wrongly with her medicines. Once the cheeses were all on the table, he brought out a half gallon of gin, a fifth of vermouth, and then he stomped crushingly on both emptied bags.

"Only cheese and liquor?" she asked.

"Not sufficient?" He was using a large piece of cardboard as a cheese tray, unwrapping each portion only partially. "And here I thought it would be very uptown. Understated. Cheaperoo."

Then he stared chasteningly at her. "I probably bought more food for tonight than your museum serves to an opening night crowd of hundreds of starving folks. I bought eight whole flounders from my man, Frankie D., at the Fulton Fish Market. It was down there, at the Seaport, where I also got us our uniforms." He touched the bill of his cap. "Two ladies I do some carpentry for, they own a crafts shop. I build them shelves, they pay me, I get the money for this blast. They threw in the uniforms free."

"Does our team have a name?"

"But *mais sur!*" He thought a moment. "Huft's Hellions!"

"Are those two women coming tonight?"

"And when I say the word, my eight *flounders* will be wearing uniforms, too. Wine sauce, black bean sauce, a very spicy chile sauce (I'll
tell you which is which, I'll warn you off). The rest will be a surprise.
I'm also leaving all the vegetables and noodle dishes up to him."

"Who's him?"

"Willy Kee. We're ready here; I call Willy; he gets to work; then he
brings it all over. Now what?" Huft rested his hands on his fringed hips
and surveyed the stocks. "Cool the booze, I guess. Hand me that." The
gin jug required two hands and lots of muscle from Judith, yet Huft
took it from her with but two fingers. "The vermouth, too."

When the downstairs bell suddenly rang twice, Judith grabbed those
two of Huft's slender fingers, squeezing them: "Tell me who you've invited or I'm not letting you go."

"Time to put on your cap, Cap"—his fingers sliding like eels out of
her teentsy grip, the bell ringing a third time. Dressed as he was—in
fringed vest, green satin baseball cap—Huft went to buzz whoever it
was in, opening the door and going out to the landing. Judith ran to give
herself a last quick check in the bathroom: wig straight. With two
hands she beat a dust rat from her skirt. Her toenails could have stood
some polish.

First through the door, followed by Huft, came a rangy hippie with
straight limp hair down past his shoulders and a middle-aged face; he
was holding a white bakery box by the knot and kept looking behind
him at Huft's getup. "Hey, fontastic! I didn't see so goodt out there in
the dark."

Huft took the hippie's cake box from him, put it down on the table,
and marched promptly to the phone: "Time to call Willy Kee."

The hippie—whom Judith judged to be forty at least—wore a tan
poplin suit over a dark green tee shirt that read "The Nosherie, Ann
Arbor." Lank, he must have frozen in only that. She offered a hand:
"Hello, I'm Judith."

"Pitter." They shook while he looked around. "Fine loft. Hardt to
findt one this nice."

This? Nice?

"Have martinis, both of you," Huft directed from over by the phone.
"Or at least Peter. Genever, Peter. He's Dutch."

"Bols?" queried the hippie.

"Genever."

The hippie repeated, "Bols?"

Perplexed, Huft looked at Judith. "What's he saying? *Genever.* Gin. Blue ruin. *Genever!* In the fridge—and there's ten pounds of ice in the freezer. These chinkies, I swear, are still afraid of this invention: it rings and rings and they go their merry w—Hello? Let me speak to Willy!"

Judith took out the vermouth, leaving the heavy gin jug for the Dutchman to remove. "Glasses, glasses, now where do you suppose he keeps them?" (She couldn't help it. She preferred it be made clear to the hippie that she wasn't a permanent resident here.)

Huft held the phone away. "In the cupboard, top shelf: the bag that says Discount Job Lot. I bought them yesterday: very Puerto Rican." Peter was opening the seal on the gin bottle. Huft advised further, "Use any one of those Maxwell House cans over there—they're all clean—as your mixer jar. And be sure to make those dry."

The hippie had isolated three tall water tumblers: amber, with warts. Judith told him, "I don't, so pour only for the two of you."

"A teetotaler," Huft reported. "I'll get her to drink yet, though— WILLY? WILLY! HE'S HERE. YOU TOLD ME TO CALL YOU WHEN THE FIRST GUEST ARRIVED. HE ARRIVED. SO HOP TO IT AND MAKE US PLENTY OF DELICIOUS THINGS."

The Dutchman had wandered into the work area and was looking at the assemblages on the walls when Judith caught up with him. "Are you also an artist?"

"Yes. Ho—look ad this!" "This" was "The Seduction of Quinny."

Huft, now off the phone, stayed back near the table and the liquor— "This you call dry?"—correctively filling his glass to the top with straight gin, drinking some off, then pulling over the Morris chair to serve as the fourth seat around the table. "Of course he likes that one. He loves them that age."

The hippie was amused. "I give you the inspiration, Billy?"

"What no one's ever explained to Hans over there is that he can go to *jail* for playing around with little girls."

"What kind of work do you do?" Judith asked Peter. "Painting? Sculpture?" The hippie's lecherous joshing had let her down a little: he looked so pure and unearthly.

"Carpentry."

"Couldn't you guess?" Huft had seated himself at the table to tackle his glass seriously. "Looking like Our Lord Himself. That's why those dirty little girls from the Catholic high school down his street stand there and stare at him for hours."

An unbothered, throaty laugh from Peter to this.

Huft sawed at one of the cheeses with a plastic knife; nibbled; screwed up his face; put the rest down. "He makes couches right in his window. And chairs. Look at him laughing—he thinks exhibitionism is funny. What happens when your brain gets pickled by genever." Huft got up just long enough to remove from the cupboard the stacks of iron-stoneware Judith had previously let sit.

The Dutchman continued to wander. In front of *The Teachers' Cafeteria*, she asked him, "Did you really build a couch in the window of your shop?"

"Just one time." He touched the cheese sandwich on one of the teachers' trays on the off-chance the bread might be real. "Billy kidts me about it."

"Give her one of your cards," Huft suggested. "Buy a couch from him and then I can come to your house and sit on it. *I* certainly couldn't afford one. Especially not since I spent all this money on all this putrid cheese that no one is eating . . . It's not putrid—I'm only joking. Actually it's delicious. I dropped forty-one dollars and it's just going to sit here?"

The downstairs bell rang. Huft didn't bother rising. "That's not the food so soon—it's got to be . . . Hey, you, who's not wearing the hat I gave her—another guest."

"You go, Huft, I won't know them. Besides, I'm talking to Peter."

"Sure, why don't we argue, let our guest meanwhile stand out there, figuring no one is home, it's been a practical joke . . ." A crankiness in the grumble—and he obviously wasn't going to stir. Judith gave him a half-meant dirty look on her way to the door.

After buzzing back, she walked out to the landing, prepared to make the necessary apologies to the climber for no elevator, no stairwell light.

"Hi, Jude."

Alex? "Alex?" It was Alexandra!

Alex waved matter-of-factly as she reached the top of the final flight. "No wonder the woman I passed coming in wished me a happy ascent."

"What," Judith whispered, "are you doing here?"

"Being out of breath. Here." Alex pushed a bottle of wine on her. "How would you spell Aquarius?"

"I know, it's wrong down there . . . You know Huft?"

"I don't, no, but he phoned me last week and said you were giving a dinner party here. I tried calling you to see what it was all about. I could never get you. So here I be. Later you'll fill me in on all the deetles, like where you met him and when. I had this feeling— Later. Hello."

Huft had appeared at the door. Baseball cap and buckskin. *"You,"* he pointed dramatically at Alex, "love flounder. It's perhaps your favorite fish."

"I look the type, right?"

"And plenty of strong martinis. That's our menu—and no substitutions. I don't hold with this variety rigamarole. Study any book on mythology and see if the gods aren't always eating a single food, drinking a single libation." His small-town pharmacist's face under the silly satin cap, this artisty frothing about: Judith discovered herself charmed by it despite everything. He was trying so hard.

Huft said, "I'll take that from you," and immediately loaded Alex's coat onto Judith, who was already holding the wine. He squired Alex into the loft. "That chappy down there is Peter Orint—in case you ever want to buy pretty good but insanely priced furniture. Right, Peter?"

Judith joined them just as the hippie was shaking Alex's fingers. "Hallo."

"Hello."

"How'fe you been?"

"Not bad. Yourself?"

"Now a drink!" Huft said from over by the table. "I make them dry, dry, dry. If you don't drink them dry, you don't drink them! You see my cocktail shaker?"—holding up the Maxwell House can for approval.

But Alex and the hippie were continuing to exchange looks: layered, fond, ironic looks. Something was afoot.

"You two know each other?" Judith asked.

Peter kept his eyes on Alex as he said: "She didn't give me a jobp."

"Only a tumble." Alex now had on one of her full calm smiles. Huft had joined everyone again and was handing Alex a glass which she took absently. "Do you remember, Jude, a few years ago, when Lee was on that commission in Washington for six months and I was the acting director? Peter came in for an art handler job. I hate to remember this."

The hippie patted her arm good-naturedly. "It wasn't so badt."

"It was and you know it. Me deciding to be very official and tight-assed, I wanted a formal resumé. He didn't have one. So I gave him a bad time, I began to grill him on contemporary art. Did I also ask you to lift my desk? I think I did, didn't I?" Alex put fingers in front of her eyes. "How awful I was. I wanted to see what it was like to deny somebody a job. Ughh."

Huft, who'd been listening with his head inclined, drew himself up. "You were smart. He would have insisted on working in a window. He would have been an embarrassment."

"I hired the very next applicant, pure caprice. Then I felt so *guilty.* I called Peter up, we met . . ." The hippie's eyes narrowed, pleased, as Alex went on: "And I'm pretty positive you were the last guy before I went heavily into the women's movement. Grand farewell performance. Of course grand or not's for you to judge, not me . . ."

Judith always loved Alex's way of running her personal history by you like a book's flipped pages, the whole story in the breeze itself. The enlightened hippie, too, was saying, "Ah, ah," and looking completely grudgeless.

But once he caught on to what Alex was saying, Huft was felled. The host was being ignored, left out, beside the point. He irksomely went striding back to the table to mix and pour himself still another drink from the can. "You're all wondering where the food is already," he offered, largely to himself, "and I suggest that we all sit down at the table here and concentrate—we'll conjure it to arrive! Worth a try, I'd say. (But who's even listening.) Let's all sit. (All right, let's not sit.)"

"He said something before about a window?" Alex was asking Peter. "You're a window designer now?"

"Nah." The hippie cocked his head complacently toward Huft: You know *him.*

"Did you ever go to work in London like you said you might?" Alex asked next, heading for the table with Peter right behind her.

"This is a catered party, you know: the timing is split-second. Everyone has to start *now* on this cheese!"

To pacify Huft, Judith pulled a chair out by the table, asking Peter as she sat, "What sort of thing do you do in London?"—but Huft had stopped her with a hand on her arm and was pulling her back up:

"No, no, not here. You're seated over there, Peter at the end over there with you. *Never* go to London."

"He makes playground equipment." Alex took the chair Huft was indicating as hers, the one next to him. "For damaged children. That's right, yes?"

Judith: "Damaged how?"

Alex meanwhile wanted to know from Huft—a side conversation— what he had against London.

The hippie, sitting, pointed to his head. "Brain."

"I mean *people* can—just not *some* people, like artists. Artists have to be careful about seeing new places. Travel overloads you with images. If an artist travels more than once every ten years, that's not good. Image overload."

"I hadt to go back a few times," Peter explained to Judith. He tasted some cheese. "Something that I made wasn't goodt."

Alex, listening to both men, turned to Peter. "I remember. You were worried about it."

Huft glared. "An artist needs about a dozen basic memory images. Out of that, six will maybe be nightmares—"

"It was a slide, wasn't it?"

Peter nodded. "A playgroundt piece. I hadt ribbedt the endt of the slide, so that they wouldt bump a little at the bottom. I thought it wouldt be fun for them."

"Taste this cheese, this one here. Wow!"

"But they criedt insteadt. It was explainedt to me." Peter rose to remove his jacket, revealing ropey but powerful arms; he draped the jacket onto the back of his chair and resat. "Like what Billy is saying about artists: these children don't let themselves have too many sensations. They will cry if the taste of a foodt is strange. They will vomit it right out."

"Six, as I was saying, will be nightmares. If you're lucky, one or two will be very pleasant . . . For a chappy like Peter here, sure, travel is okay—he's an artisan, not an artist. You see, what he does, he imposes what he has—his skill—on the places and experiences. Not vice versa." Huft looked pleased with this.

The hippie objected gently. "I am an artist. A woodt sculptor."

Alex now was staring at Huft. "And I'm not sure I follow. You're saying—"

Huft: "Yep!"—to whatever.

"—that artists should be hermits."

"Didn't they used to be?! In the monasteries, illuminating manuscripts . . ." He took a large gulp from his glass, which each time Judith looked was again full. The downstairs bell rang, and Huft asked Peter to get it: "I'm in the middle of an important conversation here." The Dutchman smilingly went.

"Monasteries were societies in and of themselves," Alex argued.

Judith (why not, a real discussion about something other than her health) added: "And when you look at history, geographical cross-pollination is important. Rembrandt seeing copies of Raphael, for instance, or Picasso being influenced by African—"

Huft, while she spoke, began to whip his head from side to side: "No no no no no no No No No NO NO NO NO! Artists are like those kids he was talking about: vomiters. That's all. No no no no." He subsided into a sulk.

Peter was calling from by the door: "Billy?"

"Yo!" Huft rose ungracefully, thudding his foot against something beneath the table before weaving off.

Judith could feel Alex looking at her, a plea for explanation. Instead she bent to peer under the table, where she found a fifth of gin, half-empty, on its side.

Back came Huft and Peter—and with them a young, short-haired, and chubby-cheeked Chinese girl wearing a down jacket and jeans. "This is Marilyn, everyone," Huft announced brassily, taking two shopping bags from the girl. "You tell your father, by the way, that he shouldn't send you out on deliveries after dark—that's not too big on brains. I figured he'd send one of the waiters, not you. I don't like that. He's not too big on brains to do that."

Judith smiled at the girl. "Huft," she warned.

"Sit down, Marilyn. Oops, you need a chair. Take that stool over there. We're having good talks about art—it'll be educational. This girl, I want everyone to know, is a genius. She goes to Stuyvesant High School, which I hear is pretty elite, and she takes calculus and physics and all the hardest stuff. Sit down, hon."

"I have to go," the girl said shyly, staying where she was.

"Beautiful English, too, did you hear? You ought to hear the tic-tac-toe that comes out of her father's mouth, though. A great chef, but when it comes to English—"

Loudly enough to drown Huft out, Judith asked Peter: "How did you first become involved with retarded children?"

Peter retook his place at the table. "When I came to the States, first I livedt in San Francisco. My neighbor hadt an impairedt little girl."

"No chopsticks?" Huft was removing cartons from the bags. "No, wait, I see them."

"One day they askedt me to help them with the patterning. It was a fontastic experience for me personally."

"'Personally.' Of course 'personally'—it happened to you, didn't it? 'Personally.'"

Peter was asking Judith, "Have you ever?"

"You never mentioned to me that you actually worked *with* the autistic children," Alex said to him. "I think that's so great."

Huft, busy with counting chopsticks, pronounced: "All children are innately artistic. Only three pairs here; someone is going to have to eat with a fork."

Judith reminded Huft that Marilyn was waiting to be paid, then she started to tip one of the containers toward a plate. Huft lunged and re-righted it. "That'll make it cold!"

"We now are working with a boy namedt Carly, on East Third Street—a group of about fourteen of us. We always needt new people, especially during the week."

Alex, mounding up some rice on her plate, asked Peter, "What does it entail?"

"We pattern him. He has special exercises that we do with him, over and over—"

Alex turned away from Peter for a moment, toward Huft. "You said this is what again—flounder? I'm always fearful it'll be abalone. Something about the word: *abalone*. It's flounder, though, right?"

Huft smacked his forehead dramatically. "Stupid me! I should have served some Greek food also—in your honor. Just occurred to me."

"Why?" said Alex. "I'm not Greek."

Judith got up. "Marilyn is still waiting, Huft. If you like, I'll pay her." When Judith left her chair, so did Alex hers—moving immediately into the seat vacated next to Peter. Huft took two bills out of his hip pocket and thrust them at Judith blindly, all his attention ragingly on the pair at the other end of the table.

Peter was still explaining about patterning when Judith returned after seeing Marilyn out. "In London, they have a very bigk center . . ." She took Alex's original seat, next to Huft. There evidently had been another foray by him under the table—his glass was once more full. "They are enlightenedt about this, the English." Peter had put a casual hand on the back of Alex's neck as she listened and ate.

"*The* most constipated people in the world," Huft declared. He stood up. "The Magna Carta—think that's an accident? No, not at all. Very repressed nationalities—the English, the Dutch—have to get it all in writing. Their painting is wooden for that reason. That's a well-known fact."

"Dutch painting is wooden?" said Alex, at the same time gently removing the hippie's provocative hand from her nape.

"Well, English painting is." Huft sat again, heavily.

"Wouldt you have any time to help us?" Peter asked them all.

·

Alex said she couldn't. "I'm very clumsy. I stumble over words, let alone exercises."

The hippie looked to Judith: "You?"

Huft broke in excitedly. "Everyone try this. Say *I'm much less well read than you are* three times fast."

"If we don't have enough teams, it is very hardt. Enough teams: easy. An hour a week wouldt be all you wouldt do."

"The guy usually never says two words"—a mumble from Huft—"Now we can't shut him up."

"I'd be willing to give it a try," Judith said.

"And you're sure not you?"

Alex swallowed a mouthful of food, shaking her head. "He's tiny, right? No, I know myself—I'd cry. Too emotional."

"We were talking about art," Huft said, "so let's continue. Here is what I have to give the English credit for, though: no rigid gallery system. That's what kills good art off in this country. That's why I gave it up. The older way was better, one on one, the artist and the collector. Point of origin to point of collection: a straight line. My prices are cheaper that way, and that whole stock market mentality is kicked right in the old ass, in the old ass."

Peter had gone on talking straight through Huft's diatribe, trying to persuade Alex. "If you saw him on the street you wouldt not know Carl was different. In the house you wouldt, because he is five and he still wears diapers—but in the street, no. You wouldt just think, This is a beautiful childt."

"... drowned in Hebrew taste in this city, everyone knows that." Chin down, Huft addressed his vest, but twice he raised his eyes under the cap-bill to see if there was any reaction. Judith had heard him; Alex and Peter apparently not.

"You know what I bet?" Huft said further to Judith in an overlarge yet conspiratorial voice. "I bet that he's got some of his parochial school whores helping him grope up that kid. Let's both ask him that. Bet. With their brown plaid little skirts that come up all the way to their cunts, their dark stockings, their fuck-me shoes—let's ask. He gets into plenty of that, you can be sure."

Peter leaned over the table to better see Huft. The indulgent smile came, but slower: "Ah, Billy."

"Ah, Billy yourself"—and Huft suddenly finger-catapulted a single chopstick at the hippie, sending it across the table end over end. It hit

Peter square in the throat, but the Dutchman only set the stick back on the table, saying nothing.

Alex, whom the stick had missed by an inch, jumped up and was charging around the table toward Huft. "You're a rude bastard, do you know that?"

Judith stood up and touched Alex's shoulder. "He's been drinking."

"And what *you're* doing in all this is completely beyond me. Can this be good for you? You don't look great, I saw you shiver before—why? For what? Who *is* this?"

"You'd know. You'd *know* who it is—if the damn art magazines didn't refuse to print articles about young painters and instead run the same tired shit always about Torng and Relverio and Alice Stemmack and Dornish and those asses—you'd know then!" Huft's chin dropped immediately thereafter, welding to his throat as he desultorily played with his fringes, sunken into himself, the eye of the storm.

"He scares me." Taking Judith by the elbow, Alex was walking her down the hallway toward the front door.

"He's confused about art-world politics, Al, that's all."

"Which of these is your coat? I see it. This your pocketbook?"

"No, I have to stay. He's a wonderful artist. You saw the kind of work he's doing—it's very touching."

"I can feel how hot you are even through the coat. The man is a boor. Everyone and his brother is a 'wonderful artist.' He's a boor, Judes. He obviously used you." Down the first flight of stairs. "You didn't even know I was invited! And some dinner party—out of cartons. It was all to get me down here to see his work. Oh baby—you're burning up, your hand is so hot. Last few steps."

From three floors above Huft's voice boomed down upon them as he leaned over the landing: "At least they're honest about hair—their legs are like men's. And if they've got mustaches, no problem!"

"There you are. So much for wonderful." Alex was opening the downstairs door.

Exhausted from the quick walk down, Judith leaned against the outside of Huft's building. Alex had stepped out to look for a cab; she returned, reporting, "We'll have to go to the corner."

"I should go back up there. But I can't."

"Now you're talking."

"No, I mean I *can't:* the stairs. Shit," Judith whimpered.

Alex touched Judith's cheek. "It'll be all right. I understand that you want to do it all by yourself now—"

"Do what?"

"You know. Anthony called me to set up an appointment—something to show me, he didn't say what—and I got a sense, from the way he was talking, that—"

"If we're getting a cab, let's get it, okay?"

"Hold on to me. Walk slow. You'll come to my house to stay."

"No."

"God, that cap. I've been to lots of lofts, met lots of artists . . ."

"Let's stop. I really have to go back up there."

"We're almost to the corner."

"I have my bag up there, my overnighter. I have clothes in it."

"It's only a bag." Alex's arm, as good as steel, was around her.

Jeans. A shirt. Underwear. Her other shoes. Toothbrush. Deodorant. The new hair dryer. And it suddenly flooded her: this is what it will be like. Her first real taste.

Not being able to go back and get your things.

Another hand, not Alex's, was touching her shoulder now: Peter, in his thin jacket and holding the cake box he'd brought to Huft's, was patting her while Alex said, "Let her lean on you while I run out and flag a cab."

"Billy, he's a goodt guy, he really is," the Dutchman said, arm tightly around her. "But he shouldn't drink."

Judith tried wresting free. "I have to go up there. Is he very upset?"

Peter looked surprised that she'd even think such a thing. "No. He's eating."

11

"I dream about wide plazas, esplanades, big rolling lawns like the ones they have at Versailles," May Dornish Tenzer explained to him. "And when I wake from these I feel absolutely wonderful. Why? Because they're telling me that there's room inside me yet."

Anthony nodded. The train ride out had tired him. The suddenness in deciding to make the trip had something to do with it, too.

"You don't buy it."

Anthony said there was nothing not to buy.

"Haven't you ever had a vivid, exhilarating dream?" May pressed.

"I was flying once."

"Well, you see." Leaning across the foot or so of space that separated their facing chairs, she took his hand in hers, gratified.

"I was flying over the Interboro Parkway. Walter was on my back. I kept yelling up to him 'You all right?' like the old-time pilots, front seat to back. We were going beneath underpasses, over a golf course, made banked turns, the works."

May removed her hand and sat back.

Anthony smiled. "Offended that Walter was on my back—not the other way around? I remember waking up scandalized."

"I was just thinking about the rides out here, before he knew how to drive: holding a hand over his eyes whenever Gold would cut someone off or run a red light." She rested her head back against the chair's headpiece and silently mused for a minute, sucking on her plastic cigarette.

Anthony pierced his own nighttime reflection in the living room window nearest to him and looked out at the bare-treed street. When the rare car would hiss by, the darkness seemed to be smoothed of one more wrinkle.

May said, "One of Matty's boys sent him a book recently, which I looked through, that claims we're not very different than bugs: we obey a species law like any other animal. We don't know it, we think we arrange our own social behavior—but actually it's all been biologically wrapped for us and ready to go. I can't tell you the degree to which that saddened me. I'm not sure, first of all, that it's true; but even if it is—what good does it do me to know it? My dreams, what comes involuntarily from inside me, *they're* of use. Indicators I can trust. From them I can get an idea of whether my spirit is free or is all knotted."

"Fried foods an hour before bed must play havoc."

May snorted, exaggeratedly lifting her chin to turn away. She looked fine. She wore jogger's pants and sneakers. A man's shirt, blue oxford, was opened a few buttons down her speckled chest, and despite the chill in the room she was sweaterless. Her red-grey hair as always was braided, the rope then draped and pinned laterally mid-scalp, like a gasket. When she got up to refill Anthony's cup with rose hip tea, her breasts, unbra-ed, bounced cheeringly firm. Age told mostly, if anywhere, on her skin. Her neck was a fluted column of tendons and vertical folds; on the backs of her hands and dotting her temples were sun-induced livermarks as big as nickels, sites for potential trouble. She'd always been a little leathery—which Walter seemed to have had a taste for. Once, in a hardware store on Fourteenth Street in the old days, he had put a young Anthony to the blush by pointing to a box of pumice stones and saying, "Take one of those, and a square of chamois, to bed with you—a woman's entertained for hours." In all, May still was a woman of strong good looks, well preserved both by her natural independence and her money. The heart specialist she'd married a few years back had been able to pour his own fortune into hers without causing a discordant splash, and she seemed content.

"Such a skeptic. The I've-seen-it-alls, you know, are usually the smallest minds. If you want proof, though, that the spiritual is roaming within you while you sleep, I can give it to you. And you'll accept it— because it has to do with your pal. You know that before Walter and I met—when we both were teaching at Boys' in '40—he had done some bumming around. That he had boxed oranges for a few months in California in, I think, '38. That he was getting paid ten cents an hour—or was it fifteen? I don't remember."

"Whatever."

"—No, it was ten. Listen, five cents was a substantial difference in those days and under those circumstances. In any case, it was something ridiculously low. With one hand he'd crumple tissue paper, put an orange in the box with the other, then crumple another piece of tissue next to it, pillowing the fruit on both sides. He did that all day, everyday.

"He'd told the story to the kids many times; and one day, when Denise was—well, let's see: Paul was just starting school; Denise had to be, what, twelve?—twelve. Both of us, she and I, happened to walk into the studio and find Walter asleep, snoring away in his chair. Maybe he'd just finished a painting; you remember how he liked to just drop down and go out afterwards.

"He didn't hear us come in. When I said something, first low and then in a regular voice, he didn't hear that either. Denise was the one who had the idea. That bowl of oranges he always kept around to eat when he was working? (Oh, do I laugh when I read people calling the work 'ascetic.') Denise took an orange and a flat piece of newspaper. Very gently and very quietly, she put the orange into one of his hands and just lightly pressed the newspaper into the other. Don't you think that hand crumpled the newspaper? Like a Venus flytrap. Denise and I looked at each other, and then we had to hold back from laughing. And he was *really* asleep, too—his jaw dropped open, the whole thing. I could always tell when he was faking. He wasn't that time."

Anthony yawned under cover of a hand. "The man was an impossible card."

"See if I care whether you believe me or not. Ask Denise the next time you see her. Matty doesn't understand any of this either: he tells me that if it makes me happy to think it, then think it. The same old big tub of 'happy' that men think women are content to splash around in, but what can you do?" She touched Anthony's knee. "Go to bed, Peter Pan. I'm babbling, you're exhausted. There's a pair of Matty's pyjamas on the bed in your room, and you'll see two blankets on a chair, extra ones in case the electric isn't enough."

Anthony stood. "Forgive me. I did want to talk." He splayed the fingers of one hand widely, ever since he was a boy the only way he allowed himself to stretch in public. "Good thing I wasn't Madame Blavatsky's sole disciple. Her name would be lost forever."

The guest room smelled strongly of lemon furniture polish. Clothed only in the tops of the doctor's pyjamas, Anthony lay splinteredly awake, not sure if the sloshing scrape he faintly but regularly was hearing was the early winter sea or sounds of the narrow highway nearby. A stripe of moonlight was upon his legs from the knees down: bony legs, old man's legs, the ankles lately starting to come up colors, blue lines and purple. May had set out a glass and pitcher of water on the night table, to which Anthony had added his vial of sleeping pills, his Dalmane. He put out a hand to them now.

It could not have been done tonight in any case. He would have found it impossible to stay and sleep a night in the house afterward; besides, he'd have been too tired, too inattentive in case something threatened to go wrong. Still he wished it was already seen to: the back of a monstrosity was less frightening than its face.

And there was a time element. J.'s midmorning call a week ago had rocked him; she hadn't sounded good. He didn't like, as policy, to be away from the city and out of reach. But her call had also reinvigorated him, reminded him that he was *always* going to have less time than he estimated, that things had to be done *now*. Anthony sat up, shook out a pill, poured water, and swallowed. He hoped for a blotting sleep.

May was in the kitchen preparing coffee when he came down in the morning. Her back was to him, the sink tap was running. Not wishing to startle her, Anthony coughed . . . and then couldn't stop: when May turned it was to discover him gripped by a blinding, dry-lunged paroxysm.

She laughed while he went on hacking uncontrollably. One of May's palmier traits: she didn't believe in wasting a hilarity. You stepped into dogshit, broke a zipper, any momentary and harmless predicament— she laughed "And you don't even smoke. What's in store for me? Here's water."

"I'm all right," he wheezed, accepting the glass.

"Matty hated missing you. Did you hear him come in?—it must have been around one-thirty. He had two emergencies, then he drove straight out. The expressway is surprisingly nice at that hour; you feel that the road is yours to shape as you like, it's rolling under you like that machine in the penny arcade. I think it does him good actually, the ride—it unwinds him." Living as little as possible in the doctor's Fifth Avenue apartment, May was always a bit guilty at the separations during the week, the long drive back and forth she imposed on her husband on weekends.

"I took a pill. I heard nothing."

"Bah on pills. Do not approve."

"I don't especially myself."

"Then why do you . . ." She pushed at a chair idly. "Well."

Now?

Not yet.

"All the poisons are neutralized by the olive oil in my veins anyway. You know that." An old joke of Walter's.

May poured two cups of coffee. "Matty won't be up for hours and I

have errands to run in the village—you'll come with me, won't you? By
the time we get back, the bear will have emerged from his cave and we
can try lunch."

"I have to make the four-eighteen train back."

"I haven't forgotten. There'll be plenty of time." She glanced with
concern at the wall phone. "I just wish I could uncradle that. He has
patients whose idea of urgent is a lot different than mine. But there's
nothing I can do. The poor man."

While driving the doctor's dough-colored BMW, May continued to
have telephones on her mind.

"I did do that with Walter once—leave it off the hook for days."

"Weren't people, though, pretty good? We knew not to call and disturb."

"Yes, you, but not everyone. There were people less intimidated. I'll
never forget how he stormed once. Someone called, I don't remember
who. I wasn't around, neither were the kids—so he had to take it himself. Did he give it to us later! That was the period when he was wearing
the eyepatch. *The Caballa. Contraction. The Vessel.* Staring at the picture for hours at a time—"

"The concentration ordered and *dis*ordered the perspective."

"I know, I know, but he really got on us. And that was a short period,
all told; he complained about the phone before and after it, too. So finally one day I did something about it. My God, he squirmed. But he
couldn't say anything. I was telling this to Marc Bassine of the Met a
few weeks ago. If they could figure out a way to exhibit Walter's life-
style, his image of himself, then they'd have his greatest, most carefully
done creation."

Anthony kept deliberately silent. He didn't want to endorse her approach. Reject Walter completely, or else cherish him; do him in *(as I
have?)* or leave him be. But not this shallow chipping away at the base
of a sphinx.

While May shopped in the drugstore Anthony sat in the car. At this
middling early hour, most of the village stores were still closed, fortify-
ing his long-held impression of the town as a basically unserious place.
Two black plastic garbage bags outside a stained-glass-windowed bar
caught the pure shore light in an angry luster. May stopped at the car to
drop off a small white bag and a newspaper for Anthony. "Or you can
come with me into the A & P."

Health so constantly on his mind, Anthony didn't want to be tempted into looking, alone, into the drugstore bag; he got out of the car. The supermarket was an old one. Wooden floors stank of soured milk. By the dairy case someone gripped his elbow: "Here to visit May?" It turned out to be Larry Rogg.

Rogg, in the old days, had been the manager of the Template, a jazz club on Third Avenue, now long closed; he had also picked up extra money by illegally tapping gas lines for painters, twenty-five bucks a shot to run a loft's meter into that of the closest neighboring factory. He went on eventually to become a well-known record producer.

Bronzed and wiry, he was smiling down with pride at his boy-child—five or six years old, beautifully dark-eyed, who was banging himself against a fatherly knee while busily pointing to and counting the containers of sour cream in the dairy case. "Noah, say hello to Tony."

The child peered up. "Hello, Tony. Hello, Tony. I'm a parrot. Hello, Tony, Hello, Tony." He went back to his count of sour creams.

Holding a wire basket containing packages of chicken, May joined them, and Rogg extended an invitation for drinks over at his place that afternoon. Speaking only for himself, Anthony declined. Noah had skipped off and was being given a ride on the conveyor belt by the checkout girl. Rogg and Anthony reminisced briefly at the cash register—a brawl at the Template which Monk played straight through, undisturbed—and then the four of them were outside, May kissing Noah goodbye, the boy asking the same of Anthony.

May said in the car, "Have you ever met the second wife? Maxine. He's so rich now—they've got two other houses aside from the one out here—but she keeps it remarkably simple. Nice girl. I doubt she's even twenty-five."

"The first wife I knew a bit."

"Chris."

"Wasn't she killed?"

"They had just separated a week before the crash. Imagine the guilt—but look at him now. The terrible things that are introduced into people's lives, and that they then go on and disarm—it perpetually amazes me."

Anthony was thinking a little about Noah. Rogg was six or seven years younger than himself—he had fathered Noah, then, at forty-four, forty-five. Oh for a child of his own, a little daughter: blonde, sweet, dependent. Blonde was unlikely—but sweet and small and dependent.

Anthony lamented for himself: the needlessness! The truth was that the only thing he'd ever loved enough in the world to foster was his own capacity for sacrifice.

They had left the village. They were on a two-lane road that periodically scratched against the beach, the margin of the greytop salted by dunespill. The hard light tired the eyes. May said the next stop would be the last, and quick: "My lawyer's. Ted Poitras."

A trap? Anthony's groin tightened automatically, although it was too improbable: the bad feelings between widow and ex-dealer ran too deeply too long; what besides could Mallelieu have told her without incriminating himself?

"Don't you use whatshisname in the city anymore: Hendel?"

"For the estate—of course. I'd be lost without Sy. Ted is our man out here: you have to have a local lawyer. Years ago we bought a large lot in Sag Harbor, which we let sit. Now Matty and I want to dispose of it. I hate to tell you what sort of filthy price it looks like we're going to get for it, too."

Tell me, Anthony thought. Tell me a half-million dollars; to know that money like that floats around freely, valuelessly, that every asshole and his monkey had it to spend for an acre of sand, would give Milan an even greater dignity by perspective.

"Walter told everyone it was his choice for us to originally build in town like we did and not on the ocean. But actually it was mine. He first liked the idea of a beach house. He said it would be good for seascapes—as if he'd ever cared about them. He never painted from nature. He had said it simply to pressure me, as a test. Counting on me to say no, but that goes without saying."

They were turning left beside a yellow and white house surrounded by shore bush and dwarf pines. May continued down an elongated driveway and, after swinging around, stopped at a bungalow-like outbuilding, the lawyer's office. "I should be no more than fifteen minutes. Matty had an even better FM put in, so play it, don't worry about the battery."

Parked in the sun, the car grew warm inside. Anthony turned, getting on his knees to move the paper sack with the chicken out of the direct sunlight on the back seat and onto the floor. As he faced front again, about to fool with the knobs of the Blaupunkt, the back door of the main house opened and out waddled an elf in a blue snowsuit with peaked hood, heading straight for the car.

Anthony rolled down his window, the cold air an absolution. "Hello, button. What's your name?"

The small mouth on the tiny swaddled girl's face opened, a perfect O, but no words came out.

"Tony's my name. What's yours, sweetheart?" He looked to the back door of the house but could see no one there.

What happened next took all of half a minute.

With a rush more like a stumble than a run, the little thing beelined for the right front tire of the BMW. And her mouth, which had yet to close, clamped itself to the tread.

"Don't do that!" Anthony immediately cracked open his door—at the same moment that a young woman in a housecoat was tearing from the house, clutching up the bundled child, stashing her under an arm, and running back inside with her.

Anthony was unaware of May's return until he heard her say: "You moved the chickens to the floor. Thank you."

"Did you see—?"

She held up a hand for him to wait. "Your window is open."

"We heard you shout," she said once they were again on the road, "and we saw through Ted's office window. Ted doesn't even blink anymore. That was Sarita. Who's eight."

"How can that possibly be."

"Eight. Mentally, eight months. So they're all not Noah Roggs, you see—I was watching your face in the supermarket. You can also get a Sarita. You take what you get and love them no matter."

"*Eight!*"

"It takes a certain simplicity of spirit—pardon the word—to be a really good parent. Not everybody can do it. Walter never was an honest man with me—"

Anthony looked at her through a corner of an eye.

"—Candid, yes, but that's something else. Once, though, he really let me see inside. Paul was having some trouble in school, the third grade; the teacher sent us a note to come in. I had to threaten to leave him if he didn't go with me, but he went. Complaining that the school building was depressing, a prison (the Henry School: some prison)—and just before we found where the classroom was he said to me that he probably would have been happier with one of those pictures of Indian kids. Do you understand what he meant? He meant those magazine ads, Save The Children, you support a poor child with a monthly donation.

"Tell me, was I destroyed when he said that? I wasn't. I was just surprised that he even noticed those ads. I know very well that he suffered over failing the kids as a father—"

"Do Denise and Paul think that, that he failed them? Why are you so sure?" He couldn't help his annoyance.

"All fathers fail, Tony. Didn't yours? Mine did. And look at Matty. His boys love him, but you would have to say that the good times are when the level of mutual disappointment is dormant. Otherwise he hardly ever hears from them." Driving back again through the village at reduced speeds, May waved to an occasional someone she knew. "I'm not saying that you wouldn't make a good father. A better one than Walter, that I know. You're different."

Craven curiosity controlled him for a moment, long enough to ask.

"Less ego," May answered. "Less inflexibility."

"Less talent," he corrected. "More cowardice."

May thought about it. "Maybe. I'm not sure."—her sometimes terrifying frankness.

Matty was standing on the porch as they got out of the car. "I was just about to go call a lawyer," said the burly doctor. He was dressed in both halves of a jogging suit like the one May had worn last night and a pair of eyeglasses hung from a chain around his neck. "I figured the two of you ran away together on me. You leave me with not even a newspaper, no way of knowing how much money I lost yesterday—pffft, you're gone, and my marinade sits with nothing to marinate but itself. Good to see you, Tony. How've you been?" He peeked inside the bag Anthony was holding. "Nice birds. You did good."

Later, while Matty built a fire in the grill, Anthony sat with him out in back of the house. In defiance of the thin, chilly air, the zipper of the jogging suit top was pulled three-quarters of the way down, exposing a scramble of silver-grey curls upon the doctor's square chest. "You never bought out here, Tony—any reason?"

"A down payment alone would empty me."

"Not now, of course not now—now's crazy. I meant then."

"I suppose it was possible, but the big boys bought; the rest of us rented."

"May likes to remember the softball games."

"Simpler days."

"Better ones, probably," said the doctor.

"I don't know." Strong, errant winds were blowing the charcoal smoke in every direction; Anthony hunched, slightly chilled, and Matty zipped his jacket fully closed.

"Two mules, May and me. We won't admit summer's over. Go inside, Tony. Help May. I'll be in in a second."

May refused assistance and steered Anthony into the living room, where she left him alone. An afternoon fire had been started in the grate. He couldn't for anything remember Walter ever sitting in this bare room. In the kitchen, upstairs, on the porch—but never in here. This was advantageous. Memory ought to be as strict and stylized as a police lineup. You can see them. They can't see you back.

May could demythologize all she wanted—I still forgive him everything. Solely because he's dead and far. And I wish for the same courtesy from him, on the same cross-territorial grounds.

Toward the end of lunch, before coffee, Matty sent an eyebrow signal to May, and she gave it flatly back. Hands on his thighs, the doctor said, "We ought to talk something over, Tony."

The paternal tone—out of the blue—sent fishbone apprehension up the back of Anthony's neck.

"I spoke to a colleague of mine this morning, while you were out. About Judith. This man is down at the NIH in Bethesda—"

"Explain what that is," May ordered. "What the initials are."

Anthony said he already knew—National Institutes of Health.

Matty said, "I explained the case, the history—everything that Saul Wellitz told me." May was glancing at Anthony culpably. Matty went on: "When May called me yesterday to say you were coming out, I took the liberty of phoning Saul—we interned together at Bellevue, you know."

"No, I didn't."

An edgy May said, "Who cares?"

"Anyway, I gave this chap Stanton, down at NIH—who's as brilliant an oncologist as they come, take my word—the exact presentation Saul gave me. We of course all know what the most serious hitch has been all along: the fact that the initial treatment given her was not as skillful as you and I would have liked—"

May broke in dryly again. "The way you put it to me was that it was inept."

"It wasn't up to standard," Matty conceded. "Small hospitals often don't have the equipment, don't know the fine points of a modality. But big hospitals, you know, can be ignorant too, can miss—"

"Don't excuse," May directed.

"In any case, this isn't what's important now, what was. She was treated; it didn't do what it might have; her tolerance for radiation was reached; there's no looking back." Deeper color had come to Matty's face, like a tint of his great decency. "Saul tells me that you already know—he says he told it to you in person—that she's gone into Stage Four. You also know that there is some opportunity even for Stage Fours to be greatly palliated, even good remissions. It's harder when the disease becomes invasive like it has, but some of the new drugs have been known to hold it. You would be surprised how often."

Anthony listened, staring down into his lap. The time was wasting: he had only about two hours. "Some of these drugs you mention were developed in Italy, weren't they?"

"I really couldn't say—not my field, remember. But to get back to this man Stanton, at NIH. If you can imagine a medical seminary—it's a little bit like that down there. There's a section for leukemias and lymphomas only—and, oh, before I forget: it would be totally free.

"Because it's free, though, there's normally only a fifty-fifty chance of being accepted in. I know this is going to sound terrible to you"— he eyed May defensively as well—"but the case has to be interesting enough for them. Stanton, though, told me that he would need only about a week's notice—she'd be in."

May had Anthony pinned with a caustic stare—*Do the right thing for a change*—as Matty went on: "Two things that you and Judith must know, though. On a ward, it's strictly inpatient. I know she likes her freedom to come and go—"

Could they know that J. had left him? People were frequently on to more than you gave them credit for. And held invisible cudgels.

"—and this would be locking up a big chunk of her time. Open-ended," he added significantly.

Pebbly sounds all at once began to come from May, squeaks which she tried to mask as throat clearings, a hand against her stringy neck like a choker.

"The other thing to keep in mind is that it's an experimental ward. Now what does that mean? It means that, once she's there, they are either going to try totally new drugs on her or else variations on ones already tested. This isn't kept a secret—she'll have to sign a paper beforehand which spells out her 'assent and comprehension.' I can tell you now: it isn't easy to read. But, although he couldn't absolutely promise, Stanton did say he would do his best to see that she not be enrolled in randomization trials."

May hawked, reaming her throat violently in order to recover her voice. "Do you know what that is?" she asked Anthony. Now the doctor's wife, and before that the painter's—twice married to bearers of strong news; and both times herself the ombudsman, the translator, the go-between.

"No, I don't," Anthony said. (By now, probably only an hour and three quarters.)

Matty explained. "Clinical trials sometimes involve giving one treatment to Patient A, another to Patient B, and none at all to Patient C. Then you see which worked best against the nontreated control. They call that randomization."

Revolted, Anthony nodded anyway.

"Stanton assures me that he'll track her only into what's in her welfare first and foremost. But look, it's going to be very rough, tougher than anything yet, and it should be considered in light of what your choices now are. Saul Wellitz, as far as I'm concerned, is a great man—no such thing for him as too much effort. This NIH deal, though, would have to be seen as extraordinary, heroic treatment—with the risks being equal to that. The power of some of those damn drugs . . ." Matty ran the meat of palm pensively over his chin. "Think of it as a long long shot, and *please*"—both his hands flew anxiously up— "whatever you two decide, don't for one minute feel you have to do anything on my account. I made a phone call, that's it: you're in no way obligated. This isn't like me telling one of my heart patients to go away for Cape Cod for two weeks. It's not easy, by-the-book advice."

A corner of the tablecloth was rolled around Anthony's two first fingers on his right hand; he unshrouded them so that he could point at Matty. "As far as I'm concerned, you're the great man."

This did May in. The throat clickings, wetting swallows, the sinusy echoings all solidified into a woeful groan; her chair was shoved back; she left the room with a face hot and messed.

Matty watched her go. Built-up pressure was meanwhile starting to arch up inside Anthony; his lungs had begun to feel dangerously light and dried, like right before laughter.

"The shittiest part, of course," Matty said, a quiet coda, "is that they're young. Either they're denied a chance at a life completely—or, like your girl, the life they've worked so hard to develop is spoiled early."

"She manages." Anthony was solemn—Signore Terrezza, in the melodrama *Addio, dolce svegliare.* "People are managing animals."

Only then did a door slam, one high up in the house—May must have first listened a while.

Matty raised his eyes. "Apparently no coffee for us. Not that I really wanted anyway. You? No." He stood up and began clearing the table.

Anthony didn't help, he did not move, debating whether or not to ask the doctor what he knew of Italian cancer research. But then, remembering randomization, it came to him that there was no need anymore to ask anything further. His mind was firm and set. In Milan, who would bother with—understand even, make the slightest sense of— "randomization"?

Now. It was time. The sensation of owning more air than could be accommodated in his chest was floating him to his feet and lifting his legs consecutively as he went by the open door of the kitchen—Matty sitting at the table in there reading a medical journal, a hint of damp eyes?—and to the stairs.

In the guest room Anthony opened his suitcase to remove the carefully padded package. He loosened the wrapping. Leaving the room with the package in hand, he walked down the hall and then up the three small steps to the sub-attic.

No answer to his knock—but he went in anyway. May was sitting at her desk. A small high-intensity lamp, the kind he had no love for, burned there; daylight was still in the room, but it was turning to tea. May, facing the wall, didn't turn around even as he took a seat on an angular chair he remembered as once having belonged to the porch.

Anthony rested the padded package on the floor, against a file cabinet. The room was functional: the chairs they sat in, the files, no books, an aged office typewriter on a grey steel stand. The dormer windows were all uncurtained and from the north two it was possible to see a colloidal dab of the sea.

May's shoulders started to make small, hunching motions, then stopped. She stroked her cheeks. "I'm sorry," she said to the wall. Her voice wore through patchily.

The hit man emptied his barrel for good measure. "I wish you knew her better—only those few times we've gotten together. I feel unworthy of her, May. She makes it seem—the time she has, how she fights for a little more—as if it's only a matter of perfecting her attention."

Rended, May wailed, "And *isn't* it?" She raised a hand, erasing her outburst from the air. "Don't tell me anymore." She gazed at a window.

The swivel chair squeaked as she turned. "What's that?" She pointed to the package on the floor. "I hope I already know."

Anthony took hold of the package and brought it to his lap. He unwrapped the two unframed canvas boards, getting up to set them on the back sill of May's desk. His hands shook just a little, not badly.

She looked at them without curiosity. "I thought so. Good. Good." She started to cry again, then caught herself. "You think I'm bitter . . . ?" She let it pass.

She was studying the paintings more closely now. "I don't remember these at all. I suppose that's a good sign. What do they say? that if you can't forget you'll never amount to much? There's hope for me yet maybe. I only wish I could get you to do some forgetting also."

She took one up in her hands. "These did something for him—because otherwise why would he have bothered? But I tell you, it torments me to think of the collateral he put up in exchange. Denise, Paul, me, you. Look at these. Look at these.

"You have nothing to say? Maybe I am bitter. It's better than what you've been—responsible. Are you still going to be responsible to him now? Are you going to worry about this? You are, I'm afraid you are. They're beautiful, but so what—Judy is more beautiful. You're going to have to bypass—I'm sorry to have to say it—your masochistic nature. Is Fred Mallelieu selling these for you?"

Heart in his throat, Anthony borrowed a voice. "No. I think I have a buyer lined up myself. I've already sold another."

"Years ago."

"No, just recently."

"Well, I hope you weren't stupid. I hope you robbed them, and that you rob whoever on these, too." Throwing her head back, she shut her eyes and inhaled deeply. She opened her eyes. "I assume you need letters." Pulling at a drawer in the desk, she took hold of a note pad and a portfolio of stationary. "What years are these?"

"Both nineteen fifty-four." Anthony stiffly accepted the note pad. For a moment the titles he'd made up and put on the pictures, and the dimensions, wriggled from his memory; but he recaught them, jotting them down on the paper with his own pen. He handed the pad back to May, who meanwhile had taken both pictures and laid them flat on the desk.

"The paint is so fresh. He used to say he was philosophically opposed to technique. Who can count the things he said that weren't true, that he knew weren't true? Go. Take them," she said, swivelling away. "I don't want to see them anymore."

Fifteen minutes later she knocked on the door of the guest room. Drained and dazzled by unsureness, Anthony was sitting on the bed, his packed and closed suitcase beside him. He had spent the time trying strenuously not to think.

"Here." May handed him a sealed envelope. "Menopausal women come apart, you know, and they have to be indulged. Come downstairs. Matty is all ready to drive you to the station. I'll come along too."

Anthony asked that his lightning visit not be held against him.

May leaned over and kissed his cheek, then rubbed the kiss away with a thumb. Tears started in her eyes again.

"This is all—no more after this—but please just let me. If Walter can be pardoned, the only one who has to do it is me. Not you. You can't afford to give him any more of your time. He's taken more than enough. Let me be the widow, all right?"

PART THREE

At the Sun

12

A painty gloss still was on the parking lot stripes of the new Mall and over every store was a fresh unbroken facing—like a brow—of shiny plasti-cedar shingling. The small parking lot-side windows bore signs advertising back-to-school and pre-ski sales.

Jack drove to the western end of the Mall, turned right, and right again. There, in back, were the construction trailers he'd hoped to find, sharing the mud with a stray backhoe, a tractor, humps of excess steel mesh piled up like ocher biscuits of shredded wheat. Jack stopped the car, got out, and climbed the wooden steps to the management trailer.

Inside—browned blue carpeting, space dividers, yellow hard hats resting on bare, veneer desks—all was silent and deserted. Yet the door hadn't been locked. "Anyone here?"

Silence.

Jack knocked atop one of the veneer desks.

A flash of yellow behind a corner partition. Jack took a flinching step or two backwards toward the door.

"Jackson?" The yellow, swarming forward, proved to be Pellegrino, in matching daffodil golf cap and windbreaker, checked madras slacks of mustard and green. "I thought I heard that door open. I peeked out. Could it be? It is!" Coming at Jack with arms wide, he nonetheless stopped two feet short; rather than a hug, there was a pull-pump of Jack's hand in both of his. "Hey, can't you do any better? You only look one hundred and fifty percent perfectly healthy."

"And you: one hundred and fifty percent filthy rich."

"Taken a tour inside yet? Now that the atrium's finished, and the fountain, I've got to say it myself: it is pretty. Up to a long walk?"

"Can walk, can talk, can fix, can rent, can manage properties—" Jack checked his overeagerness. That could wait.

"Been back long?" Vic asked.

"Just since yesterday. Who, by the way, is this Burke person, across the hall from me now?"

Vic straddled a desk corner. "I can't get over how good you look. Like nothing had gone on. How long are you up for?"

Jack was surprised. "For good. Permanently. I'm back. I called you last week, left a message, but— So, anyway, whatever happened to my old neighbor, the Asian. Back to Pakistan?"

"Asian neighbor," Pellegrino repeated pensively, with obviously no idea who Jack meant.

"Tariq Qazi."

"What? Oh. Hm. Asian . . . You know, I'll tell you the truth, Jacko: you know that I don't think I know? I'm way out of touch with anything about the Slope. The office has been taking care of all that. But if you're curious about your friend, I can find out from Tracy"—he leaned sideways, almost flat to the desktop, and touched a distant phone.

Jack called him off with a headshake. "Not important. Who's been doing maintenance for you, by the way, while I was gone?"

Vic plucked at his creases. "I signed on some firm up to Syracuse, and they subcontract out local men by the hour, different ones for different jobs."

"Sounds bulky."

Pellegrino nodded, but said, "It's worked out so far."

Clutching at reasonableness, Jack said, "As a stopgap, sure. Of course, they can't be all that familiar with the properties . . ."

Pellegrino confessed ignorance with two opened hands. "There again, the one to really ask is Trace. She's been in charge of the day-to-day."

"And will, I'm sure, be glad to pass off the headache." Jack could see now that it had been a miscalculation on his part: his surprising people in the flesh like this. He had wanted to savor every sinking turn of himself back into the core of things, but other people apparently required more warning. Proof of that was in Vic's overbright stare, his ossified grin. "I'm all set and ready to go again, Vic. I wanted you to know."

"Well, when that contract runs out . . ."

"That'll be when?"

"Eight months more? A year? You can see how much on top of things I've been. If it doesn't have to do with that big monster out there"—pointing in the Mall's direction—"I'm at a disadvantage. I drive up here in the morning, I look at it—you know, I still don't believe it's not a mirage, that it's actually—"

"That's an unusually long contract, isn't it?"

"Is it? I'll tell you: Tracy will know specifics." Pellegrino listed almost flat again, a hand on the desk phone. "Maybe it's less time, maybe more, but if anyone's going to know, it'll be her. Hold a sec."

Leveller than he would have ever imagined himself to be in these circumstances, his anger stunned as quiet as the rest of him, Jack said,
"Why don't you show me your Mall first?"

Nesby, always a little deaf, didn't raise his eyes as Jack entered the manager's office. The secretary outside being nowhere around, Jack had been able to walk right in. The *Courier* was spread out on the desk, and Nesby was eating a meat sandwich as he read.

"Lunch, Hank?"

Nesby's small brown eyes rose and grew wider by the moment, fixed on Jack. "They always do this to me. No messages. No one tells me anything . . . So how are you doing? You look pretty good. I wish they'd give me a little warning . . ."

He lifted the sandwich in order to close the newspaper. "See the job Clara did of getting everything of yours in boxes? Are you going to want help taking them out to your car? Not too many people around; I guess I could give you a hand . . ."

Jack said, "So I've been fired, too. Bonsell and Richmond."

Nesby clambered out of his chair, looking thoughtfully at what remained of his sandwich and rewrapping the foil around it. "Edward wasn't terminated. He was reassigned to Eau Claire. Three months ago. Why do they leave this all up to *me?*—it isn't right. Here, you sit here and call New York: best thing." Lifting his lunch in the sling of the *Courier,* he came round the desk and made for the door. "You won't be disturbed."

Jack didn't bother sitting. As the switchboard girl put him through to corporate headquarters, he looked out Bonsell's—now Nesby's—window, at the niggardly view: an oval patch of blue-dyed gravel, three evergreen shrubs planted in its center, and the windows of another office not five yards away. It swam, the whole it, in the blanching, dulling Delphi light.

Fewer cars were parked in the plant's entire lot when Jack drove in than there had been waiting in front of the Grand Union at the Mall. The smokestacks were plumeless; inside the office wing, half the desks sat unused, typewriters and adding machines snoozing beneath their dour grey hoods.

"Jack! Hey!" It was Phil Cincotto first on the line, V.P. for Operations and a sharpie only a few years older than Jack. "In the city for the day? Could you manage lunch?"

"I'm in Delphi, Phil. You remember Delphi."

"It's all right, Phil, let me take this," succeeded another voice quick-ly, either on a different extension or the same conference box. "Jack, it's Ed Haxlin. Good to hear from you."

Haxlin was First Vice President and Chief Officer. Jack sat down in Bonsell's—Nesby's—chair, turning away from the detestable view.

Haxlin asked whether Jack wanted the situation in a nutshell. In March, the entire Delphi operation had come up for review—Jack's good memo as a basis—and it was then decided unanimously to close down all productive capabilities in order to convert the site to a North-east distribution center of precartoned plasticware.

A line operation was still extant at Eau Claire, if Jack felt really strongly that he needed to be involved in a plant milieu; but, frankly, it would be cramped. And of course they all understood that Jack wouldn't have a taste for HQ anymore, once having been out in the field. About Eau Claire: Haxlin couldn't honestly say, though, what kind of medical care Jack might count on out there—that certainly being a major factor in Jack's decision, right? One way or another, of course, the remaining two months of leave benefits Jack was entitled to would still be forthcoming, and whenever he needed anything along the lines of letters of reference and recommendation, he knew that he just had to sing out, didn't he, and it would be taken care of.

On a Monday afternoon (a Tuesday?), Jack heard noises out on the land-ing. It was not the paper boy, who had already come and gone. This was someone else. This had to be one or both of the as yet unseen Burkes.

Jack hadn't left the apartment to go downstairs and outside for days; the Burkes he'd heard coming and going before, but to no great interest of his. He'd eaten Chunky Chicken or Chunky Beef Soup night after night. Contact with the outer world was kept minimal: a call from Ir-win; one from someone named Nestora, a fellow-Twelve-Thirty-Clubman who said he'd seen Jack the week before at the Delphi Mall and was wondering if Jack would consider appearing on a local TV pro-gram about beating cancer (put that way, it was difficult, unlucky, to refuse; and if he went on, it might show them a thing or two over at Scofield; and, a day before, he'd cancel out anyway—so why not? and he'd said, "Sure"); one to Judith for more grass, his baggie was low. He smoked morning, noon, and night. Empty days spent rolling deadened patches of irradiated skin off his chest and into clayey cylinders, sleep at night that felt like dehydrated waking.

But now he decided that he wanted a look at his neighbors, the Burkes. He rose off the Hollywood bed slowly, his timing distinctly off, seconds either feeling too gaping or too pinched. Likewise, when he got to the door, he opened it too soon.

He'd only wanted a glimpse of Burke backs, as they descended the stairs or entered their apartment. But instead now he caught them on the landing, still occupied with the business of keys. They turned to look at Jack.

The woman, Mrs. Burke (the first thing about her Jack noticed was her wedding band—an indication of the wantonness of his stoned attention), was freckled, red-haired, pretty. But Mr. was a buzzardy longhair; where she wore the business clothes of a breadwinning secretary, he had on a tie-dyed over-the-waist shirt and a pair of gauzy, billowy pants.

Both of them were smiling at Jack with demure knowledge.

His dope fumes were filling the landing, he realized only then.

For the Burkes that stood as introduction enough. They knew him now. They grinned mellowly, and so thereby he knew them as well. A little generational transaction.

With gawky overemphasis, Jack made as though he'd come out only to see if the paper had arrived at his doorstep—looking down avidly, snatching it up—and then he slammed the door shut, scalded by those we-gotcha grins.

Tracy, at the realty office downtown, looked confused. "Does Vic . . . ?"

Jack pointed to one of the empty desks in the office. "This one here all right?"

Tracy said, "I guess," dubiously. She examined her crimsoned thumbnail minutely. "Mornings, you know, Jack, are usually pretty d—not much to do. Would it be better if you maybe came back after lunch, you think? You're going to be so bored."

"The discipline will be good for me," Jack answered. "I hear you've been doing a great job, taking over the Slope."

Tracy looked around the office purposelessly. "Would you like to see the newspaper, Jack? I'm finished with it."

"No, but I tell you what I wouldn't mind seeing: the contract with the maintenance firm in Syracuse. You have that handy?"

Jack himself understood how unfair this was; and Tracy, beset, was chewing at the inside of her mouth by now. "Vic has all that sort of paper over at the Mall with him."

"No, I don't think so. He told me you were keeping it."

"Mmwhh . . . Jack . . . I don't—excuse me"—eyes doubled in size by worry, she picked up the ringing phone. "VIP Realty, good morning. No, I'm sorry, we have nothing that's open at the moment. But if you give me your name and number I'll make a note of it. We'll be in touch with you as soon as anything comes free. That's right. Yes. Thank you for calling."

She put down the phone, which then rang again a second later. Jack made urgent motions to Tracy that he wanted to take this one.

"VIP, Richmond speaking." Tracy, pocketbook in hand, was getting up from her desk and heading toward the back of the office, to the washroom. Jack noticed another button light up on his phone; craning around, he saw Tracy standing by the last, furthest back desk, dialing.

"I'm sorry," Jack said to the caller. "None at the moment. But I tell you what—why don't you give me your name and number. When something opens up, you'll be the first one I call. A promise." He wrote the girl's name and telephone number down on a blank file card, which he pushed into his shirt pocket—the start of a client's list of his own. "Great."

The phone didn't ring for a while after that. Tracy was staying in the washroom a long time. Soon the front door opened from the street and in walked Vic Pellegrino.

"Boy, like old times," Vic said, very cheery. The toilet at the rear of the office flushed, the washroom door opened, Tracy was marching back to her desk, eyes on her shoes. "You two been having fun? I was saying, Trace, that it's like old times. Doesn't he look great?" Pellegrino touched his own belly. "I'm hungry. I haven't had any breakfast yet. Come keep me company, *paisan.*"

Jack, on the street, immediately had peeled off west, toward the Hearth; whereas Vic instead went in the direction of his car. "No, they changed owners while you were gone," he said, opening the door of his Riviera. "It's not the same. I know a place."

They drove directly out of town. "The Hearth isn't the only place to fold. God, business is bad." Pellegrino said he wondered if he'd picked the right time to go and open the Mall. The writing was on the wall as far as the economy went. Stores out on the Mall, once the novelty wore off, were going to have to fight tooth and nail to stay afloat. He said he tried never to kid himself—it looked like a long hard time ahead. "They use the word slowdown, but every businessman knows it's just a fancy term for depression. You've had more pressing things on your mind than to read the financial pages, but it's damn scary."

Pellegrino said that he had pretty well decided to let go of all his Slope properties. "I'm not making a cent." So what, then, honestly, would that leave Jack—a percentage of not a cent? "The world is going insane. That bunch in Syracuse, the maintenance contractors: they wouldn't even hire Karlyn—he's back, by the way, couldn't stand living with his children. They said no, only the subcontractors on their list." The whole thing, he said, was a headache; the minute he could get out he would. Real estate had seen better days in this town.

Jack asked to be let off at home.

"If you ever get really strapped, Jack: please. And, look, about the truck: use it for a while if you need it. Whenever it's convenient, just drop it and the keys off at the Mall. Hey, and stop in to say hello to Mamma sometime—she asks about you. She'll cook you up some ziti."

How much could he smoke? The whole contents of what was left in the baggie rolled into one great joint? Or tiny snufflings, on the half hour every half hour?

And where now should he live? In Delphi? Or go back to Bethpage (taking with him, stealing, Pellegrino's goddamn truck)? But what then would he do with his own car, the Valiant? How did he come to have cancer, no jobs, no place in which to comfortably live, and two vehicles to get there in?

Jack slept eighteen hours, and awoke knowing what to do. First thing: go get his car, which he'd left still parked near the realty office downtown on Main Street. He set out on foot. He'd never walked the streets of the Slope high before, and they came up interestingly beneath him. No one else was abroad at six in the morning on Adams, on Burdell, on Cliff, on Woods—Woods!

At first Jack thought they might have moved. The coffee sheets of mimeograph stock were gone from the window, as were the photos of the Red apostles. Instead, covering every inch of the glass from inside were badly seamed-together sheets of contact paper, a stained-glass pattern. A white card was taped inside the door that Jack walked closer to read, noticing that the door too had been fitted inside with something to make it opaque: a sheet of green ribbed plastic. The white card was lettered plainly, by hand: NEW MORNING PRESS. PLEASE RING BELL.

To the side of the transom overhead, bolted into the masonry of the doorway, was an additional something new: a gunmetal box with vents. An alarm system.

Lights were on within the store. In the whole neighborhood of sleepers, of wasters-of-life, only Jack and Salco seemed to be up. Jack knocked; he couldn't find the bell the card referred to. There was no answer. A shadow moved—an adjustment of density through the milky ribbed plastic—but no one was opening up. Jack knocked again.

"Salco?"

Out of the corner of an eye Jack saw light; he turned just in time to see a half-moon flap cut from the inside contact paper close. Someone had peeked out to see who it was, peeked out and still wasn't opening up.

It was ludicrous. They were treating him like someone he no longer was.

"Salco, you poor bastard, why don't you just open up?"

Silence. Nothing.

"All right. Don't open."

Then, after he retrieved the Valiant and was driving back up the hill to the Slope, Jack changed his mind. It wasn't farcical. No, it made him furious. The only ones who took him seriously were these Trotskyites?

He was back the next day at six again. With him, this time in the truck, he had a thermos of coffee, a giant bomber of a joint, and his suitcase: he would leave directly from there for New York, scheduled for a clinic appointment tomorrow. He didn't drink the coffee and smoked only half the joint as he watched first a watered ink, then a dark coral, a manila, a tan, and finally some blue squeegee over the treetops along the adjacent campus. Rags of cold air enlivened his face through the half-opened window of the truck. Parked nose facing away from New Morning, Jack surveilled through the side mirror and the rearview.

A little before seven, a car—a lime Datsun—pulled up before New Morning and a man—it was Parmenteer—got out and opened the trunk. Someone else—Salco: Jack recognized the shallow drag of the right foot—came out of the storefront and stood at the edge of the doorway. Parmenteer meanwhile removed two shiny and industrial-sized cans from the trunk of the Datsun: solvent, or ink. Salco, bare chested, wearing no shoes, in only a pair of black corduroys that color-matched the heavy frames of his glasses, walked out to receive the cans, taking them inside.

Parmenteer got back into the car and drove off. Jack had jammed himself against the truck door, trying to catch a corner of the mirror that might let him see inside New Morning as Salco reentered, but it was impossible.

Jack waited ten minutes, then left the truck.

"Salco, it's Richmond again. Why not open a second? Just to give me the satisfaction. I don't have anything to do with you anymore."

Jack's cheek gradually come closer and closer to the glass window of the door, and finally was touching it, forehead and fingertips flattened. He took a certain cold peacefulness from the position. What he would do if Salco actually did open up he couldn't say. Hit him? Laugh at him? Offer him the other half of the joint? Simply stare dumbfoundedly at the odd, misconstrued pass his, Jack's, life had come to—and which Salco had a part in? Not a dier, not a liver— a what, then?

"One quick look inside, Salco. Unofficial. You have no idea how un-official. Come on. I'll wait here all day if I have to, because eventually you're going to have to come out. You can't stay locked in there for-ever—you'd suffocate, it would be dangerous. All those chemicals."

A volley of clicking tumblers—the door starting to slowly open—Jack had to straighten up fast. Salco, standing in nearly total shadow, said grimly from inside: "You can come in."

Two seconds too late it occurred to Jack that he might be hurt, beaten up, if he went in—but by then he was already inside, surrounded by walls painted the dark blue of a serge suit. Salco was resetting all the door locks. Nearest to the front was a rexograph machine and what looked like a small printing press. Running against one of the length-wise walls: a long, narrow banquet table, a typewriter at one end along with stacks of paper.

Salco remained busy: he went immediately toward the back of the store and pulled a folding screen across the width of the space. Before it disappeared, Jack was only able to make out a cot, a half-sized refriger-ator like the one in Donna's trailer in Priory, and on top of that what seemed to be a small jeweler's scale, and a clock radio.

Salco came back, to within three feet of Jack—where he stopped, crossed one shoe in the front of the other, and leaned his weight against a hand propped to the banquet table. He had put a shirt on before letting Jack in—white, buttoned up at the neck—and when he hopped his hand around the table edge, looking for a more comfortable yet still casually commanding posture, a roll of pudge hitched around his middle—surprising to Jack, who'd always pictured Salco as a severe collection of sharp black angles.

"We'll be out of here in a few weeks," the Trotskyite started in forlornly, "once we find another place. You should know, though, that we work for two—and later this week it'll be three—fully chartered student organizations, doing printing and getting paid out of student-fee monies disbursed through the office of the Dean of Students."

Jack gave it less than his full attention. The sight of Salco's living quarters in back was staying with him: a solitariness, a cut-offness Jack was able to understand too well. The stained-glass pattern of the paper pasted on the windows lent the light inside an indistinct, after-imagey color, pinpoints of red in the air as though behind a sun-insulted eyelid.

How did Salco live here day in and day out, only his zeal as company? The top copy of a stack of leaflets on the long table: *An Analysis of Student-Labor Bonding In The Formation Of A Communist Vanguard Party, With Special Attention to Workerist-Reformist Tendencies (Schwartz-Tallyism) And Why They Are Bound to Failure. By Comrade Len Salco. 50¢.*

"A best seller, I bet," Jack remarked, looking at some of the other leaflets as well. He was even beginning to feel oddly comfortable in here, like a monk who visits a strange yet affiliated cloister. "Do these actually pay for the groceries, though? I'm curious, sincerely. Something pays the rent."

Salco drew himself up more stiffly. His fingertips were pressing so tightly against the table that half his hand, heading toward the wrist, was blanching. "We do our work. We haven't done anything at all illegal. And as I said, we'll be gone by the end of the month."

Salco had begun to rock back and forth on his heels, and his urgent behavior was just starting to get through to Jack, whose grass-high and honeyed mood still, though, made no sense of it. "Do you all take the same course in paranoia, or is it self-study? I'm joking. Do you know if Trotsky had a sense of humor?"

"So any arson against us, first of all, would be against a University-sponsored entity. Secondly, there are often students in here—"

Then suddenly Jack remembered his call from Bethpage to Sleighlin.

The thought jumped up to the top of his mind and sat there like an atrocious bug . . .

"—and they'd be torched too, remember." From the back pocket of his corduroys, Salco was removing a folded sheet of paper. "This is a letter expressing our intention to move. A copy will also go to the *Observer*, which did the story about the fires. That way there'll be a record. We don't intend to be fried in here one night like that girl, and leave everyone only guessing who did it. Here."

Jack didn't—and couldn't—raise a hand. "Keep that. I don't know what you're talking about—what girl was fried where? What newspaper story?—and, anyway, I have nothing to do with anything anymore."

Salco, holding the paper, went to the front door, unlocking and opening it. Speedy daylight ran burning through the dim store.

"Really, I'm not involved with this anymore," Jack said, hearing an unmanned tremolo of pleading sneak up into his voice.

"You asked to be let in; you were; now you'll have to go." Salco, standing by the door, stuffed the letter into Jack's shirt pocket as Jack walked meekly, confusedly, by him and out.

The woman at the library's information desk was trimming folders with scissors, a task she apparently found soothing, because she seemed offended, her peace disturbed, by Jack's pressed and demanding barks of "Back newspapers! Where do you keep them?" She turned slowly, pointing her whole body in the direction of the newspapers.

The *Observer* was the student daily of the University, and each issue was thin, six or eight pages at most. Grabbing a hank of them was equal to months, months that Jack had been away and sick. President Mollon Nixes . . . Campus Cops Deny Onyx Fraternity . . . Dining-Service Firm in Audit . . . Is the Slope a Firetrap?

Not breathing, Jack rubbed his eyes along the letters. Police and fire officials attributed it to a burning candle knocked accidentally onto a sofa third-degree burns over ten percent of her body incurred while running back into the burning apartment to rescue her pets recovering at the home of her family in Buffalo *Observer* however had learned of a complaint filed by Ms. Zoeller five months earlier with the Delphi Hot Line charging harassment by the landlord's agent, but Victor Pellegrino, owner of building, denied Gowall concurred with the landlord's assessment of his and other Slope properties fire-safe can be categorical denial of any investigation being planned—

Sleighlin's office in the Savings Bank Building was dark—according

to the card taped to the door he was on vacation. In the lobby Jack called
the emergency number listed for Sleighlin's service. Did Jack want an
appointment with Dr. S.'s sub, Dr. Carter? He was very good, "a lot of
patients swear by him."

Being called a patient drew Jack's knees together momentarily. He
had to be in New York by tonight; the clinic began its day early, blood
taken at seven-thirty in the morning. A patient. Halved between having
a life and living it. As if you had to assemble your car from parts each
time you wanted to take a drive.

From a rest area alongside the highway, on his way to New York, Jack
again called Sleighlin, this time at home; the number was unlisted, but
Jack's voice alone may have convinced the operator that it was indeed
an emergency. No answer. Five hours later, haggard with dread, he
called again, from Bethpage—Irwin trailing after him like a dog, repeating over and over that he didn't like how Jack looked. Jack called Sleighlin twice more that night and then the next day from the hospital, before his checkup and after. Judith was supposed to meet him in the
coffee shop in the lobby at noon, but he had no time for that, he stood
her up.

He made Delphi again by six in the evening. The autumn nights
came on sooner, and lights were on inside Salco's still as yet untorched
New Morning. Jack pulled the truck over across the street and cut the
engine and lights.

Now, temporarily, he was safe. And if Salco came out and wondered,
Jack could explain: for your sake, for your sake, I'm doing it for you: go
back in, it's all right. But the cab was cold and Jack's eyelids felt stony,
like a part that was older than the rest of him. Hours of driving with
fear-rigid muscles now were backing up on him; he soon began to shiver. Putting the truck's heater on didn't much help. He would have to
go home. He would have to trust to luck, luck and will, that Sleighlin
would not creep up under the furry October night and do a terrible,
Jack-induced thing.

The next two days passed in a fumy mist of calling Sleighlin at home
every few hours and just as regularly driving or walking over to Woods
Street to check that there'd been no fire. Finally, late Thursday night,
the dentist's phone was answered after fifteen rings—and Jack nearly
folded in two with relief, hanging up without ever speaking.

The dentist turned the corner onto Main Street shortly before eight
the next morning. While waiting, Jack had bought himself a pack of
cigarettes at the smoke shop, smoking four of the Winstons in quick

succession (although he couldn't have said what they tasted like, what it was like to smoke again after all this time). Sleighlin, Jack saw as he made his move to head him off, had a tan; he was tanned even on the backs of his hands—and this for some reason was terrifying, it seemed to suggest a kind of cured and utter fullness to the man that Jack would never be able to counteract.

As soon as he was close enough, Jack began to blab uncontrollably. "That store on Woods Street I called you about? From New York a few weeks ago? They're not Trotskyites. I was wrong. They're a bunch of kids doing University-contract work. They're fine. Forget I ever said anything about them. No problem. They should be left alone."

But Sleighlin, saying "Isn't it a nice morning?" took him by the elbow and marched gently with him further down the street. "Ever at Hilton Head? Quite a place! We were down there this last week."

Jack refused to walk any more—he stopped under the marquee of the closed-down movie theater that was now used as a food co-op. The sidewalk in front smelled distinctly of the in-turning odors of old vegetables. "It's all off." (How to impress it upon this silverfish?) "No fire. I mean it. Really."

"I don't think I exactly know what was 'on'—but whatever you say. You were sick, I do know that. You're better now, though, right?"

After Sleighlin had turned around and left him, Jack pitched away the pack of Winstons and experienced a great urge to run. He told himself not to: running on the street alone always looked bad. Walk. Why run anyway? Everything now was settled. Still he wished he could run. And for the next three days, never emerging from the house, he still wanted to run. Had Irwin wanted to run this bad? Was that why he had plunked himself down on the floor of Penn Station, unable to move— because mere moving was a pale zero beside the need, the urge to run? He grieved for his father, he grieved for himself.

He grieved for Judith, too, when she showed up. Her phone call on a Thursday morning: "You're probably down to about nothing by now. Time for a delivery. And I miss you. I'll take the ten-thirty bus, if that's all right. Is it?"

She brought with her a new, full baggie. She wore a blue kerchief, in a style that was unflattering and made her look timid. She was sallow, pasty, yet her cheeks were sickly bright. With a lunatic casualness she admitted that she was getting treatment again, that she'd "slipped a notch."

They lay there together the first night, two time bombs. Jack didn't sleep, running over again in his head the whole of the last two weeks, the worst in his life—for this he had clawed to get well? Judith's hot and temporary body rose and fell beside him.

The next morning she asked what time the TV taping was scheduled for. He only vaguely remembered mentioning it to her; in fact, he'd forgotten until now about the whole thing. Then Nestora from the station called, a reminder—and there was no time, no space in which to back out.

The cameraman at the studio turned out to be Lex Parmenteer. Here is truly where I go crazy, Jack thought to himself—and while the show was going on, it frighteningly seemed to come true: all of a sudden he wasn't getting enough air to breathe, he had to stand up, he had to get out of there. Only outside, in the parking lot, did he feel himself just barely pop back in again, like a lid reestablishing a seal.

13

The father—whose name was Joe Sultan—was taking her by the hand, leading her to the middle of the floor, where he then knelt. Judith got down too.

"And last but not in any way least"—releasing her hand, Joe waved his fingers in the air with a flourish of glory-be—"SUPERKID! The one, the only—Carly!"

It made her shy. "Hello, Carly"—the scrapiest whisper.

The child, hugging himself and rolling side to side, slathered a smile on everything.

"Louder," Joe urged her. "Really tug at his attention."

His and also everyone else's in the room, but she reluctantly fed it a little more gas:

"Hello, Carly." Hello, little lump: blissful and couldn't-care-less-looking. Knolls of cream-white fat—or were they knobs of muscle?—bunched at the back of his little knees and neck. His elbows were chapped dove discs that looked like stale vanilla wafers. Something was the faintest bit blunt to his eyes and his nose, though perhaps not, possibly she was only imagining this, needing to find something visibly out of whack on his face, something pathetic. A mark that would explain why a five-year-old should be lying on the bare checkered linoleum floor of a nearly empty room, wearing only a diaper under a pair of rubber pants; and why three kneeling adults should be attending him. (Reminding Judith, in the way that they were all hunkered down and distributed around him, of something familiar—but what?)

Peter the hippie, sitting cross-legged and looking right at home, was massaging the child's back now; his nodding smile invited Judith closer, to lend a hand. She put two less than resolute fingers to the small indented spine, on the rounded levees of flesh to either side of it.

(Did she just now hear someone say "snake"? At the very moment she'd been thinking *how dry* and smothering the impulse to pull her hand away, repelled? But maybe it had only been "shake.")

"He likes you," Peter said, taking a handful of Carly-flesh at the thigh, jiggling it roughly. The boy cooed, giving out a long deep gastric razz. Then Peter flipped him over (which allowed Judith to stop desperately stroking) and rubbed an ear on the miniature potbelly. Carly cooed some more.

I like *you*, thought Judith, apropos the hippie. The fact that you have both long hair *and* a lined face. That you're compassionate and maybe a little dumb. And, mostly, that you call me. Not once but twice; wanting something—to enlist me in this—but that's still more than I can say about some other, sufficient-unto-the-day types: Anthony, Jack, now Huft—I can really pick them. Love the one you're with.

Getting back up, Joe Sultan helped Judith out of her crouch and walked her in the direction of a card table, one of two in the room, this one holding a coffee urn, a tray of pastries, paper cups, stirrers, and sugars. Two vacant folding chairs stood beside.

"Sit, help yourself to the goodies—we're going to run through a protocol or two to get warmed up. Great, isn't he? He took to you immediately. Once we start repeating, when you've seen it done a few times, in you'll come. Outtasight!"

He was short and very muscular, irregularly pigmented around the eyes with foldy branny dark rings. (Judith originally thought they were shiners, but who would ever hit the good-natured likes of him?) As was Peter, he was wearing overalls, white ones. And they were staying white: the linoleum was spotless. The whole house was.

She'd been so astonished when Peter first drove down the block: in the heart of very bad Lower East Side crumble, this row of manicured, one-owner Federals, stocked inside with *Times* readers and bicyclists and kids with private-school backpacks and bowl haircuts. According to Peter, some of his best clients in the city lived here.

The Sultans weren't among them—because, for one, Joe did his own carpentry. Until Carly came along, he had been (Peter told her) the most innovative industrial-arts teacher in the city high schools. For two: the house—at least the downstairs part of it that Judith was seeing—had little need for furniture. It was a palace of therapy, strictly functional. In one room (which had mats on the floor) stood an adjustable bar apparatus used for hanging and swinging exercises—and it stood alone. All there was in another room was a wooden slide (built by Peter, gratis) of the gentlest downslope. Every window was covered with a heavy green shade. And the flooring all through the house was the same: big ballroom checks of black and white linoleum. For visual stimulation, Peter said.

"People?" Joe was back on his knees in the middle of the room, facing Peter. Carly lay between them. "How about it, everyone?"

One of the two homely girls who'd been sitting with the mother, Ruth, at the other card table (which had no food on it, but a Christmas wreath on the wall above), put down a brochure she was looking at and said, "Coming, coming"; a big-hipped waddle brought her over to the others where, after folding herself down to her knees, she took up position behind Carly's head. She bent to kiss his forehead; Joe then kissed the right wrist, and Peter the left one.

The moving began. When the girl turned Carly's head to the right, Joe, on that side, would flex the boy's pudgy arm and pull the plug-like leg straight. Meanwhile Peter, across from Joe, did exactly the reverse: extending the left arm, bending the leg. When the girl pushed Carly's face in the other direction, the process reversed itself: Peter flexing arm and extending leg, Joe the opposite. Everyone was working as smoothly as pistons.

(That was it. What she'd been reminded of before. Carly looked like a carburetor or some other engine part that was being tinkered with by a ring of street mechanics—a sight she used to see on Anthony's block at least once a week.)

The girl who had remained at the other card table with Ruth the mother suddenly got up—"The water"—and left for the kitchen.

These were Ruth's students (of flute, Peter had explained). When Judith arrived, the three of them had been sharing a gaudy, knowing laugh: "Well, I'll tell you what always worked for me with Leonard, whenever he'd get too prissy," Ruth was telling the girls. " 'But Maestro' "—her voice pleating into that of a coquette—" 'what do I need *you* for if I'm not going to make a few mistakes?' "

"Mistake lib!" piped one of the girls. Both students, in their late teens, were overweight, of a steady, packhorse substantiveness. The one who'd gone to the kitchen had the most beautiful black hair Judith had ever come across (while the one now holding Carly's head was cursed with recalcitrant Brillo).

Ruth, the mother, was small and light haired, hard to assign an age to. She wore pink slacks, the cuffs and pockets edged in gingham check; around her neck hung a stopwatch attached to a braided lanyard. Harlequin eyeglass frames gave her face the look of someone who knew better and didn't care, as if some part of her remained angrily faithful to a simpler past.

Now she had gotten up and was coming toward Judith.

Stand up? Only smile? Small talk? "It looks like he enjoys it," Judith said. (Very poor.)

Ruth stirred sugar into her coffee while making severe, canopying motions with her upper lip. It was certainly not a smile. A pout then? Was she going to cry? "This is your first time here?" she said finally. Then more queer lip business—ah, of course, embouchure exercises!

"First, yes," Judith responded quickly. (In her own home, strange hands on the flesh of her flesh—and she doesn't keep track?)

Without much spirit, Ruth said, "That's good. Joe loves novices. When he taught, the first day of the term was his favorite: getting those sophomores. He'd hand them each a block of pine and tell them to hold it. All they did that whole first period—hold the wood. Speaking of which—" Abruptly, she turned and walked back to the other table across the room, yelling "Time," without consulting the stopwatch. She stooped to a box under the table and removed two blocks of wood, which she then went over and gave to the Brillo-haired girl on the floor. Peter and the father helped Carly onto his back again.

There was a tremendous rifle shot. The coffee in Judith's cup went lurching and the Italian cookie she'd been taking at that moment from the platter snowed powdered sugar all over her other hand.

The girl with the wood blocks was lifting them again, this time slightly behind and to the left of Carly. *Whaaacckkk!* The boy placidly and slowly craned his neck back.

From the doorway of the kitchen the other flautist announced: "Whenever you're ready, the water is." Peter, giving Carly a last belly kiss, lifted him up, hugged him, and handed him over to a waiting Ruth, who hustled him off. Both men, kicking out the knee kinks, then approached the refreshment table.

Judith, finished wiping off her fingers and checking her blouse for spills, asked, "Bathtime?" of the hippie—who looked down at her blankly. "Do you bathe him now?" she tried again, this time on Joe Sultan. (Peter's command of English, she saw, would be a problem. Did she have time to say things twice to somebody?)

But Peter had just got it: "Oh. *Bathtime* you said." He wrung out his ear, long hair undulating, glorious open smile. "The blocks."

Joe was pulling at her hand: "Go in and see the tactile stim."

"Anything I can give you first? Coffee? One of these nice cookies? One of these?" Whatever tactile stim was, she preferred to play hostess rather than have to stand up and move to go watch it. Peter was indicating something small and cream-centered—"One of those"—and she gave it to him, centered in a napkin nice and neat. "Joe, for you?" But Peter wasn't done: "Coffee, please," he ordered. "Black, one sugar." (A lord, like his pal Huft—who'd have thought?)

While this was going on, the crew from the kitchen returned, Carly in tow. Something distressing must have happened, because the girl with the wonderful obsidian hair had gone to the box that had held the wood blocks and out of it now was taking a clear plastic facemask attached to a thin cannister of oxygen. Ruth and the other student were sitting Carly upright on the floor, then helping the girl with the oxygen mask fit it onto the little boy's face.

Oddly, no one seemed in any great hurry—and Peter and Joe weren't even turning around. Judith was going to have to alert them . . . But, finally, Peter did happen to look—and then he went right back to finishing his gooey sweet. "For the brain, you see," he calmly explained.

Joe took a quick look back, then smiled. "*That's* why your expression changed so suddenly. I saw it in your eyes. Which are lovely, by the way." Balancing down on his haunches, he took her hand. "I'll explain. A normal brain receives oxygen according to need. An injured brain, though—we're not sure. So we supplement. We try to create as complete an awakening of normal instinct as we possibly can."

"Makes sense." (She wished he'd drop her hand.)

Stroking, stroking the hand, gazing intensely at her through his coon-ringed eyes: "The aim is to try and teach the hurt stage of that little fella's brain its own function, not just to condition his muscles to an exercise."

Over Joe's head she could see Ruth, standing, observing them. Carly now had been unmasked and left by himself on his back in the middle of the floor. The black-haired girl, at the other card table, was springing open the clasps of a velvet-lined instrument case; she removed and assembled a silver wand, and then issued a run of loud, creamed notes, a scale. Peter, putting down his coffee cup and pouching a last cookie inside his cheek, was going back to Carly. Finally letting go of Judith's hand, Joe went as well.

Another flute was out now across the room—Ruth's. Looking sharply at Judith, she blew a few flatted notes. Joe and Peter had resumed their previous positions at Carly's sides, and Joe was calling to Judith: "Lady needed at head! Lady needed at head!"

Did that sound dirty to anyone else? She was afraid to look over to

Ruth. And now it was too late to back out: though she didn't have the strength for it, she had to participate; she couldn't let Ruth think she'd come just to be someone Joe Sultan could make googoo eyes at. Pressing down hard on her thighs, Judith rose from her chair—a nervous upthrust that sent her back to the day of her level-three piano recital, when she was eleven ("Miss Judith Kornbluh, who is going to play 'The Shepherd's Lullaby' by Moselli. Judith."). Then as now, some of her stomach remained seated. But she pressed on, heading for the middle of the floor. (Was it just her imagination, or had the female flutes at the side of the room struck up a mocking march?)

Carly was lying face down, nose mashed to the linoleum, making content, humming sounds. "You saw what Berta was doing," said Joe. "Knit your fingers together under his chin. Get your hands however they're most comfortable. And don't be afraid of turning vigorously— you're not going to snap his neck."

Did he have to say that? She lifted the head in her hands now as though it was made from packed sand. Joe, oily-gentle, was saying "Whenever you are," but Judith's palms were still shifting all over Carly's cheeks, sticking and unsticking, trying not to press in anywhere that's painful . . . Peter was giving her a look of impatience.

"Oh, right, okay, you want a signal? Okay. I've got him . . . I guess, then, now—wait. Which way am I going to turn him first?"

Joe: "To whomever you like the most."

She turned (Please God keep the neck unsnapped) the small head toward Joe, to the right—a harmless, kindly lie. All three flutes were going at once now, dissonant tooting, so Ruth probably had been too busy even to notice.

Peter, he and Joe already smoothly in motion, shouted to her over the din: "Three-segond intervals!"

One thousand, two thousand, three thousand—Carly's head toward Peter now . . . One one, two two, three three—back to Joe. To Peter. To Joe . . . From inside Carly's neck, a cartilage rub, louder than any flute and was it ever sickening . . . To Peter. To Joe. To Peter . . . Wasn't anyone timing? Can they time and play at the same time? . . . One thousand . . . The three of them were very good, but meanly loud; she was starting to shrink under the assault, more pooped, weaker . . . To Peter. To Joe . . . Carly's head, so light at the start, now was a bowling ball as mists of sweat started to form brooks at her ankles, her spine, her chin . . . To Joe—whose scent she could smell (it must be reciprocal: how embarrassing] . . . To Peter . . . Wetness, wetness, suddenly it was all she could think of . . . To Joe . . . A drop of sweat fell off her chin—oh!—and plunked into the soft red hair at Carly's neck, sitting there like a dewdrop . . . The simplest job—to hold and turn the tiller—but, oh, her fingers were starting to skid, slip, skid—

"Oh, God, I'm sorry!"—wailing, scrambling, crawling blindly away, the image of the little forehead bouncing once on the linoleum burning on the back of her eyes.

All the flutes stopped. Joe, jumping up, put an arm around her and brought her up to stand. "No problem—he's a tough old bean. It happens sometimes. He probably thought it was fun."

Flute in hand, Ruth had come strolling over. "I guess she forgot to take her vitamins this morning."

Joe said, "It was time for bathroom training anyway."

"Not quite," the wife disagreed. "Forty-eight seconds left."

Peter had sat Carly up and turned him around to show Judith: no damage.

It didn't help. "He *bounced!*" A sob, and another—but the sobs were not enough, weren't scooping down anywhere close to the offending image: that small and innocent forehead rubberly dropping, rising, dropping. That was what she had to get rid of, that's what wasn't going to disappear until *she* disappeared. On spaghetti legs, she ran from the house.

Peter, out on the street, let her quickly into his car. But before he could come around and slip behind the wheel himself, Joe the father got there first. A knee up on the seat between them, he groped for Judith's hand.

"We're here every single day, so I expect to see you again, hear me? And if you ever feel like just coming over—not to pattern, to say Hi— that would be a great pleasure, I'd love to see you. I'm here. I'd love it. Ruthie's out on Thursdays—she teaches uptown at Mannes all day until nine—but I'm the full-timer, I'd be here. Just drop by. Carly would dig it—I know I certainly would. So, look, Happy New Year—and drop in, anytime. Thursdays are especially good." Leaning, he was going to kiss her cheek. Dodging late, though, she allowed him half her mouth. Pleased, he patted her elbow meaningfully and got out of the car to let Peter in.

"You crud!" she screamed—but it was at the windshield, where was the knob for the side window? she found it, cranked it down furiously.

"With me? Someone who bounces your baby's head on the floor? *Me?* Someone who looks like I do is who you want to fool around with? You crud! Stupid, stupid, you . . . crick!" The car was moving out into traffic while she still was yelling, leaving Joe and Ruth and the Brillo-headed student behind, all standing on the stoop of the house, all wearing one face: who *was* that?

Peter drove in silence while Judith continued to sob. Squeaking, puffing, blowing, leaning almost laughing over certain pits of hopelessness so steep they were funny; and then, with a phlegmy hitch, sidling away toward others, throat-bathed and tear-white. Sob, sob. The only time Peter moved at all close, it wasn't to console her but to roll up her window when the car was stopped by a red light at a derelict-infested corner of East Houston Street.

As she cried, Judith thought: This is *good* for me, being as I am scared and being as I am angry; being so scared and angry, then, this is probably good for me. (Peter steered the car up onto the East River Drive: openness of vista, dock and shore and sky and water.) But, oh, it's also phoney-baloney, what an act—poor baby crying over being poor baby . . . Winding down her window again, she said, "I like the smell of the water."

"All garbage in it. You smell only that." Peter glanced at her hoodedly, long thin lips bunched as though he were holding something nonedible in his mouth. "Are you okay?"

"What is Amsterdam like?" Stopping crying was worse than starting: it left you so dry, a parched fool.

"Not like this." He cocked his chin disdainfully at the hard, unlovable river.

Stopping crying also usually made you feel like you were looking at your reflection in a mirror hung at the other side of a long room. "Dirtier? Cleaner?" Judith leaned into the stiff window wind; it numbed her face, and she vised open her mouth against it, complex dirty/clean waterside atoms bumping over her teeth.

"Amsterdam water is not clean, no. Maybe cleaner than this. But what is that expression?—comparisons, they can be odious? One in Dutch is similar."

Watching a powder-blue helicopter start to angle down for a landing at its pierside pad, the windshield crazed with golden glare as it turned momentarily straight into the sun, Judith thought: No, I was definitely never good at it, crying. Since age twelve or so, the reason behind certain aspects of it have eluded me. The business of crying *over*, crying *for*, crying *to*—were you required, like a pilot, to file a flight plan first? And then how do you stop? One day her I'm-being-silly gauge will break along with everything else, and then what? Turn into that horse in *Guernica* with its mouth always open, never closing? Better not to start.

She looked at Peter, his eyes on the road. "Peter, tell me. Did you and Ruth ever . . . ?"

He leaned across her once more to roll the window up. "Too cool for me."

"I bet your shampoo is European, isn't it."

On her street, Peter parked and wanted to take her upstairs. A fine sight that would be—one rattled, weepy, parched, embarrassed, cancerous lady; and, looking like some hip attendant at a pricey sanitorium with his white overalls and sneakers and Christly hair and leather pouch tied into a belt loop, Peter. "No, no, that's all right. You're dismissed."

He slid closer. "We can sit down, we will talk. I'm not a badt guy, and I may be able to help you. You are very depressedt, yes?"

"And your toothpaste—also not American, is it?" She started gathering herself up before opening the door.

"Wait, Then at least I will give you my cardt." He jammed a hand into the pouch hanging from his pants. "You will call me please if you want to talk to someone. I am concernedt about you. Here."

PETER ORINT

MASTER CARPENTRY   LOFT RENEWAL   PSYCHOTHERAPY

53 Stanton St. N.Y., N.Y. 927-7839

"What?" he asked, puzzled.

"Nothing, I'm sorry. Don't mind me." But another squall of laughter, helpless and explosive, shook her. "I have this image of you buying this in Times Square, where they sell those novelty newspapers: EXTRA! EXTRA! JUDY KORNBLUH PROMOTED TO SIXTH GRADE! EXTRA! My friend Betsy Heller got one of those once for her birthday. She never bothered to read what was on the front page, the faked news stories below the headline. For me that would have been the most interesting part, those fake news stories. Not the seeing of your name in bold letters: you know your name already. But those fake news stories."

The hippie stared at her. "Please let me come up."

Was he going to be a problem now, on top of everything? "You can't. Go back downtown. You can't." When she got out of his car, however, he followed.

"I wish I couldt give you a gift, something to start the New Year off with right"—he was rummaging inside his hip pouch while trying to keep up with her—"but I don't . . . just, here, these." Into her hand, the one already holding her keys, the Dutchman stuffed bits of newspaper, varicolored confetti. "I go. Happy New Year. If you needt you have my cardt."

Not confetti, no—but cents-off coupons. For Sanka. For Alpo. For Gainesburgers and orange juice. When she looked up, his car was pulling away.

Fumbling her apartment door open, coupons and mail in hand (a Con Ed bill, an envelope from *Who's Who of American Women* that's marked "Third and Final Notification. Please Answer Immediately. Dated Mail."), fully looking forward to collapsing (I bounced his head!), the first thing she did when inside was fling her cape, the coupons, the mail to the floor.

The trouble with collapsing, though, is that there's nothing very on-going about it. You do it, it's done. She picked up her cape from the floor and brought it to the closet, hanging it not very carefully over a red slinky party tunic and blue velvet pants, both of which immediately slipped to the disorderly floor. She went around picking up Peter's coupons and dropped them in a heap on the desk in the kitchen, among other odd papers. (One that caught her eye, a scribble in her own handwriting, read: "Delphi 273-0800." Not Jack's number. The number of the connection upstate that Tom at the museum had given to Alex to give to her to give to Jack—which she had never done.)

"I forgot," she said to herself aloud now, a total falsehood. She hadn't forgotten. Deliberately avoiding going even near to the bed *(Don't lie down)*, she returned to the closet, to pick up the tunic and pants. Party wear. New Year's. If Peter (how sweet: those coupons, and what a hard time he'd been given in return) hadn't said something, she wouldn't have remembered. Anthony would be in Phoenix with his mother, but he hated parties anyway. This'll be the first year without a party in a long time. She loved parties, the pure ones of her girlhood especially: putting out Fritos in Tupperware bowls in Lisa's rec-room, not giving the poor hapless boys like Rickie Lebo and Howard Kaufelt a chance to sit down before the seriously romantic songs began to plunk down along the fat 45 spindle of the record player: "First a boy and a girl meet each other . . ."

While she's here already . . . off with her jeans and sweater, on with the tunic, the blue velvet pants. And? The spaghetti-strap heels. She pushed the wig straight, squeezed her eyes to slits to blur the definition in the closet door mirror. Stockings? Definitely, runs and all. She looked.

No: too mincy and old birdy, overdressed. Put a drink in her hand, and a napkin: it would scream out spinster. (Is it premature, under the circumstances, to face up to these final designations?) The heels alone, wobwobbling inches too high, exposed solitude and desperate habits.

Off. She slipped on next the Lanz print jumper which had been stuffed all the way over to a side of the rod with the rest of the don't-wears. Neat as a pin in it, sensitive. Whatever happened to what she used to think of as her "brown" aura, a woody and depressing serious-ness smart girls got away with (though often by hedging: a single green ribbon in the hair, thus achieving the best of two dishonest impres-sions)? Jack would really hate this if she wore it. (A ribbon in a wig? Ghastly thought.)

Jack. She couldn't put it off any longer. No more punishing him. (It's the only theory which salvages some self-respect: that Huft had been revenge on Jack, Peter on Huft, Joe (and Carly) on Peter. Call her Tor-quemada.) If Peter could give her a New Year's present, mercy only de-manded that she do the same for Jack. Not that there'd be any party or anything up there, she realized, walking over to the phone in the kitch-en, maybe just a nice dinner out together . . . She dialed the bus termi-nal. There *were* extra holiday buses on the Delphi route, the clerk snotted; which did she want, *to* or *from*? To? Well the next *to* would be in an hour and three minutes, then nothing until tomorrow. You're *wel*come.

No time then! *(Don't lie down.)* Off with the jumper—oh, no, would you look! Every day, all through Firenze, she'd worn this, and no won-der she'd been pinched! Yellow, with blaring red stripes, coming just a tad over her hips, looking like a nightshirt. One thing that can be said about lack of previous taste, she thought, wriggling into it just for old time's sake—and that's the proof it offered that your life was change-able after all. Closets were a kind of carbon dating.

Off. Now she had to be serious, she hadn't much time, there'd still be a taxi to find to take her to the Port Authority. The blue silk blouse: for sure; she left it unbuttoned for the moment. Then this Jaeger tweed skirt—or the grey suit? The suit's hanger caught on the bar, and when she yanked, down tumbled a robe—she gave it a vicious kick back inside of the closet: no more robes!—and a white terry beachset she never wore once.

On with the grey suit (the choice was narrowing down)—but, once the best tailored garment she owned, it now was enormous on her, a clown's getup. Off. Off. Away. (I'm so *scared.*) So: the blue blouse and the Jaeger skirt it would be. Look at the mess she'd made.

Now shoes. Her good boots, and a pair less good—there must be snow by now in Delphi, probably plenty of it. She wished she'd had the time to saddle soap both pairs, something she neglected to do this fall, and which would have to wait until next . . .

And what about the wig? No. And not a kerchief either. A stocking cap, for warmth, and he'd just have to accept it.

Less than half an hour now to get to the bus station. She went around grabbing the slip of paper with the connection's phone number on it; her keys; her suitcase (too large, but there had been no time to find a snugger one). Ready.

And she had been victorious. Never gave in, never lay down.

14

"Did I already say that Doughnut was shot?"

She hadn't. Even if she had, she could tell it to him again, though.

Donna said, "But in the head, so that at least I know it was immediate. No suffering."

"He was *killed!*" It had taken Jack a moment to understand. "Did anyone see who shot him?"

"She. Shot *her.* My neighbor, the one two trailers down, Mackellson—I don't know if you ever saw him, big fat guy, he works for the Highways Department as a grader—he brought her back in his arms."

"Did he see the shooting?"

"He *did* the shooting. At least I've been assuming that: they were his rabbits that she'd been ripping to pieces. One of the gals on Peeds is married to a vet, and according to him, Collie mixes—when they get a little senile—go feral. And, remember, Dough was twelve. Now and then I'd see her slinking around about six in the evening; you could tell by her eyes that she had this urge to go off and do some business. The first two times, Mackellson was able to chase her away by yelling; and the second time, also firing in the air with his gun. She'd actually clawed open a hole in the wire and just about had her mouth on one.

"So what do you do? His bunnies, my dog. He's this big white hunter every fall, some poor deer always lashed to his hood, so at least he knows how to shoot. He may not be much, but I don't think he's cruel. She wouldn't have been long for it anyway, you know. Once they've killed, they don't just trot home. I'd lost her one way or the other."

The story disturbed Jack. Was this how, he wondered unhappily, she took my being sick also? A bad turn of nature? no use protesting? accept it as it comes? He needed her balance desperately—but up close to it, it frightened him a little. Earlier, taking a ride together in her Volkswagen, Donna driving as she had the first day they met, he kept knocking the question away (too capable of backfiring) and yet out of his mouth it soon enough leapt anyway:

"Why didn't you ever call me?"

Donna's eyes levelly swept the road, the snowfields. "But I did."

"Later on, I mean. Once I was back."

"You were busy. How could you not have been? That was why you didn't call me, either. When you could you would. And you did."

That simple? "Busy"? That while he'd been hiding out of harm's way, she'd been keeping out of his—and keeping out of each other's way was, for them, a way?

She made it sound so rational, but the truth was profoundly more headless: he had called her, remade the contact, out of the severest, most exhausted need, rattled from one misadventure after another: Salco, the *Observer*, Sleighlin. Then Judith, that fiasco of a visit: the TV show, the disastrous outing to the cider mill, the feel of her skeleton in his arms as she rubbed maniacally against his thigh.

After Judith's bus left that day, Jack had gone directly to the Big Blue and stocked a week's worth of the cheapest food—canned macaroni, soups, frozen french fries. Then he holed up at home. Mail accumulated in the box. He kept the phone off the hook for hours at a time. He sparingly smoked the new, not very potent grass Judith had brought up, hating his own parsimony. He watched it snow during the nights. He didn't shave. He kicked the newspapers delivered to his door across to the Burkes—and, pigs that they were, they took them right in. Once, during a spell of the phone being on the hook, Pellegrino called, wanting to come by and get the truck. Jack went down and fit the keys in the ignition. When Pellegrino showed, Jack made as though he wasn't home; he heard the truck rev, leave.

He lived for two weeks (three? four?) like this. When he came down to the city for a checkup, Irwin would give him money, then Jack would hurry back upstate. The questions in his father's eyes *(Why? How long can this go on? A job? How will you live?)*—questions no one asks the sick or the newly recovered, yet which sit like gatekeepers at the front of a concerned mind—were too painful to see, since Jack himself shared them all.

For this I got well? Death-in-life?

And, finally, just this morning, when his baggie was completely empty, he had called Donna. Nothing calm and predetermined about it: pure Mayday. She had come by in the afternoon, around three, and brought with her a single yellow carnation. (He kept glancing at the flower with unmasked apprehension.) But she couldn't stay long. She had previously signed on to take over other people's shifts at the hospital during the holiday week.

They took a drive together in her car. Tina, she told him, had been

dismissed from Delphi Community. ICU negligence was the adminis-
trator's charge, but everyone knew it had actually been because of the
petition Tina had been passing around inside the hospital: Health Pro-
fessionals Against Legalized Infant Murder. A botched abortion had re-
sulted in a live baby, which ICU then took care of for thirty-six hours,
until the pathetic little thing finally died. Tina began to have nightmares. Some people said she'd been fired not on account of the petition,
but because of her relationship with Sue. But Donna didn't think so.

Jack didn't ask.

Sitting in the small car, Donna seemed taller than he remembered.
And her breasts, which he used to think of as disproportionately
large, really weren't so big after all. Her physical image always had
eluded him, her body a surprise, but now it seemed that she had grown
truly taller and slimmer. Racked by worry over him? Gnawed down
by fear? Jack hoped so.

It grew dark; they ate a supper at McDonald's. A plastic noisemaker
came along with the food on both their trays. She would be leaving the
trailer soon, Donna said, once Bert was gone: she didn't want to be the
last soldier in the fort. Bert was moving in with this very kind woman,
Lois Tealsen, into a house by Canaford, near the falls. And Tina had
been gone ever since she was fired; she and Sue lived in Rochester now
and were very much in love.

After, they returned to Jack's apartment. He went around turning on
lights (protectively: if Donna had to leave for work at eight, going to bed
together was rapidly becoming a topical question), while she went into
the kitchen and made tea. (She would see his radiation burns, the scars
on his feet, the skinniness. She would be disgusted.)

"No bread, no milk, no sugar—you're living here totally without
staples," she said, giving him his tea. At the end of a straight arm, the
cup and saucer rattled, a tiny tremor. (Suddenly he did want to go to bed
with her . . . maybe.) It was then, settling into the other Danish chair,
tucking her legs underneath her, that Donna told him about Doughnut.

"Bert did have a point, though. Think, he said, that at least she went
happy—with her teeth in some nice juicy meat. I *have* thought that.
And it does help."

"How is old Bert?"

Head on her arm—the arm draped across the chairback, where the
upholstery was slick and dull from years of Jack's greasy hair—Donna
narrowed her mouth and set her eyes to a mild scold: "I must have just

had a dream. I dreamed that you and I were in McDonald's . . ." She smiled.

"Lois, right. House in Canaford. I'm sorry." (But with nothing else to say, bed was the only alternative.) "What about the sculptor, the Armenian? Whatever became of him?"

"Larry was fired, but I think he received a grant and moved back to New York City. He and Sue had broken up a long time before that, though." She raised her head, sipped tea. "All your favorite folks."

"I was very stiff-necked, wasn't I?" Much better than bed perhaps would be this: as though he really had died and now was back to ask of the living where he'd fallen short. "I can tell there's a difference now. Now I seem to be more—impressed. Whole days go by in which everything seems amazing to me." Jack found himself beginning to relax. "I don't exactly know how to handle it. I'm not accustomed to being one big response and nothing else."

Donna sipped at her tea. "Oh, yes you are."

"Do you want to go to bed?"

"Can we? They didn't radiate that off?"

Jack was speechless for a moment with love. "No, the only organ that required immediate care was my brain. I heard them conferring: 'Leave the nodes alone, the man has something much bigger—a lump of bullshit lodged in his head that's got to go. If need be, we'll resort to surgery.'"

"And?"

"And now I love everybody. I love you. I love Bert . . ."

Laughing—oh, this was rarer, more precious, more important to him than bed!—Donna put her cup down and got out of the chair. "Am I in the right apartment?" She walked theatrically to the door and opened it as Jack laughed. "Very fishy. No name on here." Then the next moment, she was looking at something on the stairwell, she was saying "Hi."

A familiar voice, but one that Jack couldn't precisely place, was answering back, "Hello."

Jack stood up.

"It's so hot in here," said Judith. She dropped her bag outside on the landing, freeing both hands to tug at the neck of her cape, the weight of its bow-knotted tie seemingly about to strangle her. "But I guess where the landlord lives, the landlord does live."

Two hours later, as he sat immobilized in one of the Danish chairs hearing the drag-chain bass of the Burkes' stereo rise and fall each time their door opened (New Year's Eve, he was reminded), Jack's phone rang.

"It's me. Is your friend all right?"

"Just chilled—the bus was cold. And tired."

"Jack, she was breathing kind of harshly."

"You're the expert." Why was he acting curt and defensive?—it was absurd. To right himself, he offered a simple fact: "She's in bed now." But, no, that didn't sound very good, and he hastened to add, "I'm in the living room."

(As if he could ever have gotten into bed with Judith. Bad enough simply to watch the yellowish bare arm grabbing for the nightgown Jack had held out for her. Her breasts as she sat up were, shockingly, almost shrivelled, pinked from exertion. When she slipped the nightgown over her head, tugging down and flattening the hair over her ears, streaks of baldness appeared on the crown, a stutter of white. He had stood by the bed in horror.)

"Can I ask you something?" Donna said. "Does she have what you have? Had?"

An impulse to deny it came and went. "That's how I know her. From the clinic."

Gently, Donna said, "I figured."

"Why, do we look the same?" It had shot from him before he could lock it off.

"It's really raw out now. They say tomorrow also—so try and keep her inside. And Jack? You'll call me if you have to?"

"Can't I if I just want to?"—a brutish, stupid insistence to his voice.

"It's pretty slow here now. The E.R. won't get busy until later, after midnight—all the drunks and crashes—so it shouldn't be too bad for a while. Of course call. Do."

"I wanted to spend tonight, New Year's Eve, with you."

"We couldn't have anyway, I have to be here. We'll do our own celebrating another night. I promise. Jack, I have to go."

Totaling up the damage done, he felt like holding his head. He had reminded Donna that he had cancer. In the process, he had come across as erratic, whiney, and closed to her. Why bother to call her back? He'd never hear from her again.

The Rolling Stones continued to pound on from behind the Burkes' door. Jack read the *Courier* Donna had left behind, then read it again with a mindless thoroughness: the ad for the electrologist on Main Street, the hog-futures table. The television, on without sound, kept throwing ten-second teasers of Guy Lombardo and his band, the party hats and ball gowns at the Waldorf, preparatory to the big moment. When there was a diminishment of the music from next door, Jack took the opportunity to tiptoe to the bedroom door.

He believed he heard breathing. Belief for now would have to do; he was afraid to actually go in there, though sooner or later he'd have to. (And find all of Judith's breaths collected on the blanket, spilled from her nose and mouth into a mound like grated cheese?) How could she have gotten so much worse so quickly? That wasn't supposed to happen, it was against the terms of their pact. And certainly not here, not now. The miner's canary didn't go and collapse in a cage in the living room. Jack tiptoed away.

On the TV, more snatches of the band silently playing away, the bobbing silly hats. He would have called Donna—but was afraid that, at the sound of her voice, he would begin to whimper and cry. What he did instead was pass out: close his eyes and suddenly he was in a restaurant with his father and the Burkes. The breadsticks seemed to be bolted into the dish, and to get one out you had to pull and yank and haul—

When his eyes opened, Judith, standing over him, stopped tugging at his finger.

She was dressed again; the stocking cap covered her head. "It's a quarter to eleven. You said you'd wake me, but you didn't, did you? Wash your face, wake yourself up. We have to go."

The bass of the Burkes' stereo thumped louder than ever, submerging Jack's alertness. Why was she dressed? Was she dying?

"Your coats are in here, right?" she said from over by the closet. "Please get up. I'm afraid we won't make it."

Her face was a very frightening rose color. Jack asked, "Are you all right?"

"I hope you still have your blue parka. I told him we'd be a woman in a brown cape and a man in a blue parka."

"Told whom? Jack's legs were hollow boles—they'd mash if stood on yet.

"Here it is, I found it. Good. I didn't see the truck outside when I came—don't you still have it?"

"Only the Valiant."

"Ooh, I told him a truck. This is a heavy coat. Here, put it on. We're going to be cutting this so closely. Please, let's go."

Jack took the parka from her. "Do you want to go to a hospital?"

"A *hospital?* No, I don't want to go to a hospital. Let your friend go to a hospital on New Year's Eve—I don't mean to be catty: she seems very sweet. Aren't you getting ready? I don't know how long it takes to get there. The railroad bridge that runs over the road right outside the north end of the Ag campus—is that far?"

Jack laid the coat down on the floor next to the chair. Her specific description surprised him. "There *is* a railroad bridge north of the Ag campus."

"And we're getting later and later—" She was glowering at him, but then she fell back with a surrendering bounce on the Hollywood bed.

"All right," she said, "maybe I shouldn't surprise you anymore. Maybe I've surprised you enough to last you for a while. Although, for a change, this one you would have liked." Her arms jumped in place, a shiver; she fixed her cape more securely around her. "Do you have twenty-five dollars in cash on you?"

"I'm not sure," For emergency room costs? He raised himself in order to dig into his back pocket.

"It doesn't matter—if you don't I can cover the whole fifty," Judith said. "I've found you your very own connection. Unless you've been planting seeds in a greenhouse, it's something you need badly, isn't it? You can't have much of anything left from what I brought up last time."

"Some," Jack fibbed. "A little."

"Then you've been rationing, and that's no good either. The person who's been selling to me at the museum is going out of the business. And even if he wasn't, you can't keep on going down to New York every time you need to buy. And I can't keep delivering to you."

Standing again, she went over and picked Jack's parka from the floor. "Well? Are you coming?"

I can't keep delivering to you. "This 'connection' is in Delphi?"

"No, in Kuala Lumpur—please!" She consulted an imaginary watch on her wrist. "If we don't show up he'll leave."

"You've already called this person?" Jack hated how interested he was.

"From the station, after the bus got in and before my taxi came."

"And you gave him my name?"

"I had a number, that's all: no names involved. No, actually one—Tom Gordon's: I had to identify myself somehow. He said he knew Tommy very well. I explained the situation—that you and I were chemotherapy patients. He was very pleasant. He said he'd try to supply us only with the best."

The phone rang—Jack jumped. "Is that going to be him?"

"I don't see how it could be."

"Hello?"

"Jack? Happy New Year!" Sure enough, the Burkes' party had just erupted more noisily than ever; on the TV, silent mayhem in Times Square filled the screen. Judith was watching it without expression.

"I can't talk now," Jack said hurriedly to Donna, "I have to go."

But after he hung up, Jack found that the imposition of another voice had steadied him, recalled him back to some sense. He looked up at Judith, who stood holding his coat and glancing occasionally at the celebration on television. I can't keep delivering to you. "Put down my coat," he said.

"No, you've got to wear it: I told him we would be a brown cape and a blue parka."

"We're not going to be anything. You can give me his number. And if I want to call him some time, I will. That'll be your gift, all right?"

"Why are you patronizing me? I don't like it."

"I'm not patronizing you. You know very well that you shouldn't be going outside—"

"Who says? Your nurse? You say? I know whatever I want to do, I can—*that's* what I know. Sometimes you can be a awful boor."

Her bitterness was a surprise. "Just that you're obviously sick, weak—"

"As opposed to you? who's tip-top?"

"I don't see, that's all, what you think this business of being brave is going to get you. You don't see that it's only grotesque? This is something that I've learned lately here: that you can deny being sick all you want, but believe me, no one else bothers—they've all got you written off. If you don't comply right away, they bear down and write you off a little harder. Look, *they* know who the odds are with."

Ignoring him, Judith again looked at her watchless wrist. "Meanwhile time is wasting . . ."

"I'm trying to *tell* you something." Something important—why wasn't she listening? "To be brave for them is not worth the trouble.

They may think they're impressed and uplifted, but all it is to them really is an entertainment. Amusement. You can't keep going like this, running yourself into nothing, coming up here, finding connections, making believe that—"

"Shit. *Shit.* Shit!—you're supposed to under*stand,*" Judith said, tight-jawed, turning to face a window. "But you never have, *never.*" There was a crash; when she stepped back, Jack could see the parka lying on the floor beneath the window, clear splinters all over the shiny blue.

"I wouldn't do this to *you.* I wouldn't rush you. I'd be brave, I'd be scared, I'd go out, I'd stay in—I'd be anything I wanted to be, because as long as I'm here, as a person, I'm here. A person—not someone pure and crazy like you. So don't tell me how to be. You're sick too, remember. Don't scrape yours off on me." She sat down heavily on the floor—not a collapse exactly: a folding up, a placing of herself.

Jack, who had bounded over, inspected the broken pane: that a soft thing could break a hard thing—a coat a window—only seemed to drive the moment more askew, made all lurking physical laws feel threatening and malevolent. He threw a momentary, imprisoned look out at the street through the one rectangle of absent glass, tasting the cold air that rose from the innocent street and innocent bushes and innocent snow and innocent Mustangs, none of which knew a thing about the intricate indoor pain going on right here and now.

Snatching up the parka, raining bits of glass onto his cuffs, Jack screamed, "Get into bed!" at her as he might have to a bad child. She had started to cough now—awful, custardy coughs. "Jude—"

She shook off his hand. "Angry at you. You jerk," she gulped. "All you do—all you *all* do—is let me down. I'm trying to do you a favor and the only thing you're in a rush to do is spoil it."

The chinkless grumble of the campus power plant behind them was like a retaining wall, a backstop. Giant icicles, the tips scintillant with reflected light from the long sheds and barns across the way, hung down like incisors just under the railroad bridge. Jack had made sure not to park directly beneath the bridge itself, but, instead, in the wide slot of a maintenance shed's loading bay twenty yards short of the bridge. He didn't want to be hemmed in. Moonlight was sugaring the ice crust on the piles of snow.

The Valiant's heater was going, but Jack had his window wound down an inch. The fifty dollars inside his shirt pocket, tens and fives, seemed to be as heavy against his harrowed, excited chest as a roll of quarters.

"Well, he's prompt."

A small car (from the sound of the engine) was pulling up under the bridge from the opposite direction and stopping; for a moment its headlights stayed on like a query in a foreign language, then they died.

Judith, who hadn't spoken a word to Jack since leaving the house, put a hand to her door handle.

Jack's eyes again were adjusting to the dimness. It was a Datsun—and the driver was getting out, walking forward a few paces, the right foot slightly slow. He stopped, a bit out from under the bridge, and stood there in the broth of Jack's parking lights.

Jack touched Judith's arm. "Let me. By myself."

"But he's expecting a brown cape."

"It's all right. If you get too warm, that lever there shuts the heat. Pull it way over back to the left."

Later Jack would wonder why. Salco had had plenty of time to turn around the moment he recognized the Valiant (and Jack was sure that he had recognized it). But instead he had parked. Jack, too, when he saw it was Salco, could have driven off. He didn't.

Jack would later decide it was because he and Salco were both in bad need of a mortgage. Mortgaged, hooks into one another, the better your chances of not simply disappearing, floating off without a trace. The last thing any sane person wants is the upper hand.

Now that they were within speaking range, Jack expected that at least one of them might smile. But it wasn't happening. "It's fifty, right?" Jack asked softly, and Salco said as quietly, "Yes, right, it is."

"Well, here."

"Thank you. The extra envelope is for the lady—and that's no charge."

Their breath vapors were twining and layering. Jack thanked him. And then couldn't help himself. "How much did you know? Did she tell you that it was going to be me?"

"Who are you?" Salco said.

Nodding, Jack agreed—"Right"— as Salco fit the money into a pocket of his field jacket and without another word walked back to the Datsun.

Jack, nothing left to be done, returned to the Valiant and to Judith.

15

Howard, inside the travel agency, was vacuuming. His gate, unlike Anthony's, the halves of which had to be pulled creakingly left and right each morning and then back again each night, was the stronger, more costly kind that rolled up vertically. At this early hour, before the agency was open for business, it was raised only waist high: Through the chinks of steel mesh, Howard could be seen going over his carpeting with an old floral-bagged upright.

Anthony bent down, restraightening on the other side of the gate. (His thighs, at night lately especially, burned with neuralgia: in Milan he'd take the waters a few times himself.) At the sound of the rapped-on glass, Howard looked up from his back-and-forths. He seemed to take a deep breath before stepping over the snaking cord and leaning to open the door . . . then went right back to his vacuum cleaner, which, still running, was propped against a chair.

The desks of the agency were arranged pyramid style. Three of them, shoulder to shoulder, were nearest the door. Behind them were two more. And, finally—as the pinnacle—the one furthest back was Howard's own, which sat beneath a large photo mural that was periodically changed. (At the moment it showed a daylit panorama of Sugarloaf and Rio.) Anthony, going directly there, turned Howard's clients' chair around to face the front.

Howard merely vacuumed on. He stopped only once, to remove ship models and airline advertising cards and a splay of brochures from one of the two carpeted window ledges; all these items were laid down carefully atop a nearby desk. His back to Anthony, he said above the whine of the vacuum, "I was sure you still were in Phoenix with your mother. That was the consensus opinion."

"Not this Christmas. Too busy: I didn't go."

"I see. We thought wrong, then. Your place has been dark on unusual days." Howard, having lifted the vacuum up onto the cleared ledge, was gliding it to and fro like the parent of a toddler, a supporting hand on rump and belly.

"I need some assistance from you," said Anthony. "First you can shut that."

Howard didn't shut it; he brought the vacuum down off the ledge, reordered the display, and then nosed the machine into a tight corner created by one of the front desks and a wall.

Insulted, Anthony guessed. He had half-anticipated it—that their feelings might be crimped by his dropping so mysteriously out of the morning shape-ups, going so squirrelly on them without warning or explanation. If there could only have been another way . . .

"I need two one-way airfares to Milan. And then, there, a moderate hotel—less than ritzy but not a shared bath, either. If it's got long-term rates, all the better." He was being forced to cry this out, to jump it over the machine's wow. "Whatever you suggest I'll give a try. Are there direct flights?"

As if he'd heard none of it, Howard continued to vacuum.

"Hey!" A particular rage had been gestating inside Anthony for weeks now, a hatred not for time running out—he couldn't entertain such assbackwardness anymore—but for time that came on too slowly, a dawdling and disciplineless stroll through precious moments. It galled him terribly.

Howard shut the vacuum and rested an elbow on the stalk. A carefully composed and guarded look had come over his face. "Do you mind me asking why one-way?"

Anthony gazed at his fingers for a moment before saying: "I'm taking J. over there. This is not, by the way, please, to be general knowledge yet. I know I can trust you."

Howard's lips drew tightly back.

"There is a tumor institute there, apparently very famous and very gutsy. They've developed some of the best drugs that are now used routinely everywhere. It'll take some doing to get them to accept her for treatment, but I think it can be done. No finesse: the play will have to be one stubborn wop against another. We go, we dig in permanently; we make as though we're there to stay, sick *or* well. I then don't see how they can turn us away."

The vacuum cleaner dropped when let go. Howard set the backs of his knees gingerly against one of the desks. He changed the date on a roll calendar. Near to a whisper, he said: "Suddenly you come to me."

Anthony, too far away, couldn't hear. "Repeat? I still have the vacuum cleaner going in my ears."

"It's the first time," Howard said, only slightly louder.

"The first time what?"

"You've always done your booking directly with the airlines. But now you're wanting me to do it. That's all. Just noting it."

Anthony leaned forward: he was missing something here, something that was jailed behind the slabs of strain that made up Howard's face. "Is there a special reason why you're busting my balls?"

Howard reached over. Wearily, he pulled toward him a large and obesely stuffed looseleaf binder; strumming the pages, he cracked it fully open as he slipped a pair of half-glasses from his shirt pocket and put them on. "New fares started yesterday, the first of the year. I've got them all—the problem is where. Milan, you say." He flipped pages. "Each airline sends its own notification and you try to put them all in. But some always get lost."

He closed the book over his index finger. "You want to be sure of the lowest fares. You know what my suggestion is? Honestly? You cab up right now to Fifth Avenue, the Alitalia office or Pan Am's, and you speak to them. At this stage, when the fares are brand-new, they're going to know them much better than I will."

A muscle was working tensely beneath Howard's right sideburn— even from ten feet away it was obvious—and watching it, in time to it, Anthony grew more and more peevish. Here he was, required to move like a hart, and instead he was being mired in a pool of muck, age-muck; Howard—growing old, old and tetchy and ill-timed—bringing up a hidden longstanding grudge after all these years: that Anthony had never brought him any business before! Incredible. The health of all of them, all the hangers-on, was good—no cancer, no heart disease or diabetes (the less you try, the less you lose)—but grouchiness seemed to be their ailment, Anthony's included. "Are you hung over? Were you so pussy-whipped on New Year's Eve that it made you feeble?" Anthony got up from his chair. "I've got someone dying here and you're telling me to go to Fifth Avenue and comparison shop."

"Tone—"

"Tone nothing—fuck you, Rosenman."

With a melancholy nod, a turn of the hand, Howard agreed: Yes, fuck me.

"Superb behavior."

But Howard's finger delayed Anthony as he was passing by, grabbing at a raincoat button. "Don't. Stay."

"That'll help me how? You don't want to do anything for me." Close up to it, Anthony was made aware of the ring on Howard's pinky: unspeakably vulgar yet not a cheap thing, either: a Tiffany or Cartier silver band.

"Sit. I'll do." Howard's eyes closed, opened. "First you ought to hear, though, what I've already done."

Anthony touched the side of one leg to a desk, the most comfortable he'd allow himself to get.

Howard ploughed his palms upward along his forehead and into his hair. "The riddle is, which came first—the shmuck or the shmuck."

Anthony erected.

"No, will you please sit? Look, you've got trouble. I think I got you into it. No, that's not true: the one who got you into it was you—but I may have at least made it worse."

Howard wasn't able to look directly at Anthony. "Since that gonif landlord of mine began this co-op business, I've been very involved with a housing group, The Artists Committee for Fair Housing. Heard of it? Jeannie—I don't think you've met Jeannie: she's the lawyer for the committee, she volunteers her time—well, she's been great for me, not letting Becker pull little tricks, calling his every move—"

Anthony shifted weight from one leg to another.

"To make a long story short," Howard hurried. "Jeannie and I have been seeing each other. Tony, she's great. Very uptown—her friends are all Connecticut, yachting, the Blue Hill Troupe doing Gilbert and Sullivan, that whole shmear—but she's right there on this housing thing, very very sharp. To raise money for the committee she came up with the idea of a *dansant*—"

"A *dansant*," Anthony echoed, no restraint at all in cruelly tincturing the word; and Howard blushed beneath his Aruba tan—he was suffering richly.

"It was one of those expensive tickets per. Plenty of museum types, directors and such. Lee Morrowing and his wife shared a table with Jeannie and me. Afterwards he went back to my place for a nightcap. He liked your painting."

"No, you don't still have that, do you? And still are hanging it? Throw it away," Anthony said sharply, touched.

"Of course I have it," Howard said, and then his shoulders dipped back down: it must have dawned on him that this one small fidelity was like beating back the ocean with a paper fan. "We talked a lot about the old days—Jeannie's very interested. You'd like her, Tony. Anyway, Morrowing asked me to come up to the museum the next day to see about doing some consulting work.

"Tony, could I possibly have known? I went naively—naive greed: a hundred dollars an hour—and of course also the vanity. He brought out two small canvas boards and asked me if I thought they were Dornishes. I swear to you, that's exactly how he first put it: 'Do these look like paintings done by Walter Dornish to you?'—leaving the impression that they'd found these things, unattributed, and honestly couldn't make up their minds."

Howard's voice was dragging lower and droopier in a dust of shame. "I looked and I told him what I thought. What's bad is that I was emphatic about it, I went on and on—you know these WASP bastards, they like a scene, something dramatic. And here I was, flattered that they were asking me— When he pulled out letters from May that vouched for the pictures, I got even stupider. Was he trying to trick me? I really laid it on: that May had been fooled etcetera . . . Nothing registered— you know me for twenty-two years now, you *have* to believe me—until I got home that night and looked at your picture on the wall. Then I realized."

Anthony was looking out the window at the street. The morning was settling, the sludginess of the light thinning away. Passersby were on the increase, some sending a glance in at the two men inside the gated-over travel agency.

"What you can do about it at this point," said Howard, his eyes swimming in pain, "I'm not sure. Whatever, though, do it fast. And you can see now why it can't involve me. The one who does the arranging for you to get out of the country a week after he was the one who—"

"A *week?*"

"I didn't know what to *do.* I thought you were in Phoenix. Actually, it was that I was paralyzed. I never tried you. Guilt. Eventually—today, tomorrow—I would have told you."

Howard put one hand to the back of his neck, the other flat atop his crown; his head kept thusly on, he studied the ceiling lights in agony. "I keep thinking what I would have done in your place, but I don't get very far. What I think I understand is that you wanted to help Judy, that this was what only you could do for her—but that's when I lose it. The other people enter in. It isn't just you. It's May. Was she tricked or did she know? Walter watches out for her, you know—because he's dead doesn't make a difference. All his life my father belonged to a memorial society, people from his little _shtetl_ who came here like he did. I used to think it was morbid, those meetings to talk about financing stones, the upkeep of plots. But you know what?—it was politic, it wasn't morbid at all. They were keeping on good terms with the ghosts. Ghosts don't care about morbid. They want respect."

As Howard had done, Anthony opened his own gates only enough to be able to slip in behind them. He left all the lights off inside but for one small lamp in back, by which he dialed Alitalia. He would make the reservations, ask them to arrange for the hotel as well.

Everything was still going to work out. Howard's breed of despair no longer threatened Anthony. Ruined faith—this was something he had learned from painting the canvas boards—made only for a grittier walk underfoot; but the path itself didn't disappear. Besides, there was still time, the world didn't ever exactly spring into action like a firehouse. Fear imagines it does, but fear is wrong. Nothing ran faster than death—and look how surprisingly, cruelly poky _it_ was. What you were really worried about was that its brakes might fail.

Anthony still had brakes of his own left. (Alitalia answered, a recorded voice explaining that all service representatives were busy at the moment, and if he'd hold on . . . Taped music—"Close to You"— followed.) If need be, he'd go uptown to the museum, meet with Morrowing, and spill a little blood: whose opinion as to the authenticity of any one Dornish was the museum director readier to accept: Anthony's own (with letters from the widow, the executrix) or a travel agent's?

Someone was knocking at the door up front. Howard probably, come to juice some solace—the queer way of things by which the screwer is always begging balm from the screwed. And he evidently wanted in badly: the gates were being shaken impatiently. Anthony pulled the phone cord as far as it would go so that he could see around the partition.

When he saw, he set the receiver down on top of a cabinet.

The telescoping luggage caddy Alexandra Somogyi pulled into the shop carried a small load: a canvas tote bag. "I've been at a window seat in the coffee shop across the street since seven-thirty," she said, making her way resolutely to the back. "I would have caught you out on the street if they hadn't gotten busy in there suddenly and made me wait

for the check. But my eyes," she said accusingly, "were on you the entire time."

She began to undo the elastic cords of the caddy, freeing the tote bag
from bondage. "Your phone is playing music, did you know?" When
she lifted first one and then the other wooden box out of the bag, Anthony experienced a light quaver of perverse pleasure, a momentary
threat of laughter like that which goaded him the day with May. The
boxes, their stickers: the museum registry numbers, the "Walter Dornish"'s, the titles and dates and dimensions all neatly typed and officially
affixed.

Anthony thought, This is happening—and yet it isn't. Everything
seems so hypothetical to me always. When did I get this way?

Somogyi, a finger circuiting zig-zaggedly in the air before the mason-
ite toolboard over Anthony's worktable, found what she wanted: a long
flathead screwdriver. Working fast, inelegantly, tongue flitting out, she
went at prying open the boxes.

"Which is your ban-*nnk*—got it. The one catty-corner, across the
street? Or the one two blocks down the side street? That one opens at
nine, but this one starts doing business at eight-thirty. Obviously I
checked."

Anthony asked why she believed that was any of her business—and
then lost himself again in the observing of her tizzied fierceness. She
slammed the unboxed paintings down on the worktable like sides of
fish, chipping one frame. She said Anthony ought to know that she
spirited these out of the museum at six that morning. "Your ass was
saved—if you ever in the future want to thank anybody—by the nicest
person working there, a guard who'd die before he ever asked me to
show him what I was taking out in a bag." She was saying Fred Mallelieu's name, a remark of his about European collectors having some
doubts about fake Dornishes. "That seeded it, you see. He only had to
tell Lee that one thing." Howard's name then came out of her, too, as
she went on. "So now Morrowing has two strong opinions—enough to
go to the board with. *Ah-hem, our lady curator has made, rather im-
prudently, two acquisitions which later information leads us to believe were not of the best . . .* I can hear it all—and just how much he'll
be loving every word of it."

A shrunken lozenged voice was bouncing on the metal cabinet.
"*. . .talia—may I help you? Hello? Hello?*" Anthony took the receiver
and hung it up. He sat down in his workchair.

"Don't sit!" She wanted everything done before noon, before Morrowing got to the museum. "Your check on his desk."

No longer able to deny himself, Anthony reached for a square of chamois and a fingertip of oil; he touched it to the chip on the frame.

"I should have just let the D. A. come down here," she said, hoarse with frustration. When Anthony replied absently that D. A.s were partial to framing, Somogyi cast around and found a gum eraser, which she threw and which pinged off one of the canvas boards. Anthony, at this, let go of the chamois and gave some thought to killing the woman: taking her around the neck and bringing her head down repeatedly against the sharp corner of a cabinet until it was a punctured mess of gore.

"You still think it's a game!" she was saying incredulously. "But it isn't, though, no game. Lee already's been making noises about Judy—"

Anthony—this *was* happening—snapped to. "She's had nothing to do with anything."

"—Saying that we were going to have to think about how long we should carry her, about how valuable her office space was. And some much less subtle number only yesterday: something about 'possible implications of influence mongering and conflict of interest.'"

The room started disintegrating on Anthony. Somogyi said, "Yes, real nice, huh?"

She jammed the luggage caddy short, making it into an open rectangle with wheels. "Let's go get the money—you can't have spent very much yet. I've been thinking, and I guess a bank check would be best. And those" —the paintings— "are yours again. He was already calling them 'the evidence' by five in the afternoon yesterday. If you care, by the way, I still like them. They're good."

(To Anthony's great disgust, the compliment spread pleasurably across his teeth like a film.)

"I have nothing against sentiment. But you, you're a shit—I *hate* it that I'm saving your ass. So which one of the banks is yours?"

Anthony stood up, knees crackling. "The money's all in traveler's checks. I'll have to sign them all. It'll take time." He almost added: *And I'm an old man.*

Somogyi arched an eyebrow. "Where were you off to?"

"Milan."

She shook her head. "You're some pip."

He grabbed hold of her coat sleeve. "Nothing of this *ever* gets back to J." His head felt like it was melting.

"And that's another thing—where is she? With you? I've been calling and calling her at her apartment, but no answer. I called her parents once—she wasn't there—and then I didn't want to call again and scare them. Where is she?"

"I don't know," Anthony said.

"God," said Somogyi.

16

Every breath she was managing to win contained a small wet sound-mechanism, something like the pocka-ticking of a backpedaled English bike.

To Jack, lying next to her on the bed, knees locked and shoulders pointy, taking up the least possible room, each one of these breaths was like a scratch on the walls of his every vein.

And they were changing—Jack narrowed his eyes in order to hear better. The segments now had a hiss to them. Jack sat up and put on the light.

"Get dressed."

Judith's eyes were already open. "I think so too," she said quietly.

She sat like a sack on the edge of the bed while he helped her on with her blouse and boots. The skirt she did herself. Jack rounded up the rest of her things; the suitcase was so terribly light. Turning to her once, Jack saw her nostrils open, then pinch closed, her mouth leading the pain away over to one side.

Through an alkaline night, buff clouds distinct as dumplings in the dark overhead, they drove to New York. Jack had asked but wasn't surprised when Judith said she didn't want the Delphi hospital. He didn't want it either. They'd both trust to her stamina, the alternative being Donna in the Delphi E.R.

Mostly the car seemed to run on hysteria, ten-mile intervals of it, spasming it along. The roads were asleep, they were wakened momentarily by the application of the Valiant's hot tires, they slept again. The interstate felt no different.

Once Judith whispered sharply: "Damn!"

"What is it? Should I stop?"

When she answered, "Nothing. It's my fault—I keep twanging it. Like a stitch that popped," Jack grew ashamed of his speeds: sixty, sixty-five—the proper, the safe, the expected.

Later she seemed to be deliberately slumping against her door, pressing her left arm tightly against her ribs.

Again from Jack: "What?"

Judith smiled. "This is good now. If I have something to breathe *against*. Pretty stupid, isn't it?"

Seventy-five after that began to feel like coasting; only in the precincts of eighty was there some seriousness, some progress. Turns danced a little this fast, but Judith said nothing and so Jack kept on.

Authority was disappointing him, though. Eighty-five—and no one cared? He was honestly afraid to drive this fast, afraid for himself. The Valiant was unused to such continuous speeds. But, outside of Liberty, they finally did catch a siren. Judith, making some weak noise of concern as Jack pulled off the road and slowed, pressed herself harder and lower against her door.

In his side mirror Jack watched the broad bland hat approach. When he pulled at his door handle, the trooper's crisp voice immediately said, "Stay in the car, please,"—and a spear of loathing went through Jack for ever having stopped. The trooper asked to see Jack's license and registration, prepared to read both by the light of a flashlight as long as a newborn baby.

In the emergency room of the hospital in Liberty which the trooper had led them to, Jack was all ready to demand and yell and brook no foul-ups; but it turned out to be a languorous, charitable place, much like Delphi Community, as cousinly to modern medicine as a college drama-club production is to a Broadway play. Judith, very crumpled, had been helped with unhurried gentleness from the car by the trooper and a nurse.

In the eerily quiet corridor (too quiet, as though everyone politely dozed to postpone the reality of illness), Jack was afraid—and didn't want—to hear a doctor's voice saying, *"Hm, rough"* from behind one of the swinging doors. He left and walked outside to the parking lot. Day was coming. The light was starting to move up, fitting as close behind the night sky as two people caught moving in the same sector of a revolving door. The mountains looked so free and dumb, bluish.

Who wanted day, though? Not him.

Jack stood out there another ten minutes before realizing he was cold and foot-heavy. When he went back inside, the nurse at the emergency admitting desk told him she'd been looking for him. "Dr. Mal was out to see you, but you'd gone off. Now I'll have to call in and see if he's free again. He may not be."

Jack nodded sheepishly—but what he would have liked to do was reach out, collapse her cheeks with thumb and forefinger, causing pain and saying: *It's so busy here that you can't be nice, right?*

Dr. Mal was the color of cooked mushrooms. His tripping speech reminded Jack of Tariq. "Mr. Kornbluh?"

"No, not—" How to explain? "I'm—" (I'm what? A fellow sufferer?) "—a friend."

"It looks to be a pleural effusion. However, you may desire to order an ambulance so that she can be brought back to New York. Tonight she will be all right, but better for you to do that, I think. She has an advanced lymphoproliferative disease, and there is little we could do here."

The huffy nurse turned out to be of large, patient help in arranging for the ambulance. The phone receiver went into the hollow of her thin throat as she asked Jack: "Will you be riding inside with her?"

"Is there room?" Not expecting it, the question had flummoxed him. "No, no," he waved urgently at her as he came back to himself, "I can't. I forgot: I have my car."

The ambulance, an old Cadillac, strung Jack along behind on the route back to the expressway, then for some miles on it too. But near Suffern Jack lost the tailgates completely, the siren evaporating into distance. The yawn growing ever greater, that was the end once and for all of catching up.

"This guy—" J.'s father pointed to Anthony for the benefit of the thin brother-in-law in beltless slacks who sat one-cheeked on the edge of a solarium sofa while balancing on his lap a two-pound box of butter cookies he hadn't been able yet to let go of (no visitors at the moment). "Once I mentioned to him that I'd seen a game where Maglie had the Reds not knowing if they were coming or going? He gave me the line score, all the final totals. He's got one of those memories."

"I know," Steve the brother-in-law nodded courteously, "there are people like that. Real fans."

"Hal took one step into the room—they told him to leave," J.'s mother was in the meantime recalling for her sister, who with her husband had come directly to the hospital from the airport after a flight out of St. Louis. The sister—short grey hair and reserved blue wool dress—was a strong contrast to J.'s mother: her dramatically large eyeglass frames, the Afro'd permanent, the caftanish shift, heavy jewelry at throat and wrists. "Right then we could sense what was what."

Anthony had posted himself with care. In his line of vision, from his solarium chair, were the corridor, the elevators, the doorway of Intensive Care, and, through the window, something of the nurses' station. The chair was hard, the glare bad, but he'd never move, never.

"We forced ourselves to expect, though—right, Gen? I promised myself years ago that I would not, I would not act like this was something we were completely unprepared for. The good memories, they don't go away ever." J.'s mother began to cry. Steve the brother-in-law scanned away from the men's diversionary talk and grew wet-eyed as well.

Shortly after four o'clock in the afternoon, the elevator discharged Alexandra Somogyi. Anthony watched her heading for Intensive Care, reading the sign that detoured all visitors to the desk at the other end of the corridor; he then saw the nurse there point out to her all of them sitting in the solarium. Not since the day he'd returned the money had Anthony seen Alexandra Somogyi. He realized that that was only four days ago.

He rose to head her off before she could enter the solarium, nodding permission to the nurse meanwhile. "All anyone's allowed is two minutes," Anthony told Somogyi.

She was bashful. "Hello, Tony."

"Alex!" J.'s mother had spotted her, risen, was coming over.

"Mrs. Kornbluh." They hugged, and Somogyi was refusing to cry.

After seeing J., she returned to the solarium—white. The sun in the room had sagged off. Radiator heat prickled the back of Anthony's wrists. Somogyi sat beside J.'s mother, the aunt having made room. They held hands.

"I told her, and I know she heard— (Do they really need all those tubes?) I told her that when she gets out of here, she's coming with me for a whole month to a place I go to in the Adirondacks that's very wonderful. It's a theatre commune, all women, good food—Jude'll love it. She can get her strength back there. She can sit and sketch. And because it's only women, there's so much support."

Anthony took no offense. It was embarrassing, that was all. No one spoke in this way any longer. The rules changed so liquidly. You told by how she felt when you held her. There'd been internal bleeding, but then it was checked; still Wellitz, holding Anthony at elbow and bicep, was making no predictions. "If she got herself enough ahead to produce some platelets I'd like it better." Anthony got the identical information by holding J.'s toes, her long cold toes under the white stencilled sheets.

While each step (Each step)
Draws you closer (Closer) . . .

How funny that you never know at the time when you're being happiest. The boys wanted to throw potato chips at each other, wanted to revert to roughhouse (so much less mature than we were). But it wasn't tolerated. They could do that on schooldays, not at *our* party. Dancing now! (And they obeyed, they obeyed—first glimpse of power.) My cupcake-sized breasts against Rickie Lebo's Cloroxed shirt; and very boldly, for a quick second, a pinky slipping down under the sewn-on belt in back of his Ivy League pants . . . Tell me that I wasn't more serious then and there than I've ever been since. And happier.

Why?

I know. Because with Rickie Lebo was the last time I ever got to lead.

" 'How is the bed?' I asked her. In that teentsy croak, she said back, 'It's all bed—no artificial filler.' Can you believe it? Still that beautiful sense of humor."

"Don't say 'still,' " J.'s mother chastened her husband. She looked to Anthony for support. " 'Still' infers . . ." Then she gazed out the window. "The river is so black. You can say it, Hal. Say whatever you want."

Jack?

But without a soundbox anymore, all the question can do is rumble over the banked surfaces inside of her, like a roller derby.

Anthony told them what Wellitz had told him about the new bleeding.

"They're afraid of a tamponade."

Her parents, back after a few hours of sleep, absorbed it with downward eyes. Hours later, Hal asked, "What *is* a tamponade?"

Anthony had to say he didn't really know.

Night so soon? It was just day. And more green moon men—different ones—dropping the siderails down. Rolling her over a quarter turn.

It's all housekeeping. If they fed me the sheet, would that be a good blotter?

Anthony and her toes—always her toes. And now Daddy creeping in—*you* I should cheer up. Something that I remembered before: a goat doing what a goat's supposed to do—Santa Claus Land, Lake George, the summer of nineteen fifty bifty—it butted me right in the perfect little tush while I was staring up at the sky at something. And you laughed.

You did. You laughed. Sometimes I forgive you for it and sometimes I don't.

Everything is washed but the walls. The four faithful thumpers, standing guard.

Day. And a *hole. Smooth. Absence of handles. Whooo–pack that smell. I want that. Good smell.*

The different kinds of hairy arms there are, watches.

This is no good, after all.

Can I be held? Someone?: "Ccccchhhhhhhhhhhhhhhh-ccchh."

Tip– No.

Lean.

Goat jump.

Almost.

And once more–jump! Rest. Everything rests roundly.

And not bad, even nice.

Rounder.

The pair of arms J.'s mother was bouncing into next was his. She wet his shirt.

"You were very good to her, Tony."

Oh, the abomination!

Jack came every day. Delphi was not his home, Bethpage was not his home—this hospital was his home.

Under the entrance canopy, the very first morning, he by chance had run into Wellitz. "Everything all right?" the doctor asked. "I'd been under the impression we weren't supposed to see you for another month yet."

Jack told him why he was here.

Wellitz let his smile go and firmly led the way over to a lobby sofa. "She's in the ICU, Jack. Outside of family—"

"I'm friend: same thing. And I was *there.*"

"Where?"

There was no good answer for that, Jack discovered. "If you're worried, don't be—I'm not going to be shocked at the sight of her."

"You know that for a fact? My responsibility includes you, too; you're my patient also—and I don't want you up there now. I'm not kidding around, either. If it comes to that, the nurses'll be given orders specifically not to admit you. Let it be enough for now that she knows you're here and close and fighting along with her. You being at the bedside will do nothing for either of you at the moment."

Jack had waited until Wellitz disappeared down a corridor before heading for the elevators. When for the longest moment none of them came (and not wanting to be discovered by Wellitz, who might easily stroll through the lobby once more), Jack instead found a staircase, went to the second floor, and rang for an elevator from there. When it arrived, it opened empty; Jack stepped in, pressed Six, and the car ascended.

At Six the doors opened. Jack had expected to see a closed-off unit—and he did, it was; and that there would be a door, of course, to have to go through—and there was that, too; and that the atmosphere inside there would look very quiet but also very charged—which seemed the case. And still from within the elevator he could see that all the nurses inside there were wearing sweaters; and the slight blurriness to the glass window, was that steam or cold vapor maybe? . . . and the doors closed and the elevator started down again. Jack's feet hadn't moved one inch.

On Wednesday, called to the house phone, Wellitz stingily informed him that they were transfusing her heavily now. Jack asked, "Would my blood be of any . . . ?"—and there was then a block of embarrassed silence jammed between both ends of the conversation.

After that, Jack mostly sat, spending whole long days staring at the glass walls of the lobby's gift shop. He didn't know how to give up—and so if maybe he just continued to sit here . . .

On Friday morning, around ten-thirty, while the gift shop windows were being washed—dolls and peignoirs and chocolates obscured by suds of ammonia—Jack happened to be turned in his seat toward the elevator banks.

Out of an elevator stepped her parents and the boyfriend. They were moving without power. The boyfriend held a shopping bag tightly to his chest . . .

Jack was instantly to his feet and through the main doors, out onto the street: bread trucks, trees, sky, Chinese restaurant, cars, hotdog cart, people, sneakers, doctors, corners, buses, sky, Con Ed crew, sky— the whole thing overgrown horribly, room and more room.

PART FOUR

A Little Country

17

He had a few diversions.

He enjoyed watching the neighbor's airplane go up on clear weekend evenings. The pushing of the lower wing around so that the plane faced in the proper direction for take-off, the farmer's climbing back into the cockpit, the sprint, the leap up into the springtime air at that coral hour.

And Jack liked to barbecue. The house he and Donna lived in, twenty miles out of Delphi, was actually half a house: five small cube rooms at the rear of a building divided in two a dozen years before by the owner, an old widow named Timiny. Their entrance was at the side, facing the pasture in which the feedcorn farmer who owned the neighboring land kept two horses and his airplane: an old former crop duster that was flown, in good weather, in from the Delphi airport on Friday afternoon and kept there until Sunday night. Jack would set up Donna's hibachi just outside the door, on a square made from cinder blocks, a patio. He'd get a fire going. Wary of grilled meats (which Donna had read were possibly unhealthy), he mostly barbecued bread, garlic bread: five cloves of garlic minced and cooked in a stick of butter and then spread on the split loaf, which he in turn wrapped in foil and set onto the hibachi's small square grill. Jack was able to eat an entire loaf like this by himself; and he often did, deeply hungry for the saltiness, the sweet unctuous centers, even the crackling crusts. Cooking the bread in the oven would have been easier and faster, but preparing the hibachi was part of the pleasure: a lot of work for an odd and transitory happiness.

His only serious daily chore, other than to keep the house moderately neat, was doing the small shopping. (Donna, on her day or night off, would drive alone into Delphi and get the bulk of the groceries at the supermarket.) Taking Rafe with him, Jack always walked the mile and a half each way to the Tylersville General Store; he could have driven the Valiant, but didn't. This part of the country, more rural even than where Donna used to live in Priory, consisted of wastes of open land. For miles, not counting silos, the only structure rising taller than two stories was the drive-in theatre opposite the general store, with its gatehouse and its old-style stuccoed screen-slab painted powder blue. Jack was able to walk for five and sometimes ten minutes with his eyes to the sky before having to lower them to watch out for a passing car or truck. Rafe would meanwhile be ranging ahead, sniffing out the culverts.

One day, in the late morning, returning from the store, Jack saw Mrs. Timiny opening one of her front windows. It looked as though she'd been waiting for him, and sure enough, in a high but clear voice she called out: "Put what you've got away, and then come around to see me."

Jack obeyed. If he had learned anything at all it was Irwin's lesson: obey; be less of a target. Shelving the milk in the refrigerator, he went back out front and knocked on her door.

"Ed Kaslin usually does this for me, but he stayed down in Florida this year on account of his arthritis." Jack followed her into the living room or front parlor, a dark place that was papered with a pattern of brown fleurs-de-lis. A white spew of summerweight drapes was laid over the back of a venerable port-colored sofa. "They're all hooked up to the valence already, so you take the ones up there down, put these up, and you'll be all right."

Jack looked at her—how did she mean that?—but she'd gone poking her way out of the room, a scissoring walk, fists closed; she had a hump, but it seemed almost delicate on her.

While Jack worked, sweating and wishing she'd given him a less rickety chair to stand on, Mrs. Timiny returned with a plate of Fig Newtons and two cups of tea. Climbing down, he asked what he should do with the armful of mustard brocade winter curtains.

"There." The old woman indicated the sofa. "Leave room for yourself." She handed him a cup of tea.

Jack took the cup, wiping his face with the back of his free hand, while Mrs. Timiny, sitting in a wing chair matched to the faded vermillion of the couch, was studying him.

"One of my great nephews had what you do."

Jack bit into a Fig Newton, surprised. Donna must have told her. Ordinarily so private and covert, Donna must have felt some explanation was due the old woman for why Jack hung around the house all day, had no job. Jack sensed once more how very unsurely he knew Donna, if at all. Living all day (and sometimes all night) alone with her things, he'd come to know them better than he knew her. Among her books was one on how to perform magic tricks and one on speaking more effectively. In a drawer he'd come across a bag of barrettes and hair bands that made him realize her hair hadn't always been as short as now.

And now she was superstitious. At the hospital, near the phones in the lobby, the floor was inlaid with a black mandala-like design with compass points; whenever Jack came to fetch her, he noticed that she made a point of never stepping on the dark circle; she steered around it each time. And one night she spent an entire hour unkinking the chain that held the Spanish longevity charm Jack's sister had given to her, working and working on the twisted chain but never removing it from her neck. They were for his sake, of course, these superstitions: he had spooked her into a need for vague and future defenses. He knew that. Yet they also seemed to put her so far ahead of him. At this rate he would never know her, only love her—and he didn't know if that was allowed to be enough.

Mrs. Timiny was continuing to fix Jack straight on, now with glittering eyes. "He *died* of it"—a laminated note of accusation and triumph.

And then Jack suddenly decided that he wouldn't let the old bird get away with it. It came clear: at eighty-three (Donna had been told her age, and had passed the information on to Jack), she was *jealous* of him. The almost-dead like to feel unique. "Well, that's too bad," said Jack, calmly taking another bite of cookie. "When was this?"

"Oh, I would probably have to say ten or twelve years ago."

"See, that explains it. He missed out on the drugs that can cure it."

The old woman looked at her shoe, digesting this and planning her next move. "I don't know about that," she stalled.

"Too bad," Jack shrugged callowly, "for him."

Snorting, beaten, she turned her cup a quarter way around on the saucer. "Are you looking forward to your birthday party?"

"My what?"

"You know . . . Oh, maybe I wasn't supposed to say. I guess not. That's why—I didn't think—she must have come in here and asked me to keep that wrapped package in here until the day. Forget I said anything"—as she got to her tiny feet, ready to sweep him out.

Back in his half of the house Jack found, in Donna's address book, a piece of hospital-chart paper.

Sandy and friend ✔
Mr. R. ?
Bert and Lois ✔
(Mrs. T. ?)
(Mr. and Mrs. E. ?)

Jack called her at the hospital without waiting.

At first Donna admitted to nothing. "Can we discuss this when I get home?"

"I want you to call them all up right now and say it's off."

"Maybe we can talk about it first. Not now, though—I've got to take out a catheter. I'll be home around four-thirty—"

"No, *now*. Or when you get your next break—go down to the lobby and call from there, charge the calls to here. But take *care* of it."

"I only thought you might—"

"Well, I don't. The idea's a bad one." Bert and Lois, Mrs. Timiny, Irwin—this was now his *de facto* circle? "I won't be able to handle it." The truth. "And I doubt it's good luck." Also the truth. While Judith had been alive, a lightning rod for disaster, he had felt more safe.

Mention of bad luck scored with Donna—as Jack knew it would. After a pause, she said, "I'll make the calls. I would never have planned it if I knew it would make you so upset."

Wretchedly, Jack assured her he was all right.

Yet by the time she returned home that afternoon other thoughts had intervened. She was making the party, Jack at last had concluded, more for herself than for him, as something to assuage her loneliness at being stuck out here with him. How, then, in good conscience and love could he torpedo it? After she showered and changed her clothes and came out to sit on the cinder block steps leading to the house and dry her hair, Jack told her not to make the calls after all.

"I've changed my mind. I've got to be mature about this."

Shielding her eyes from a brilliant sun low in the shirred warm sky, Donna looked up at him. "It has nothing to do with being mature."

Jack was firm. "We're having it. I want it."

She said, "I made the calls already."

"What did you tell them?"

"That I have to work that night."

"Do you? That the truth?"

"I plan to. If that'll make you less uncomfortable."

Two weeks later, on the morning of the twenty-eighth, Jack opened his eyes to find Donna already staring at the ceiling. "What are the rules for me?" she asked with seriousness, still looking upward. "Can *I* celebrate it?"

"Wish me happy birthday," said Jack.

She turned to fit herself to him. "Happy birthday, sweetheart. Many

many more." She kissed him, then rolled away and left the bed. She was getting into her clothes. "We're going to go somewhere."

"Not at ten to seven."

"Get up. You'll see."

Ground fog was over the fields. She was heading the Volkswagen in the direction of Priory (she had skirted Delphi as best she could), and Jack's only guess was that it was going to be something sentimental or superstitious. She had never called him "sweetheart" before. Inapt as it was, Jack still warmly appreciated it.

Donna gave him half a smile as they came down the road beside the airport. Turning in at the entrance, she went surely in the direction of a particular green and white hangar, where she honked the horn three times and cut the motor. Their farmer neighbor stepped out of one of the hangar's side doors and waved at them.

Donna took care of the introductions. "You both kind of know each other already. Jack, this is Dan Eltman. Dan, Jack Richmond."

"The birthday boy." Eltman, wearing a mesh-crowned cap and steel-rims that made him look like a math teacher in a country high school, offered his hand. "Ready for a ride?"

The planning that had gone into it startled Jack into being what he wasn't very often lately: gracious. "Be delighted"— he swept a hand down, for Donna to lead the way to the plane. But she said, "Just you and Dan. Not me."

"Me and the birthday boy," Eltman concurred.

The plane wasn't the familiar ex-crop duster that Jack watched take off from the house but a single-engine Cessna, red and white. Eltman explained that the morning air was a little too cold for outside cockpits. Jack climbed carefully into the small cabin. The throttle before him, identical to the one Eltman would fly by, was shaped like a sad clown's mouth. Two small seats were behind. The plane taxied onto the field's only runway. Jack was growing accustomed to the loud but then somehow not-loud-enough roar of the single-propeller engine at the nose. The tower cleared them over the radio. The airplane began to speed, to strain, and then it rose.

Jack turned around, looked at Donna's waving form growing small. Then she was getting into the Volkswagen and driving it out of the airport.

Eltman spilled it: "She's going to meet us at the other end."

"The pasture?" Jack grinned. "Home, Jeeves," he said—which embarrassed Eltman, who scratched the side of his mouth, wanting to find a comeback. "We aim to please," the farmer finally overpronounced, like a high-school actor's first line on stage.

How clear! Below. Above. They were under the clouds when flying over the University, which turned on its side like a mock-up on a board when Eltman yawed left to head out over town. Pellegrino's new Mall, nothing more than a puny indentation, slid under them.

Jack had never felt more densely tied to earth than he did seeing it slither and bunch beneath him like this, being used up and passed by. It was like drawing a map with a burnt match.

"You about ready to take over?" asked Eltman loudly.

Jack yelled back, "I hope you're kidding."

"You hold on this thing right here in front of you—"

The purling rush of the engine in front caught, grumbled, was silent for an instant. While Jack smiled, Eltman—saying, "Oh, looka-here"—scanned his instrumentation, lifted his hands briefly from the throttle. Jack didn't appreciate the joke. The nose of the plane was starting to dip. Eltman said, "Hell."

It wasn't a stunt—and when Jack realized this he put his fingers to the window frame beside him and gripped the gasket, a train commuter's instinctive brace. He kept his eyes only on Eltman's hands, forswearing any look out at the endless soup of sky they hung in without assistance: he wanted to see indoor skill, not an airy plunge. "Don't go croupy on me," Eltman warned the craft. He hit a toggle switch, pulled at the throttle; the motor coughed again, it recaught.

Jack's fingers stayed on the window frame for the rest of the flight. Slowly, he began to look out and down again. Over the lake, the Cessna's shadow smoothly inked the water. The hospital came up on their left, then the cornfields of Tylersville.

Donna was running through the Queen Anne's lace to meet them on the ground. Through the still-shut cabin door, she called in, "How was it?"

Jack opened his door and quickly jumped out. "It was good."

"Only good?" She invited Eltman back to the house for coffee, but the farmer declined. She gave him a kiss on the cheek. Jack, after shaking Eltman's hand ("Sorry about that up there," said the farmer; "It made it interesting, more interesting," said Jack), walked away, in case any money might next be passed.

Going across the meadow to the house with him, Donna asked Jack what that had all been about. Jack was unable to say yet, hardly had a voice. *That,* up there, was being afraid to die. Down here, it had all been something amateur.

In the house Jack went directly to the bedroom; from the back of the dresser where he'd hidden it he took the present he'd bought for Donna: a yellow velour overshirt. He'd bought it yesterday at an expensive clothes shop downtown in Delphi, one of the few quality stores not to desert the town for the Mall. Driving in, entering the store, picking out and paying for the shirt, driving back, he'd been like a horse with blinders on. He brought the wrapped box out to the kitchen.

Donna stepped back from the table. Candles were going on top of a decorated cake. Jack froze.

"Yes you can," Donna said, taking him by the wrist.

Holding out the box, dry-mouthed, eyes on the cake, Jack said, "This is for you, for my birthday."

"You sweet man. I'll open it after you're done." She was putting a knife into his hand.

"Is that mine?" Jack pointed to a box on the seat of one of the kitchen chairs. He put down the knife to open it. "Why suspenders?"

"You don't like them? We'll get something else. I thought they were cute. But put them down now and take care of the cake."

"It's nine in the morning," Jack said.

"They're starting to melt onto the icing, so hurry, blow. Remember, a wish first."

He didn't wish. He blew. She directed his wrist toward the cake and he cut it. He prayed not to faint.

"What now?" he asked.

Two plates were waiting. "Let's have a piece. Let's eat the whole thing. Let's throw it out. Whatever you like."

"We throw it out."

Donna didn't flinch. "Okay."

"No, that'll hurt your feelings. We take a bite. You, not me. Is it any good? No? Yes? You're not going to tell me? You are? You're not. All right, let me try."

Design by David Bullen
Typeset in Mergenthaler Trump Mediaeval
by Robert Sibley
Printed by Maple-Vail
on acid-free paper

DATE DUE